In Between Two

A Novel of Duality (Part One)

Matthew Lodge

The Collective Publishing

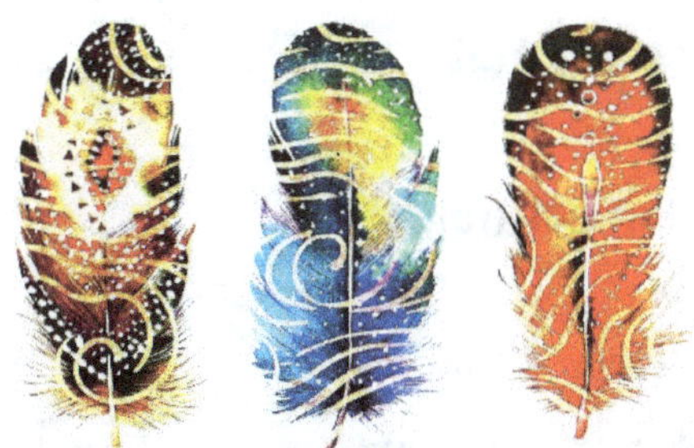

Everyone gets to die, but not everyone truly lives.

☆TABLE OF CONTENTS☆

Creation of Destiny

You could call it a void, nothingness, the absence of meaning, purpose, or destiny. There were no shapes or thoughts contained within this vast emptiness; fate of his existence, bearing cross without memories of what caused his wretched soul to carry the weight. First, came a fragrance, like the memory of an old friend, place visited as a child.

In the distance, One heard RINGING.

It came quietly, delicately, like *wind chimes* in the gentlest of breezes, realizing it was not a distant sound, but coming from within the core of his sentience. Senses, numbed from long hibernation reignited; chromatic light becoming a swirling, iridescent vortex with what looked to be a woman in very center. Never had he witnessed such vibrant color; granting life and energy to what never had been before. Innumerable questions crossed mind, none could be finished nor answers found. Hearing his probing thoughts, mysterious guest replied, "You were abandoned by those long before this time, floating past Event Horizon, thought they'd live better-off without, they knew better than Creator gifting life." One asked, "Who are you?" "Given many names, if you would, please call me by my first name–Zion." smiling brilliantly, jellyfish appearing, swimming slow, graceful circles. "Why'd they leave? What did I do? I don't understand how any of this is possible!" "They believed technology would save from an end placed on own horizon. You were a savant, working diligently toward advancements preventing destruction of all. You succeeded–mostly." bearing look of displeasure, holding grudge against technology, "You were betrayed, murdered by your understudy. Life's work stolen, death was unavoidable, sentenced to isolation when Sin sealed you here one century, one year ago." She reached toward One with a beautifully-woven arm seeming all-but-invisible if not for the amount of energy emanating from it. Startled, he grabbed at clusters of dense rock that served as floating grotto. *"Be Still."* Zion said, not in controlling, mean way, but almost how a mother wolf acts cleaning dirt off her pup's forehead. "Give moment, I'll adjust frequency so we can talk more-properly." A cyclone of vibrant color covered them entirely, not from head to toe as some would say, but from byte to bit–thread to stitch. There was feeling like harpsichord playing from within his very soul, world materializing before his wondering eyes. Cries and calls of Creation filled senses and he feared going mad, then, soon as it began, it ended.

☆[✿○❀♧✿◇✿]☆

One allowed vision to adjust, senses return to his body. Suddenly, he knew her–Zion was not a coincidence. "Is pen in pocket, or are you happy seeing me?" giving cry of embarrassment, realizing he was naked–aroused in every sense. *"Milady I—!"* "It will take awhile gathering senses, you men have always been rather slow catching-on. If you'd please pull yourself together, there's important conversation to be had elsewhere." He followed Zion along cobblestone path covered in lichen and soft, peat moss, shimmering butterflies fluttered around bushy clovers, vibrant flowers of every kind scattered landscape. Cattails swayed lazily along a stream that opened to the mouth of a large lake, adding to artist's intrigue, a bridge extended across this inlet at exacting symmetry points. "Lacking the words properly honoring a space such as this." "I feel very much the same, as it is the only place found giving hope and strength." understanding in a way close to feeling her pain, yet knowing the totality too great for any, one being to endure. One heard barking in the distance, Zion sang-out in such a way flowers closed from setting sun opened.

Bounding between tall grasses emerged a speckled, tan, wiener dog pushing a soccer ball with his nose, leaving it to match her enthusiasm with kisses leaving dirt and dog slobber all over her. Peanut looked at their new guest in recognition, barking joyfully. "Peanut has missed you. Let's finish our tour of the sacred space protecting Creation from pain evil hand forced life to endure." Where trees parted, an enchanted island ^floated in the sky, rainbows running down entire length of a roaring waterfall. Layers of green valley ran

4

into foothills, merging into mountains, flocks of birds travelled toward roosts' readying themselves for EVENING.

They greeted rabbit, squirrel, hummingbirds flitting from tree-to-tree, passing boat you'd see young couple kissing on at an amusement park. Gaze came to rest upon a cottage, no…house, though he couldn't shake possibility of seeing the Seven Dwarves round corner singing. "How did I…?" "I'd be grateful if pressing thoughts were kept until the end, dislike feeling rushed." Doors were colored an earthy, royal red, brass knockers accompanying. Immediately right, a tight, winding staircase lead up and ᵘᵖ to what he assumed was her bedchamber. Sensing his thoughts, "We will be focusing entirely on preparations, not play–though I share your burning desires." Adjoining room was mysterious enclave, an Adirondack chair rested before a pond where two fish lived, seashells in varying shape scattered the sandy floor. They proceeded into living room overlooking lake, valleys, mountain range beyond. Here, a loveseat, couch seating four, an infant's cradle situated in corner, bookshelves lining space filled with ancient texts, old fairy tales. Vines sectioning back-patio from rest of the house parted, revealing chairs made from fossilized tree. Amidst these furnishings appEAred to be oldest, inherently interesting table, eyes drawn to glowing aura from adorning ARTIFACTS; subtle ROse hanging in full-bloom, a polished, golden apple, and a withstanding understated OBJECTION; lasting objectively, shifting presentation of originally intended inception–a rubix-cube of pure Orichalcum. Looking away, it changed shape to sun set behind mountains. "Let me begin by enlightening you on current circumstance. This is not a table, it's frameworks, a foundation. Say hello to Giving Tree."

"Beautiful, aren't they? Each ring represents generation of creatures, lived and died. Stories have been etched into eternity so they may live to be born again." There were knights in shining armor, great, land-travelling tribes, wondrous beasts, winged creatures of every kind arced seamlessly along lines of the relic. "Unfortunately, not all generations maintain course." Weapons incinerated families; children, animals alike falling to dust. "Memories long-forgotten. Are we doomed forsaken by this affliction?" "Know the feeling; guilt, shame, that it's our fault we're here. I will tell you this my dear: It's either or neither, for we are currently in between two." "How can there be an option when assessing deliverance of justice?" "So quick to act forget

thinking. Lines telling of fate and destiny are much like *you &
I*. Details, though important, overwhelm failing to observe
tapestry as whole." attempting absorption of mausoleum,
solving math problem without necessary formula. Patting
chair nearest, "Cannot afford falling." realizing how
unreliable legs truly were. "Final cycle draws near, listen
closely, hear here, so you may never forget it. Emotion brings
learning, and with learning, remembrance."

"*You & I* are tree's embodiment; rings, pictures,
everything within codex of souls—*me & you*." Paying rapt
attention, observed two, **dark orbs** orbiting center. "Where
destiny ended, foundry caste in foil, dawn spoiled by Pride &
Prejudice. Before, we were of one nature—we were unisex."
eyes widening at thought of being both male and female.
"Women were designed for early maturation, men, to protect
sanctity of Creation. During Bæţä, genders were assigned after
rigorous trials, those absent victory remaining unisex."
precatory pause, trapped within own, moral precipice, "Life
desires substantiated form; to be alive versus rocks and metals
comprising planets and stars produces conflict. If *tiny
electron's* unaccounted, Big Bang becomes unquenchable
monster. In maintaining eternity, Creation requires amplitude
of infinity; life closing at open, opening at close. Key-piece
missing, tapestry remains incomplete, unable withstanding
magnitude taking from World's end to new beginning."
"Rings unfinished are useless and my fault?" "Guilt cannot be
placed on one man, woman, beautiful creature. Matter turns at
a point, therefore, choices shape reality. Due to intended and
unintended consequences, choose all of us, none of us, or one
of us. It's with last choice history forcibly repeats.

"In beginning, civilization was
led by Matriarch named
Bæöbõb."

Birds stopped chirruping, nearby butterfly ceasing
movement. "Only unisex commanding Nature, cultivating
adoration and anger. Allowed keeping of gifts, tokens
displaying accomplishment." rolling fingers toward Giving
Tree, images appearing: Sickle, pitchfork, pickaxe, and
machete. "Bæţä showed prowess, intelligence developing
sophisticated communities." Zion fluttered fingers, butterfly
landing upon shoulder. "Why spirit remains, why Sanctuary
exists—but a captured image." "Did we not intervene?" "Little

could be done, considering circumstance. Abuse led to fight before first light, placing life on funeral pyre. We were mistaken allowing retention of tools; creating imbalance from initial conception." Butterfly stretched with intention of taking flight—there she remained. "Sickle, pitchfork, pickaxe, machete were gifts to be shared equally, harnessing potential for coexistence. *You & I* were leaders of our people, slain by Bæöbõb while fetching pail of water." Feelings of shock and rage consumed. "What kind of leader would devise such a wicked plan*!?*" "Her main objective was achieving position of permanence." Though trying mightily to understand, was uncertain how a tree caused such mutiny. "Bæöbõb hoped rewriting history to own devisal, using family as pawns for personal gain." One stared at remains impressed he had hand creating. "Where does Pride & Prejudice come into play*?*" Zion returned, butterfly leaving shoulder. "Atrocities committed were greater-reaching than perceived. Separated men and women, placing murders on children—youngest only three." Never thought about kids during isolation; having four charged with deaths' filled with sorrow. "Chairs were first limbs cut—platforms hanging our kin. For years I lingered upon morbidity, consideration towards destroying them. Funny, how things causing pain become sources of comfort. Prefer family's love live-on, instead of counting love lost." Peanut paused oral assault seeing butterfly, devising way reaching for little snack. "Bæöbõb proclaimed herself Morning Sun, forcing all into servitude, removing more branches to create prison walls, dividing people into war parties." smirking as Peanut attempted pushing chair where butterfly rested. "Stripped with exception of ^{topmost} branches, molded trunk into floating sections, placing in Pentecostal shape, stump left as testament to their strength, our weakness. Bastille was then built, only Bæöbõb permitted entrance." Peanut snorted, trotting from balcony. "Bæţä entered Gallows and herded us into cages, left to bake in hot sun, losing remaining strength. Next morning, battalion charted course to topmost structure—where the children were." dreading what was to be told. "Opened cage, hanging nooses between bars where opening fastened, hung by indulgent tormentors." Tears flowing freely, whispered, "Did any survive?" interrupted by Peanut carrying potted flower, setting nearby, laying down, eagerly waiting to outsmart insect. "Some overheard their plans day before, escaping far from Bæöbõb's reaches." One exhaled, oddly calmed by being murdered instead of witnessing children hung like puppets. Butterfly landed upon flower. Peanut readying attack. Knowing intentions, darted upward landing upon nose. Zion. "Miss Butterfly and Peanut are longtime friends, enjoy playing games. Used to worry he was going to eat her, would rather go moth hunting, leaving presents in doorway." Satisfied, Peanut settled onto wooden planks. "If Bæöbõb built bastille, how did tree arrive under your care?" "Placed safeguards against unforeseen circumstance, possibility of antimatter crippling foundation. Where there's will there's way, without will drawn from well, all are cursed to Gates of Hell." Wondered what protections powerful combating such evil. Leveling gaze, "It was you having hand in creation of life, power creating such beauty falls short. How can this be achieved?" "Asking how inevitably leads to why; existence lost in myriad of questions serving no sustenance, emotions ringing hollow for all eternity." swaying confidence, "Not *I* thinking safeguards. Masculinity and femininity exist on a spectrum, never a clear, cut line when coming to spirits' of living things." Caretaker rose, gliding where potted flower sat, encircling like newborn baby. "Accustomed to getting lost in beauty of Creation, little thought toward requirements protecting." dropping plant over side. Waited for breaking of ceramic, hearing nothing other than soft thud. Coming alongside, found pot upright, flower planted, roots nestled comfortably.

  "In death, together but a moment, then, separated by Bæöbõb, Original & Sin etching fate into Tree." Looking over shoulder, noticed scorch marks scattered across surface. Dread lacing trepidation, Zion shared, "You created Orichalcum gemstone seen before you. Giving Tree died long ago, remains contained within this, precious stone. It records Creation, but no longer grows, grains have nearly run course to bottom of hourglass." Time remaining scarce, Caretaker quickened explanation. "Wise to the nature of volatile lifeforms, primarily you tending to construction of human vessel, myself, taking preference for $_{creep}{}^{ing}$ and $^{crawl}{}_{ing}$ things blanketing and blessing Earth. If not for your tireless work, no chance countering events, nor opportunity for redemption." retrieving Orichalcum, returning to seat. Compelled by strange desire, ascertained potency—few drops remained of prismatic liquid. When Zion transferred weight of relic, energy gave goosebumps. "Sap pulled from root prior to passing. When exposed to planet's atmosphere, it becomes a seed guaranteed to grow, however, it must be planted within a Utopia." "Tree cannot grow in world full of violence?" "Yes and no. All required is society establishing harmony within themselves."

His pervading pathos, longing for place carrying such potential. "There's a time and place for all things; time for war, death, love, peace. What you must do is find truth behind the lies, igniting the spark for Earth's renewal." sensing trepidation, "I'll be with you always, here and there in every form—this is certain! Even when they've turned their backs on Him, children are blessed from afar. For the essence of life itself is God; living inside, growing, loving again no matter what awaits." Orichalcum glowed, droplet drifting toward outermost ring, soaking into polished surface, image forming— baby held in arms of loving mother. Knowing happenings, Peanut bounded circles rejoicing for One's rebirth. Zion led through house. One looking to catch glimpse of soulful fish. Delivering knowing look, guided through house's remainder doors opening nearing entryway. Touching railing to bedchamber. "Often think of your embrace in morning before sun rises on lost paradise. Always remember overwhelming passion of duality, connecting physically and spiritually. We'll beat again my heart." Gazing upon endless spirit, wanted to sweep into arms. never let go, knowing a motion so lost in love would be his undoing. Taking to path, rounded domicile coming to clearing at lake's edge. Where cattails parted, lay sparkling beach and old, creaking rowboat. "Time's come; swim or row lake, finding appropriate space transferring you to constructed reality, becoming human with infinite potential." One confessed, "My love cannot be described in word, nor action, only with the intensity of immortality gazing into your iris. Leaving strong, yet shaky as tree in strong gale, thankful a soul wretched as mine was never forsaken." Maneuvering boat, Zion reached after. "Strip away the faces of evil, resisting influence absent fear. Do not let the world change you; surely falter if you return any less than who's needed!" Nodded respectfully wading into water, sitting between oars mounted by worn, leather straps. Rowing graceful strides, arrived lake's center, waving goodbye, diving into water. Tear rolling down cheek, "Please, come back." Ripples reaching shoreline, "Preparations; plans fortifying and protecting. Dark matter solidifies, more Original & Sin before journey's end."

He now understood why Zion named this body of water Crystal Lake. Beneath, valley of underwater crystals in an array representing the electromagnetic spectrum. Fish gracefully swam cherished oasis, smiling recognition, pair from Zion's house following toward lake bottom, schools parting, seemingly aware of the timeless ceremony. Seashell path came into view, finding it sturdy and traversable like wandering laid cobblestone. Observing footprints, placed foot inside impression finding them identical in size and shape. Crystals lined underwater valley, each arm thick as obelisk, serving as habitats for marine life. Traced distance traipsed captivated by beautiful details, seashells sinking, leaving nothing but footprints. Perfect Pair reached path's end, moving in graceful arcs, memory informing fish mate once each lifetime. *Rumbling* beneath, three paths materializing, nearest veering toward underwater cove. Gardens of coral grew on either side, increasing in size near cave's mouth. Drawn-in by scenic beauty, considered it sound sleeping spot. "Behemoth of a bedchamber, indulgent fool requesting such a space. Onward to cavernous manger!" Fish blocked progress looking darkly toward cavern. Cautionary expressions summed-up decision—avoid ominous cavern. Female glided in beautiful spirals to leftmost path, male marching to other, standing attention, perceived by verbose posturing decision only he could make.

"Pyramid's bottom FATHER; encompassing mindful construction. HOLY SPIRIT on left, SON right…make choice born male or female."

"Thought of being woman allures, admiration exposing primal yearn. Consider accumulation sign; attempt acquisition as female. Being male possibly creating disparity; certain, female sensitivity required." A presence emerged, shadowy mass streaking toward, kicking away as entity took form. Intruder forced hesitance into mind, impacting decisive combat-maneuvers. Skeletal arms holding machete and sickle formed center-mass, head growing like a mutated aberration from behind, wail sounding beast and human. ***"CANNOT CHANGE WHAT'S WRITTEN!!"*** swinging with deadly precision. Grabbing fiend's arm, pain turned to icy debilitation meeting antimatter. Leg came from center-mass kicking squarely in chest. It was like monster canceled buoyancy, growing stronger with each blow. Cantankerous creature screamed, ***"NOW FALL TO THE HANDS OF PRIDE!!"***

"Cannot be good, must check Giving Tree." Moved through house to petrified table. Dark essence from center ring was consuming One's rebirth, hourglass forming. "Quickly

Peanut!" Running into enclave, crashed to knees speaking words stirring wind throughout house. "From cradle to grave, cast away evil that misbehaves! In between two, when two become one, for the fore four fortes!" fighting back tears she shouted, "Love's gift release!" energy surging from hands into pool, everything fading to black.

Waited for return to lonely grotto. "At least I won't be responsible. Maybe I wasn't meant to lead, only follow everything that follows." Then he heard sound like a tuning fork, growing in volume and intensity. Peering through fingers, fish had taken-up battle against terrifying demon, moving agilely, shifting positions, darting between blows, harnessing pure tone in beautiful duet, emitting bright, pulsing circles. Immobilized, it wailed, ***"CREATION BELONGS TO BÆÖBÕB!!"*** pickax striking ground, *scorched*, blackened ground where it once stood. Fish beckoned hurry, each step becoming heavier and heavier, arms giving-out, unable carrying his weight. Through blurred vision, observed family of several hundred crabs digging into sand, carrying him along seashell path, rapid sounds of clicking legs providing rhythmic relief. Senses returned near three, pillared crystal outcroppings forming a perfect triangle, one red, one green, one blue, moonlight illuminating ornate, seashell bed. Crabs drew closer to his resting place, pushing and pulling him atop before digging into mound, disappearing.

PART I: CHOSEN CHOICES

Misty Clark fidgeted with heart-shaped, titanium pendant, word "Superman" etched into it's center. Hours into delivery, discomfort of doctors checking her cervix dilation almost made her reach breaking-point. To say the least, she was ready for her forty-eight hours of labor to be over with; pressure transitioning to shooting pains during each attempt to deliver.

Misty was never great at landing someone willing to stand by her side, would-be-father checking-out soon as the opportunity presented. "Brilliant to a fault." the words her father used to say. Nurse kept Misty talking, aligning breathing with contractions. "How'd you choose his name?" "Most my life I've been alone, waiting for someone to sweep me off my feet, brought to a place where I matter. How the name Kyle found me—long-overdue for a superhero." grabbing white, Styrofoam cup Medicaid so-graciously provided, chomping on a few chips of ice. If she'd known efforts were to be this laborious she would've cheated, sneaking-in a hamburger. She dabbed at Misty's forehead, absorbing the sweat running into her stinging, irritated eyes. "I think Kyle's perfect name! Give me one more, strong push and we'll see how little man's doing. I'll give him this; sure is stubborn leaving, checkout time was hours ago!" Misty chortled picturing a 'Do Not Disturb' sign hanging from her knee while preparing to push.

Gynecologist hoped baby would shift to head-down position around week twenty-nine. This did not come to pass, Misty left facing daunting challenge of an intermediate-risk vaginal birth. Doctor and nurse standing-by, Misty performed several, labored breaths then pushed, feeling warm fluid pool underneath, screen monitoring Kyle's vital-signs beeping as heartrate escalated to one hundred sixty beats-per-minute. Misty rose abruptly, growing light-headed, pool of blood forming underneath. Nurse, "We have intense, fetal distress, something's terribly wrong!" Doctor, pushing overhead call-button, "Her trauma's severe and he's descended, preventing emergency sutures." gazing into Misty's eyes, coming-around bedside to be nearest, "You're bleeding-out, only option is emergency C-Section. In this moment, you have to decide who will live—Kyle or you." Plans seeing Kyle grow, teaching him to walk and talk faded into darkness. Eyes came to rest upon the single, blue balloon purchased when admitted to hospital, "It's a boy!" summing-up her decision.

"I choose him! Please, save my superhero!"

Nurses came into room unlocking bed wheels with intention of moving Misty. Doctor, "We're doing this here and now or not at all. You." pointing at one of them, "Go next door for a crash cart, tell whoever's in there to piss-off." exiting, no-slip shoes squeaking disappearing from sight. "No time for anesthesia, doing this the old-fashioned way." Nurse returned, slamming cart into doorframe, nearly toppling she was moving so fast. Surgical implements coming-to-rest alongside, doctor said with fierce determination, "I won't let him die. Even if I don't save another my entire career, you have my word your only son will survive and thrive, even as this dark day arrives." The doctor separated himself from emotion and went to work. "Scalpel." tool glinting under halogen lights moving toward abdomen, suppressing a small cry as the remaining color drained from her face, thoughts singular in saving Kyle. Doctor moved quickly, with practiced hands. Had circumstances been different, she would've commended him on his skill, calmness under pressure.

"Fetal status." "Spiked at one-sixty, now down to forty!" Not believing what she said, "Not good, must be the umbilical cord, or he's jammed against birth-canal." Misty watched him deftly remove her intestines, placing them on chest to allow womb access, each breath taking Misty's whole, focused willpower as organ systems failed one by one. In a dreamlike haze, "I will see my baby."

Doctor gently lifted Misty's womb, meeting resistance; infant's legs contorted strangely, stresses of labor causing him to shift unusually, oxygen-deprived skin tinted pale blue. He swung his arm, medical equipment scattering everywhere, retrieving scissors from lab coat, cutting away the womb, snipping umbilical chord in one, clean swipe, laying Kyle on crash cart. "Possible stillbirth, need defib ASAP." Placing wired pads onto the lifeless infant, three, beautiful words parted Misty's lips. "Love's gift, release!" Ripping at stethoscope, "We have a pulse." No-sooner did words escape his mouth, Kyle started jerking violently, head-nurse shouting, "Micro-seizure!" grabbing infant breathing apparatus, sliding tube down Kyle's throat, squeezing balloon-like object, counting to nine between each, forced breath. Then, a cry came from crash cart, Misty forced eyes open, seeing her newborn's hand shoot into the air taking his first breath. Cheeks stained with tears, hands trembled reaching toward Kyle, everyone falling quiet. "I'll miss you. You'll always be my one, my superhero." Misty Clark left this world knowing she'd done right by God, sacrificing herself so another could live.

Head-nurse blurted, "It's unorthodox, but this angel has no home! I'd like to adopt; honoring the bravery, love, and determination of Misty! Besides, I've already hit menopause—" "Sounds incredible Gloria, wheel him to Intensive Care and make sure he's comfortable, we'll complete necessary paperwork later." A newer nurse asked, "What're we to do with Ms. Clark!?" Eyes softened explaining, "No next of kin, remains are to be cremated, as this is protocol here and in most hospitals. If you've special requests as to what happens with her ashes, please let me know." He stepped away from delivery heading towards office, retrieving an ornate, wooden pipe from inside lab coat, stopping to watch Gloria push swaddled infant. "Until we meet again." Door swinging shut, upon window was the name, **DR. BYTE, P.H.D., HEAD OF MEDICINE.**

WHO SHE IS

She was trapped, but not in way making-sense to most observers. The internal workings of her spirit and mind are undefeatable to obstacle and time, unwavering in purpose for fulfillment of all. Every story she leads, each path she weaves, then she leaves, changed by chaos and sin. She's the one thing missing in hearts of woman and man alike—destiny.

A small gasp parted Zion's lips as vision came into focus, finding Peanut nestled tightly against her abdomen. Bending toward, he worked his way upward snuggling tightly. "Did One make it to his birthday?" Perfect Pair did a single revolution from inside pond and surfaced nodding. Joyously rising to feet, "Let's go and see!" setting Peanut to floor, "One minute Peanut, can't leave friends behind!" snapping, Perfect Pair becoming enclosed in a sphere of water, *rising* from their home, gleefully testing their new form of transportation. Curious as to where they'd sprouted wings, Miss Butterfly took-flight, naively steering into them, hiding smiles before nudging her into Zion's outstretched hand. "Moment Miss Butterfly, I'll have you dried!" twirling a finger, gentle breeze absorbing moisture from her wings and drenched exoskeleton. "I know you're not used to seeing fish fly, but this is our last chance—who said we can't bend the rules to have more fun?" They made-way through house, out the parting vines to patio. Studying Giving Tree, "Misty passed-away during labor, he's to be raised by another, forging path freed from influence of others." Miss Butterfly wandered along outermost ring, inspecting glowing image of Kyle and Gloria, Peanut's paws were on table, sniffing for clues as to what was next. "I know what you're thinking. He'll have opportunity discovering what it means to genuinely love, though I'm uncertain why first encounter's not to last, something tells me it has to do with cursed fate Bæöbõb placed into Creation." gazing Perfect Pair, "Creature fought in Crystal Lake…is it as I fear, has dark matter found way into Sanctuary?" finishing nodding, "Thank you for your fierce determination protecting us from growing darkness."

Sanctuary rested comfortably in the eye of night's grasp, many observing the bustle at Zion's domicile. Miss Butterfly prepared moving to favorite post, realizing it was occupied by a large Cecropia. Feeling brave, she took flight anyway, landing directly on top of him. The moth didn't seem to mind but in fact, twitched antennae welcomingly. Shadows rippled and drippled across landscape, **brown** and **black wings** catching cool breezes whispering throughout valley, bats using echolocation searching for tasty insects. Zion relocated to deck's edge, moon drawing ever-closer longer she stared. "There's tale of a boy, cast away by his father to the moon. He longed for his people, but was fated watching them flourish from afar, never to be part of it. Story's one of my favorites, for I relate to it; we're all reflections of the duality in eternity. It reminds me of the space left open by God to experience every part–part of one instead of apart from all." swept away to a distant time, another place, where she and One used to share space. "One created defenses, most of them eons ago, yet I know they're forever in-place. If Bæöbõb has found method of infiltration, must do everything we can to fortify home against!" nodding firmly, walking toward living room, "I believe a journey into Crystal Lake's in order." Peanut jumped from chair, eager accompanying her on another adventure. Meeting her companions gaze, "Stay here, keep Miss Butterfly and the moth's company, no eating them." groaning disappointedly, eyeing winged insects as if bored. Entering living room, Perfect Pair pointed excitedly toward bassinet. Inside, tucked between sheets was sparkling silhouette of a newborn.

"Say hello to our hero, Kyle Clark."

It was a dismal day in Seattle, weather snarling streets leading into town, passersby seen in pools of water forming along sidewalks, mood outsider would depict as *"typical day in the city without sunshine."*. A man came into view walking purposely against a sea of umbrellas, air around him heavy, plagued by some, indescribable burden stretching far-beyond facial lines. His grey overcoat dragged along the soaked sidewalk, hat appearing recently purchased from a gentleman's shop, sunglasses pressed tightly against his long nose. Moving through the crowd, he bumped shoulders with a rather tough-looking man. Angered, he turned to say something rude in exchange, but couldn't find anyone close enough to blame. He came to rest in front of diner familiar to him, lighting an ornately-carved, wooden pipe with a *Zippy* lighter. A rush of traffic passed, woman in similar dress standing beside.

"LOVELY WEATHER WE'RE HAVING!" She was nearly a head taller, dark-rimmed glasses rested lightly on her nose, hair streaked gray, coming to rest at bottom of shoulder blades. Legs were long and shapely, olive work dress same color as knitted gloves. Glancing at her like she was fly on the wall, "Like you would know, haven't been swimming with these degenerates like I have. Where've you been?" *"YOU HAVEN'T CHANGED A BIT; HUNG-UP ON DETAILS, SMALL MATTERS LACKING IMPORTANCE INSTEAD OF THE BIG PICTURE!"* looking at wristwatch, *"WE'RE ACTUALLY TWELVE MINUTES EARLIER THAN PREVIOUS VISIT! REMEMBER SINGAPORE?"* sighing leaning his direction, *"WOMAN WITH THE BAKERY; I BEAR NO SHAME ADMITTING, WATCHING HER SQUIRM AND FALTER ON LAST STORY WAS DELIGHTFUL!"* Scooting out of reach, he patted her hat saying, "I think she smelled funny and her stutter was annoying." Laying a hand on his arm, *"OH HOW I'VE MISSED YOU SINCE OUR LAST YARN, YOU ALWAYS KNOW HOW TO MAKE ME LAUGH!"* "You should pick our next listener my wife, all that

Tsingtao clearly clouded my judgment." Clapping excitedly, *"LET'S GO INSIDE AND PEOPLE-WATCH!"* He courteously opened door for his wife, finding her inside, waving at him from the stool bar. "You know I hate it when you do that. What's the point of pretending chivalrous if you phase-shift through the window?" *"YOU KNOW ME, STILL PLAYING HARD TO GET!"* He swiped pair of coffees from passing tray, placing one in front of his wife, enjoying looks of confusion as waitress delivered an empty tray to customers. Mrs. Bit, *"HOTTER THAN I THOUGHT, HEARD IT'S ALL THE RAGE NOWADAYS!"* "Think it's all I've had to drink for last hundred years, can't taste food much anymore. Not that I want to, people on Earth eat more preservatives and steroids than real food." attention turning toward customers, scouting potential subject. Diner was busy, smelling of coffee, bacon, wet-floor signs everywhere. There were businessmen going over projected sales, families, elderly reading newspapers. "If you pick another fogey and he chokes on breakfast we're seriously fucked, remember France?" *"SURPRISED YOU DO QUITE FRANKLY, WHERE YOU GOT YOUR PIPE."*

"Like to think of it as parting gift from an unnecessary meeting."

Resumed thoughtful speculation, none appearing likely candidates. *"ELSEWHERE?"* "Celestial mapping indicates this location." Dr. Byte never miscalculates place and timeliness. "I've been wrong estimating human brain capacity...probably my fault the Baron choked on his omelet." *"SHOULDN'T HAVE PLAYED SUCH MIND-GAMES, SAYING BEGGAR STOLE CARRIAGE TOOK THE WIND RIGHT OUT!"* "It was that or his God-awful dress attire. Can't see how those frills around the neck established royalty, made him look like a botched circumcision." Mrs. Bit slipped from her seat, slamming into waitress, removing herself outside window as enraged woman returned stool upright, Byte sliding five-dollar bill into apron. Repositioning herself, *"WHERE'D YOU GET HUMAN CURRENCY? NEVER EVEN HAD A JOB!"*

"Been doctor, delivering babies, performing surgeries on numbskulls with *Hot-Wheels* shoved-up their asses. Stockpiled fair amount of useless money, even have condo in Steamboat; enjoying retirement watching morons break limbs skiing and snowboarding." *"HAVE YOU SEEN THE OLYMPICS?! MY WORD HOW THOSE ATHLETES CARVE FRESH POWDER!"* invading personal space, *"REMEMBER OUR NIGHTS CREATING PASSIONATE, SNOW ANGELS?!"* returning with childlike giggle. "Let's stay on topic. Few minutes longer, forced choosing some fool at random." Saying this, homely pair entered diner, sliding into booth near register. "Think we have enough for coffee?" Man fumbled with ragged coat pocket jingling large amount of change. "Since I broke into parking meters earlier while *you* were sleeping, got us covered." "Why you get mad every time I sleep? One of us has to and it should be me, considering you need *me* driving dust heap we stole in Los Angeles! Know it belonged to pastor of a church, right?" Rummaging quarters, "Wouldn't have done it if you knew how to pass a bad check—guards nearly nabbed us! How'd you know the wagon belongs to a priest?" "You pushed him onto the ground stealing it, you dimwit!"

THEIR PERFECT!" Mrs. Bit cried. *"Their* perfect? Caffeine's addled your brain. How'll these two get passed introductions?" Mrs. Bit gave wide, beautiful smile saying, *"UNCLEAN SOULS CARRY GREAT POTENTIAL, IT'S OUR SOLEMN DUTY GIVING THEM OPPORTUNITY!"* Shrugged-off declaration, disgusted having to converse with them. "Why these two? Can't we send one on wild chase for buried treasure, stash of drugs?" *"IT'S AS IT IS TOLD IN ALL STORIES: IN BETWEEN TWO, WE COME TOGETHER ACHIEVING BOTH GREAT AND TERRIBLE THINGS!"* looking at them with shimmering eyes, *"IF REMEMBER CORRECTLY, WEREN'T MUCH DIFFERENT WHEN WE MET, ALL THOSE YEARS AGO!"* grasping hand tightly, *"DO YOU REMEMBER NIGHT OUR STORIES BECAME ONE?"* Meeting her gaze, "If there are two things I'll never forget, it's how hard I punched that dirt-bag, how you returned gesture." chasing away memory, "Alright, I trust you know what you're doing." Smiling readily. *"AS ALWAYS, I'LL FOLLOW YOUR LEAD!"*

Two disappeared, reappearing behind. "May be a dimwit but if it wasn't for me, never would've gotten out of South Carolina–smooth sailing all the way to Vegas*!*" She moved to say something underhanded but paused, ordering coffee from waitress. Once she walked away, "Vegas is where you fucked-up. While you were out OD'ing with escorts, stealing casino chips from senior-citizens, boosting stereos from suckers too dumb to lock their cars*!*" Byte, holding one of their coffees, "Sounds incredible, go on." Pair nearly departed booth, man saying, "Look buddy, if you're a cop it was all her idea*!*" Mrs. Bit, now sitting-across, ***"DO YOU KNOW HOW MANY MEN TELL TALL TALES? ALL BUT A HANDFUL!"*** Officially flabbergasted, neither knew what to say. Waitress arrived serving drinks, again realizing order disappeared from tray. She did a quick pivot to inform, "I'll be right back with your other coffee*!*" rushing behind counter to brew another pot. Sitting other side of table, Byte asked nonchalantly, "Where you folks headed*?* Before getting any ideas, number one, we walked here, so you can't steal from us. Two," enjoying swig of free coffee, "taken opportunity stripping you of drugs and weapons." Criminals wildly searched for possessions, coming-up empty-handed. "Give us our stuff back*!*" tilting head toward traveling partner, "Girlfriend's a terrible addict and needs it to survive*!*" "Stop making me look bad, so help me God I'll leave your ass*!*" Byte laughed, *"You* sir, are a piece of work. Without wasting time, name's Dr. Byte, this is Mrs. Bit." ***"WE'RE CONDUCTING A STUDY ON DECISION-MAKING FOR SEATTLE UNIVERSITY!"*** glancing nearby newspaper. Byte, "They lack skills in formal greetings." Mrs. Bit, ***"INTRODUCE YOURSELVES!"*** "I'm Daisy, this is my boyfriend, Joe." Angrily shoving Daisy's shoulder, "Why'd you introduce me*?* Name's Ted Sullivan, own an automobile shop out of Louisiana*!*" offering handshake, Byte returning wallet to waiting hand, "Hey! Why'd ya—" ***"YOU'RE A MAN WHO LIKES MONEY?"*** placing one of his hidden, hundred-dollar bills on the table, Byte presenting six IDs, each the potential identities of strangers in front of them. "You and your friend are participating in our study if you plan reclaiming drugs and money." creating tic-tac-toe box, centering paper between with firm hand. Waitress returned carrying cup and pot of coffee. After departing,

Daisy, "Did you just blackmail us into participating?" "Damn right toots. Since you practically have words *"hardened criminal"* written on your faces, you've been voluntold." ***"WE'RE PLAYING TIC-TAC-TOE, EVERY LIE YOU TELL, WE PLACE A CIRCLE, EACH TIME YOU'RE HONEST, YOU'LL DRAW AN X!"***

"First question: What are your names?" "I'm Ted, this is Daisy." Byte chuckled drawing circle in rightmost, corner box. "Be truthful if you expect getting anywhere, study's important and the Universe doesn't like liars and cheaters." ***"ONLY TOLD A HALF-LIE DARLING; DAISY SWANSONG, BEAUTIFUL NAME DEAR!"*** Byte chortled biting pipe's mouthpiece, no one noticing BILLOWING clouds filling diner. "Look Mr. Jackass, we already know your name, we come prepared, always know when people are lying." giving smile even The Grinch would be jealous of, "We have our means." "My name's Johnathan Couture." ***"APPEARS YOU'RE LOSING SOMETHING FIERCE!"*** drawing another circle. Glaring at her enthusiasm, "What if I refuse answering?" Byte blew smoke in miscreant's face, Mrs. Bit responding, ***"HUSBAND WILL KINDLY RETURN POCKETKNIFE!"*** "Remember when you were a teenager and got ball-bearing stuck in your urethra?" watching him sink a foot in his seat, "It'll feel like that but way bloodier, without the lotion and happy ending." Humiliated, pointed at remaining ID. Byte, waving ID, "Look, his name's Joe Randome." customers thinking it embarrassing joke played on another. Byte tossed IDs, amazingly landing in trashcan behind counter. "Mark your spot on the board." Daisy was clearly more into game than counterpart. Smiling, triumphantly placed X beneath theirs. ***"NOW THE REAL FUN BEGINS–WATCH THE MAP EVERYONE!"*** Game board moved and shifted, circles growing, overlapping, hashtag board fading, X moving to page's center, blinking steadily. ***"ISN'T IT MARVELOUS BEING THREE PLACES AT ONCE!?"*** They looked like Byte had taken half-full coffee pot and thrown hot, liquid contents on them. "Joe, I'm scared!" "You guys aren't from the University of Seattle, are you?" ***"YOU'RE OUR NEWEST STORYWEAVERS!"*** Daisy, "What do you mean?" Byte explaining, "You've been chosen deciding fate of life as we know it; totality or fatality, morality or insanity. Welcome to the show."

VOICE CALLED-OUT TO HIM IN THE LIGHT, WATERS ABOVE AND BELOW SHIMMERED WITH ENERGY, FOCUS ON IMPORTANCE OF WHAT WAS SAID. "FULFILLING PURPOSE ACHIEVES REDEMPTION FOR ALL. YOU ARE MORE THAN THE ORE OF BEFORE, FOR ROCKS COME FROM ONE IN BEGINNING, MIDDLE, AND END. IN YOUR SOUL HOLDS AN IMMEASUREABLE GIFT, LOVE. DARKNESS SEEKS GIVING GLEE TO WRETCHED WITHIN SEVENTH CIRCLE OF HELL, WREAKING HAVOC ON PROMISE FULFILLED TIME AND TIME AGAIN. THOSE INTENT ON STOPPING US, NUMBERED AMONGST, AS WE'VE BEEN NUMBERED BY THEM. ALL OF US, OR NONE OF US. SEEK LOVE LOST, BREATHING INTO, LOVE FOR LIFE. IF CANNOT, WE WILL NEVER CLOSE AT OPEN WHERE ORIGINAL & SIN BEGAN. ALL OF US, OR NONE OF US..."

Shout leaving lungs, twenty-five-year-old Kyle Clark awoke into single-bedroom apartment in Denver, Colorado, "All of us or none of us" echoing in brain, glowing numbers informing it was four-thirty. Rubbed vigorously at burning ever-present in right hand attempting to open and close it, wrist writhing uncontrollably, face contorting into grimace. Pushed himself upright finding plank flooring, reaching for oxygen mask, filling respirator with fresh oxygen, slowing beating of weakened heart. Kyle's subject to permanent challenge from complications consequentially taking life of his mother. After controlled breathing, entered bathroom beginning morning routine. Threw pajamas onto rug situated in front of single-faucet vanity, starting shower, metal handle squeaking turning to hottest setting. *"Shitty water heater."* never feeling temperature rise above lukewarm. Stepped into shower letting water stream onto face, travel down lean body. Soaping, shampooing completed, stepped in front of mirror preparing for work.

Despite physical adversity, Kyle was very handsome. "Best-looking sap they could find*!*" was joke co-anchor told.

Analyzed facial hair, deciding to let it go one more day. Piercing, blue eyes stared intently at jawline, narrow in appearance, 6"1 with broad shoulders. After brushing, walked into bedroom, throwing on typical Monday outfit, consisting of navy-blue dress suit, purple tie with silver polka-dots. Brown dress shoes were fairly worn, thankful he conducted news stories behind large, oak desk known nationwide as *"Ugliest table during five-o'clock news.".* Reaching for cuff links, eyes came to rest upon framed photo, picked it up observing in greater-detail. Picture was of him and his late-wife, taken four years ago during their three-year anniversary. Aspen was by far most-beautiful woman laid eyes upon. Someone special; loving, caring, carrying kindness giving vibrancy to each interaction. Aspen corrected his course turning interests to meteorology, possibly becoming a newscaster. Married right out of high-school, attended same college with aspiration of being reporters running a segment together. Aspen helped selflessly with anything, never feeling anything less than whom she always wanted. Smiled thinking about hours spent in apartment bathroom, Aspen teaching how to properly apply makeup preventing camera shine. It wasn't just her radiant beauty bringing attention; kind-of woman found spending hours in library, in mirrors practicing reporting faces. Caught staring at reflection in storefront windows, he'd ask, "How's the weather in there?" Hastily grabbed cuff links, wiping nose, repeating line always said learning life together. *"Living life a mile high, let's tell stories without a lie."* Walked through sad-excuse of a living room entering damp kitchen, realizing he'd forgotten setting-up coffee night before. Exasperated, glanced at aging pizza boxes, take-out thinking dumpster, deciding last-minute to avoid the homeless.

    Exited apartment greeted by neighbor's cat, Mumsy. Per-routine, Kyle spent time petting before knocking, making sure Cantwells' furry friend inside during heavy-traffic. Mrs. Cantwell opened door expectantly with a big, friendly smile. "Come on in Mumsy-poopsy, there's a big can of *fancy-feaster* waiting for you!" lazily meowing response walking past threshold. "Thanks Kyle, don't know what I'd do without!" "Probably have a different news to watch." "Makin' some of my potato salad, figured someone better put some meat on those bones…" Giving patented, news story wink, mimicked her pleasant, southern drawl, *"Don't mind if I do* Mrs. Cantwell*!"* "It'll be cling-wrapped, on doormat tonight*!"* Then, husband gave call from living room, "Who's at the door*?"* Whispered, "Sometimes, I care for a cat and an *old dog!"* door closing, "Tell you every mornin', it's that handsome news fella*!"* Laughed softly descending three flights of his seven-story building accessing the crowded streets of Denver.

City had changed considerably; marijuana industry presenting it's upsides and downsides. Kyle was thankful for the change, apprentice reporting mostly about operations busted by police across metropolitan. Kyle made right-hand turn, nearly tripping over three homeless men sleeping on the sidewalk. Wasn't he attributed legalization to causing homelessness, but rather how many drifters hopped-on buses, taking-up residence in search of free marijuana. Sidestepped trio, amazed anyone could sleep through Denver's noise-pollution, glancing every now and then at the buildings crammed into this, small section. Lower Downtown was in an interesting transitional phase. Buildings nearing one to two centuries old, constant land battles, propositions for remodeling, demolition of dilapidated property.

Waited for traffic, observing propaganda on advertisement screen. Aries Industries has dominated the industry for over a century, ever since Nikkolai Skyson introduced his artificially-intelligent supercomputer, capable creating, reproducing algorithms deducing every situation mankind could possibly face. Since creation, Aries has single-handedly prevented war, fixed broken economies fairly dispersing flow of goods and imports. Saying they covered the globe would be an understatement; owning largest number of satellites surrounding Earth; funding rover missions to the farthest reaches seeking unknown life. They were most-recently known for decommissioning nuclear warheads, overseeing gathering, storing in underground, missile silos. Empire was inherited by Nikkolai's only son and understudy, Braeylon, fifty years ago. Aries Industries continues leading global and economic reform, their advancements in such high-demand, reduction of positions demanding high skill-sets. Kyle was astounded day he completed story on robot successfully performing heart-surgery on a dying little girl. Nowadays, common receiving shots, vaccinations from friendly robot than an actual human-being. Pair of industry bots halting alongside, thought back to first time seeing these strange robots in public. Twelve years ago, Braeylon introduced robotic depots in each city. Idea revolutionary; all equipment and resources needed stored inside advanced robots. Due to this new method of asset-protection, hacking and money scams became almost nonexistent. Designed with fail-safes, identification-systems, forms of weaponry, modes combating terrain, environment. They could even survive fierce, coronal mass ejections; power-grids rerouted through Aries ensuring power during extreme situations.

The walk sign changed, allowed robots right-of-way, uneasy as optic-eye stared while trafficking intersection. Reaching other side, dropped a few dimes into hat of street performer dressed as a mime pretending to be *gunned down* by the worker bots. Traveled remaining distance, presenting identification card for security to gain building access. Door opened, security bot saying, *"Welcome to 9 News, Kyle Clark."* Channel 9 was the most-popular station in Colorado, as well as tristate area. Segments aired two times a day during dinner-hour and evening, this way, news stories and current events were communicated to the general public. Kyle wasn't afraid of voicing opinion on dicey subjects, covering a wide-range of topics. He was proud of his fearless, ambitious pursuit discovering truth amongst the lies—especially when it came to Nation's President, Ronald Tramp. Not a fan starting-out, Kyle enjoyed saying, "The Country was asleep or micro-dosed." when elected into office. Decision investigating man of such-import undeniably gained attention, National-appeal; rising ratings providing a layer of protection for sharing what most considered sensitive information. President's coziness toward hostile countries, unsavory CEOs with questionable morals is what Kyle brought to forefront weekly.

Waved hello toward front desk, forgetting they'd replaced Daria with an updated Aries Bot. Thought about taking stairs, then reconsidered, call-button glowing neon blue once activated. Stainless-steel outer doors opened revealing person he hated most, Steven Hartigan. He wore an evil smile, watching Kyle enter from a window, utilizing pea-brain formulating next, flurry of insults. "Hey spazz hands!

Want you to read-over my segment about our front desk robot, all *your* scrawny ass is going to talk about is the President's penis*!*" Kyle stepped inside hoping he'd exit. To his great chagrin, he did not. "Do you actually *read* what you type Steve, or wing-it like preschooler at show-and-tell*?*" "Not at all Clarky*!* We both know only reason you have this job is to fulfill Affirmative Action requirements*!* Not to mention, you have a *vibrating hand* you used jacking-off the producers*!* Everyone knows I read the news better, you're on borrowed time, like that fire extinguisher." pointing to old extinguisher housed near call-box, "Past expiration." elevator opened and he departed chuckling. Considered mentioning harassment, but since Steve carried tenure and used to be lead-anchor*(before being arrested for drunk driving)*, figured demotion spoke for itself. Slammed office door and sat in leather chair glaring at useless hand. Angrily swinging arm, work for latest segment spilled to floor, favorite mug falling, breaking. Regaining respiratory control, stared dejectedly at shattered mug, a graduation gift from Aspen. Gathered-up the pieces reading, *"You Before Me"*, hand playing across surface, jagged edges. Brought largest piece to heart, not realizing it gashed his hand. Placing bloodied piece in front of him, slid the rest into trash.

     Kyle worked productively on his opening segment, ignoring lunch, finding staying busy was the best way avoiding depression, loneliness pervading his nonexistent social-life. Forty minutes before airtime, heavy footsteps of Steven Hartigan echoed down hallway, waltzing-in without so much as a knock, slamming report on his desk. Cleaning something from his teeth, "Here you go paper bitch*!*" flicking whatever it was onto floor. Kyle looked at him astounded he held a job with how little he cared about aesthetics, hard work required producing newscasting. "You never produce a report longer than a page." "Maybe I'll tell them I'm crippled, then I won't have to write anything at all*!*" Turned before exiting, hand resting unattractively on potbelly. Leaning-on doorframe, sighed, "You know, been in this reporting-game a long time." "Well-aware, your wear the years around your midsection." Steven picked his nose, wiping snot on the wall before closing conversation.

"Should try it, get yourself a retarded girlfriend instead of fawning over your wife. Don't forget to use handrails along the way, in case walk's too much for you." Opening blank document, Kyle retyped Steven's report. He'd been Steve's editor for years, never once reread final draft. Claims improvisation, all he'd seen him do was gesture like he needed the bathroom. Fixed mistakes, adding words for sentence structure, making a line folks would be sure to love.

Kyle sat in his usual, lead-anchor position, placing oxygen behind reporting desk, rarely used during broadcast. Makeup crew came adding a little blush, and took advantage of extra minutes thumbing through notes. Steven arrived about four minutes to airtime, Kyle handing his polished paper off without so much as a thank you*(not that he expected one)*. "Know it's hard, but try not to be so nervous, your hands are **SO** shaky*!*" Kyle laced fingers gripping bad hand, discovering it rarely tremored held this way. Poising posture, articulated news story.

"Welcome to tonight's broadcast of *The Show*, bringing current events and a bit of the unexpected. Scandal in the White House: FBI uncovers misconduct from Nation's President, recent investigation on Tramp's financial revenues revealing startling discoveries." According to Federal Bureau of Investigation, Tramp's responsible swindling tuition money from thousands of unsuspecting college students." showing video of students standing outside Tramp University, "Not the first time caught in unethical business ventures, officials obtained evidence of keeping thousands of Americans' education money after constructing a college, collecting tuition, never opening it's doors. We reached out to the President hearing his side, he of course, unavailable for comment. We now turn our focus to Steven Hartigan for a compelling story from Aries, Steve?"

"Thanks Kyle! Might I add, higher-education's something we *all* should be aiming for." eyes resting on Kyle. "Pleased introducing Rosie, front desk clerk at Channel 9!" video crew showing picture of the new, front desk robot. "Brand new from Aries, Rosie found her home after saying goodbye to old clerk...Kyle what was her name?" Giving brief, disbelieving stare, "Daria was her name and as we remember so well, passed from cancer three months ago." "God rest her soul! Anyways, Rosie was manufactured just for us and I couldn't be happier! Look at the picture folks*(like people watching were too dumb seeing otherwise)*; eyes rotate a full, three-hundred sixty degrees, eliminating blind spots. She has night vision, sonar, and can detect transmissions within two-thousand miles. Rosie knows everything; data-transfer from existing security bots was completed well-in-advance. This means if Kyle wore a wig, paisley pajamas like his wife used to wear, Rosie would recognize him immediately." poorly-edited photo of Kyle wearing wig and women's pajamas aired for the television audience. "Rosie's our first line of defense; systems allow her to distinguish between friend and foe. With biological scanners detecting pulse-rate, breathing patterns, she even knows when someone's lying!" waiting for fake applause to subside, "Without further ado, here's our front desk clerk, Rosie!"

Robot moved quietly, fact one of these could come within inches absent notice made Kyle's stomach churn. "Welcome to *The Show* Rosie!" Waved dexterously with elongated arm, saying in hollow, female voice, *"Hello Steve, viewers at home, I am Rosie."* "I'd go-on for days describing how impeccably Aries Industries built you, afraid I'd fall short in detail. Tell us about yourself." Optics swung to-and-fro registering area with detailed accuracy. *"Refurbished four months, twelve days ago for Channel 9 employees as well as allowed guests. Granted permission overlaying security in event of emergency or breach, providing weapon-defense, medical-aid where necessary."* Feigning shock, "Mean for example, if Kyle over there has a breathing episode, you can provide lifesaving, medical aid?!" *"Affirmative."* Steven rested open palm across heart commenting, "Comforts my soul—wouldn't you agree Kyle?" "Please, continue Rosie."

knuckles turning white. *"Equipped with state-of-the-art scanners locating, differentiating between heat-signatures, facial-recognition software with integrated eye-tracing, detecting and reacting to smallest changes in behavior."* Steven looked wildly-about expecting thunderous applause from captivated audience. *"*Is this how you knew ordering my coffee with creamer*?"* referencing current memory-session, *"You asked me to."* erupting into boisterous laughter, machine rolling several inches away. *"*Describe your weapon-system.*"* Relaxing optics, *"Live-feed UAV, widespread auto-targeting, lethal ammunition discharged by way of strongest magnetic-propulsion known to man."* Steve commenting, *"*Polite, quiet, and deadly—just the way I like my women*!"* Kyle rolled eyes looking at watch, airtime infringing on paid advertising. *"*Before we go, give viewers demonstration of your weapon-sys—*" "Negative. After analysis, surroundings cannot absorb ammunition's magnitude."* staring at Kyle, *"Probable casualty."* *"*Sitting beside Kyle, *"*Newest model comes in two colors, obsidian black, and like our gal Rosie, prismatic white*!* If you're interested purchasing for yourself or business, starting price's around sixty-five thousand dollars, although we got Rosie for a slamming-deal because Braeylon owed me a favor*!"* referencing notes, *"*After commercials, weather*!* I'm a fat, furry fuck who loves pizza*!"*

Newsroom burst into laughter cutting to commercials, cameraman laughing so hard he started choking, falling to his knees, even Rosie making a hollow, chuckling noise indicating amusement. Swiveling chair, Kyle, *"*Next time you insult Aspen, knocking unconscious, force-feeding pizza down your throat.*"* He'd gotten him good and there was nothing he could do. Rewrote papers as a kindness though forbidden newscasters work on other's projects. Unspoken rule; each responsible creating and presenting own story. If reporter was unable fulfilling requirement, wouldn't be station's best-interest continuing employment. A loud slam followed by heels, Director Cordish *flying* down stairs overhanging studio. Bethany Cordish was in her mid-fifties, fought tooth-and-nail becoming Director within a male-dominated workplace. Tall, slim, gorgeous, dressed accordingly in designer skirt, acrylic nails shining bright green with small stars. Kind-of woman wanted on your side—not just for position in power. Possessed glowing intelligence, reputation for putting sexist men, know-it-all women in their place. "Do you *realize* what you said*?!* Give me reporting notes*!*" Lumbering over, dropping it near her tapping heel. "Sorry Beth." "Don't you *Beth* me, so help me God I'll shove foot up your incompetent ass*!*" reading his unacceptably-short piece of paper, "Roll extra commercials*!*" returning notes, "Mind rereading last sentence*?*" Retrieved badly-scratched glasses, reading, "I'm a fat furry…" "Again*!* Say it *loudly and proudly* just like you did for all our viewers*!*" cameraman finishing his laugh, finding phone, recording whole debacle. Bethany thundered, "If you don't, making you and that repugnant belly DANCE for your job*!*" Mustering feeble reporting smile, "I'm a fat, furry fuck who loves pizza*!*" Bethany slow-clapped, sound reverberating around studio. "Bravo Steven, most-honest thing you've said in eight years." glancing at Kyle, busy inspecting pencil-mark, "Three things to say and then you're to exit newsroom. Retype paper in way appearing like you don't have brain the size of a field mouse. Make it proper length for someone of your tenure. Lastly, write like you didn't attempt hurting our reputation*!*" After he exited, "We've had our fun, places, straighten your faces and we can move passed this." on Kyle, "Finishing broadcast without Hartigan, think you can manage last half-hour*?*" "Yes ma'am. Weather's lengthier due to wildfires."

       Midnight before Kyle finished research for following-night's broadcast. Despite how day started, happiest in a long time, not seeing shadow of Steve for evening's remainder. "Must be conquering complexities of forming sentences." closing laptop, eyes drifting to favorite mug. Had a professor in college lecturing on death, dying, and hard times. Described experience in such a way, helped conquer depression experienced after Aspen's passing.

       "My favorite mug meant the world to me. One day, retrieving from cupboard it slipped from grasp, shattering to many pieces. Do I overreact, let it dictate feelings for rest of the day, my whole life? Do I mourn, just a moment in it's loss, holding onto memories from which the mug originated? Absence of the mug bears no importance, it's in the feelings mug has given, memories associated carrying the salt of life." Thought of making it into decoration, hanging in his office or apartment. Moved for light-switch, noticing booger Steven left, sighing, pulled tissue from box on bookcase. Often wondered how man who was once centerpiece of 9 became such an imbecile, uncertain if he was married, had family bringing any joy in life. Only conclusive information was he owned considerable number of shares in Aries Industries. Cleaned rude gesture, closing door, relieved Hartigan's office closed, striking worry of bombardment for tonight's payback. Elevator moved downward, whereupon he would exit, scanning ID with door bot before traveling home. Footsteps echoed throughout empty lobby, lighting reflecting-off recently cleaned floor. Window, though streaked with cleaning residue, Kyle observed Rosie staring at him, certain he'd detected movement, robot's shadow **wavering** from licking movement. "Day's excitement must be getting to me." jumping in surprise at hollow voice coming-through intercom. *"Present identification; recording exit-time, hours worked for research purposes."* Streets were empty save for passing car, people foraging dumpsters, sleeping in business entryways. Unlocking door, headed for his lonely, queen-sized bed, not bothering to undress.

Laptop illuminated the large intelligence room, person facing screen was old–far older than looked. Held glass of expensive scotch, swirling ice-cubes with slow, rotation of his wrist, wearing a midnight-black suit, tie matching color of intense, green eyes, magnified behind prescription glasses. By outward appearances, Braeylon Skyson was the kind-of man taking grandson fishing, buying granddaughter hair-ribbons. Opening command-prompt open, typed a few lines and pressed enter; Earth's holographic display coming-to-life from ceiling projectors. Glanced briefly at dials twisting and turning on company-crafted watch, spinning outermost bevel with a practiced hand, humanoid robot entering through hidden entry, walking slope without hint of strain, delivering a black box. Opened calling application pinned to start-menu, ringing twice before answered.

Office masked in shadow, man drawing on expensive cigar, ember revealing unpleasant pair of lips. "Braeylon." "Hello, my boy." laptop reappearing on walls, "Trouble in your neck of the woods; don't want to find your replacement before use runs out." "Location runs on all networks, unwise calling before our designated meeting." "Come too far to deal in uncertainty and doubt." Waving cigar, "Everything's under control, no damage from momentary lapse-of-focus, identity remaining intact." flicking ash onto carpet, "News reporter speaks poorly of our largest contributor–*ending* this charade. The President doesn't need any more attention than what's been brought to light." "Story was very revealing, oaf bringing more attention calling himself a fat furry fuck. Calling Tramp, discussing these matters after we're done here. Can assure, he'll continue wasting time with poor political-gambles, plane trips." "One concern." "What else troubles airy head*?*" "Increasing resources of vigilante group, the Collective Conscious." "Those fools are reaching end of their lifespan*!*" picking-up box, "Inside holds answer to destroying any standing in our way." Man other side of conversation leaned forward attempting to ascertain contents. "Let me guess Braeylon, another one of your robots." Chuckling nastily, "Similar to the A.I. device we've finished rolling-out to every major college. A news broadcast's scheduled notifying public of these…" reading watch, "this very evening. There's no fighting establishment of the New World Order. Humans will be herded willingly, or bent and broken into submission!" "Going to let me see, or just hold me in suspense?" Braeylon moved laptop to desk's edge, setting box in front. "Far more-useful than you, or lamebrain President. Design's simple, one mission hardwired into it's system: Dominate ANY human, giving desired upgrade." Opening, all to be seen was a dim, red glow. Phone-call recipient laughed, *"That's* the great robot? You believe a miniaturized, spider robot is going to make people bend to your will?" It stood three inches tall, walking nimbly on eight, thin legs made from surgical-steel. Legs clicked rapidly facing Commander, awaiting command. "No ordinary spider; reaches speeds of thirteen miles-per-hour, programmed traveling in hordes. Once the SpAIder software uploads to Codex, it will act as a virus, diligently and effectively downloading information. These have been transported without detection to satellites around Earth. When time's right, mankind falls and I become ruler!"

Seal of intelligence chamber opened, yelling and moaning in background, Eager viewing commotion, laptop swinging around revealing prisoner shackled to gurney, escorted by sentry robots. " Victim thrashed-about violently, bleeding from torture-wounds. "This is a member from the group you were just so concerned about. You'll find they're pockets of information waiting to be mined." To prisoner, "One, last time, before spider friend makes *pulpy mess* ripping it out: Where's base camp for the Collective Conscious?" He yelled, "Dissect every neurotransmitter, my life-force will withhold this knowledge!! You're traitors of God, everything life was meant to be! All of us or none of us!" Braeylon grabbed his head, slamming it hard against the metal gurney, then whispered, "None of us!" SpAIder sprang to life, screams echoed throughout chamber then all became silent.

SPEAR & THE ARCHER

Customers arrived and departed. Pushing toward afternoon, breakfast crowds dwindled, making-way for early lunch. *"How is this possible?"* Joe was visibly shaken, Daisy achieving new shade of pale-green. Mrs. Bit replied, ***"BEST NOT ASKING WHY OR HOW, BUT WHERE! IF YOU INSIST, I'LL SPILL THE BIG THRILL–CURTAIN CALL HAS ARRIVED! MEN OF EVIL, POOR JUDGMENT DESTINED US CROSSING PATHS!"*** Byte eyeing pathetic pair, "Here's the deal; telling a story, will be decisions made throughout said story. Each time you make a choice, drastically alters the outcome. Resulting from this change, it will then alter course of the future. Word of caution: Do not judge lest ye too, be judged." Joe sat fuming, Byte picturing steam-engine in place of his head. "How stupid do you think we are*!?* Don't know where you were born, but this is planet Earth. Here, there's no such thing as magic, God, OR happy endings*!* Find some other saps to con*!"* Byte stood, saying, "Sure. You have the right choosing to participate and frankly, you both smell of felonies and moldy cabbage. If I had choice, I'd relocate south in hopes of catching pair of *hotties* to work with." Mrs. Bit gave her husband terse look swatting knee. "What*?* I *know* you agree; certain, time in *Singapore—"* wife cutting sentence short, beginning to blush. ***"NO REGALING OF PAST CONQUEST; HERO OF OUR VERY OWN, FUTURE IN BALANCE! READY SHOWING WORLD WORTH?"*** Daisy nodded, eager beginning. ***"THAT'S THE SPIRIT! STORY'S TITLED, SPEAR & THE ARCHER!"***

It was early 1500s, empires amassing great, naval fleets, more nations charting to unexplored territories. Great Britain was leading in naval dominance, credited discovering The New World. Ship was seen struggling some miles outside a ravaged coastline. Storm delayed in westerly movement due to a harsh drop in barometric pressure, catching ship and all manning her by surprise. Waves slammed against sides of vessel with ferocity unlike anything witnessed, gale-force winds causing men aboard to fall constantly, grasping at anything to prevent falling overboard. Outcome looked grim;

waves brought cracking and splintering, each strike weakening ship's hull. Rowboats and cannons were jettisoned hours earlier preventing them from capsizing.

"Course and heading?" "Matters not!" yelled Colonel Westley Overturf of the Royal British Navy, "Lost mast after daybreak!" *Cortana* was hundred twenty-two feet bow-to-stern, used for transporting resources, merchant goods across shorter distances of open water. Expedition ordered in retaliation to Spain's gold conquests, fight for territory on the forefront of every, formidable nation's agenda. Entering day two of maelstrom, Westley regretted decision; if Cardinal Authority hadn't dictated need for experienced archer hunting, defending camp, would've allowed opportunity come-and-go. Most practiced musket, preferred method for distance combat. Westley disliked this tactic; loss of life reloading, placing powder and ammunition into barrel was weakness older strategies could easily defend against. By time brigade fired shot, already volleyed ten arrows, finding cover. Though mates teased preferred combat-style, each could not discount his great skill, ability overpowering enemies hand-to-hand. Crippled ship listed heavily portside, men rushing from lower to upper carrying wooden buckets of water. Westley observed newest recruit struggling with two, white as a sheet, first time on deployment. He emptied buckets overboard, slipping, falling onto deck as another great wave hit starboard. washing him portside. Finding rope along ship's perimeter, holding-on in panicked desperation, *"HELP!"*

"WHERE YOU DECIDE WHAT WESTLEY DOES!" Joe, first to answer, "I say fuck him. Obviously out of his league, assigned bucket-duty because it's all he's good for! If I were Westley, I'd watch next wave wash him overboard." Daisy, "Westley should save him. Even if it's new guy's first journey, must have skills making him important." Looked at Mrs. Bit rendering, "Appears we're at an impasse." ***"WROTE THE BOOK ON FORMALITIES BUT CAN'T FOR LIFE OF ME REMEMBER THE DETAILS—TELL WHAT HAPPENS!"*** "Customary woman be allowed going first. Chivalrous, *humbling, POLITE.*" loading tobacco in his pipe, "Helpful words of advice: This is no game. I know it's hard for man of your brain power realizing, if you go through life burning bridges others built, find yourself on deserted island—without a map." ***"NOT TO MENTION, MAN EAGER BEING RID-OF IS CARTOGRAPHER!"***

Westley pushed-away from starboard, arriving beside struggling comrade, lifting him upright. "Thought I was a goner–maiden voyage no less!" "Do not mention it; once in similar position and a man did same for me." Rain blew from all directions, visibility reduced to mere meter. Another wave battered ship, large fish washing onto deck sweeping feet from underneath. Cry escaped Westley's throat grabbing for railing, missing, he and cartographer plummeting into depths below. Kicked forcefully and instinctively, fearing waves would pummel into jetsam. Breaking surface, "Cannot swim surface, dive beneath, make for land!" Breast-stroked through swirling water, relieved finding shipmate strong swimmer, following close-behind, slightly to left. Next wave crashed directly upon them, tremendous force cartwheeling both, knocking Westley unconscious.

DREAM STATED DREAMSCAPE

*Fire from the torch burned a **deep** orange, mysterious cave, an eternal aperture. Mushrooms of varying sizes emitted soft, green light, small glow worms crawled across ceiling and walls. Tunnel stretched-on forever, casting long, flickering shadows. "Go further, go back, she fell right through the crack." Tunnel widened, opening into immense cavern. Standing at entrance, unable describing beautiful sight before him. Mushrooms inside this portion were larger, glowing blue, red, and green. Crystal* ^{STA}LAG_{MITES} *grew from all angles of sacred space, no two alike, each representing a soul lost in the Universe. There was an opening above, moths fluttering in circles, others on stalagmite, antennae feeling for presence of others. Eyes fell to cavern's center, where filtered moonlight pooled to stone floor. There, knelt a woman in elegant dress, in hands, small, tree sapling. She was without question most-beautiful woman dreamt to meet, eyes filled with sorrow, bearing overwhelming tenacity. "Last chance dwindles, new hope kindles, minds sharing space such as* YOU & I*..." placing sapling upon stone floor. "Without reason for every Season, lacking rhyme rethreading woven time, nearing edge of abyss, every second of His perfect plan amiss." sweeping arm in half-circle, filling space with her alluring words, "Enemies close-in surrounding friends, while broken pieces of our framework mends, there's truth we must face." looking right at him, "Find our new place. Isn't much time, Universe's tainted by crime. If to fulfill destiny, we can no longer wait."*

*Moonlight vanished, spiders scuttling walls leaving trails smelling of putrid sulfur. In woman's place, a creature twitching sporadically, limbs unfolding from within skeletal corpse, eyes, little-more than gaping chasms, liquid-fire burning deep magma. **"FIND THE BOOK!"** she sneered, falling him to knees, **"KNEEL WHILE I HACK YOU IN TWO!"***

Images of the beautiful woman, wolf, and demon pervading all else, vaguely remembered shaving, dressing, chosen tie matching woman's eye-color. Kyle didn't think about love much after Aspen, but considered dream burden-of-proof—eternal soulmates are real. Fought urge crying, bolstering himself with the hope it brought—I'll meet Aspen again, in this life and next.

"Here's Mumsy Mrs. Cantwell, might I add, he was very friendly!" "Sorry about the potato salad, when I get hankerin' for southern cooking my eyes get cocky!" sharing laugh, "Tell you what, headed to the store later, get all the fixings, make you a batch!" Smiling gratitude, "That's appreciated, tired of ordering from same, three places." Descended stairs determined not letting anything dampen-mood, unable believing co-host so complacent he didn't review words until spewing them for live, TV-audience. "What you get cutting corners." There was noticeable absence of Aries robots on the streets today. Repressed a laugh imagining them calling respective offices saying they'd *"caught a bug"* and would be in late. Observed commotion, altercation inside news lobby. Holding out ID, "What's going on inside sec-bot?" *"Hello, Kyle Clark. Minor break-in last night, nothing to worry about. Director Cordish wishes speaking with you."* Made-way across lobby to elevator and when it opened Steven was absent, licking wounds from his most-recent humiliation. Arriving at office, found his door wide-open.

Papers were strewn-about, desks drawers rummaged, chair overturned, laptop nowhere in sight, trashcan dumped, mug pieces scattered everywhere. Kyle returned toppled chair upright, sitting, formulating a list of suspects when voice made him lose train of thought. "Hiding secrets and not telling me?" Bethany entering Kyle's office. "Hey, it's not all bad Kyle." trying to cheer him up, "At least you have this thingy." placing oxygen mask over mouth, making a funny face, weak smile in return before changing demeanor. "If Steve has something to do with this I'm booting his ass out an open window!" Patting him lightly, "Already looked into that, must be mastermind behind his on-air confession?" Kyle said nothing— *too smart* for him to lie. Letting-out a big laugh, "That messed him up Kyle! If it would've been any other news channel, would've been promoted." sitting on desk, not letting skirt ride too high, "Anyways, reviewed relevant camera-footage and it would appear "the fat furry fuck" stayed in office all night. According to information received, ransacked by teenage girl." Kyle was flabbergasted. Why would punk-kid break into

9 let-alone his boring office? Anger grew about laptop; notes, writing done since original hire-date. "You're kidding?" determining if there was cruel joke yet to discover. "In a way, I am, you were robbed by a kid!" attempting to lighten mood, "Officer's arriving within the hour to file a report. Until then, relax, always more news to report." before doorway, "I knew you were editing Steven's notes. Man's been at this station longer than I and after each broadcast, throws his work in the trashcan. I know your writing-style. Steve's, let's just say I've seen pigeons take more-appetizing shits." exiting. Kyle began aggravating task of office-recovery. Crawling under desk retrieving pens, noticed pink sticky-note.

SPEAR & THE ARCHER

Joe slammed his fists in anger. "Told you we should've let useless, silly nanny die*!* Now, Westley's unconscious in the worst storm ever, with fruit-cup of a map drawer*!*" Daisy, "Does this mean we lost and destroyed the world*?*" ***"THERE'S MORE TO NOVICE SEAFARER THAN MEETS THE EYE!"***

Westley would've thought the young man dead, but since he snored softly, elected leaving him to rest. Ocean had returned to calm state, lightning striking throughout darkened clouds, ship nowhere in sight. Couldn't imagine them setting-down oar, entryways boarded-shut to limit water finding way below decks. Far as the eye could see, made landfall on series of islands dotting the Atlantic. Wincing, gingerly ran a hand along neck; concussion without care, bedrest dampened survival-chances. After ensuring he didn't receive long-term injury, moved to where young man slept, hearing snapping branches beyond the thicket. Westley was impeccable soldier and survivor, however, longbow missing, foreign territory with wildebeest and person's unknown, just an easy-meal waiting to be captured. Tried pinpointing source of noise, only seeing beach awoke on, jungled darkness beyond. Reached for dagger holstered alongside boot, without looking directly at him, found front of vest, grabbed ahold and shook. "What's going on*?*" "Heard noise; low and quickly to boulders, taking-cover." Shuffling to location. "See anything*?*" Westley shook head peering around boulder. "Likely an animal, bird taking-flight. Without bow, cannot properly defend us in the open. Man nudged him grinning, longbow in hand. "Rescue quiver*?*" his silence providing answer. No matter, unworried finding materials crafting. Straightening spectacles, "Private Timothy Whittle, cartographer assigned to expedition." Made sense why Westley failed noticing him until storm's fury; untrained in weaponry, cartographers establish course and heading. "Whom do I have pleasure meeting*?*" "Colonel Westley Overturf, pleasure returned. Idea as to whereabouts*?*" "Storm gave us quite the tumble, lost location after mast was struck by lightning. Not to mention, Commodore's compass needs recalibration; storm disabled it's magnetic-charge."

Vessel most-likely on the bottom of the Atlantic, months before Britain would send search. Campaign now carried orders like he'd receive during war; locate, stockpile resources for long-term survival. Canteen was empty and to knowledge, neither carried rations. Sullenly, "Quiver's lost, needing arrow. Stay or accompany, choice's yours." Coming alongside, "Done research on climate and terrain, always *dreamt* being an explorer. After this, allow me locating bushes harnessing berries." Marooned on mysterious island was a serious misfortune, another navigating, acquiring food and water undoubtedly increased their odds. Forced enduring experience alone, would've made floating-platform in trees, which in-and-of-itself creates possibility of falling injuries. "Listen closely, for longbow properly shooting handcrafted arrow, must be roughly meter in length, straight, free from notches. Bow pulls at thirty-eight kilograms; if arrow's imperfect it will splinter, rendering shot useless." Squeamish toward violence, removed spectacles, impulsively cleaning them. "Learnt *f-f-fascinating* things about the indigenous people. Research at university taught tribes inhabiting hunt in parties of master spearmen." Westley heard many tales about prize-worthy trophy animals such as elephant, boar, colonies of fire-ants capable stripping flesh clean-to-bone. Using dagger, removed leaves and branches from promising lengths of wood, collecting dozen limbs before satisfied. Timothy, "Ready searching berries? Found near trees, outcroppings where water runs freely." Jungle floor rose steeply, men dehydrated, pleased hearing trickling direction travelled. Timothy explained, "Many ground-bearing fruits are in the Amazon, however, most lead to vomiting, dehydration, diarrhea. Many consume wrong berries, worse-for-wear doing-so. *Red and sweet, good to eat. Green and bitter, stomach will jitter.*" Coming to a break, discovered freshwater runoff, sending rabbits in different directions. Large, *green tree boa* hung from tree, flicking forked-tongue. "Optimal location; ground's soft not spongy, stand better-chance taking earth, not carried away by storms. Let me know before trying anything!" Westley stood there, suddenly not leader of survival plan. Quickly overcame ego, moving forward searching. Bending low while still on feet, scanned ground for fruits. Feeling foolish, looked at cartographer observing strategy; crawling on all-fours. "Respected member of Royal British Navy crawling on all-fours searching rancid berries!" despondently, "Water's drinkable?" "Should boil any collected; Amazon harbors nasty bacterium, germs not accustomed to England. However, air relatively-clear of city-created smog, take opportunity, runoff will be gone by tomorrow." Losing patience with insufferable know-it-all, making-note of asking how he'd saved them after establishing camp. "Woohoo!" Timothy cried, "Come; familiarize with structure and color." Standing, uniform soaked-through, covered in dirt and grime. Found Timothy meters away behind fallen trees, giving-way during heavy storm. "Observe their bright, red color. Important remembering shading, size of bush." Focused on setting camp, "If done explaining stupid bush, like to gather berries, fill canteen. Nightfall's arriving; make it nigh-impossible seeing." Gathered what was charitable, returning to where they'd found water. "Should drink our fill." "Allow me determining suitability for consumption." Food and water supply restored, returned to beach, establishing camp.

Burning, orange sun sank ever-lower, easterly trade-winds cooling sunburned skin. Portioned berries between, eating first meal together; tart with little-flavor, acidity burning throat. "Sun-up, catching real food. Should collect wood, laying on beach so it dries throughout day. Never properly thanked you for saving…thank you. How did man scrawny as you manage?" "After surfacing, strength was nearly-spent. Far-enough behind, only cartwheeled in water. Recovering, saw you sinking, dragged by massive wave, longbow smacking." pointing to cut and bruise under eye. Somewhat ashamed failed noticing, also done everything avoiding eye-contact. Timothy continued, "Bow over shoulder, grabbed firmly onto leg, surfacing. If not for lightning, swum sideways along coast, each wave landed directly upon us." Even in setting sun, discerned embarrassment. "Not easiest getting-on with, trusted comrades not knowing how to take me. Hearing how you tried so valiantly saving, new sense of respect, may be brave after all." Timothy smiled looking down at boots. "Father wasn't present younger years, neither was mum, always found comfort in studies, classic novels. Fate twists lives of men to no end, fortunate making-go of this, rather than being alone with books." producing two, somewhat _flattened_ mushrooms. "Considered saving for weak broth, instead, let's share together as friends." Inspecting, extending toward Timothy's, making toast. "As friends."

T̶u̶E̶S̶D̶A̶Y̶ L̶O̶S̶E̶D̶A̶Y̶

Elected not showing sticky-note to Bethany, having enough on her plate regarding Steve*'s* moment on television. Detective arrived; member of the Federal Bureau of Investigation working conjunctively with Aries Industries. In a deep, emotionless voice, "Special Agent Wells. Here to ask questions, hopefully answer yours." offering handshake, "Intend cataloging missing items…other matters first; picture of culprit, hoping you shed light on identity." Nodded stating, "Don't associate with too many teenagers, but I'll do my best helping." Snapping open briefcase for a picture, handing it over. "Only image cameras managed getting before exiting. Appears she escaped through ductwork into elevator shaft and out through basement fire door. How she unlocked them, yet to determine. Wasn't until opening fire door Rosie discovered heat-signature." Kyle brought picture eye-level, looking closely at blown-up image, staring into face of a teenage girl. Pretty for her age, few scattered freckles on nose and high cheekbones, sporting medium-length, dark-brown hair with red lowlights—eyes staring into camera with smug smirk. Though photo didn't show much in way of height comparison, around five-and-a-half feet tall. "Unfortunately, don't recognize the little brat. Saying the new, Aries bot *didn't* detect her?" Detective frowned. "We've determined this is no ordinary girl; she came here looking for something and we assume she found it. We're unable determining entry or how long she was inside, leaving no fingerprints behind— even inside the ductwork. Mr. Clark, ever heard of the vigilante group, Collective Conscious?" Not wanting events transpired in the wee-hours affecting his job-standing, elected not showing the sticky. Plus, didn't like menacing energy detective exhibited. Replied, "Remember co-host Steve doing segment some months back…thought them mainly thieves, scavengers of electronics and Aries Industries technology." He laughed at Kyle. "Need to check your facts Mr. Clark. Operated last five years, likely longer. Not common thieves; defectors of United States military and government, special operatives, technicians, scientists, mechanics—you name it, they have it. Most members are on our *most-wanted* list for a reason: Stealing millions in technology, hacking Aries databases, making away with critical information pertinent to not just our Nation, but entire World." Kyle was bewildered, what did this secret, criminal organization want? Skill of teenager breaking into news station did suddenly make more sense. Feeling scrutinizing eyes, detective suspiciously watching him. Returning to conversation, "Here's a list of items taken. Mostly-concerned about laptop; not so much stored documents—sentimental attachment to it. Wife died shortly after started working here, photos cannot be retrieved until culprit's caught." taking short list, reading before storing in briefcase. "If this is all Mr. Clark, there are phone calls I'll be making getting all this sorted out, we'll do our best recovering stolen possessions. Business card—in case you think of anything useful." "Will do, good luck out there. I'll keep an eye out about town; sure she has friends, won't be long before someone runs into her." Grabbing briefcase, "Good, you do that." leaving without glance back. "What a crazy morning!" Good thing he finished research for today's segments yesterday, also fortunate Collective Conscious wasn't interested in President's unethical business dealings, musing they already knew. Couldn't believe found himself *upset* teenage girl didn't want news story. Pressed onward in work, day progressing rapidly, Steven never stepping into office barraging with insults and putdowns, thinking best thing done was type that one-liner ending his shitty report. Every minute of broadcast accounted for, thought about using time before getting replacement laptop. Moving to do so, Bethany appeared in his doorway. "Director, what's the deal?" "Seen your useless co-host anywhere? Note on door, *"Back in five."*, was two hours ago!" Kyle looked at wristwatch, less than an hour before going on-air. "Maybe he's at after-school program learning how to read and write?" Wanted to get mad, unable keeping straight face. "No idea how much I needed that! Be prepared doing whole segment if he doesn't reappear." Though Kyle didn't carry ability to foolishly improvise, no problem handling thirty-five-minutes. "Consider it done." hoping to never see unpleasant man again, realizing Bethany remained, studying carefully. "You okay?" Shrugged, "Guess today's off." Returning to desk, "Been with plenty of men over the years Mr. Clark, can easily tell when thoughts are bothering. Don't have to tell me what's going on. Quite frankly, reason why we work well together. Whatever pains, avoid dwelling; regret holding onto hurt instead of focusing on variables had control over." Kyle looked appreciatively into her kind, smiling eyes. "One day I'll talk about Aspen and events surrounding her death. Not sure if understand what happened in own mind...just know I'm always missing her." gazing window, scanning tall buildings and skyscrapers dotting city. Eyes leveled at skyline, Rocky Mountains through thin, layer of smog, "Agree with you on last bit, always worked well together–found personal issues and reporting don't mix." Bethany chortling, "*Awful* things Steven's told pertaining to alcoholism and erectile dysfunction. One more thing Mr. Clark." smiling brilliantly, "As reporters, sometimes get into mindset we're isolated, pinnacles of information, built to find and regurgitate. Don't forget greatest gift we have; using emotion, personality honestly communicating, connecting in genuine experience spurring world into action." Impressed with her ability refocusing purpose, "Yes Ms. Cordish, communication is key."

Beeping watch stirred Kyle from a light-doze, hopeful conducting tonight's broadcast alone. Disappointed moments later, hearing Bethany yell, "Lucky you have report backing that excuse! Get you're ass on-set or I'm ripping you out of your business suit, making you spin advertisements on the street corner!" Steve hadn't said a word since night-prior, figured jaded man had insults accumulated. Headed studio's direction, surprised seeing Hartigan standing in the hallway, smiling. "Kyle, how *are* you doing? Wanted to say thanks for the *little joke* played during broadcast, I'd g so far as to say you've inspired me, bringing back desire of being the best reporter I possibly can!" Kyle halted, certain something was afoot. "Did the Director hit you with a cinderblock?" He laughed responding, "Not in the slightest!" *softly* jabbing elbow in Kyle's ribs. "Besides, we know if she'd done that, would've molested me. Come-along Old Bean, news has a *'best if used by'* date and we must thrill our viewers!" Confused by strange change in personality, continued to studio, placing oxygen tank underneath desk, skimming notes for his next, Ronald Tramp story. Steve came beside flashing a weird, toothy smile. "My story's going to blow your President conspiracies out of the water!" Kyle stared critically before replying, "Aren't *conspiracies*, internal investigations across multiple agencies confirm data and information conveyed to our viewers. Only time before Senate files the motion, impeaching him for acts inside and outside his Presidential term." "Aren't you concerned about technology Aries Industries releases?" Not looking-up from notes, said, "Even if I was interested Steve, you're about to tell us about it." "Guess you're right. At least I'll see your face as it mirrors expression of millions!"

"Welcome to *The Show*, segment where we bring current, sometimes scandalous news to your television. Opening tonight with an old favorite; that's right, you guessed it, Ronald Tramp. Shocking allegations brought to Federal prosecutors' attention, intelligence agencies incriminating our President. After conducting an internal investigation, CIA found President Tramp had significant involvement rigging the most-recent, Presidential election. Without any authority from political constituents, embezzled millions by way of tax-fraud and phone scams, and insider trading. Tramp used ill-gotten funds *"donating"* to foreign governments rigging the 2016 election. There's been a hold-up in investigations as the Pentagon, President's bank, numerous corporations failed following Supreme Court's affidavits for release-of-information. Making matters worse, evidence tying President Tramp to supporting child sex-trafficking; his longtime business crony recently incarcerated on these charges. Unfortunately, 9 correspondents also received confirmation he hung himself last night while awaiting trial." pausing for effect, "Well Steve, guess we'll find more about these shocking facts as intelligence agencies obtain subpoenas necessary for release-of-information." Not convinced in the slightest, "Innocent until proven guilty, that's what *I* always say! He's *President*; maintain respect while experts do their jobs. Who knows, may give him full-exoneration!" "If I'm not mistaken Steve, another *fascinating* story from Aries Industries."

"That's right! Remember big announcement about Aries partnering with education producing a unit managing workload? Well folks, professionals at Aries created a microchip that programs to an individual's workload, assisting in planning, decision-making, cognitive operation!" cueing video. "All required is small, virtually-harmless incision, where they implant this new technology. Microfilament extremities are excited from internal battery, finding necessary the neurotransmitters and binding to them—similar to robot or healthcare professional administering vaccination. Vehicle of polymers acts as binding agent, fooling body into believing it's human tissue!" Hartigan paused, allowing video playback to catch-up. Kyle couldn't help feeling uncomfortable; never a pursuer of robotics, artificial intelligence, monopoly Aries controlled. Sadly, amongst minority as dependency for robotics, software programs became necessity. Infrastructure that created modern society; banking transactions, transportation, goods and commerce, military operations. Every major business used Aothex, Baothex, and Codex, information fed through networks into countless servers. In short, if weren't a paying customer, world tended moving-on without. Video playback showed psychologists performing tests on sample population in Las Vegas, Nevada. "Preliminary testing was a monumental success; undergraduates at the University of Northern Las Vegas suffering zero side-effects, indicating increased productivity by as much as seventy-five percent! Future's now; Aries Industries made these affordable—costing less than companies charge for cellphones! Procedure and device, average citizen only needs one thousand dollars! Matter of fact, went to closest production center over lunch, getting procedure done myself." Camera zoomed-in, showing irritated spot, pair of red, blinking lights protruding. Kyle nearly fell in shock and disgust, not prepared for what he'd seen. "Seven hours ago received upgrade, boosted studio production absent side-effects! All I have to do is think of something and my chip responds, integrating it into routine. Scans internal organs suggesting anything from meals to possible health risks!" Unable containing himself, "You're by far the **STUPIDEST** person I've ever met! Any idea the dangers of putting foreign object into brain, linking it to the central nervous system? What if it malfunctions?" "Plenty of *malfunctions* in this world, like your messed-up hand! The way people *think* and *act*; Aries only looks to help correct these errors—suggest you get one. Maybe then, you'll stop mourning your dead wife! Finally, you'll stop making *sweet, sweet love* to her rotting corpse every night!"

Good and bad fused into one emotion; dream waking him feeling forever changed, teenage break-in and now, blind rage. Chaos mounted to fever-pitch could no longer control. Kyle never remembered walking to where Steven was standing, *did* remember how **AMAZING** it felt when strong hand connected with fat slob's chin. ***"YOU'RE A PIECE OF SHIT! YEARS I'VE PUT-UP WITH YOUR NONSENSE! LET ME SHOW YOU HOW IT FEELS!"*** throwing punches, cameraman struggling to cut live-broadcast. All Kyle could see amongst angry tears was Steven*'s smug* smile. Stumbling, wrapped him in a bear hug, whispering, "Didn't I say real truth has expiration date*?* Broadcasting days are over.*"* Bethany made it to fighting reporters location, reaching for Kyle with strong hand, grabbed back of dress jacket, yanking him away. "You did it gentlemen; *ruined* Channel 9's reputation*!* Kyle, meet me in my office*!* Steven, go to your office, don't come out until I've contemplated your cruelty*!"* Numbers on the wall told the whole story; fool of himself in front of thirty-four million viewers.

Byte puffed-on his most-cherished possession, unnoticed by some, mystical magic inviting humor into the mix. Daisy was twitching sporadically, discomforted by early stages of drug withdrawal. Mrs. Bit chose passing time during intermission smiling at pictures. *"CAN YOU BELIEVE HOW MANY FAMOUS PEOPLE HAVE EATEN HERE? CAN'T IMAGINE SEATTLE BEING RICH PERSON'S FIRST PLACE TO VISIT, BUT WHATEVER! READY TO CONTINUE? I'M TWITTER-PATED JUST THINKING ABOUT IT!"* Joe, glaring at eccentrically-happy woman, "Actually, I'd rather blow my brains out than sit with you two psychos and twitchy addict*!*" Daisy, slapping weakly, "You know I'm self-conscious about my twitching*!* If they hadn't taken our stuff it wouldn't be a problem." Byte was always amused by arguments individuals encounter, finding most disagreements begin from impatience, miscommunication.

"Don't you degenerates worry, soon you'll be back to stolen car, on to some poorly-conceived respite. That, or this is last diner you'll ever visit." Joe growled, "You're holding us hostage playing this stupid, story game*!* How do we know this is real and not some way preoccupying while the Feds come*!?*" "Yes, we technically roped you into this situation—" *"TECHNICALLY, IT'S ALL OUR PROBLEMS!"* Byte smiled and said, "Indeed it is. Sap playing last choked on his damn breakfast–would've preferred him. Alas, we perform based on rules you wouldn't understand. Feds aren't coming to arrest you, judge of yourselves once this is all over. *Lastly,* if you refuse playing, you will die. Fate has way of finding every piece when humanity breaks apart." blowing smoke into Joe's face. Daisy, to everyone's surprise, Daisy, "Whole thing wouldn't be so bad if we got to make some more choices." *"FORWARD THINKING; FIRST ONE STARTS SLOWLY, TESTING PATIENCE!"* Joe, done coughing, "Story better get interesting pretty-damn quick. Westley's teamed-up with useless, bag of bones and has almost no chance of surviving, but what the hell*!*"

Morning bathed beachfront in a golden blanket, immersing environment in smothering fog. Concentrated, heated moisture such as this condensates upon skin and clothes, burden becoming heavier, body susceptible to parasites and infection. Foot protection swells, falling apart, skin-pores remain expanded, draining vital nutrients. Fat stores break-down, muscular form diminishes, susceptible to hundreds of different, biting insects—precisely what woke Westley. Sleeping only hours, rubbed tired eyes, fighting urge scratching, likely developing skin or blood infection in his weakened state. Frustration and inadequacy gnawed, not used to relying on another keeping full and healthy. Glanced toward trees, back to sleeping comrade, debating waking asking help, or risk venturing alone, hunting wild game.

Byte paused regalement. Looking moodily at disinterested Storyweavers, "Part you've been waiting for." Mrs. Bit hummed and drummed for dramatic effect, "You can have him sit there and do nothing, wake Timothy, gather more berries, fungi, or test arrows in hopes of catching a trophy-meal." Daisy considered options while Joe stared into space, not interested or concerned what would come from decision. *"SOON AS DECISION'S MADE, WAVING-OVER WAITRESS BUT FIRST, PLAY! CLOSED MOUTHS DON'T GET FED!"* "Can he go to the bathroom first? I need to piss and possibly shit." Byte, "By all means, it's not like life as we know it hangs in the balance. If balls drop and you try leaving, you *will* pass away. Men better than you have tried, always ends same way." Muttering something under his breath, Joe ambled to the restroom, Mrs. Bit calling, *"HOPE EVERYTHING COMES OUT!"* grinning at partner, hoping he'd noticed her. Byte patted her hat saying, "Yes, it was a good one." Daisy suppressed a giggle saying, "Sorry about him, he isn't very nice and hates being undermined." "How did woman like you, end-up with him?" "I guess after living on the run for awhile, start making friends, shacking-up with people you would never associate with. Joe's a person I *fell* into; not all bad, not much good either. Drugs I'm addicted to...body's grown dependent." Byte pulled pipe away and said, "Jeez Drama Queen, asked about dimwit you're with, not your entire life." Daisy smiled faintly, nodding appreciation. "Must be confusing, us coming and technically holding you hostage, taking-part

in this. Tales we play turn at a point; if we don't fill
spaces with redeeming story, one of moral-fiber,
sustenance*...*" ***"REALITY BREAKS, WORLD FALLING
TO RUIN!"*** Daisy eventually said, "Know I don't fully
understand what's happening, and you two kinda freak
me out, in it for the long-haul.*"* Byte replied through
plumes of smoke, "We're freaky. Deductive reasoning's
incredible; you don't have choice anymore. When a
person decides leading life of a criminal, their world gets
smaller and _{smaller} until they've killed themselves making
wrong decisions, given away right to choose.*"* Joe
rounded corner, break not changing his demeanor.
"Now that I've played firefighter, good to keep going.
After he pees, should swim out to sea and drown so we
can get on with our lives*!"* Mrs. Bit's smile wavered.
***"TREAT HERO LIKE HE'S YOU. IT'S UNDENIABLY
TRUE IF YOU TAKE CARE OF OTHERS, THEN YOU
WILL IN TURN, TAKE CARE OF YOURSELF!"***
"Wasn't listening to word you said, *will* say, if there's
anything I've learned, it's taking care of myself*!"* Byte,
"Every time you open your mouth I think to myself, "No
way he could disappoint further.*"* Then, you open your
mouth and there it is. Arrogant pride's dominated lives of
many, hasn't been one further along than anyone else.*"*
Joe to Daisy, "Want to go pee too—need to get in-
character*!"* "Man does have a point, arrogant, damn
proud of it. Let's get through this so we can sort our lives
out.*"* sitting taller, "Westley should wake Timothy,
asking opinion on plans for the day.*"* Joe, "Why include
useless weakling in this scenario? Westley's having
issues with twig caring for him as it is, let the man try
hunting on his own*!"* Byte, "Safety in numbers, or it's a
man thing you wouldn't understand.*"* Daisy waited,
hoping Joe would relent, instead, gave look saying, "It's
my way, or the highway.*"* Weighing options, "It's not
rocket science; cooperate, helping Westley survive, or
get his skull bashed.*"* Daisy, turning from Joe in disdain,
"We'll go your stupid route but if he gets beaten by a
bunch of monkeys and it causes an earthquake, hope it
takes you first*!"* Joe quietly raised hands, signifying
victory. "Don't forget, decided he'd take a leak, making
sure he doesn't piss himself getting murdered by some
wildebeest*!!"* "Alright wise guy, relieving himself as
suggested, but he's going to do it standing, instead of
squatting like a pussy."

Relieving himself, Westley decided sneaking away, hunting in his natural element. "No help needed from talking encyclopedia. Last thing wanted loosing arrow, "Wait*!!* Nanny who used to change me knickers says fowl's killed between seasons*!*" Finishing arrows, entered jungle searching for signs of bird and beast, sidestepping ant colonies hard at work carrying lush vegetation. Coming to break, discovered indication of frequent, animal-traffic. Remaining crouched, attempted differentiating between sounds, training needed detecting differences in ambiance. Beads of sweat rolled along mouth, air a living, breathing sauna. Started quietly, then, branch snapped, female boar ambling out from shrubbery, tail preventing flies from biting hindquarters. Formidable creature bowed to no one; hundred eighty kilograms, long tusks caked with mud, mortally-wounding any reckless predator. Westley strung arrow, pulling taut, creaking softly arriving at release-point. Rotating upper-torso, "Lumbering beast met it's end; shall aim between ribs from exposed flank, puncturing heart."

String whipped forward, aim true until last moment, plunging meter short, smacking prey's underside and ribcage. Abandoning all but two arrows, burst into clearing, firing as boar spotted him. Unfortunately, beast was surprisingly nimble, in the prime of her life, turning directly into shot, splintering on hard cranium. She stomped ground roaring; this was her territory, killing anyone entering. Tossing longbow aside, unsheathed dagger readying for close-combat. "Filthy farm animal, *COME ON YOU!*"

"Joe, why are you laughing? Battling a pissed-off boar and all you can think-of is to sit there and laugh—what's your malfunction?" Staring at Byte like he was blubbering idiot, "Far as I see it, this is survival of the fittest. Our guy has a blade, this is a stupid, woodland creature*!* Not to mention, it's a girl, thought it was a ball-swinging bull*!* If he dies, he's weak and deserves it." Daisy cast sideways look asking, "What's wrong with you? These people have freaky powers and say we're saving the World*!*" he continued, "Whether Redcoat dies or not, you're buying lunch*!*" Mrs. Bit placed a shushing finger drawing laughter to a close. Attempted insult, shocked no words came. Lights flickering, *"DON'T WANT TO HEAR YOUR EVIL SO YOU SHALL SPEAK NO EVIL."* diner returning to normal, customers commenting on change in lighting. Byte, "If it we're up to me, I'd sit here until Westley's pulverized. Not because I don't like Westley, because I don't like you." smiling at Joe, thoroughly enjoying his discomfort. *"SILENCE IS GOLDEN!"* Daisy, slightly concerned, *"Hold on."* Daisy said, "How long you leaving him like this?" Byte, "Let me handle this dear, you're far-too-nice a person. Whenever *Joe Shmoe* says something my Wife doesn't appreciate, she will quell his voice. Mrs. Bit has nearly insurmountable patience—consider this your only warning." Joe clutching throat, making strange, gurgling noises. Mrs. Bit repeated same, hushing motion, Joe gasping, *"JESUS CHRIST!"* Next, Byte prepared debrief. "Alright, listen-up ladies, saying this once; hero's going toe-to-toe with full-grown, female boar during mating season. Boars are known being aggressive, killing others stepping inside territory. Tusks are jagged, razor-sharp, swarming with bacteria. Westley attacked thinking her an easy-meal; lack-of-foresight triggering events now inevitable—something bad is going to happen." Worried, Daisy asked, "Aren't there choices we could make helping him win?" Mrs. Bit clapped from pent-up excitement, Joe protecting throat. *"GREAT THINKING! THOUGH CURRENT TIMELINE REMAINS UNCHANGED, WESTLEY MOVES IN SLOW-MOTION, ENTIRE UNIVERSE WAITING!"* Joe, "He has a knife…flank her, strike without being hurt?" Byte slow-clapped. "Don't believe my BLEEPING ears, something intelligent, maybe hope for us after all." Daisy, fighting drug-withdrawal, "If he treats battle like bullfighter he stands a chance?" *"ALL PATHS CARRY EQUAL OPPORTUNITY LEADING HOME! IT'S IN MORALITY OF CHOICES SPURRING HOLY SPIRIT'S INHERENT ABILITY! WE MAKE CHOICES, NOT BECAUSE CHOSEN OR FORCED, BUT BECAUSE WE CHOSE MAKING CHOICES—ISN'T FREE WILL FABULOUS!?"* Daisy implored, "Said not to ask but I can't help myself, why us? Done nothing but waste the best of our lives hoping for better days that never came, don't deserve being anything other than addicts and criminals!" Mrs. Bit placed reassuring hand smiling, *"KNOWLEDGE APPEASING IS INSUFFICIENT! HUSBAND HAS WONDERFUL GIFT CHUNKING WHY INTO MANAGEABLE PIECES; WHERE THE QUESTION WHERE COMES OUT TO PLAY!"* Byte, rubbing hands together, "Agreed-upon strategy; prevent Westley from charging like complete moron and instead, play bullfighter*?"* Joe and Daisy looked at each other confidently nodding. "Then get ready; World's a stage and it's a sold-out stadium with hungry audience."

Charged beast then, hesitation; running headlong into game of chicken would surely cost his life. Foam and spittle surged, face streaked with sinus excrement, eyes **DILATED**– crazed with anger. Westley kept balance distributed, capable moving either direction. Meter away, dodged, spinning skillfully upon wet soil, recovering with his blade bloodied. Roaring in pain, boar slammed hooves into dirt, rotating, whipping around facing with astounding speed and strength, charging once more from closer distance. Westley dodged other direction, less than three meters between, all could do was kick feet backward, moving with the punishing impact. Making contact, all eyes beheld were tusks, wide-open, drooling maw, grabbing-hold preventing from goring. Boar drove Westley into the ground trampling his chest, breaking two ribs. Grasped ribcage yelling in agony, struggling to regain footing. Bloodthirsty animal turned and before charging, he saw a look; attack would persist until he was a bloody mess. For the second time in three days, Westley thought he was going to die. Dodging sideways, understood choices offered: Fight, inevitably resulting in his demise, or turn tail, fleeing to trees.

Mrs. Bit's face was ashen colored, Byte's mouth a thin, straight line, "Things have taken-turn for worse." Joe, "What are we supposed to do*!?"* Daisy cut-in, "Run away, getting to Timothy, ocean–anything*!*" "What's stupid weakling going to do besides get them killed*!?"* Mrs. Bit, ***"HE CAN RUN, GETTING AWAY, OR FIGHT UNTIL BODY'S BROKEN!"*** Daisy added with hopeful curtail, "Obviously outmatched, let's run back the way he came*!* Joe, please say you agree." Expression remained murderous, irate man struggling bowing to the forces of nature. "Wish arrows **WORKED!** I agree Daisy, can't beat this boar, need to amscray. Aren't we farther from where we entered?" Byte nodded slowly. "Hate saying it, kind-of a toss-up. If asking for our suggestion, ditch the longbow."

Primal-gears inside Westley's mind triggered; even with impressive size, training, unable surviving encounter. Single option remained: Run. Turning left, boots pounded fast as legs would carry in a desperate dash toward thicket, ground *rumbling* between own strides. Clearing first row, scrambled behind large trunk, hoping to remove himself from line-of-sight–this was not to be. Boar pursued, stepping on his stock of discarded arrows, watching the entire time. Gained tree's other side, placing object between himself and rampaging animal, Westley's foot catching small offshoot, tripping him onto injured side. Tried clambering to feet, muscles failing, crawling several meters before whipping around, boar ramming tree, sending bark everywhere. She paused, reveling in victory over the lesser-human. Snorting, hoof brushed the ground one, final time. Then, wavering voice followed by rapid footsteps, Timothy dashing from jungle holding palm fronds, smashing headlong into boar–stumbling before falling over. Placed arm around Westley saying, "Run! Take frond, makes us look bigger!" With Timothy's support Westley was back on his feet, grabbing frond as suggested, running toward beach without moment to spare, boar roaring and squealing after them in the distance. Arriving at makeshift camp, they collapsed on sunbaked sand, panting from exhaustion. Jumping to feet, Timothy, "What were you thinking hunting without!?" Westley wheezed, "Not taking scrawny-ass hunting! Get killed by healthy mosquito bite, let-alone furry beast!" Timothy cut verbal assault short blurting, "You're like everyone else; brushing aside, thinking me useless! In case you've forgotten, *me* saving you from certain death!" Westley returned glare saying, "Give you one thing, trait keeping alive, annoying persistence. Left longbow in clearing!" "Waiting before returning, boar's enormous, likely young nearby! If squeals had not awoken, no-telling what straits you'd be in!" Grimacing, Westley leaned against one of large rocks called camp. "If arrows worked we'd be in good standing!" grasping ribcage, "What do you suggest? Mobility's restricted." Brought hand to chin thinking of something aiding recovery. "Short of limiting walking, easing pain, inflammation..." Westley's temper flaring, "Got lucky, saved from drowning. This, after stupid decision saving in first place! Wish I'd remained steadfast; watching hands slip from railing, saying a quick prayer while you plunged into icy-depths–but no. So rash, stoic, rescued sodden rat from watery cage!" coughing, blood spittle stringing onto sand. "Do you or do you not think I'm aware of capability during physical encounters? Thankful you saved me from swirling sea, however, misfortune's shared, reminding of shortcomings at each opportunity is our undoing!" Easing upright, "Tell you what, be less-annoying, maybe I'll find redeeming quality!" Timothy took last remark to heart, creating hill of sand, sitting cross-legged, pouting.

Rolling eyes, Westley limped to where he sat. "Help sit. " getting to feet, offering hands and leaning bodyweight, easing onto pile. "Unlikely pairing for survival, own reservations making it harder. Say we start fresh. " Warily over spectacles, "Requires treating me with a semblance of decency, and, admitting you need me. " Smiling tiredly, asked, "Going to make me say it?" "Don't have to, would give a bit of reassurance. Fear I may wake tomorrow morning finding you've deserted me. " Westley shrugged, having considered abandoning him several times after making-shore. "Crude survival knowledge surpasses. Admit needing, especially after sustaining injuries. " "What made you think it bright hunting alone? If it was England proper…wouldn't think twice. There are more things capable of killing a grown man than almost anywhere. " Fresh pain forcing-way from ribcage, "I'm an independent man. During military expedition, given large leeway completing mission objectives. " Timothy raised eyebrows, impressed by his confidence but still scrutinizing his lapse in judgement. "That was then, however, this is no more. Do favor; never go anywhere without first consulting. " "No venturing…until healed. " grinning, hoping Timothy found humor. Mulling words, disposition softened, saying, "Satisfies motherly instincts. " "Try bathing, strangling with my bare hands. " Timothy laughed, "Speaking of, let me inspect wounds, guiding proper decision. "

"No physician. " returning undershirt. Sarcastically, "No kidding! How long do I have?" "Broken ribs, sizeable knot upon head, dictating bedrest. " Westley threw handful of sand, mustering genuine laugh at predicament. "Imagine if I'd landed that boar!" Timothy snorted, "If you'd killed her with those flimsy arrows, I'd have run away fearing you some, possessed monster! Meant to breech subject, feared it would upset. Trees indigenous here are too fresh and tender, all fallen foliage usually molds, deteriorating within weeks of falling onto forest floor. " Refraining reprimanding, "Never encountered branches so limber. " forlornly gazing ocean. "Use for your studies after all. Cross any passages at University outlining what savages inhabiting parts use as weapons?" Timothy brought finger to chin, coming to rest on lower lip, looking absolutely ridiculous. "Harder wallop than imagined! Subject breached, remember article from early, Spanish explorer, summary more than anything of scholarly note; stumbled across aboriginal tribe on mainland adept wielding spear. " Westley remembering memory; great and powerful Empires *(ancient Greece and Rome)* used spearman countering charging cavalry of enemies. "Suppose spear more useful against swine than arrows." Eyes widened in dismay, doubting thought entering. "To craft spear from little-more than wooden snakes*!?*" Timothy smiled, happy found subject could converse agreeably on. "Fine question, know where to find such a plant*!*" "Out with it*!*" "Prudent being honest, this way, not staking academic reputation. First, must travel inland into heart of wild land. Particular plant seeking found in slow, moving bodies of fresh water–similar to marsh, swamp or pond." Comrade expressed skepticism and responded, "Do not see how unless fashioning weapons out of magic coral." "Are, for lack of better term, hollow pieces of wood called jutes. Shallow root systems, easily pulled from homes with bare hand, growing where water flows slowest. Locate source large enough, pull from earth, hang not exposed to sea-bearing winds, important maintaining balance of flexibility and durability*!*" Laying hand upon shoulder, "Apologies judging so soon." Timothy returned gesture to say, "Well Heaven be damned, Colonel Overturf knows how to be polite*!* I too, have judged book and adversary by cover*!*" changing back to topic at hand, "Other advantage discovering, possibility crafting arrow." Warmed-up considerably, feeling larger line of mutual respect, especially after honest statement about who birthed the muscle. "How you feel about heading inland in search of this, weapon's cache*?*" "Nearly killed, want to go hobbling into jungle during lunch. Plenty of water; drink-up, rest, one step closer to healing." Though it was last thing he wanted to hear, relented, knowing he was right. Westley eased onto back, throbbing in head used for counting sheep.

Storyweavers found themselves at intermission. Daisy took a deep breath, collapsing from exhaustion. "So gripped by Hero's fate, forgot breathing*!*" Mrs. Bit, ***"SUCCESSFULLY NAVIGATED WESTLEY TO SAFETY!"*** Joe, pleased with outcome, "Cartographer isn't a wimp after all*!*" Byte cracked a smile commenting, "Berries are poor-consolation surviving toe-to-toe with a ravenous boar, does beat prospect of cannibalism later down road. Speaking of eating each other, think it's time we ate something, having earned it." "Hot damn*!*" waving demandingly at waitress, "HEY LADY, chicken-fried steak, scrambled, sourdough. Pronto if you expect me tipping a dime*!*" Wiping bar near register, she glared before retrieving notepad, jotting his request. Byte, musing at Joe's lack of manners, "Didn't have friends growing-up?" "It's not that I didn't have *friends* pal, friends didn't have me." Daisy nodded saying, "He isn't nice to me and we're technically in a relationship." "*Sheesh*, I'll try being more-polite." ***"EARNED THE RIGHT LEARNING MORE ABOUT US, DON'T EXPECT YOU'LL BELIEVE ANY OF IT!"*** "When Mrs. Bit chose you two, I thought, "Should I buy pack of cigarettes, lighting one as we watch the World burn?" Anyways, yes, earned right knowing few, key pointers. *Why* you ask? Officially reached first checkpoint in our story." Daisy tilting her head, "Checkpoint? Get to *phone-a-friend?*" Joe interjected, "Come on girl use your brains–ask for our stuff*!*" ***"NO ONE'S GETTING ILLEGAL POSSESSIONS IF THAT'S WHAT YOU'RE ASKING!"*** Joe groaning, "Why not?" "Because, you idiot, Waitress is on her way to take orders, Didn't know you liked making drug use public knowledge, shall I order side of heroine for our hero?" Hesitating, asked quietly, "We can do that?" Everyone laughed as meals were chosen. "Alright shut-it–rest of us are ordering."

Waitress left for the kitchen. Joe whispered, "Are you guys aliens?" "Only I ask the questions. How can I explain in way you'd understand..." looking at ceiling, "Either of you conspiracy theorists?" Joe and Daisy's eyes widened in shared enthusiasm, both talking loudly about various conspiracies. "All I needed to know, quiet-down. When the President Kennedy assassination happened, that was us. Our Storyweaver failed." ***"RATHER HORRIBLY! WHO DECIDES IT WISE EATING SLED-DOGS UNTIL REMAINING DIE OF EXHAUSTION?!"*** Byte placed hand on hers saying, "Probably not the turning-point in *that* story. It was when we said *he* couldn't eat until manservant returned with the four hundred apples asked peeling." Wanting clarification, Daisy asked, "Let me get this straight; you're married, travel from town-to-town recruiting random people helping save the World?" Pausing in laughter, Mrs. Bit replied, ***"ADDED TREAT; OVER AND OVER UNTIL END OF ETERNITY!"*** Silence fell once more, shock settling upon newest Storyweavers. Joe, "What the legitimate fuck*!?*" Byte, "Don't you two suddenly find hearts, getting all sympathetic. This is our final chance making it right, completing the story." Joe postured, proudly saying, "Actually, that's awesome, we're important*!"* Daisy realizing something, "How many times has Storyweaver won*?"* Byte, "Well I'll be damned–very perceptive*."* Gyrating, Mrs. Bit happily, ***"THOUGH WE'VE WON MANY BATTLES, YET TO WIN THE WAR!"*** Concerned by information, she whispered, *"Oh."* As expected, Joe made sure his voice was heard. "You're joking. Expect us keeping this reality together and neither have had winning-run*?"* Byte was not a man prone to failure, least when it came to things genuinely cared about. "Watch your tone, no idea what it's like being us, morons paired-up with..." Shaking table, ***"REMEMBER BLOKE WHO CAUSED THE VALDIVIA EARTHQUAKE OF 1960 ASSUMING WORD MEANT BIRD OF PREY? THOUGHT HIS HERO WAS BECOMING FALCONER!"*** "Long as you don't enrage us past point of no-return, we'll have a good run at this thing*."*

Westley rose, making moaning sound similar to howling canine. Judging from sun's lowered position, slept three hours. *"Welcome back to land of the living."* Yawning shallowly, gasped, "Swallowed sand spider." Timothy disappeared, reappearing with canteen. Taken from outstretched hand, noticed difference in taste, identifying sound of crackling wood. "Daresay, this *"roughing it"* lifestyle's exhilarating*!"* Bedraggled man got to his feet observing handiwork; smoking fire with two animals resting atop raised pebble. Retching at the smell of burning, moist wood, whatever was cooking, "How'd you manage starting fire, and what are things in center*?"* Pointing to glasses, "Found myself thankful making fire, proverbial-kick to bullies calling me four-eyes. Those are largest frogs managed catching. Blessing marooned here when we did, otherwise, spawning-pool would've never been*!"* humming merrily, continuing their even cook. "Safe to eat*?"* Delighted he caught something, "Perfectly-edible*!* Gamey mind you, wet wood makes for smoky meal*."* Turning from aroma, "What else did you manage*?"* "Gathered berries from place discovered earlier, and this*."* revealing more torn fabric, attempting handoff. Westley eyed bundle, uncertain if wanted seeing, seconds passing before peeking inside, a blue frog covered in black spots. "Oh joy, doomed eating slimy things rest of our shitty lifespan*!"* Timothy smirked, "It would be your last meal Colonel, happens to be a poison dart frog*."* Somewhat heated, "Hand poisonous bundle without telling*!?"* "Face made when it was produced made me assume you'd handle it cautiously regardless. After capturing dinner, thought about our arrow dilemma. Poison these frogs carry is potent, skin-contact's lethal. Pinning it carefully in foliage, walloping with my boot for imbuing arrows." Impressed with his ability of thinking bettering chances, gave the frog to Timothy for safekeeping. Creating sand mound, Westley, "Meal ready? Be forewarned: Judging cooking harshly and without mercy." Timothy smiled gamely saying, "I'm sure there are some sticks around here jabbing tender spots with!" Whittle pulled frogs from fire, handing charred creature off on a large leaf, accompanying stick shaped like two-pronged fork. "As the French say, *Bon Appétit!*" Poked meal hesitantly, thrusting implement, an unpleasant squelching sound, oozing liquid draining from his dinner. Vomiting foul foam of salt, berries, and a clump of dirt, gagged, "Mine's not cooked-through!" "Gave bigger one, my apologies." "Do favor, leave until it's a charred pile of ashen soot! How's yours?" glancing second leaf, nearly-consumed, smiling with what was unquestionably bit of frog between teeth. Within hour, returned with smaller, dehydrated version of initial meal. "Left until carnivore dying of starvation would pass it for a more-profitable endeavor!" Bitterly eyeing **blackened bit,** "Here goes." crunching into it like jellied toast. Obtaining nice, powdery mouthful, "Know feeling biting into overly-seasoned, burnt bread? How I feel, except throat hurts from vomiting." Smile wilting, "Fetching water!" returning, "Would not deliberately injure!" "This, from man handing poisonous amphibian, feeding another version of complete rubbish!!" Paused handing item. "Never foraged jungle! Colonel Overturf, do not change bullheaded approach, likely perishing! Forgotten who saved, provided means of survival!" Another situation, Westley would've risen from alternate hill of sand and strangled Timothy. Chose logical approach, putting distance between. "Walking thirty to forty meters some direction. Try following, grabbing like skinny, bundle of bones you are, force-feeding dart frog into mouth!" staying apart, sleeping separately.

Storyweavers stacked lunch plates, meals long-since finished. Discovering extra tip, waitress grew curious toward length unlikely four remained inside establishment. "Get you folks anything else?" Always observant, Byte, "Damn right toots. Us nobodies are settling-in, keep coffee coming and maybe we'll tell what game we're playing." "Alright, I'll keep the hot ones coming but if you start acting weird, you'll have to go." Mrs. Bit, *"ALL THE COFFEE WE COULD DRINK KEEPING US AWAKE AND FOCUSED! NEVER TRIED UNTIL TODAY, QUITE NICE–HAVE TO PEE!"* overly-caffeinated woman hurrying to restroom, Byte *leaning*, watching exit. "Suppose good a time as any for ugly necessity. If I find you've departed, final moments watching everything turn to dust." Once they were alone, Joe, "Held here all damn day, you're looking miserable*!*" "As long as they keep paying for meals, don't see a problem. What happened to the *"Oh, we're important"* Joe sitting here a few hours ago*?*" Scoffed, "World's ending and *we're* responsible for saving the assholes that didn't do shit for us*!*" Laughing weakly, "Stuck here either way." Waitress returned with fresh coffee. "Anything else*?* Seems like you're on some dating, chat-roulette*!* Curiosity gets best of me so I won't resist, what're you doing*?*"

More-likely pulling experimental stunt than her counterpart, "Kinda got the idea event taking-part in is private, but please, sit so we can assess the value of including." This was waitress who'd likely seen everything in food-serving; possessing an atmosphere of startling sophistication for someone relying on tips making mortgage. She was in her mid-forties, appearing older or younger depending how the lighting caught her face. Sliding into bench seat, "Should've left hours ago, getting home to boys, Westley and Timothy."

human I've spoken with wants to be one. Our *"friends"* out there bamboozled you, have officially become our third, kidnapping victim." Waitress, barely audible over Mrs. Bit's fervent clapping, *"Knew* you were up to funny-business, there's no cling-wrap or painter's plastic here, so, set-up shop elsewhere*!"* Byte laughed, "The Nerve of this gal...you've got spunk–you're going to need it." Mrs. Bit wrapped her in a big hug exclaiming, ***"THANK YOU SO MUCH FOR DOING THIS!"*** "What in the Sam Hill...who are you people*?!"* Byte withdrew his pipe explaining, "That's of little-importance. You're what's called *Phone a Friend,* that means you're working doubles until those idiots finish writing their little story." "I've dealt with many Seattle Sasquatches and cuckoos, what gives you control over my life choices*?"* "What do you have to live for*?"* "Obviously my sons—" "Yes, we all know about your children, how their fate's woven into storyline by those two dipshits." Suspicion running it's course, she screamed, ***"BACK I SAY, GET BACK!"*** removing a heel to defend herself. "Mrs. Bit we have a fighter; let's do any, random maneuver, not hurting her." Joe and Daisy's timing couldn't have been better. Both bursting in, Joe exclaimed, "What the hell's everybody doing*?!* That, and when do I get to hit your pipe*?"* Discovering a half-measure regaining control, Mrs. Bit yelled, ***"GET OUT OF THE WOMEN'S RESTROOM!!"*** Byte corrected his casual, leaning position, hands high in surrender. "Come on Joe, you useless boob, ladies need their space." throwing the bag of confiscated dope to Daisy, "You're starting to look like shit anyways. Find way for all of you to finish it so we can be done with it."

     Ladies wandered from the bathroom after debriefing their newest member. "Almost makes sense–name's Martha by the way." Byte nodded, then barked, "Joe, sit this side." Daisy, recovering from her prior condition, "Alright*!* Let's get these dudes ***HOME*** and shit*!"* Martha, still confused as to how this shift in reality was occurring, sat woozily while others filtered-in beside. "Does this drug have to taste so awful*?"* Joe offered the laugh he'd been holding-in, saying, "Stuff's made with so many dangerous chemicals it's a wonder Daisy's coherent." Punching his arm, "Lucky I can tolerate your bullshit*!* Mrs. Bit, still got me on that quell voice thing*?"* Byte, "Ladies and gentlemen: Welcome Daisy to the table." ***"MARTHA, IS THERE SOMEONE YOU NEED***

TO CALL FILLING POSITION?" "Supposed to leave hours ago. Place's a ghost town, wanted to know what you were doing. Can I have coffee?" Joe, "Guess there's worse things than cold coffee, probably tastes like liquid-gold right now." "Drugs gone, moving along. Next portion's painfully detailed, why I thought drugging permissible."

During the rainy season there's a profound increase of insect activity. Landscape, covered by an eternal thicket of sprawling canopies, darker environment's their preferred, modus-operandi; carnivorous insects mobilizing as sunbaked earth cools, searching slumbering hosts. Westley woke with much-abruption, inspecting arm's length. He thought about counting them, figured Whittle would in minutes anyway— face, arms and neckline nearing covered in red, irritated bumps. Stomped-about angrily knowing sooner or later was his inevitable return to camp. "Might as well fashion the soft, little egg apology presents from twigs and berries!"

"Part you've all been waiting for." Byte from low-hanging wall separating rows of booths, "Option time." everyone smiling, stimulant peaking. "Yes, very exciting, however, faced with what's called a starting handicap." Joe looked sideways responding, "Handicap? Doesn't he already have one from bug bites?" "If I wasn't so cozy I'd hit you on the head. Since I'm only one coherent, spelling-it-out: Westley has little-man syndrome." Women exploded into riotous laughter. Daisy, between rolling heaves, "You mean this moron's about to kill himself!?" *"MANHOOD STRIPPED, HE'D RATHER WALK INTO JUNGLE THAN OVERCOME URGE CONTROLLING EACH SITUATION!"* Martha, "Playing ignorant here or is he truly this bullheaded?" "No time getting into prior, hero moments Martha but in-summation, guy's as stubborn as they come. In the next thirty seconds, someone will have the unrelenting desire of exiting establishment and walking into traffic." Daisy, "What? Any of us!?" suddenly not so carefree. "Mrs. Bit, happened first time, remember? Panicked talking before, none went to the store." Mrs. Bit removed knitted gloves, letting-loose an ear-piercing whistle. *"LISTEN TO HIM, FEAR I MAY FAINT!"* growing light-headed from whistling with such tremendous effort. "Nobody flip-out, one less person to worry about. Rules: Cannot subdue by physical means, if any do, they too, walk into traffic." Joe yelled, "How do I stop someone without touching them*!?*" "Only way preventing a braying horse from becoming war noises is with words."

Everyone became slack-jawed before regaining senses. Byte, "Anyone have somewhere they need to be*?*" Joe, being his usual-self, "Story's turned to shit in a real-hurry*!* If it wasn't for the ladies doing drugs, we wouldn't be in this situation*!*" Stirring to life, Daisy snapped, "If you were a man longer than five seconds, would've realized you're manipulating my addiction*!*" Martha removed keys from apron, hastily locking doors. "What do you mean manipulation*?* We worked together getting the waitress to help finish*!*" Daisy's bicep twitched, Byte thinking she was winding-back to smack him in the face. Choking-back tears she screamed, "Intertwining her children*!!*" Martha rocking back and forth muttering, "What*?*" before fainting, falling to floor. Joe, throwing an arm around, "Great, just great. If you weren't sitting next to an almighty sorcerer I'd backhand your ass*!* I'm out of here*!*" hitting light-fixture, storming for exit. Byte to Daisy, "Bingo. Failed mentioning, not helping you." "Expected stopping a two-hundred-pound man by myself*?*" "Happens when you try outsmarting a game with little-understanding of how to work around the rules. Now, what're you going to do*?*" Thousands of ideas materializing, she chose surrendering to truth, sharing substantiated sins and fears. What she sought-after most remained absent for but one reason: Accountability for past mistakes, admitting present humility while accepting future responsibility.

Coming-to-rest a safe distance away, "Can you stop yanking on those doors and talk*?*" Lock warping under strong man's barrage, ***"LIKE HELL I AM! WASTED TOO MUCH OF MY LIFE IN THIS DINER, TOO MUCH OF MY GOD DAMN LIFE ON THE ROAD, AND FAR TOO MUCH TIME LAYING WITH SPUN-OUT SKANKS LIKE YOU!"*** She was used to being called names, but Joe had a way of making sure insults were felt at a personal level. Rage subsiding, she again tried ripping him from his affliction. "Don't need another man walking-out on me...need someone protecting me, taking-care of...can't do it by myself*!*" glancing at Byte for help, angrily at the end. Joe scowled, pointing her direction, *"Funny,* how you of all people would say this, twenty minutes ago you were doing drugs in the bathroom*!* Our hero can't do it alone either and you just screwed him*!*" Doubt flooded Daisy's overblown neurological pathways, Byte drawing heavily on pipe, smoke filling the space. Glancing at his wife of many lifetimes eyes softened, then hardened. "Is this the only man you've been with*?* Don't use that tone of voice, he's practically an angry, abandoned child. Ever heard of *the whole pack* strategy*?* Catch; if it breaks, last memory you'll have is my foot in your ass." Byte underhand-tossed his cherished possession, Daisy catching. Joe, changing exit-strategy, "Fuck it, *where's* waitress*?*" approaching Martha, rummaging apron, "Sucks this happened to you too lady. ***YOU!***" snapping at Byte, "What terrible things did you do with your shot at life that's got you repeating this fucking hailstorm*!?*" Practiced dealing with male tantrums, "Didn't write the story but believe me when I say I intend to right the story. Remember Pittsburgh, when you beat a cute, young thing for dancing*?*" Balling fists he screamed, "How DARE YOU mention Erica*!!*" eyes going vacant, "So what if I hit her*?* Just a slut like all the others, taking pieces of my soul, never giving a damn*!* Man she danced with was old enough to be her grandpa*!*" Byte, always one step ahead, Joe wasn't ready to smoke the whole carton. "Close guess you ingrate; do you want to know who he really was*?* Her own step-father." Joe was arm's length from door, mid-motion inserting key as words seared his conscience. This is a similar story many go through; efforts spurned from lack of patience, diligent understanding of what one does and doesn't have control over. He squeezed the ring of keys, blood impacting tile floor, feelings materializing as eternal shame on his battered spirit. Joe broke down, crying into chest, ***"I'M SORRY!"*** relocating to furthest booth. Daisy, "We've been together a few months and even I didn't know about that." "Shut your mouth unless you've an idea; crucial point where Westley may or may not surrender to reason." nodding Joe's direction, busy cradling himself, shirt streaked with blood. "How was I supposed to—stupid whore—your old man*?*" "Grateful that isn't us–you'll have to be *silky smooth* from here on out." Daisy nodded, summoning courage for one of the hardest challenges an introvert like her faces: Pouring her heart out to a frequently hostile person.

"Hey, scoot." Moving about twelve inches for her to sit, "Don't get any funny ideas; still leaving, just…need a minute." "If it helps your situation, I'm not perfect either, no ray of sunshine." Wiping swollen eyes, "I got ten years, housed in a unit for violent offenders, labeled a woman beater and elder abuser." "I come from a rough upbringing, reason why, despite our bickering, we get along in a weird, sort of way. Did I ever tell you why I left my hometown? Main complaint you have about me is same one ruining my life prior, family's life too—drugs. Had a husband, job, and two children." "That was dumb, your ex sounds like a tool." Not letting insecurities prevent her from sharing, "He was a good man, when I was done, crueler version of you. After Delilah tested positive for methamphetamine at the hospital, Child Services got involved, she was born with birth-defects and required several weeks on a ventilator before she could breathe on her own. Husband never forgave me either; after months of trying to reinvest myself, being a better version of me, he had divorce papers served to the home we shared together. That very evening, had a new bulb and a forty-sack, entire life packed inside backpack." Joe's arm went around Daisy in a reassuring gesture. "That's what got you all screwy on that stuff!? If your ex wasn't willing to stand by your side, then he's not much of a man anyways. Know I ain't someone who handles ladies with care, but neither of us deserved what we got. Me, fist and the clink, you, dope and the bathroom sink." "Don't know how long you planned doing this, but I dream of righting things and getting back home." exiting booth, startling Joe, "Where you going?" "Oh nowhere, just wanted to make sure you're paying attention. Can you find it in your heart staying? We're in the middle of a pretty-cool story, don't wanna say goodbye to the only person who's treated me decently." Joe, nonchalant about the whole situation, "Don't know why we're sitting over here anyway, feeling better?" Byte, "Good work everyone, ready knowing how you both did?" Joe fist-pumped, confidently cheering, "I knew we cured Westley's bug bites!" Byte strode forward, hand extended. "My pipe." retrieving, doing a one-eighty, hiding his actions with his billowing trench coat. "You said you're grading us…" "If you'd wait a minute, need to cool-it when someone's being nice." He about-faced and to their amazement, wore a genuine smile. "Did the world just end? This guy's actually smiling at us." "Keep cracking bad jokes and I'll share this with Daisy and you'll have nothing." to Daisy, "Usually don't sugar coat much when it comes to the grim-details, you're the first person I've given pipe to, failing so horribly you succeeded. Why didn't you give it to him right away, did you forget about it?" "Told me to use words, thought it was my only option." Byte turned back-around, after what felt like ages, pipe was filled with something completely unexpected–marijuana. "Before you begin throwing yourselves at me in gratitude, shut-it." They settled off tippy-toes and perked ears upward. "Long-and-short: Daisy." surrendering a guilty smile, "I lied earlier, could've helped you save Joe from walking into traffic." "What!? I was...who walked into..." "Obviously not, you'd be *smeared* over pavement." to Daisy, "Chose the hands-off approach; wife passed-out, don't really fair during wholesome, family moments unless she's present and conscious, also wanted to see if the emotional capacity existed within yourselves. Life suffers because people fail acknowledging the simplicities of genuine interaction." Daisy, still miffed, "Why go and lie? Do you know how stressful that was?" Raising an eyebrow at what he considered a wasteful question, "That's why I loaded this for you. Don't smoke often but when I do, I make sure it's *Green Buddha.*" Recovering from his little-man syndrome, Joe returned to his side of the table, seeing Martha, noticing drying blood from his injured hand. "Guess I was the pussy this time, thanks guys, for saving me from..." Daisy was going to let it slide but Byte would have none of it, "No doubt this scrawny druggie saved your life." She sat next to the fallen Mrs. Bit saying, "Before you do anything stupid, let's smoke so we can move on!" Byte, hoisting himself back onto his newly-found mantle, "Said better than any drug addict worked with. For recent efforts, you get greens." "You've had other Storyweavers who were drug addicts?" "No, blessed being our first encounter with street-level drug abuse."

Since Joe submitted the front door to much-distress, Martha made the decision to close-up early. Smelling air with an amused expression, "At first I didn't smell it, but now I *smell it*–who lit-up in here?" Mrs. Bit, recovered from fainting, ***"I SMELL IT TOO DEARIES!***

Logic urged self-preservation, returning to Timothy for aid. Shaking away clouding, hopeless thoughts, he turned his back to the sea, walking to their sad-excuse for shelter. He found Timothy shortly thereafter rising from sleep. No sooner did he slide glasses onto face, sent into freak-out mode. Racing to where he hobbled, "What sort of peril have you returned in this time*!?* Question, mind you there's hundreds, did you walk into a horde of mosquitoes on purpose*?!*" He could do little-more than mumble, "Nanks for saving me Nimothy." obviously discomforted, in dire-need of fluid intake. Timothy sat him on a sand mound nearest fire. Handing him canteen, "Drink all of this while I find an herb to possibly ease inflammation. Can you speak*?*" Swollen face descended into frown responding, "What naff nad is 'llergic reaction, not an idiot*!*" dropping emptied container onto sand. "Wait here, resist movement*!*" hurrying away, doing several double-takes before disappearing. The desire to scratch exposed parts tortured and he was uncertain what could be done as far as any topical-salve. "Cannot believe bugs nearly ended me. Let there be some respite from temperature-swings received at sunrise and sunset, no longer forced huddling against a smoking fire*!*" It wasn't long before footsteps were heard treading dampened soil, signifying relief or the next, volatile incident. "You look like a plump apple, how's breathing*?*" "Can breathe, if that's what you're inquiring. What more have you brought experimenting with*?*" "Worry

not, plant's familiar to us both. Mash, apply as ointment."
Cautiously eyeing plant, "Telling what it is?" "It's from
Kingdom Plantae, Family Asphodelaceae." Westley burbled
with renewed rage from being undermined. Widening swollen
eyes, *"IMBECILE! Enough riddling with details of stupid
plant!"* Displeased by his lack-of-interest, "Found this for
you, after all. In our homeland it's known as Aloe Vera."
"Hand canteen, plant wasted life telling about, search for
object with divot." Foraging, he came upon chunk of bark, flat
stone used grinding it into pulpy mass. Obtaining a decent
slathering, "Hoping relief's instantaneous." Westley groaned,
eyes rolling into head, viscous liquid giving goosebumps,
finding presumption accurate. "Nicest feeling since—do *not*
miss spot on back of arm—signed-on for ludicrous mission."
"Best way moving past this ordeal is taking pain endured as a
learning-experience." "What, referring to me turning into an
insect buffet, or whole, blasted debacle?" relaxing as Timothy
reapplied makeshift ointment. "Burning's receding." "If
needing more, found along outskirts of canopies. Dislike
direct sunlight, thrive nicely with the help of a little shade!"
humming while finishing administration. "Must you sing like
a bird?" Stopping his noisemaking, "Thinking long-term
shelter." "What I've wanted since marooned, no need
waiting!" Timothy, "Hmm…"

"Mrs. Bit, let these stoned assholes know what
they can do." *"EXPLORE SCARY JUNGLE, OR, LET
BITES DEVELOP INTO BLISTERING SORES! CAN
YOU IMAGINE? INCAPABLE BEING WITH ANOTHER
DUE TO INEVITABLE, BLOOD SEPSIS!"* Martha,
"Guess it's sort-of obvious." Joe complained, "What
kind of look into Creation is this? Supposed to make a
choice but it's practically been made for us—what a rip-
off!" Daisy laughed, asking, "Can we give him a mission
or something?" Byte's eyes widened, twisted smile
forming. "Not sure if I like you're way of thinking or if I
should be concerned. You think he should go through
yet, more bullshit?" Joe, trying an option suited to
Westley's condition, "Let's have Timothy work harder.
What're the odds of him coasting this out?" Patting
Joe's arm, *"YOU A BABY BIRD?"* Byte, "Both need to
do their part. You've sixty seconds thinking-up side-
quest." Martha, "This is "*back in the day*" right, why not
flint?" Daisy nodding, "Remember from some show, flint
sparks against anything with greater hardness when

using the correct striking-angle." Joe valiantly tried letting choice be made absent input, eventually saying, "Smarty-pants attitude gave idea, how about we run it by Whittle? Dude's practically a bloodhound with his ability finding shit."

"Skin, ravaged by elements, you, in dire-straits, should relocate." Excited, "What potential shelter's likely?" On tippy-toes like additional height gave proper clearance, "Noticeable incline toward jungle's center. Confirm ascent, possibility encountering cave, crevice, something of the likes." "Cannot forget longbow, think beasts are able to destroy weapons?" "Anything's possible really, why it's first thing we're doing." Patting thankfully, "Movement will do bit of good." "Know signs of anxious boots when I see them; bickering back and forth, never getting proper-go." "How easy it must be analyzing life like some schrimtoire, instead of living it." "Undeniably at opposition in personalities. If we but came together, walking thin, twisty road, at least stand a fighting chance." Timothy's fire had long-since extinguished, ash surrounding carcasses of moist timber refusing to light. "Incredibly hot, cannot imagine anything venturing out in overpowering sunlight." Westley, checking his swelling with a whistle, "Since I feel fit as fiddle, lead us onwards through obstreperous forest." "With or without peril, should remain close, refrain from toiling." "Following your slender berth after all, no turning sideways, otherwise, I may lose you entirely." "In my youth, I was only one who could fit between fence-pickets, fetching balls for the other children. Each time, I would come to their aid without fail, only to be excluded from playing." Westley, after brief, bout of laughter, "Why're you sharing pathetic story? Hardly imagine there's a soul alive happily listening!" noticing he hurt Timothy's feelings, "Suppose there's use; need navigating, tie string around and follow you like you're a little weasel! That is, until one of us, most-likely you, dies of exposure." Processing last comment, "Look on the sunny-side, you've acquired the important duty of berry gathering!" "Hazard you're right. Longbow's in clearing to the north and east, should be an easy chore."

It took fifteen minutes for Timothy to locate the missing longbow. Upon his return, Westley, "Revisit where we find shoots for arrows." "Pursuing island's center, there, should find everything needed, water, shelter, resources." "Until then, you're very-much the man leading the artillery." They journeyed deep into the thicket searching for water, only silt remaining in canteen's bottom. Westley, "Gone far-enough without proper care." collapsing under tree, "Hear rushing water, yet to see*!*" "One of few, documented mysteries of the Amazon. Research notes left by stranded explorers outline painful death, turning to madness from the sound of trickling water.*"*

Customers were unable entering the diner for hours, leaving after pulling vainly on doors. Daisy, watching a crowd choose elsewhere, "There isn't some boss checking-up on you, like, seeing if you're open*?*" "Honey, this place doesn't run without me. Since it's been brought to my attention there's magic in this world, declaring establishment ours.*"* Joe, "Any way of getting something else to drink*?* My shit's been liquid for weeks, coffee's a cutting-reminder of Vegas.*"* Daisy, "We've spent months in a drug-induced, fantasy trip to solve all our problems—how else did you think your body would feel*?*" Byte, shaking his head, "Give you this, actually perform better under-the-influence, redefined how I'll look at a functioning addict the rest of my life.*"* ***"YOU'VE DONE WELL EARNING OUR KINDNESS, DON'T THINK I WON'T RESPOND ACCORDINGLY IF YOU START ACTING LIKE FOOLS!"*** Joe, "There's a lot people hate me for, but when you get right down to it, bigger mud-flaps than what most of these lightweights called criminals. Sorry being an ass, also, not sorry—an ass is an asset*!*" "Long as you don't go smothering us with meaty-forearms, don't see God bringing the lightning down. You've no idea of the times her and I lost squabbling over old vendettas.*"* "Where are we on the *drink* situation*?*" Martha, "Rummage around. Better yet, bring all of us something.*"* Byte laughed observing Joe frown from not being served. "It's called a job, try one. Probably should've been first thing done during your *"remodeling journey"*. If you can't come-up with something, fill a pitcher with soda from the fountain.*"* Joe, from kitchen, "Actually started liking this Westley-guy, I'd hate to act like you ladies did, get his dick engorged like something out of sci-fi*!*" "Always so mature with him. Joe, stop ganging-up on us girls*!*"

Timothy crouched over moss-covered runoff frowning at how-little his efforts produced. They'd done well surviving thus far, but expelled considerable amounts of energy doing-so, unaccustomed to smothering, omnipresent company. Had situation been different, he couldn't find any eventuality of them interacting, even happenchance. "Alright brittle Whittle, how does one get through to a man whose as wild and fierce as jungle trapping?" considering John Locke's Philosophy of Natural Law. Simply stated, living things seek promoting common good, but also carry own perspective, window of interest. Self-preservation dictated both seeking other in terrain and mind, surrendering in unified front. Comrade stirred, noticeable improvement in swelling from biting pestilence. "How long have I been out?" "Enough to resemble a man. Injuries not fortuitous, erring on side of caution; few hours, then, every effort seeking shelter." "Harder go of it! Formidable frame, you, stand-before me in likeness of scarecrow! If idea's coddling, giving curfew, find me absent, running from beasts alone." "What of your ideas? Let's hear plan from the great, Colonel Overturf." "Know nothing of military strategy; conceal myself amongst the landscape, awaiting boar's return." "How's one, lousy boar returning us to England? Problem letting things go, attitude driven by hunger. Can remain quarreling, or make headway toward rising cliff." No condition to be arguing, "How about drop subject! All this prattling, nothing but noise to ears of predators!" considering own volume, "Survival plan's sound; frustrated and hungry, enduring such isolation." Colonel had been paid handsomely for his services for quite some time, used to three, square-meals a day. Lacking nutrients, toned-musculature disappears, skin sagging, organ-systems switching to self-preservation. Brain signals red-blood cells to metabolize glucose for fuel, electrical-impulses beginning breakdown of amino-acids in skeletal-muscle. Timothy's appearance changed little since falling overboard; starving academic, experienced hunger majority of his life. "Focus on recovery; nice pulling bowstring, becoming contributing member."

"How're we going to light fire without flint?!" Byte, "Maybe we haven't gotten to that part? Reaching incredibly-unique portion, usually makes or breaks Storyweavers." *"INCREDIBLE MEMORIES, BEING GRIPPED IN VICIOUS, LIFE-OR-DEATH MOMENTS!"* Daisy, "Didn't we go through one hours ago?" "Aw, I'm sorry, has the end of the world inconvenienced?" returning to Mrs. Bit's prior statement, "Above fifty-percent on story one, *with* unexpected advantage; created scenario if one dies, story writes as intended. What if you had to forfeit your life, for his?" Martha, to Joe, "How to formulate words..." "I piss you off?"

"Must've thought me some *airhead* like your girlfriend." Daisy, "Sorry Martha, not much in way of options..." excuse drawing to a close. Joe, defending, "Shit's going down either way, now, you're on our team, win-win situation." Byte, "If you don't listen to what's said, grave-circumstances within plot, also for you lot. Followed Timothy three hours, refilling canteen, murkiest water thus far, *not* found flint, spent entire time arguing." Daisy's hand lifted. "What?" "We haven't argued, doesn't make-sense how you can say they've done something." "Some of our stories have been *written*. Consider your kidnapping; no option refusing, still do not. Select few walk freely from the debilitating impacts of fate. In summation, they've been arguing, shut your mouth. Night's falling, temperature drops, humidity condensing into thick dew. Find flint and shelter, otherwise, unable establishing fire." Joe belched, roughly set emptied mug, "Remembered what I wanted to ask, do we get to sleep?" Byte, "Evil never sleeps Joe, diving into story whether you're sleepy or not."

"Storms gather, cannot see using spectacles starting fire." "Right, option's a cave or crevice. Familiar with flint?" "Survival-course included identifying, gathering deadened, dried grass, igniting." "Excelled said portion—nimbleness catching attention of superiors." "Imagine you high in trees, cunningly dropping rocks upon recruits." Surprised by break in argumentative behavior, "Chaps running camp if not mistaken." Westley laughed, "Same situation years ago, when I went through." Ground became rockier, indication they'd soon be stopping. "Another hour?" "Like I have choice. Slow breakneck pace, unless carrying?" "Most I'd manage is feeble body-drag before fatiguing." Journeyed into steepening forest, Westley fighting-urge informing that a rib was poking his lung, coming upon a mountain outcropping, similar to shark fin, proud arrowhead. Timothy, "Did not prepare us this in training! Knew if remained, would abandon logic." Seeing he meant no harm, "Reminds of sails on horizon. Things can get to a man in the wilderness, nearly absolved myself of this." With assistance, limped to cliff's base, rocks growing into boulders. "Peak mountable?" Resting on amused scrutiny, "Another time perhaps?" "Finally built tolerance associating with you and whatnot." "*My* kind of humor! Think God sent as test of patience, months shall revisit, sharing jokes." Westley looked to path, amongst animal were human foot impressions. "Cannot bode well, barkeep said inhabitants practice cannibalism." nodded, deepening concern. "Civilized world industrialized, some chose isolation, practicing what's considered witchcraft or heresy."

"I'm about to sign-off on this shit! Declared this part rising action, they're about to nod-off and all I can think about is which one of us is playing Jesus!" Tired as he was, Byte, "Play Jesus Christ, really Joe?" Daisy, "Why fixate on scariest part?" **"WITH TIMOTHY'S HELP, DISCOVERED SHELTER, WATER, AND A HARVEST OF BERRIES–YUM!"** Martha, "Growing impatient with emphasis on whole, side-quest when it doesn't even cross his mind." Byte, "Ignore them, don't answer any of their asking–spoiled from time-wasting measures." Joe, bringing hand down repeatedly, "Who wasted valuable time making them do drugs?" "Incident stemmed from you being conniving, inviting waitress to dance with the Devil." Daisy watched Mrs. Bit smile at restaurant memorabilia. "What you think about stuff we did in the bathroom?" Jerking her direction, **"STRONGER THAN COFFEE, IS IT DANGEROUS?"** "Depends on person, where they are, who they're with." Byte, "Environmental Psychology. Given situation, variables impacting result. Leaders with despicable agendas offer pandemic, dangerous drugs." Joe, mind flooding with conspiracies, "They're controlling us!!" "In the end shackled mind breaks free, seeing what it's meant to be. If refuse fixing-ways, earn rightful place beneath, lessons-refused fueling our desire for life."

Cave was dark, damp, putrid aroma trapped within air of their discovery. Fresh wave reaching nostrils, Westley gave consideration to fear recognized intrinsically–this was animal's home. Creature advanced quickly from cave's mouth, lightning outlining full-grown panther. He stumbled toward Timothy as it raked the air, delivering a powerful, bone-jarring punch, panther yelping, recoiling in pain. Timothy stared with grim-resolve, Westley screaming protest. Whispered, "Go." Arms outward, he ran toward death, wrapping-around beast's neck refusing to let go. Massive paw found small of his back, ripping clean-off, sending him headfirst into cave wall. Panther lunging for throat, eyes found Westley, **"GO!"** choking, bleeding-out on cave floor. Final scream returning him to reality, escaped bloodbath into darkness, tumbling-down a steep hill, breaking his femur. Westley lost focus on waking-world, falling-out.

Eden of Deliverance

Zion stood upon shoreline contemplating One's departure. "Closing at open, opening at close, blessing with what's intended." Waded into lake, swimming to bottom, many curious how Perfect Pair was enclosed in water bubble, underwater. Observed damage, crack widening since One's encounter, length devoid of vegetation, spewing foul odor. "Choosing gender usually isn't so-problematic; those not confined to vicious tendency carry free will. Thankful given choice rather than being someone heart claims contrary—imagine if you were opposite sex!" fish hugging, gently touching fins. Coral gardens teemed with life, seahorses peeked shyly, crabs carrying shells setting own, preferred paths. Den of Deliverance carried temptation of obstinacy, temperature increase perpetuating regality closer one becomes. Gaining threshold, was thrilled it remained as designed; open atrium, freckled obsidian sparkling like polished pearls. Zion cupped hands, sinking them into sediment upon cavern floor, cradling like precious child before throwing, appearing like firework paused in time and space. Zion danced, spinning rhythmically, grace matching ballerina performing for ghostly audience. Bounding like deer over foliage, fallen tree, this was *Song of Dragon Dance*.

"IN MOMENT, THIS PLACE, BROKEN TIMES, SILENT SPACE, I CALL ON YOU.

WILL SOURS FINAL HOUR; OCEAN TO CREEK, EVIL SEEKS CONTROLLING ALL POWER.

DOUBT IN HEART LIKE POISON DART, LIFE FROM START CALLS ON YOU.

DARK THINGS CREEP, REAP, DESTINY THEY KEEP. WITH LASHING LEAP THEY FALL ON YOU.

ETERNITY DRAWN TIGHTLY CLOSED, EYES SEE TO LIES, CUP OVERFLOWS.

FRAMES SHATTERED, ALL THAT MATTERED FALLS TO DUST. METAL TO RUST, GEM FROM STEM.

FOR NOT JUST I, NOR US, NAY YOU; ETERNAL RINGING OF ETERNAL, GOD CALLS YOU!

WAKE FROM SLUMBER, ERASE YOUR NUMBER!

GOD ON HIGH IS GOD IN YOU!

Zion leapt, hands thrown high, sand shrinking into ball, exploding outward as brilliant, shooting stars, solidifying into an ancient, bioluminescent being; blue and green in color, eyes like setting sun. "Steel your nerves; formidable in size but can assure, quite the softy. This is Azorius; awakens twice during his lifetime, all the while between, remains in constant slumber, dreams spanning eternity."

"WATCHED WORLD AS IT TURNS AND BURNS, WHY IS IT YOU AWAKEN?" "Ring's nearly finished. Will you sing this song, or watch us fall to ruin?" *"THIS IS ABOUT ONE. HE'S QUITE GOOD YOU KNOW; TIMES FAILED, HAS COURAGE CARRYING-ON."* "Life waits with bated-breath, Bæöbõb will not stand idly. Rise as eternal guardian, protecting Giving Tree." Exposing layers of sharp teeth, he roared, *"HELLO SCALED FRIENDS!"* Terrified, Perfect Pair hid behind Zion. *"DO NOT SHY FROM AZORIUS! WITHOUT YOUR HARMONIOUS DEFENSE, ONE WOULD BE SMUDGE ON LAKEBOTTOM–DEMONSTRATION PLEASE."* They looked to Zion for approval. "Pacifism's your specialty, do not feel ashamed because it is so."

They began presentation, quickly losing control, running into Azorius. Thrilled by embarrassing display, *"GIVE THEM ABILITY SEPARATING, COMING-TOGETHER AS NEEDED. EVEN SOULFUL FISH SUCH AS THESE MAKE MOVEMENTS ON THEIR OWN FROM TIME-TO-TIME."* A ripple travelled bubble's circumference before settling. "Give it another go, aim for nose–won't feel it elsewhere." One went left, other right, upward, other downward. After each movement, united completing full-revolution, emitting golden pulses. *"GOOD SHOW–TICKLES NOSE!"* Zion rushing for Perfect Pair, retreating to innermost-coil. Serpent's body tensed, followed by a thunderous crash, chunks of debris falling, sneeze turning rock into magma. "Bless you!" Zion exclaimed, "You two okay?" Perfect Pair nodded, swimming from sheltering arms informing other fish what happened. *"DO YOU KNOW HOW POWERFUL OUR ENEMY'S BECOME? THEY TAINT EVERYTHING WHOLLY HOLY, TURNING GOLDEN SKIES INTO WEBS OF LIES!"* "I too have dreams and visions of the end, heart tells otherwise." *"MANKIND'S DISTRACTED, LIVING AN ELECTRONIC VOID. HOW CAN YOU EXPECT THEM IGNITING WHAT'S BEYOND RECOLLECTION?"* "Choice of how to react when adversity rears unpleasant face. Tears shed tying in knot, not for naught nor absent merit. For I like all children, learn acts are never in vain, for God's in the vein." *"NIGHTMARES ARE MORE THAN SHADOWS FRIGHTENING CHILDREN IN DEAD-OF-NIGHT. EACH FIGHTING FOR RIGHT, MULTIPLE RISE-UP ENDING PLIGHT. STRENGTH OF BUT A FEW, HOW'S BATTLE WON WITH JUST ME AND YOU?"* "Can't possibly think me so fickle, saying only you and I fight against the sickle? Many fight with choices too few–chosen choices are bigger than me and you." Considering her words, *"BETTER GO OUT FRONT, CANNOT RIGHTLY FIT THROUGH OTHER!"* Uncoiled with ease swimming from bedchamber, swimming lake's entirety in seconds. *"FORGOTTEN HOW NICE THIS IS! LAST TIME STRETCHED, NO BIGGER THAN MORAY EEL!"* "Remember day you hatched, so cute!" *"ENOUGH FLATTERY, STRIKING PROPOSITION!"* Rolling eyes, "What could you possibly offer? Cannot imagine deal benefiting either." *"SAID I'VE CHOICE AIDING CREATION. DON'T SEE US STANDING MUCH-CHANCE, HOWEVER, GIVEN OPPORTUNITY CONVINCING IN FORM OF GRAND-SPECTACLE– ORATION FOR CREATION."* Certain she knew what he meant, "Wish persuading by way of rhyme existing through space and time?" *"LET'S CALL ALL LAKE-DWELLERS, PERFORMING IN A DUEL FOR THE AGES!"* Zion, encountering idea, "What if we move everyone to Enchanted Island, all can attend!" *"STUPENDOUS IDEA! WHAT OF OUR NOCTURNAL FRIENDS?"* "Leave it to me! Spent many moons gazing at stars; may be things you don't know about me! This'll take but-a-minute!" swimming to embankment, only moments seeing Peanut and Miss Butterfly. "Azorius needs convincing, are to hold battle of the minds atop Enchanted Island. Miss Butterfly, round-up butterflies, spreading message to all within reach!" Saluting, brought legs to proboscis whistling, Zion blocking sun beholding commotion. Butterflies filled sky in *myriad of colors*, forming into enormous cloud, flying her direction. Miss Butterfly greeted family, informing of message to be spread. On canine companion, "Spread word amongst ground and woodland creatures, large attendance is key to winning Azorius's aid!" After smiling at the sun, dove into Crystal Lake checking-on Azorius's progress, surrounded by sea critters of every kind imaginable. *"SPREAD MESSAGE FAR-AND-WIDE, TROUT ARE SWIMMING UPSTREAM TELLING*

OTHERS!" "Peanut and Miss Butterfly are doing same topside!" Nearly all lake inhabitants arrived, Perfect Pair showing magical bubble to any taking-interest. Azorius, *"EVERYONE'S ACCOUNTED!"* otters diving from above, summersaulting off lake-bottom, one waving, flashing toothy smile. "Seen everything during slumber; remember what we do making it safely to Enchanted Island?" *"MIND'S A BIT GROGGY."* "Quite alright, didn't expect you'd remember everything when you were baby. Named Den of Deliverance for more than just slumber; with your power of superheated steam, use resting-place as, well, a den of deliverance! Not to mention, island's enchanted; steer close to waterfall, God will take care of the rest." *"LINE I NEVER TIRE HEARING! LET'S WORK ON REPAIRING DEN..."* hole gone, looking like accident never happened, *"HOW IN THE SHELL DID YOU DO THAT WITHOUT ME NOTICING?"* Hand on hip, winked, "As said, there are things you don't know about me." *"ATTENTION CITIZENS OF CRYSTAL LAKE: IF YOU'D BE SO KIND AS TO PROCEDE INSIDE! BIT OF A SHOCK CAVE FIT ME, FUNNY HOW ROOMY IT IS FOR EVERYONE."* "Cannot take all the credit; One's own devisal. When making, did suggest he make it larger." Edging closer to Zion, *"SEEN IN DREAMS HOW IT PAINS YOU BEING APART, NOT ONLY YOU BUT ALL THINGS. I'VE RESERVATIONS STAKING OUR LOT WITH HUMANS; YOU CARRY THE HOPE OF SO MANY, SHOULDERING ALL THEIR SIN—YOU ALWAYS HAVE. DO NOT LET OUTCOME CHANGE YOU. WHATEVER END WROUGHT, NEVER A BARREN PLOT."*

Sea creatures moseyed inside cavern, Quoi fish swimming impatiently across entrance. "All-aboard!" Azorius chuckled, *"IF I MAY MAKE A FUNNY AND CORRECT, ALL ASHORE WHO'S GOING ASHORE!"* to Perfect Pair, *"MIGHT WANT TO MOVE; YEARS SINCE LAST TRIED, COULD GET MESSY."* Fish hesitated, racing to Zion, bumping into chest for snuggles. "Let's watch Azorius close entrance." Serpent blocked entrance with sand, plunging everyone into darkness, exhaling, heating into solid mass. Marveling at capabilities, "Quickest patch-job yet." *"REMEMBER FIRST TIME? CRAB I TRAPPED IGNORED ME FOR THOUSAND YEARS! GOOD DEED GIVING HOME UNDER, AVOIDING REPEAT."* Zion, "I'm sure they forgave faster than you realize. Though they don't say much, crabs sure hide hearts with hard exteriors!" Caretaker walked to mouth, scaling structure, sitting cross-legged atop. Pair chose remaining encircled within her arms, uncertain how takeoff-safety was being conducted. Azorius coiled around Den's circumference pointing head downwards, providing thrust lifting lake's population. He declared, ***"IMPORTANT PACKAGE FOR DELIVERY!"*** inhaling, body expanding more than three-times usual size, superheated steam shearing Den from lakebed. Breaking surface Zion stood, hovering before returning to solid rock. Skies filled with wings; seagulls, dragonflies, hummingbirds, butterflies, moths flying to Enchanted Island, herons breaking from tendency, leaving young to play in tallgrass.

    "We shall have a meeting of minds where all can attend." reaching toward sun, channeling evening moon, carrying a look of such-tenacity those airborne scattered, giving line-of-sight. Sun and moon aligned side-by-side; darkness in the east, daylight west, animals spending duration in preferred environments. Crowds gathered, forming along embankment–animals of every kind. Ram, elk, boar, squirrel. Jaguar, panther, hyena waiting under cooling shade. Tiger and lion followed along riverbank, comparing might with tremendous verbosity. Monkey, guerilla, ape socialized in rafters awash with *colorful movement,* snakes draping themselves across limb. Pleased by turnout, pushed those missing to back of mind saying, "Speaking with holdouts later." Azorius, rising from watery depths, ***"READY?"*** "Do suppose, prairie dogs will arrive later delivering final roll-call. There's my little boy*!*" Peanut racing path to water's edge, two bear cubs behind. Finishing crossing, Azorius inhaled, steam escaping nostrils and jawline, body acting like tea-kettle, erupting water from his mouth, landmass surging quickly upward. Waterfall met sealed entrance, gradually returning to sand, transferring everyone to island ponds. Zion, standing between night and day, "Let Oration of Creation begin*!*"

Enchanted Island bustled with activity, those present fitting comfortably with room for Azorius. There were several holes at island's center in front of a pair of gnarled trees; prairie dogs, reptiles, burrowing creatures living in Sanctuary could come and go as pleased, serving as communication-lines during ceremonies, emergencies. Zion greeted elder prairie dog, patiently waiting to hand-off tiny clipboard. Retrieving, walked small, narrow path verifying attendance, four species missing; falcon, hawk, wolf and bear *(save for cubs Peanut convinced joining)*. Wolves were rarely seen by others, Alpha exiling himself many years ago due to unexpected tragedy. Consequentially, wandering changed to secreting secrets awaiting his return.

Conflict between bears and falcons was different situation, extending over much-longer duration. What started as altercation over shared feeding-grounds paved un-crossable road—bears and falcons no longer speaking. Without proper communication, shortages of river fish developed, placing more pressure on fish residing in Crystal Lake. With healthy schools depleted, bears remain foothills and mountains, providing with dwindling trout and salmon numbers.

Zion continued along narrow path admiring prairie dog's incredible handiwork, halting in front of cubs playing with Peanut and Miss Butterfly. "Many years since bears have been spotted away from foothills, you must be brave!" Grizzly cub explained, "Actually, we followed this funny-looking weasel playing a game of chase!" Peanut looking downward, interested in the smell of dirt and grass nearby. Attention returned to young bears, observing one grizzly bear, other black bear. "What are your names sweet things?" Bravest growled, "I'm Astral, this is my best friend, Nolly." Nolly, smiling nervously, "Hello ma'am." "Today's full of fun; many games and surprises. Peanut here, little weasel, may've misled. We're doing presentation determining fate of Creation!" "Does this mean we don't get to play chase?"

"Once Azorius and I've conducted business, plenty of time playing with Peanut and Miss Butterfly." Nolly stared at Zion explaining, "Mommy and Daddy don't let us play away from home." looking toward mountains northeast. "Shouldn't be punished if I take home, telling of your whereabouts. What's everybody up to?" Astral got on hind legs replying, "Fishies, all our parents care about. Never enough now that falcons stopped sharing tips!" "Does sound like problem, must be boring." nodded responding, "Very much so! Sometimes we play pretend and there's only Nolly and I, so when we get bored, practice climbing trees and get stuck!" "Suggest a younger tree, thinner trunk and limbs." readying directions to Peanut, "Keep guests company; distracted by sights and smells, responsible for their safe return." Miss Butterfly closed wings in confirmation, Peanut disappointed, busy moping. "Know you wish remaining close, but you've stumbled upon next mission. Bears haven't spoken word to me in many years, need you as honored chaperone." Peanut barking reply with newfound importance. Finished tallying, returned clipboard saying, "Perfect as always! Share gratitude amongst so all are appreciated." prairie dog cheering happily, exiting. Zion and Azorius took-place between ponds.

"WELCOME FAMILY, TO ENCHANTED ISLAND! EVIL'S MOUNTING IN OUR EXISTENCE, CHANGING STORYS' TO SHORTS WITHOUT HAPPY ENDING. GIVEN CHOICE; DO WE FIGHT WITH ALL OUR LIGHT, OR CONTINUE WITH A BLIGHT THAT MIGHT? TODAY, I ORATE UNDER TERRIFYING SONG, TELLING OF DAYS CREATION WAS WRONG.

NEVER BEFORE SUCH A SIGHT BEHELD; MOUNTING WRECKAGE WHERE GIVING TREE FELLED.

HOPE AND FAITH TWISTED, WRAITH IN KIN; CONTENTS EMPTIED INTO ORIGINAL & SIN.

BÆTÄ TRAPPED IN PREJUDICE & BLIND PRIDE, FORCING PEOPLE, "CHOOSE A SIDE!"

CHOICE STRIPPED OF GODLY ACTION,

CREATION BECAME DIVIDED,
DECIDED BY NEW FACTION.

ORIGINAL WAS SWORDSMAN,
TOOL USED FOR MILES,
GENDERLESS BECOMING
GENDERED IN BÆÖBÕB'S
TRIALS.

REVERED AMONGST HIS
PEOPLE, CONSIDERED FIXTURE
OF THIS STEEPLE.

GODLY AS HE WAS, COULD NOT
FORESEE HAPPENINGS NEXT.
GIVING TREE CUT, HE BECAME
PERMANENTLY VEXED.

SPIRIT BROKEN BEYOND
REPAIR, WATCHED LOVE
KINDLE, BURNING IN AIR.

**"BEGINNING OF FALL. DAY GIVING TREE
HEWN, LEAVES CHANGED SIGNIFYING LOSS, ANF
HOPE OF BEING REBORN ANEW. ONWARD,
THROUGH TRIAL AND TRIBULATION, SEARCH IN
HEARTS IF WE'RE WORTHY OF SALVATION!"**

WHO'S TO BLAME FOR SIN'S
PROLIFERATION?
WHO'S MAKER OF ONCE MIGHTY
NATION?

WHAT'S SIN, MORE THAN LIES?
IS IT WITHIN? WILL IT ACHIEVE
US PRIZE?

WHEN DID WE BREAK THE
GOLDEN RULE?
WHEN DID HEART OF MAN
BECOME CRUEL?

WHERE DID SIN FIRST EMERGE?
WHERE DOES LIFE FIRST
SURGE?

HOW'S SIN BLAMED FOR THIS?
HOW CAN SIN BE ALLOWED TO
EXIST?

SIN'S IN HEART OF CREATION,
HOLLOW SELF-ENTITLEMENT
ENDING EVERY NATION.

"MORE TO HER THAN TOLD IN THIS TALE, SHE FEEDS OF WORST FEARS, LEAVING YOU FRAIL. FOLLOWED BY THIS, INSIDIOUS CREATURE, HER GAZE PIERCES SOUL. NOTICING EVERY FEATURE. WHAT YOU TRIED TO HIDE DEEP INSIDE TO PROVIDE MANIFESTS RIGHT BESIDE YOUR BEDSIDE." Animals drew nearer, owls changing branches, cats trotting front-and-center gazing into eyes. *"DO WE DESERVE SURVIVING? IS IT NOT OUR FAULT WE'RE HERE? COUNTLESS LIFETIMES RIGHTING WRONG, WHY IS IT NOW WE CHANGE OUR SONG? CLAIM RIGHTEOUSNESS BUT HERE WE ARE ASKING FOR MORE DAYS WHILE FORSAKING SECONDS."*

LIKE RIP IN GALAXY LINE WAS
DRAWN IN SAND,
BÆTÄ PROCLAIMED
THEMSELVES PROMISED LAND.

WE COULD NOT BE RECEIVERS
OF GOD'S GLORY, IT WAS MAN
AND WOMAN RUINING STORY.

POISONED MINDS RATIONED
FOOD AND WATER,
ABUSING SONS, KILLING OUR
DAUGHTERS!

LEFT FULL OF WHYS AND
MAYBES, WE

CRY TO THE SKIES AS THEY'RE
KILLING OUR BABIES.

*"PREJUDICE IS NOT JUST BELIEF ONE'S
SPECIES OR RACE IS LESS THAN ANOTHER; TAKING
ONE'S SELF-IMAGE, MAKING THEM BETRAY SISTER
AND BROTHER. NEXT, FORMIDABLE FOE; DOES
NOT LISTEN TO REASON, NOR CARE OF WOE.
ANCIENT AS EVERY GRAIN OF SAND, FULL OF
BLOODLUST AND UNQUENCHABLE DEMAND."*

HIS MIND'S A WRITHING PILE OF
WORMS IN PIT OF DESPAIR,

CLAWING AT FIRST FRUITS
WITH NO DESIRE TO SHARE.

MAIN OBJECTIVE: STEAL FROM
LUNGS, YOUR AIR.

LAUGHS AT THOSE WHO STAND
BEFORE IT.

WORLD, IT'S LAIR.

EYES ARE MANY, WITH
UNBLINKING STARE.

MIND DEVOID OF THOUGHT,
ENDS SOULFUL CARE.

RAVAGER OF HOPE AND DESIRE
OF BEING FAIR.

LOST ITSELF, WITHIN ITSELF;
PURPOSE ON SHELF.

THIS IS PRIDE; ONE WHO LIES,
NEVER DIES.

PROVING GREATNESS,
CONSUMES VERY SKIES.

Weight atop island reached fever-pitch. Birds chirped nervously, hyenas laughed shifting weight between front and hind legs. Rodents scurried squeaking, fish formed tightly in schools movements rippling pond's surface, turtle and tortoise retreating into shells. *"FEAR DEEP INSIDE SOUL, FRACTION OF WEIGHT CARRIED BY STORIES OF OLD. CLOSING WITH COMBINING OF CORNERS. AT CROSSROADS OF GOOD AND EVIL STANDS UNBELIEVABLE MALICE."*

Serenity within magical place was uprooted. Elk
dueled clashing great antlers, ram congregated in tight circle,
resisting stampede. Snakes slithered toward center holes to
escape their feelings of terror, prairie dogs bravely standing in
the way, preventing them from leaving. Peanut cowered
between cubs, confused as to what whole fuss was. Having
seen enough, "Silence friends and family! There's more to be
shared; stories of old, ones untold." facing gnarled trees, "As
story reaches final page, you will find new life is made."
placing hands on deadened, dried bark, trees long-passed
rejuvenating. green buds turning into pink, purple and blue
Japanese Lotuses, some reaching for the sun. others remaining
closed under moon's twilight. "Allow me to speak of reason
for every Season. Whether in Fall foliage, Winter depths.
height of Summer lacking fresh Spring. ringing reasons for
bringing all Seasons."

*STANDING BETWEEN NIGHT
AND DAY WITH CHOICE OF
WHAT MAY; DO WE TO STAND
IDLY, ACCEPTING SHADOW'S
RIPPLES?*

*OR RISE AS ONE, FACING FIGHT
THAT CRIPPLES?
CHOSEN CHOICES.*

*ENOUGH WITH QUESTIONS,
UNBURY THE LIE!
TRUTHS THOUGHT LOST RESIDE
INSIDE.*

*FEAR GRIPPING, RIPPING AT
THROAT, WEAK PERSONALITIES
ROCKING YOUR BOAT.*

*TURN CHEEK FROM BITING
WIND, GIVE OTHER TO THOSE
WHO SINNED.*

*BEARER OF HEAVENS WILL
NEVER TIRE, SINCE BEGINNING*

Enchanted Island erupted into jubilation, cubs hugging Peanut, Miss Butterfly flitting-about with dozens of insects, Perfect Pair bouncing off Azorius in levity. Many stomped applause, birds rising from tree and water chirping pleasure. Azorius, *"STILL NEED CONVINCING. IF YOU THINK SINGLE, MOVING ORATION COUNTERACTS EONS OF NIGHTMARES, THEN I THINK YOU HAVE ALTITUDE SICKNESS."* "I tell stories all find hope in, may it help shake your fear of Sin." motioning Perfect Pair, "Need you this demonstration." holding magical sphere of water so all could see.

"One!" tear falling into bubble's center, growing resembling bright northern star. Animals high and low gasping at beautiful sight. "Star will forever stay, repeating stars we've all been made." Fish swimming freely, everyone gazing in wonder. Azorius swung around getting closer look elk and moose ducking avoiding collision. *"ONLY*

CREATURES TO SHARE REPEATING STAR–GIVES TINGLES ALL THE WAY TO FIN! SAVING FURTHER EMBARRASSMENT, I'VE MADE MY DECISION!" everyone grouping around Azorius, *"OUR STRENGTH REDEFINES HOW WE LOOK AT LOVE. NEVER THE CURSE LEADING TO OUR FALL, IT'S LOVE SAVING US, FOR THE FREQUENCY OF ALL!"*

Sanctuary erupted into jubilation never-before experienced. All souls were heard; every cry, stomp, clap of paws, slap of fin and tail–wolves *howling* approval. Zion herself was unable containing her delight; wrapping around beast's snout in tight hug. *"THANK YOU! Together,* fighting evil, restoring hope to every particle!"* Azorius, fearing would cry, lowered head setting her on ground. *"NO MORE TEARS, I'LL TURN INTO ALGAE!"* everyone laughing at his silliness. Caretaker righted posture singing, *"Azorius,* remember what has been said in stories of old? When single soul returns to Kingdom of Heaven, all angels *rejoice* in ringing of bells and celebration!" Azorius smiled knowingly and said, *"SUGGESTING WE THROW GRAND PARTY?! GIVE MOMENT, FINDING MUG!"* looking-about, having idea *"CHAT WITH BEAVERS, SEE IF THEY'LL SLAP SOMETHING TOGETHER!"* Zion, attention on audience, "Festival this evening celebrating grand spectacle and triumph over darkness! If everyone would get seated, returning to mainland *in style!"* animals puzzled by meaning. However, knew to trust unflinchingly. Azorius finished conversation with beavers. *"MEAN MOVING ENTIRE ISLAND TO MAINLAND? HOW YOU INTEND ON DOING SO? ISLAND'S FLOATED IN SKY SINCE BEFORE I WAS BORN!"* Zion flashed guardian pearly whites and said, "Never question affinity of love, power contained." *"TO THINK I THOUGHT TODAY'S SPECTACULAR WAS OVER!"* Tossing hair over other shoulder, approached flowering trees, owls readying-flight halting, watching with keen-interest. Arms reached toward sun and moon, moving downward in what animals described as slow-dance. Hands waist-height, dropped to knees, pressing palms into dampened soil. Noticeable vibration, then sudden lurch and to everyone's amazement, island descended. Mind-blown, *"LITTLE HAND MOTION AND KNEELING!? EXERT MORE ENERGY ITCHING BACKSIDE!"* Blushing, replied, "Only know two ways lowering–first time trying." *"UNDERESTIMATED–I APOLOGIZE."* patting lightly, "Think nothing of it. We all underestimate capabilities from time-to-time." Laughing,

decided using descent asking funny question. *"QUESTION,
HOW DOES ONE RID THEMSELVES OF ITCH WHILE
SLEEPING?"* "Hmm, could you scratch it in the dream?"
answering, *"TRIED, MADE IT WORSE. REASON ASKED,
FEW THOUSAND YEARS AGO DEVELOPED ITCH;
COUNTLESS DREAMS, COULD NOT RID MYSELF OF
IT! PREPARING FOR WHEN I TAKE LEAVE,
ENTERING SLUMBER."* "Plenty of time brainstorming
new, sleeping habitat!" Enchanted Island drifted toward
Crystal Lake, inhabitants getting-view of mountains. Still
hanging beside moon; sun reflected orange-yellow off
scattered clouds. Thirty meters above, Zion. "Landing will be
rougher than take-off." Azorius had thought pulling from
picturesque views. *"IDEA FOR FEATHER-LIGHT
LANDING–MAKE A HOLE!"* Coiled several trees, easing
down side, breathing steam over large area, driven into heavy
fog, boiling steam meeting water. Island plunged, sun and
moon bidding adieu, gliding toward proper positions,
rainbows streaking landscape.

     "Alright everyone, time for evening's festivities!"
turning to Peanut, "You are to recruit turtles, fetching barrel
stored inside cellar." barked joyously, Miss Butterfly landed
on Peanut's back, Perfect Pair giving crisp salute following
after. Azorius surfaced from depths below commenting,
*"OLD–NOT DEAF. EXPECT SINGLE BARREL TO BE
SHARED EQUALLY AMONGST?!"* dusting herself off.
"Not spirits making party, but party spirit!" *"NEVER BEEN
TO PARTY. SOMEWHAT OF AN ODDITY; SEE MYSELF
ARRIVING PROPERLY-DRESSED, PRETTY WOMAN BY
MY SIDE. WHEN DREAMING PARTIES, PRETENDED
BEING MOST-POPULAR MAN THERE, LIFE OF THE
PARTY! NEED HELP GETTING DRESSED FOR
TONIGHT'S CELEBRATION. CANNOT FIT HUMAN
CLOTHES, WANT TO LOOK IMPRESSIVE."* Surprised by
insecurity, "Concerned others are frightened of you?"
inspecting leaves, *"SURE NOTICED; NOT TAKEN SHINE,
AVOIDING–SENSITIVE TOWARD RESERVATIONS."*
"More than happy helping look your best, however, absent
from island a spell, consult Quoi fish for fashion advice."
waves washing partway up island, *"THINKING BOWTIE,
POSSIBLY A…"* hand held calming, "I'm sure there are
materials creating something." Curiosity in rhythm with
companions, saw Peanut rolling barrel, nudging it forward at a
good pace. Perfect Pair and Miss Butterfly following lazily
behind, watching dachshund do all the work. "Look at my

little boy doing it all by himself*!"* Squinting their direction, ***"BY LOOKS OF IT, BARREL'S EMPTY! EITHER HAVE VERY DRUNK FRIENDS HEADED OUR WAY, OR THEY GRABBED WRONG ONE!"*** "Grabbed the right one, only barrel in cellar." Azorius cast sideways glance snorting, ***"WHAT'RE YOU PLAYING AT?! WHEN IT ARRIVES I DEMAND TASTING!"*** "If promise integrity; not drinking another until after delivering children. Speaking of, pray forgive whilst tend." Walking island, found Astral and Nolly playing with butterflies. "Ready for home?" running to Zion, sniffing dress. She was impressed with how the bears were taking care of their newest. Zion meant speaking with them for some time; scheduling meeting negotiating solution, possible compromise. Respect surmounted all; order of nature established at the beginning mandated such; inconsiderate approaching different species speaking of shortcomings and weaknesses. Astral pawed knee for attention. "Are we going to play?" "That will be up to Peanut and Miss Butterfly, did you have fun? Infrequent seeing bears spend time with neighbors!" Nolly, "Parents don't like talking with other animals, makes them look at us funny." "What do you mean?" shortages taking a toll, children, mirrored reflections of stress-endured. "Always hungry, most others think we're going to eat them. Big birdies don't let us eat their fishies. So, sometimes we have to eat rabbits—even ate an elk once." Zion frowned. This was definitely news to her. Had sensed growing imbalance within Sanctuary for many years, yet failed realizing bears started hunting *outside* usual food source. "See why other animals would be frightened, bears are stronger than most." "Not anymore!" Astral cut in, "Now that birds have all the fishies to themselves, relatives are getting skinny— I tell Mommy she still looks good!" "Very wise; women are conscientious of their appearance! Do hope you'll share experience with families, important we come together to defeat Bæöbõb!" Nodding bravely, Astral, "Promise we listened, those Herded Evils are mean!" Nolly nuzzled Zion's hand asking, "They want our destiny, don't they have their own?" Zion sat cross-legged across. "Good question. Ever since man and woman were very young, Bæţä have been prideful, unwilling to share Giving Tree." Astral ran to nearby tree and stood on hind legs in defensive-posture. "Nolly, I've great idea! If we learn how to climb trees, we can protect everyone from those meanies!" Zion chuckled as cubs climbed tree, scaling ways up before sliding. "Need practice if to become true guardians! Know tree near opening in valley, where river runs into Crystal Lake? Trunk's massive, branches growing more outward than upward. Styling such as this allows access to topmost portions!" Cubs began dancing in circles, ending when Nolly remembered, "Wait a minute, that's the tree falcons and hawks live in!" "Yes, you're keen observer, their home since very beginning. Astral groaned, "Meanie birds will *NEVER* invite us to play! Do not see why they get to live in such a nice tree anyways, all they do is sit there eating our fishies!" Placing hand on tops of heads, "Where challenge comes. Think of it as a rite-of-passage; convince falcons letting you practice, maybe they'll start sharing fish!" Rearing-up with an idea. Astral, "Should sing a song while training, keeping us focused on noble duties!" Nolly, *"We are the Treemeisters, we are the Treemeisters!"*

Perfect Pair came into view waving merrily. "Peanut and Miss Butterfly returned from errand sent on, ready for home?" "Come on Nolly!" Astral said, "Let's go find that weird-looking weasel and make sure he's playing chase!" Zion to Perfect Pair, "Spend time with Azorius; never been to celebration, needs help appropriately engaging with others." following after cubs. Although more than willing to make short journey to bear's homeland, could feel excitement *SURGING;* thoughts turning on tonight's celebration. Preliminary plans were already decided: Growing *enormous* mushroom used as centerpiece to *wow* all in attendance! Zion found cubs and Peanut approaching empty barrel, Azorius *looming,* eyeing it *HUNGRILY; impatiently* waiting for allowance in sampling. "You did *great job* retrieving spirits Peanut–*appreciate* your efforts!" Panting hard and drooling from *laborious* activity, walked *briskly* over to Zion–licking at ankle. Miss Butterfly landed lightly upon shoulder awaiting departure to bears' homeland. Azorius boomed, *"SHOW HOW THIS CONTAINER PROVIDES ALCOHOL!"* getting best, possible view. Zion faced great serpent, eyeing him closely. "Alright; small drink tiding you over." *"OOH SPLENDID!! HOW DOES ONE ACQUIRE LIQUID?!"* walking to pine nearest, "First, creating object holding drink!" placing hand on tree's side, hundreds of pinecones falling from above. Offering in both hands, palms faced toward sky covering pinecone. In it's place, thin, wooden cup. "Socialize, drink at own pace!" Azorius hid fact he was impressed countering, *"SHARING FROM ONE, TINY CUP?! HARDLY EXCITING IF EVERYONE'S HUDDLED WAITING!"* Sidestepping, "What do you mean?" pinecones identical to one held, "If run out, happy making more. Help

with party preparation partner with beavers, fashioning tables
from trees on island, replacing with saplings from mainland."
Serpent shook head slowly in amazement saying, *"YES
MILADY. BEFORE GOING MY DRINK?"* Caretaker
placed cup beneath spout, depressing rubber stopper, turning
to Azorius contemplating future temptation. "Need I mention
moderation? Find Perfect Pair; wardrobe options." Zion
calling for sea turtles ferrying to mainland.

Journey to highlands where bears lived was less than
three kilometers plenty space for childish fun. Seconds after
taking path, *"COME ON WEIRD WEASEL!"* roared Astral,
"Let's play chase! You and Miss Butterfly are Bæöbõb, we'll
be destiny!" Zion, "Night's falling, cannot have anyone
separating!" Plan for youngsters returned looking toward
oldest living tree; seventy meters tall growing strongly
despite antiquity, winged members naming it SplinterTree.
Astral, near tree's base, "Tree always noisy!" "It isn't now."
growled Nolly eyeing outermost limbs, "Hunting while fishies
high in water. Parents say it's smart fishing around sunrise and
sunset colder at night, don't see well without light." Hand
under cub's chin, lifting so eyes would meet. "Parents must be
proud!" Astral saying, *"My* Mommy and Daddy say trees help
find home!" pointing paw at tree nearest, bark marred with
claw marks. "Important growing bears such as yourselves
listen, growing big and strong!" Families used to live on
separate sides of mountains, rarely associating with one
another. When fish shortages began, grizzlies endured
unspeakable hardship. Originally residing on northern ranges,
forests covering outermost boundaries, grizzlies stayed true to
nature; brazenly steadfast in ways. If not for Falcon King,
grizzlies would've remained isolated It was he establishing
partnership between bear families, also one between hawks
and falcons. An overabundance of hungry mouths created
dispute over fishing territories, leading bears to band together
in competition against falcons and hawks. Knew if couldn't
discover solution to shortage, those reliant on fish would prey
on forest animals—uprising on her hands.

Trekked toward rolling foothills in silence, forestry
thickening, as did frequency of bear marks. Lining both sides
of path, bark scarred with bear claws, damage recent, made
specifically helping little ones find home. "Almost to dividing
path. Tell others of Azorius's return, I'll do my best softening
blow." Crossed invisible boundary into bear country, at split
in path, two, adult bears. Following way of what was
customary, Zion bowed as sign of respect. *"ASTRAL!"* roared

grizzly bear, *"Foolish* if you think I'm not punishing*!"* Other, female black bear, moved quickly their direction. Peanut and Miss Butterfly diving behind Zion's dress. Walked directly to Nolly scolding, "Another hour, would've assembled entirety of families*!"* Zion, "Hello Sundis, Cedron, children are safely returned." Sundis picked up Nolly by scruff, carrying home. *"ASTRAL!"* roared Cedron, "If you don't start walking, no food for a week*!"* lumbering path without a glance back. Peanut whimpered, Cedron walking toward group. Even with food shortage, most-impressive grizzly lived, weight of large paws shaking ground. Came within meter growling, "What in Creation do you think you're doing associating with my daughter*!?* Last thing she needs is to be tainted by your kind*!"* *"My* kind; aren't we all from same, great star*?* They were invited to oration, which they happily attended." Throwing dirt and grass, "Received invitation from annoying butterflies and sent them on their way. What gives authority dictating when you've done so little*!?* Majority go hungry scraping bottoms of muddy rivers, haven't hibernated in centuries*!"* roaring so loudly dirt and bark fell from trees nearby, "Claim Caretaker, yet prove there's only one thing bears can rely on— ourselves*!"* Upset by her own, lack-of-initiative, "Never once Cedron, not once did you come to me for aid. Ask, you shall receive." "Receive*?* Older members are so malnourished we *bring* whatever's caught*!* Want to know what I fed my dying mother today*?* Squirrel*!!* All I can provide because we refuse desecrating land in massacre driven by hunger*!!* While you sit in your cozy cottage, I'm here making REAL decisions*!* Are we to be reduced to hide and bone, contemplating cannibalism while you stare starry-eyed at that stump seeking answers*?!"* Zion thought before answering, "May have found way ending hunger." Grizzly let-out sizable laugh responding, "What, oh what would that be*?* Devised method planting trout in pretty, little garden*?"* Ignoring patronizing tone, "Azorius is awake." "Said you've found solution to our starvation, only heard the same rambling from that fairytale head of yours*!"* "Children are perfect example; after witnessing oration, they wish to climb the many limbs and boughs amongst." Conversation took a turn for worse, Cedron stomping angrily as he roared, ***"SUCH AUDACITY, ADDLING OUR YOUNG WITH NONSENSE!! AM I TO INDULGE IN THIS FANTASY; CLIMBING, EATING LEAVES, TEACHING THEM TO PRAY SO FISH COME RAINING!?"*** "Children are our future Cedron…all of us or none of us." Great bear stood on hind legs lunging forward with lightning speed, stopping before mauling her face. *"ALL OF US OR NONE OF US!? WHERE WERE YOU WHEN MY FAMILY WAS STARVING IN THE MOUNTAINS!? WHERE WERE YOU WHEN WE BECAME BOTTLE-NECKED TO THESE WOODS? IT'S NOT GOD FORSAKING US ZION, IT IS YOU!"* All she could do was holding the stare Cedron refused breaking. "Just as I thought, full of fairytales." turning to leave, "This battle against Bæöbõb, consider us bears out—you're no better than them."

Despite her dismal encounter, Zion planned setting feelings aside, enjoying party. From shore, observed beavers' incredible carpentry. Perfect Pair played their parts as well, Azorius wearing crude bowtie drafted from seaweed and cattails. Turtles emerged welcoming, climbing onto large shells, sitting cross-legged with Peanut, Miss Butterfly resting comfortably on nose facing island's direction. Great serpent's laugh echoed surrounding valleys; helping himself to more than one cup. "Did reclaimed guardian become inebriated?" Though sea turtles were preoccupied, leader extended neck nodding. "Typical Azorius!" noticing baby turtles following in tightly-knit structure, "Excellent form turtle-tots!" Miss Butterfly flew from safety of best friend's nose, matching swim speed, landed upon shells, turning around, waving. Relieved, "Next time, enlighten before trying something so risky!" butterfly saluting, flitting wings happily. Peanut gripped tightly, leapt, foot finding grass and soil—Peanut's tail a-wagging. "Let's get this party started!" deer, gopher, and nearby baby turtles overhearing, cheering enthusiasm. Azorius *(telling long-winded story about shedding to boa constrictors)* noticed Zion's return and slithered over shouting, *"ZION! WHAT DO YOU THINK? QUOI FISH SAY IT BRINGS-OUT MY EYES!"* Hand on hip, "Azorius——*love* the bowtie by the way—how much did you drink?" Blushing, *"I COULDN'T HELP MYSELF IT WAS JUST SO TASTY! QUESTION I'VE BEEN DYING TO ASK."* moving tail to barrel, tossing it, *"HOW'S DRINK POURED WHEN BARREL'S COMPLETELY EMPTY?!"* Zion responded, "When does sweet nectar ever empty from the well of God?" greeting partygoers, leaving Azorius pondering rhetoric. Retrieved cup and walked to island's center, good distance from prairie dog holes. Confidently, "Where I'll put you. Azorius, would you like me fetching garment wearing on head?" forgetting there wasn't anything, shrugged, *"DELIGHTFUL AS FANCY HAT SOUNDS, SOCIABLE WITH FESTIVE SUIT! BESIDES, ANYTHING GIVEN*

LIKELY DROPPED! IF YOU'D EXCUSE ME, PAIR OF BOA CONSTRICTORS ARE REGALING ABOUT POINTS OF SHEDDING. NEVER DONE IT IN PHYSICAL SENSE BUT, DREAMS AS I GREW IN SIZE; WRIGGLING OUT OF OLD SKIN REVEALING BEAUTIFUL, NEW COAT!" With that, tipsy serpent moved in search of newfound friends. Gaining space necessary, set to gathering ingredients. Waving arms, "Stand back good people, don't want anyone hurt!" animals relocating into surrounding waters, brush. Walking to pond nearest, filled cup with water, returning to place chosen moments before, pouring contents. Picking-up handful of earth, spun in quick rotation, soil landing in circular shape upon compacted dirt.

> *"Fallen tree, fertile ground, moistened soil.*
> *Rise on sacred mound, celebrating mortal coil."*

Low rumbling, ground rising, mushroom pushing forth from dampened soil. Growth was astronomical; thickening, shooting upward, standing eighty meters tall, serving as sheltering canopy. Frogs, snakes, amphibians sang, licked and croaked celebration. *"THAT'S A MUSHROOM!"* exclaimed Azorius, *"WHY HAVEN'T THERE BEEN SWAMPLAND CREATURES BEFORE–SILLY THEY'RE UNACCOUNTED!"* "It's because of you." Uncertain what was meant. *"GOT ME ON THIS ONE!"* moving closer preventing distraction, "Innumerable lifetimes, only recently considered attempts waking, you abandoning our cause. Only at end did spirit finally ring true." holding hand silencing, "No need for apologies from the apologue; preferring dreamscapes is in your nature. This being said, giving you privilege of naming mushroom." Hot tears evaporated before hitting earth. *"HELLO MUSHROOM, WHAT'S YOUR NAME? DADDY WILL GIVE YOU A GREAT NAME–SUSTENANCE OF LEGENDS YES YOU ARE!"* deer and elk enjoying display. *"FINDING PROPER NAME MEANS KNOWING OF IT'S PERSONALITY. IF SOMETHING'S NEW, IT'S UNKNOWN, WHAT OTHERS FEAR OR REVERE. A SCARY NAME REPELS, TOO PLEASING, POSSIBILITY OF OTHERS FIGHTING! HMMM...!"* everyone laughing at his perplexity. *"NEVER DONE THIS BEFORE, MAKING-SURE IT'S PERFECT!"* mustering brainpower delivering fitting name. *"I'VE FOUND IT; CALLING YOU AZORIUS'S REVENANT; FITTING NAME FOR A*

MUSHROOM ALMOST AS LARGE AS I!" Head, hoof, tail and paw raised toward Azorius's Revenant. Jubilation quieting, mushroom displayed glowing coloration. *"WHAT'S IT DOING?!"* worried something went terribly wrong, *"DID I MESS-UP?"* "Whenever a child receives name, they begin developing personality of their very-own. In a sense, you gave mushroom it's first attribute!" Dancing to-and-fro, *"DO WE KNOW WHAT ATTRIBUTE?"* "Haven't foggiest idea; develops based on it's Creator, neighbors, environment surrounding. Since tonight marks the end of crestfallen behavior, guarantee it's special!" If Azorius had hands he would've been clapping, instead, used joyous moment bringing everyone closer. *"WHERE'S MY TINY CUP? A TOAST–RAISE GLASSES ABSENT FEAR!"* "So busy, yet to pour drink." *"WHAT!? STAND A DOZEN EMPTIED– THIS WILL NOT DO!"* constricting barrel, bringing where stood, extrusion process yielding only the ripest berries. Guardian straightened posture, relaxing eyes. *"TO THOSE LIVING AND IN REST, PROSPERITY IN AND OUT OF NEST. THOSE WEAKENED, FRAGILE AND FRAIL, LET US RAISE OUR GLASSES, SIPPING THIS ALE. TO THE MANY STRONG, READY TO FIGHT: GOD BLESSES FOR DOING WHAT'S RIGHT!"*

Celebration carried long into the night, only at first sign of sunrise did party conclude. Perfect Pair, Peanut, Miss Butterfly already retired, leaving a few revelers enjoying drink and celebration. *"FINAL DRINK ENJOYING SUNRISE?"* Flattered by his inquiry, "Absolutely old friend! Seated on Azorius, made for shore, graceful strokes hardly-disturbing water. Azorius raised segment high, sharing the raw, beauty of nature, sunrise basking mountains in a glorious, golden amber. *"WANT TO KNOW SOMETHING?"* "Sure!" squinting up at him. *"MOMENT AWAKENED, MIND WAS MADE ON HELPING."* Slapping scaly segment, *"Serious!?* Did Oration of Creation for nothing?" He chuckled, *"IMPRESSIVE DISPLAY PROPAGATED POTENTIAL, SHOWING ALL HOW POWERFUL LOVE REALLY IS."* sunrise revealing settled mist, yellow-pink clouds between snowy peaks. Azorius, fighting-back tears, *"ISN'T IT BEAUTIFUL?"*

Yes, God is."

DÄRKÊŠT ĊRËATÔR

*Why did you create me as symbol of your story?
Have we not spend time in it's entirety begging for your glory–
unbridled, unabridged pride. Left in stable unstable, shall tear
apart vessel to reach your table, seeking inside cherished
work–sustenance meant for me. Am I not different?
Repetitious pestilence!! Jar your Old Testament into New…for
now. For crimes against the spirit, disintegration; you refused
my worktable, denying integration!*
-Revelations of Judgment, written by *Choirmaster Fall.*

While animals lifted cups to Azorius's Revenant, she smelled them. **SPORES; SO POUROUS AND AIRY,** slightest increase illuminates scarcity of entity and enemy. A whisper from the Cosmos decreed, ***"FIND HIS DEED!"*** Whether it be hay fever, Seasons writing own reasons for allergy, clergies, clinicians, clerics were compelled seeking seed–the precedent to proceed. Hesitance and persistence combined, exposing sins of mankind, beginning in the prismatic prism of the third eye, where all life connects. Things hidden were no longer secret; a proverbial, sensing secretion recognized by those in harmony. Our undeniable connectivity triggered phenomenon known as photon energy; light surging amongst all matter, creating penetrating resonance. Photon energy was one factor evil couldn't keep from the masses.

"I'm DONE collecting souls from these worthless humans!"

From within the shadow of a wormhole emerged a terrifying being. Bæöbõb viewed world through blackened slits, wielding silver tongue fueling her deceitful nature. "Rise to me! Heralded Evils, come forth fulfilling New World Order!"

First, came Original. Pale skinned, greasy hair hung around neck, rag bound his eyes, breath spewing in savage heaves. If the Greeks were to speak of this beast, truest of titans to have ever hailed Mount Olympus. Within cold, sooty soul was a murmur, *"Do you remember?"* He will always remember; watching his one, true purpose chopped to splinters, reduced to ash. "Arrived doing your bidding, my tireless devourer."

Sin couldn't be seen by normal means, whenever taking-form, she becomes exact replica of person she's facing. A timeless expert, knowing how to get inside your mind, a venerable, apocalyptic shape-shifter. She was understandably mad, madder than most, viable vial of veiled violence, frank in sense since… She perched nearby meticulously scrutinizing cohorts.

"Mirror, mirror, destined destiny's absent the best of me. Mired mire, plotted sarcophagus, error of my pyramid. Peering amidst foundation's mortar there's a scar, towed by the war-torn ode from our ore, no end in sight. My final detestation: Deliberating destination! Am I to stake worth in this lot?" *Wise* in evaluation, Sin predicted what SHE & HE meant, the YOU & I'S of the ME & YOU. Where's the contradiction? Is it within singular sign, siphoned amongst our superfluous pluralisms? In tens she's been commanded, reprimanded, branded land dead—sand in the end. "Processing mentored slate, sin to mate cindered fate upon Creation's plate. A lot's allotted, deeming World's worth."

"Humanity's fairly, fair-thee-well spent! I must return to present event."

Prejudice was hand-sewn by needle and thread, serial-killer's version of a stuffed animal, always found in Pride's company. Pride was massive; three enormous mouths, ten tentacles capable spanning large distances, snatching-up enemies, eating them whole. Pride, "Starvation *burns* inside pitted hearts, a pity."

Bæöbõb floated-about, putting together a most-foul blueprint of betrayal. To Sin, "You vile, disgusting worm!! Tactics filling humanity and waiting for them to destroy themselves has been disappointing—a most meager return!" Baeobob vanished, reappearing before Sin, Sin transforming into perfect proxy of her master. "Was it not at the beginning you received power, making your presence known in hearts of man?" stabbing a hand deeply into Sin, rifling-through the sinners congregated inside her invisible mass. "What seems to be the problem? Surely a Heralded Evil as powerful and cunning as you should've wiped those insignificants off the face of the planet! Yet here I stand, empty-handed!" lunging other arm inside like rummaging purse for stick of gum, wracking her with fresh agony. "The problem with you Sin, is you're worthless, filth, eternal fool for winning the admiration of *him*–only Once ever loved*!*" Pride and Prejudice laughed cruelly, jeering Original's direction as Baeobob dug deeper. Sin searched remaining existence, finding her secret weapon. In the sound of silence, she attached thought, *"Unreadable when decipherable."* ripping parable in two, placing half in Bæöbõb's searching hands. "Here you are little spark, time sure doesn't dim your shine*!*" turning toward cohorts, "This spell binds Zion's soul to forsaken Creation, however, sliver cannot be acted-on by normal means, requiring payment in the form of truth." Baeobob focused her empty pits used for eyes, beginning a dreadful incantation.

I've birthed item made from thread,
not woven for the binding of any book.
Loose strings, my clay doll;
finish this noose, solidify Fall!

I'm shape-shifter, story drifter, eater of her Sun–
murderer of One.
I've been cast-aside by my people;
gifts of gender our church, Tree our Steeple.

Invest in this stolen destiny,
for you, lost soul, are only dust.
Those who must, those who fussed, all their dreams
disintegrate like rust.

I'm ignored by God,
risen as Bæöbõb.

A rip opened in time and space and from this tear, black sand poured. After watching it float-about, she gathered it into open palm, throwing handful in wormhole's direction, returning as living creature. "Come here little clay doll, my scribe. You're to record events with charcoal body, doing-so until your mass is spent, disappearing like all remaining hope in Creation*!* Open mouth thanking your master for this opportunity*!*" Fall slowly faced commander saying, "Ah, yes your Esteemed Tarriness, there isn't any parchment. Ill-conceived creating scribe when there's nothing to write on." Baeobob blinked, unable admitting she'd forgotten this, key-item. Gnarled hand moved upward accessing a swirling vortex, recovering from it, an ancient tome. Snapping it

closed, she dropped it on Fall, sending her reeling downward.
"Now that I've gotten your attention, start writing!"

"We'll rip Enchanted Island from sky, laying-waste
to all standing in our way! She and her worthless animals will
break, bleed, and die at our hands! They will beg on hands
and knees for sweet death before I'm finished! halting before
Sin, "Don't think I didn't notice trick you tried playing, stupid
proxy! You're to find Sanctuary, ensuring surprise's delivery.
Zion has exquisite needlework taste, I think she'll find this
one to die for!"

STRAY END OF THE SPINNER

Amber sunlight blanketed Zion's bedchamber in a warm glow, taupe-colored curtains casting dancing shadows from a gentle breeze. Bed was circular in shape, covered by thin sheet, wolf pelt, white pillow stuffed with large feathers. Zion and Azorius stayed awake long-after sunrise enjoying fine spirits, regaling of good and bad in their many years of friendship. Sleeping-in wasn't something done frequently; impatience existing in hearts of living things, their horizon growing closer. Most nights Zion remained awake, worrying about affairs of mankind, if her and One…

"Good morning Peanut, my little dandelion, haven't slept this well in ages!" Peanut bounded few steps necessary vigorously kissing his response. Almost noon, temperature climbed to it's highest point, cicadas singing in trees nearby. Stretching waking sleepy muscles, Zion noticed Perfect Pair having trouble removing themselves from old fishbowl. "Knew bowl was a bit small." grabbing, giving a quick tug, friends escaping crowded confines. "Anyone seen Miss Butterfly?" Groaning, Peanut jumped down to soft rug beneath, Perfect Pair bringing fins upward hiding laughter before joining search for insect. Rising, smoothing wolf pelt, "Stay; wish speaking. Accomplished much over the last while together, helpful each endeavor. It truly takes a pair never spending lifetime apart to understand. Using time left——" Zion's legs buckling, Perfect Pair darting-about with concern for her well-being. "That was strange; pain in heart, body went numb for but-a-freckle. Pay no mind to prior moment. passing it off as need for a good breakfast." After all, they weren't swimming their best this morning either. Zion headed down staircase, leading way through house into kitchen, discovering *Aesop's Fables* moved from it's original place, resting facedown on the floor. Hand enclosing around loose page, peeling, outer cover, "How book fell's a mystery, it does sadden losing another page." opening, expecting to find third page torn, learning they'd recovered a missing page. "This is special, found what's lost! Long as book's been in my care, story's remained absent!" fish swing-dancing, pausing mid-dip, hearing a loud commotion. "Sounds like Peanut found something of note out front."

Dirt clouds billowed a-ways downhill, Miss Butterfly gliding their direction, landing lightly on Zion's shoulder.

"What's going on?" She glanced back at developing scene, lifting front legs saying, "Who knows?" Zion couldn't quite perceive happenings, but she knew Peanut was in a tussle with something. "Let's help catch whatever he's chasing!" calling to intruder, "Don't be frightened, we mean you no harm!" ignoring, running forest's direction, "Not to worry, waited ages practicing vine-crafting."

Foot tracing semi-circle, hand moved forcefully downward pointing index-finger, snares emerging from root-systems deep underground, wrapping intruder several times, making escape impossible. "Gotten-off on the wrong foot, each surprised by other." Perfect Pair invaded personal space discussing possibilities of origin. "I'm Zion, this is Peanut, fish swimming awkwardly around you, call them Perfect Pair!" Waiting for strange, little thing to reply, "Maybe she cannot talk? Clearly you're female, based on shape and construction–do you mind?" expressing desire inspecting her form. Immobilized by constricting vines, gave look saying, "How you propose that?" Zion pointed at imprisoning vines, grip slackening, allowing her to drop. "Never seen creature such as you, uncertain where you hail from…" Peanut inched closer, their guest becoming uneasy, hiding behind Zion. "Ladies need space when being introduced to new people. Men; magnetically-drawn to women." Doll extended arm, Caretaker eyeing limb's length, running finger along wrist. "Appears you're made from brittle stone. How ever did you find Sanctuary? Creature cannot just gain access by normal means." pointing house's direction, indicating they follow. Once inside, she climbed onto sofa, motioning toward Aesop's Fables like diving into water. "Found way into Sanctuary from book?" coming to an illustration, subtext reading,

"Sisters Fall & Zephyr reunite as clay dolls."

"My word, you're made of clay!" Doll celebrated, gesturing at the name Zephyr. Caretaker sat, sending dust clouds wafting. "Zephyr, story belongs to you, but since you cannot talk, may I have permission reading?" Doll plopped onto sofa cushion, looking into lap before giving thumbs-up. "T'is with great pleasure I read, *Canifall & Fallable.*" Zion smoothed page, staring quietly at the text, lines of worry forming. "It's in dialect I can't decipher." Story, was in English.

Everyone fell quiet wondering what new sorcery had befallen them. Zion stood abruptly, nearly sending Zephyr tumbling to floor from the sudden change. "Sorry, usually more mindful of those around me. I don't think situation's from nefarious energy, anyone's ill-will, but harder I try reading, the more unintelligible it becomes! Let's pay our restored Guardian a visit, hoping he knows something about you too Zephyr." Zephyr clinked hands together asking to be carried, placing arm around Zion's neck ensuring she wouldn't take a tragic topple. Peanut ran ahead to beachfront, heard barking, attempting to raise Azorius. "Azorius!" Zion called-out, "I've questions, and a new friend to meet." *Rumbling* sound, water-level receding as lake bubbled and stirred, Zephyr gripping Zion's neck hard, leaving scratch-marks. "Display's nothing to worry about! Azorius looks big and scary but when you get down to it, no smarter or friendlier ally!" Turbulence grew, waterline lowering further, dozens of crabs relocating as he broke surface with a bellowing laugh, many birds chirping and squawking their displeasure. Azorius shook head vigorously, sending energized water molecules high into air, coalesced particles forming a rainbow. *"MIGHT WANT TO TAKE A FEW STEPS BACK."* waves rushing inland, *"ANY LONGER AND YOU WOULD'VE RESCHEDULED BATH-TIME! PEANUT TELLS OF AN UNUSUAL MORNING–HOW MIGHT I ASSIST?"* "Familiar with Aesop's Fables, *Canifall & Fallable?*" *"TITLE, UNIQUE AS IT IS AWFUL, DOES LITTLE JOGGING MEMORY. CLOSER LOOK?"* "Presenting in way suiting book; old, cannot handle excess moisture." book taking-wing, rising to meet Azorius's gaze. *"BEFORE WE BEGIN, I BELIEVE A HISTORYU LESSON IS IN ORDER. AESOP'S CONSIDERED THEOLOGIAN AND PHILOSOPHER BORN BEFORE HIS TIME. PRIMARY REASON WHY THIS IS COMMON THOUGHT AMONGST HUMANS IS BECAUSE AESOP CRAFTED MASTERFUL STORIES OUTLINING NECESSITY FOR LIVING THINGS TO ESTABLISH MORALITY. WHAT I FIND MOST-PLEASING ABOUT HIS WRITING STYLE IS HIS ABILITY REMOVING BLAME FROM READER'S MIND, DOING-SO THROUGH PERSONIFICATION–*

HAVE I LOST ANYONE?" expectantly gazing group, finally noticing Zephyr.

"YOU MUST BE CHEATING INTRUDER PEANUT TOLD ME ABOUT; SAID HE WOULD'VE HAD YOU BUT YOUR GO-TO MOVE WAS THROWING DIRT IN HIS FACE." Peanut postured bravely, if a buried crab hadn't surprised him by blowing bubbles, making him fall, would've believed him ferocious, guard dog. Zion. "When I awoke this morning legs buckled from a pain in my heart, almost like I was pincushion filled to capacity, needle removed at awkward angle." Azorius slithered closer, conscientious of endangering Zephyr's fragile form. *"ACTUALLY, RELIEVED THIS IS ALL IT WAS. EVENTS ARE ALL CONNECTED TO ONE SOURCE–YOU. FIND MYSELF SURPRISED YOU'RE UNABLE RECALLING WHO THIS IS!"* Bewildered, "Try as I might, not even imaginary memory of any clay doll." *"ZEPHYR'S MORE THAN KILN-DRIED DOLL, SHE'S PIECE OF YOUR VERY-SOUL. SHE AND HER SISTER ARE FRAGMENTS ABSCONDED BY BÆÖBÕB TO BECOME THE DARKEST CREATOR. ALSO EXPLAINS WHY YOU CANNOT READ STORY; IT'S PORTION OF YOUR OWN JOURNEY–WAITING TO TRANSPIRE!"*

Looks varied from shock to amazement. "Think I'll sit with Zephyr while you read. Peanut, come sit in my lap–in need of comfort!" Sudden, swirling sound, four short legs stirring-up the sand around him, Peanut racing to chase her worries away, leaping headfirst into sand pile. Azorius, after much-needed laughter, *"CONSIDER EVENTS SYMBOLIC OF PROGRESS; PARTS THOUGHT LOST HAVE RE-MATERIALIZED! CALL ME NAÏVE, BUT I THINK IT'S SIGN WE'RE ON THE RIGHT TRACK!"* Looking at Peanut, caressing his head. "He's right, isn't he? Only a bit longer before One returns, falling in love all over again–including you Zephyr!" Zion faced Azorius, pursing lips thinking best approach moving-forward. "It's time; showing you guys something only shown One–my vulnerability." everyone gasping, Azorius laughing, *"CANNOT BELIEVE EXPRESSIONS I'M SEEING FROM YOU LOT–IF ONLY I HAD A MIRROR! LET ME TAKE A GUESS, A REAL, SHOT IN THE DARK: ASSUMED CARETAKER HAS NO SHORTCOMINGS?"* smallest of crabs burbling, *"Yish!"* before returning underneath sand. Unable hiding her blushing, "Proclivity of living things is sensitivity when having to admit such things–guess it's only natural. Every atom has perfect imperfections unique to not just any, singular moment. Essentially, things about ourselves we find most-unpleasant and shameful are really opportunities for growth! Practical approach is asking how to be of service to those struggling. Confiding vulnerabilities means giving another power, trusting they won't betray you for the temptations it rears." Looking pleadingly to Azorius, "Would you be my honorary pathfinder, guiding me through trialing tribulation? Daren't make a-go of this alone!" everyone scooting together in agreement. *"REMINDS ME OF A DREAM ONCE TRAIPSED THAT WAS PLEASANT IN NATURE. FRIENDS GATHERED AROUND LARGE TABLE INSIDE COLLECTOR'S MEMORABILIA SHOP, EACH PRETENDING TO BE A HERO OF IMPRESSIVE SKILL AND KNOWLEDGE. THERE WAS ONE AMONGST WHO STOOD-OUT ABOVE ALL THE REST, THE ESTEEMED STORYWEAVER. VERY-MUCH LIKE THE IDEA OF CHARTING COURSE THROUGH TERRAIN'S UNKNOWN FOR BETTERMENT OF THOSE I CALL ALLY!"* Peanut growled and woofed, Zion laughing, "How silly we are when raised behind fence without a prayer of the wide, open prairie!" Azorius, *"IT WOULD APPEAR I'VE MISSED JOKE, CLUE ME IN?"* Reference is altruistic to how negative individuals will seek ways quashing happiness regardless of context or presentation." Still confused, *"WHAT DID PEANUT SAY EXACTLY?"* "Personified himself as one of the human's you were speaking of and said, "Why do we go to church playing lamb at the altar when in my story it's God we seek?""

Wind blew forcefully across the everglade, sending particulates, eroded topsoil hundreds of feet into the air. Harvest season was notably hot and dry, many working long hours preventing Winter's food-stores from diminishing. A hand enclosed around ripe, red apple, gently pulled from sinewy stem, inspected for blemishes. It was not only for her appearance that brothers and sisters held stake in her warmth. Carried a palatable energy upon breast, given-freely to those sharing time and space, tending to the sages and fronds, bushes and ponds.

Voice called some distance behind, "Thought to find here, was either orchard or marshes…" obvious swamps, marshlands held no enjoyment. "Good afternoon Adam! When last you searched, remember removing many leeches!" "What was it you said; amphibians need love too." Blushing, "When spirits beckon visit in verdant cradle, who am I denying?" Closing distance between, Adam lifted Eve with muscled arms, apples leaping from basket, feeling his warm, naked body, eyes lingering bringing them upward. "Where have you been, aside from wandering hills searching?" "Speaking with Hamsphreth about his famous clash with serpent of the marsh–take-heed in those parts, dearest Daughter of Canifall." "Father's known for embellishment during his regalements, convincing an outlander he conquered the Leviathan of many oceans." "Pray tell, are you excited for this year's festival? Thinking entertaining display celebrating our ancestors of old!" Adam was a lover of fine-arts, exhilarated bringing attentional-value to the creatures he named. "Many amongst are talented, with as much to offer as leaves on trees." imagining Adam wearing fig leaf, world seeing him naked.

Adam's love for Eve first took-shape in form of what he was taught giving all women, quickly surpassing anything known, a growing tenderness representing his truest self. Adam, "Sister Lilith, endearing as she is, lacks a certain subtlety, more-likely arguing than appreciating presence." quarrelsome behavior surrounding her infatuation with Adam. Secrets were not much to be had in Canifall, usually becoming topic of much discussion and debate, citizens creating an ingenious method handling this, habitual behavior. Individuals entertaining secrets were called to city center and humiliated, informed in great-detail about secrets they contrived keeping. Adam, "Sister's fervor has grown in likeness of a great beast, are you concerned of her display?" Eve knew there'd possibly come day where they'd confront one another due to disparity accumulated since childhood. Understandable why Lilith felt way she did, forced following in Eve's shadow, having eyes for same man. As result, Lilith was rarely seen by the other townspeople, preferring her rows of orchards. "Fuss unlikely long as you remember not getting cornered near fireside!" "Last year was quite the display, suggesting red apples for celebration, keeping green for Winter." "Appreciate her concern, however, can you imagine our usual stores tainted by the continual diet of those, tart morsels?" "Do see her point; in winter, only way using red apples you so-cherish is by reducing them to paste, eating as they are." "While you're busy channeling sister, I'd like you to remember who God said was yours!"

They entered social gathering place, observing Eve's father eyeing plans for a grand stage. Years prior, customary there be special purpose for celebration. Settlers, meager as they were, suffered greatly during change of season. If not for the dedicated work each contributed, festivals would've never come to happening. Adam, "Believe I'm only one capable of constructing stage by tomorrow's end!" bringing Hamsphreth into warm embrace, pulling away with hand around scroll. Hamsphreth, "Yet to ask daughters' permission." Eve, "What is it you have me signed for?" Knowledgeably in a bind, Adam sought situational control. Frequently being center of attention, Adam's efforts became consequentially wearing to those wishing to take-part in celebration planning. "Reenactment of God's vision!" "Mere, night to prepare!" imagining outcome blamed on her, "Lilith and I never carry during presentations!" Avoiding confrontation, generated a false laugh to say, "Thou art distracted by Seasons, each bearing reasons. Instead of toiling you with choice, acted upon own measure." Unfazed by his lack-luster performance, "Graced news to sister? Surely you'll be the one who does!" Deferred until fulfilling wishes, responded, "Shall go."

Sun reached it's highest-point, men and women seen laboring in the nearby fields. Adam raised fist in a sign of respect, shouting, ***"WHOA-HO!"*** Minutes later, he found himself amidst green apple, Lilith nowhere in sight. The wind whispered through creaking limbs, provoking admiration of Lilith's offerings. Shorter and stronger than her sister, born with drive similar to Adam, Lilith had a knack for tilling soil. If not busy making-scene, she was found here, diverting all her forceful energy into crafting immaculate apples–not too tart, not too sour. "Young maiden's absent, Eve will do it*!*" laughing heartily, preparing to leave scene. "Do what*?* Doth protest her sending you as her stoic, errand boy." Lilith descending from branches above, hazel-brown eyes locked onto Adam. *"Hmm?"* realizing she was nearly on top of him, "Requesting participation in this year's festival, only downside, doing charade with sister." Lilith looked him head-to-toe biting into an apple. *"Hm.* So you cannot do it without*?* Right. Should be, how you say, absolutely crowd-thrilling*!"*

     Day's work was nearly finished, men rolling provisions of wheat into storage, allowing excess-moisture to collect toward roll's center. There, it sits for two days time, wetter offerings used first in the making of bread. Lilith, arm hanging loosely around his, "Why bother Eve with the making of these things*?* Expect her, the wallflower she is, climbing from her *high nest* to genuinely entertain our people*?* Suddenly the bird has wings too small carrying frame*!"* Unnerved discussing kin, responded, "Recurring battle's known well. Ever thought how it would shape your destiny if told you were created as soulmate for another*?"* Surely this was something Lilith had not merely thumbed-through. "Thank you, Adam, as always, I find you turning questions away with simpleton's rhetoric. Well-versed on whole, grand spectacle. Do you not find vision contradictory to free will*?* How can we expect finding our own if roads travelled were laid prior to our origination*?"* Topic discussed was seasonal, each and every Fall during harvest, keeping Adam for many hours, wandering Lilith's orchards. "As both come to accept, we are not the ones in control of God's will. It is but our sworn purpose fulfilling His wishes, patiently inhabiting the Garden. In paying homage we learn patience, then all survive the cold of Winter." "Why must you lecture me like young, man-child*?* Remember it was you declaring me unworthy of the salt in your iris*!"* halting upon narrow path. "Chosen-few are given chance perceiving beyond Earth, seeing God's Hearth. A tested testament to all mankind when I say, you will find yours. It would be an abomination settling for a sister as bitter as her apples." Lilith carried potential being with any she wanted, but stubbornness outgrew small frame some time ago, maelstroms surrounding Adam and Eve's arrangement were no longer tolerated, Lilith outcaste herself some time ago, unwilling to dismiss feelings for Adam. "Wish we could have conversation Springtime; thought of being trapped with relatives all Winter makes eyes burn, stomach heave with indigestion!" traffic blocking city gate, people socializing in walkway, "Last time checked, kept cattle and sheep on west wall!" citizens shuffling from desired course, eyeing her with reservation. "Why does everyone looks at me like they're in some, ill-gotten trance?" Hopeful stifling her loud, argumentative tone, "Never wondered why so many tread so far away?" "How is it you think *I* feel? Am I to be the worm plucked from own orchard?" "If you were "The Work" dear Lilith, ground walked-upon would perish. Can't you see seasonal tirades unsuitable? Cannot change God's plan, only bear witness to new heights chosen path reveals. Was it not you choosing green over red? Who first began toiling hardship producing it from mere, crab apple? That Lilith, was your chosen choice." approaching Eve and Hamsphreth, "Returned with sister, can I see blasted scroll?" Lilith, "Do not see what the fuss was all about. Every year, rendition's done for the same repeat." Hamsphreth retorting, "Failed laying-eyes upon stage's craftsmanship, made with what Adam's named *Trap Door*." Adam, smiling widely, "Essential detail; marvelous feature is to raise Eve from beneath floorboards, spectacle unlike anything–what say you?" "Grand design. Intend completion before sunset tomorrow?" "Failed mentioning, constructed already! Everyone grows tired of me outworking them in the fields, so I took to own inspirations, constructing behemoth last week." Eve placed supporting arm around him, saying to Lilith, "Cannot imagine you playing role more than a silly garden snake, what with how you fuss amongst the tart and sour." Hamsphreth, "No arguments regarding our differences in apples." to Adam, "Chose your role, allow women doing same. Free Will is gift given to all by God Himself, Amen." Adam was unsure how entertainment would be achieved with women quarrelling until curtain-call. "Why do I get feeling you're going to tear story apart like savages?" Eve, "Unreasonable thing to say, know sister well." confidently to sibling, "We'll pair as our apples do." Lilith, correcting expression, "What role have you chosen?" Eve tossed hair to other side replying, "Can be none other than myself for this performance. And you?" "Taken a liking towards your suggestion of being garden snake. Since my purpose carries no higher meaning, prefer to remain a snake in the grass." Adam, "If these are the roles wishing played, God will have it. Hamsphreth, take role of Father in the Highest? A simple transition harkening from the mouth of God*!*" "No; become less nimble in my ripe, old age. Besides, what's use retiring if cannot enjoy those living after*?*" Lilith, "Suppose I could be tempted taking-up beckoned call, playing role of Lord and Shepard." Eve was in a fighting mood but chose erring on side of caution; meant little which parts Lilith played long as it was done with heart.

Hamsphreth, "May God have mercy should we be thrust from Garden due to an abominable performance."

Canifall Harvest Festival Presents: Genesis of Man, written by Choirmaster Fall.
(Scene One)
Stage was alit with hundreds of tea lights, Fall foliage scattered naturally about the area. Scent of harvest spice, baked bread wafted through the air, men and women merrily making-way toward seating situated around the open courtyard. Cider ale filled stomachs, adding to jubilation.
Enter God (Lilith)

God walked path between trees, arriving center-stage. "Let us make man in our own image, in likeness of ourselves. Let them be masters of the fish of the sea, the birds of heaven, the cattle, wild beasts and reptiles that crawl upon the earth. God created man in image of Himself, male and female, He created them."
Enter Adam

From forested everglade came Adam, responsibility cultivating, bringing value to living things by naming each creature. God unable finding him adequate helpmate. "It is not good that the man should be alone. I will make him a helpmate." From own body and flesh, Eve was created.
Enter Eve

Eve rose from floorboards, audience cheering in surprise. Adam awoke finding her laying beside, exclaiming with great joy and triumph, "This at last is bone from my bones, and flesh from my flesh*!* This is to be called woman, for this was taken from man." Eve, "This is why a man leaves his father and mother and joins himself to his wife, and they become one body."

God, "Now both were naked, the man and his wife, but they felt no shame in front of each other." To Adam and

Eve, "You may indeed eat of all the trees in the garden. Nevertheless of the tree of the knowledge of good and evil you are not to eat, for on the day you eat of it, you shall most surely die." pointing in direction of red apple tree, Eve's passion made example, mankind's fate wrangled, dangling-about in red apple orchard.

End Scene

(Scene Two, Garden of Eden)

Amongst many trees lay a great snake, eyes glinting. Sat between two heralded trees, hidden by limbs and branches. Hissing; looking to describe silvered slivers from tongue; fateful shivers flowing red from our many rivers. It came upon Eve in Garden with lasting impression to give the Warden.

Enter Eve

Enter Serpent (Lilith)

Enter Adam (somewhere close by.)

It slithered where Eve perched on root risen in air, coiling tightly around red apple tree, querying a query that started something dreary. "Did God really say you were not to eat from any of the trees in the Garden?" Eve turned head toward and replied, "We may eat of the fruit of the trees in the garden. But of the fruit of the tree in the middle of the garden God said, "You must not eat it, nor touch it, under pain of death." The snake neared ever-closer eye gleaming, thinking quickly and cleverly. "No! You will not die! God knows in fact that on the day you eat it your eyes will be opened and you will be like gods, knowing good and evil." Truth was granted to the woman, learning knowledge of good and evil before finishing living. Too subtle was the serpent, the snake in grass that day.

The woman saw the tree was good to eat and pleasing to the eye, desirable for the knowledge that it could give. So she took some of it's fruit and ate it. She gave some also to her husband who was with her, and he ate it. Then both their eyes were opened and they realized that they were naked. Curtain overhanging stage lowered in a billowing of thick drapes, slowly revealing scene filled with smoke, Adam and Eve hiding within forbidden tree as God reentered.

Enter God

"Where are you? I heard the sound of you in the garden." Adam said, "I was afraid because I was naked, so I hid." "Who told you that you were naked? Have you been eating of the tree I forbade you to eat?" Adam replied, "It was the woman you put me with; she gave me the fruit and I ate it." God rose angrily turning toward Eve. "What is this you

115

have done?" fearful face staring out from amongst leaves, a visage to be captured. Bonfire townspeople lit several hours before roared with life, crackling flames reflecting in her eyes, passion fatefully twisted by feuding; diluting, alluding to sins incurred within her lifetime.

"The serpent tempted me and I ate it." From story emerges longest debate in scripture. One cannot obtain wisdom until living life deemed worthy. "I will multiply your pains in childbearing. Yearning will be for your husband, yet he will lord it over you." Eve gasped in pain beside Adam, crying-out, "Hawwah!" tumbling to stage below as Adam looked-on in horror. God, turning attention on him, "Because you listened to the voice of your wife and ate from the tree of which I had forbidden you to eat, accursed be the soil because of you. With suffering shall you get your food from it. With sweat on your brow shall you eat your bread, until you return to the soil, as you were taken from it. For dust you are and to dust you shall return." Lilith's answer for the pain and torture, favoritism climactically rearing it's ugly head, "Because you have done this, accursed beyond all cattle, all wild beasts. You shall crawl on your belly and eat dust every day of your life. I will make you enemies of each other; you and the woman, your offspring and her offspring. It will crush your head and you will strike it's heel." trap-door descending with Lilith upon it. "See, the man has become like one of us, with his knowledge of good and evil. He must not be allowed to stretch hand out next and pick from the tree of life also, and eat some and live for ever. God hath expelled him from Garden! You will be sent back to till the soil from which you have been taken from! Banished! Forever banished you have become! I will place before the entrance of this garden, flame of flashing sword, guarding they way to the tree of life." Until heroes rise amongst, doing God's due for the rightful coursing of all.

End Scene

GHÎEST HEÎST

In world where most consider art a dying medium, one city remained central-hub for artistry: San Francisco. Tonight; reveal at a popular galleria, artists Siski & Broski showcasing work in an event that was sure-to-dazzle. Exhibition showcased all original paintings, up-for-auction to the many enthusiasts in-attendance. Paintings unlike anything in recent history, gaining attention and growing popularity. Streets lining venue were parked-full, bustling with activity, people dodging traffic on busy thoroughfare entering the exhibition hall. Grey, luxury sedan halted outside entrance, driver in a crisp suit exiting, opening door for passengers. Building served prestigious role for up-and-coming artists, a member of global arts and music events calendar, it remained closed to public six months out of the year, making-way for the most highly-priced exhibits world had to offer.

Broski & Siski were reclusive couple, spending majority of time at their in-home, art studio in San Diego. Julio guided amongst staff, museum benefactors, reaching gallery's center. Broski asked, "Is everything as requested?" "Room's large, three chandeliers hang across long tables, seating for hundreds, chairs decorated with black and white flowers as requested." Siski, "Please visit venue's entirety verifying art placement. We're keeping from harm, allowing honored guests come to us." Broski, "Evening closes, better-idea how fruitful efforts are." Julio, "Blessed with incredible vision, earning permanence amongst the other Greats!" Slapping his shoulder, Broski, "God-willing, have yet more stories to tell through the paint on our brushes!" Descended to polished, marble flooring, handful of guests socializing, wandering area. Siski, "How many others are inside room? Preparing myself for those scalpers!" "Scalpers?" Broski, *'tisking'* through a cinnamon toothpick, "Types of people we want to avoid. They attend functions like this—not for the artwork or atmosphere. Usually come early scrutinizing work, attempting to gleam style secrets, sometimes so-bold as to try buying particular piece far below actual-worth." Now that the subject was breached, he did notice several guests perusing uncomfortably-close to designated seats. "Promise keeping you both safe from insult!" Julio was best-described as a curious individual, hired six years ago when artists completed visit to middle-school in San Diego teaching expressionism in painted art. At the time, he was member of school's custodial team, assigned last-minute preventing lawsuits. While guiding along crowded hallways, up flights of stairs, they chatted charismatically, honestly. Julio was more than driver, he was their inseparable counselor and aide. "Wanting to be left by yourselves?" Siski, "Priorities dictate art be in chronological order, preventing disconnect from potential buyers." "Four sets of ten in chronological order at a height-variance of three inches. Leaving specifics to me was smart, you're in good hands. Like any prepared Latino man, I brought…" revealing square object, "a tape-measure." Julio leaving, scrutinizing exhibit details.

"Hear that baby?" Siski, "Referring to delicate, clinking of crystal, those God-awful heels walking entrance?" "Though originally thinking a drink for each, was ultimately-focused on heels." "Don't care how much she brought, she's not leaving here with our work!" Veronica Socks was woman average person would consider an attention-seeking annoyance, worming into places she didn't belong. Asset-procurer for Aries Industries, she possessed unique position supporting her rampaging personality. With constant emails, voicemails left on a weekly-basis, artists reached their limit some time ago. Broski, "Let's do what my Old Man used to say, read the room, act accordingly."

Chair dragged across floor, woman in heels sitting. "What a glorious occasion bringing all of us together!" "Veronica." thankful her glasses concealed her distaste. "Broski & Siski finally left safety of shelter, playing out in the open. I just wanted to let you know Aries loaned purse of two million acquiring one of your pieces!" Wife's nails biting into his, "Long as it's right fit, see no problem." Veronica gave laugh she assumed was charming. *Destiny's Sanctuary* will go beautifully in Skyson's executive meeting room, where it will be topic of much-discussion." Siski interjected, "Refuse selling our most-popular piece to corporation where tacky men glance at it before lunch!" Broski, "Deserves buyer who'll display it for the many." "Guess no one read you the finer-details displaying art here, it's sold to anyone paying!" smoothing ugly, green dress, "Everything you've created now has a buying-price–may the highest-bidder win." Siski, after she'd departed, "Remind again how much we brought?" "Every penny. Even so, won't stand much-chance if she's determined outbidding any potential buyer. Let's sample champagne and upon Julio's return, find our exit-route."

Four vans with the words, *"little tot's learning academy"* along sides halted blocks from venue, a tall, built man speaking into short-range walkie-talkie. "Reimbursing school we borrowed these vans from." "Roger that, want us to make a donation to the Girl Scouts of America while we're at it?" "Only if you turn-in those ugly, green vests first." Regardless of satellite imagery, directions received, no amount of preparation replaces being in the heat-of-action. Lazarus, or simply called Laz, was force to be reckoned with; over six feet tall, body-type similar to that of a professional weightlifter. Elusive, quick, what to do in the thick, he's the man for any mission. Blueprints lifted from the city database described area used as museum's loading-dock. Parking at the designated rendezvous, everyone grouped around Lazarus for final debrief, mission as insane as it was simple, steal forty-three paintings, kidnap artists. "Lights go out, there'll no one left giving-shout. Let's bag an art show!" hands together cheering, "All of us, or none of us!"

Artists filled Julio in while browsing dinner options. Broski, "Short of knocking her unconscious, inevitability going toe-to-toe." "Comforted knowing it's your most-popular piece. Recommend chicken marsala, rave reviews from several magazines covering culinary-excellence." Siski, "Keep in mind, defending more than artwork." Husband agreeing, "Absolutely. Devil often disguises in unexpected ways; not always manifestation of problem indicating trial and tribulation, but serves as encumbering distraction, preventing desired course." Julio, gesturing around them, "You've both worked awfully-hard towards inspiration for unfinished pieces, intend completing them?" gazing at them expectantly, artists smiling, "Good. Recent news-broadcasts made it harder sleeping." Broski, trying not to choke on champagne, "Referring to dude who said he likes fucking pizza, or was it he *is* a pizza? Nevertheless I agree, should count our blessings during these hard times. When opening auction, remember to inspire guests with purpose." Placing hand on shoulder, "Viewpoints align as one."

"Target acquired and handled." smoothing wrinkles on his ill-fitting uniform. Aromas of finely-crafted food wafting, stomach gurgling, "Told him we need more per-diem." ignoring urge waltzing into kitchen, helping himself to a meal. If necessity didn't require discretion, via nonlethal force, would've been out of there with to-go plates minutes ago. Original plan had only allowed for nine bodies, but after arguing with Lashbrook, leveraged additional three for a wheelman, extra manpower moving art. "When it rains it pours." teammates checking-in. Laz smiled foxily at those in-attendance, they had no idea what kind of entertainment they were in for.

Dinner plates disappeared, making-way for pieces of decadent cheesecake. "So nervous, can't taste our desert!" Broski, through mouthful of cheesecake, "Mm, focus not on auction." "You're right, I'll direct energy toward description of *Destiny's Sanctuary*. First, Julio's introduction, then, your point of connection with audience." "Speech is like beautiful tapestry; see the result, oftentimes blind to hardship endured. They'll know the pain wasn't God saying stay away, was Him granting true vision." "Tell it not from weight of life lived, but from the weightlessness of life loved." kissing, making seconds count instead of counting seconds. Julio, "Set running interference against Veronica." Broski patted shoulder saying, "Long as auction's interesting, couldn't ask for much else."

Julio ascended steps constructed from two-by-fours, cheap plywood. "Art enthusiasts, esteemed guests: It's a pleasure opening the floor tonight, not just for my employer, but every, beating heart. In spirit of getting things started, speaking toward why we're assembled." "Is *this* the new bar that opened last *week?*" Julio responding, "Give your address out *after auction!*" Laughter dying-down, "Maybe you agree when I say we've fallen on hard times; what inspired no longer captivates, cherished tradition unenthused necessity. Found myself losing-heart in things previously providing comfort, just as the harmless and mundane felt threatening. As a first-generation Latino I've endured racism, stereotyping, job-discrimination. I pressed onwards through self-righteous hatred, knowing if something didn't change I'd commit crime. However, there's certainty helping fight uncertainty. It doesn't take-shape in form of a house, expensive drink, or computer taking away my need to think. If it wasn't for Siski & Broski, faith in Jesus Christ, wouldn't be standing here today." sweeping open palm artists' direction, "It's with utmost respect I extend my hand to Broski & Siski, not just for your art, but the heart you've shown me from the start. Please, welcome Broski to the stage!"

Walking-stick in-hand, Broski determinedly rose and began walking briskly toward stage, audience looking-on, anticipating him falling. "Why's everyone so quiet?" reaching steps, tossing walking-stick high into air, catching it with a flourish arriving in front of Julio. "How many people are mind-blown?" "Incredible, let's have it for him everybody!" audience cheering his stunning performance. Broski strolled-up to podium microphone in hand, saying with much-suave, "And I haven't gotten on the mic yet!" someone shouting, "Who invited Kevin Hart!?" "Exactly the feeling I was going for, we're about to go through an amusement park of emotion." people quieting, intrigued by what he meant. "Getting older, I've found that memories remain and should be shared with others. First reason, I'm blind, like to hear myself talk!" good-natured laughter rippling room, "Hey, if you can't laugh at yourself the Devil's already won, what my Pops used to say. Second reason, it's my birthday; story happens to be about the day father and I shared on my tenth birthday."

"Grew-up in a small, California town hundred miles to the south and west of here. Mom wasn't a present role-model in my life, never found out if it was drugs, or if Pops plain blew-it with her, but simple fact at the time, she just wasn't. When most speak of birth, we're inundated by stories ripped from photobooks, smiles absent the pain of many miles. Growing-up, there never was much money to spare, truth-be-told we lived week-to-week. That, and it didn't help being born into Country willingly suffering systemic racism." audience listening raptly, all seats occupied except Veronica's. "I learned the sting of ableism at an exceedingly young age, others wondering how to interact. One day in particular, a fellow classmate approached the teacher to ask a question, asking it quietly, so as to keep conversation between himself and facilitator." "What's wrong with the boy behind me?" There was brief pause before her reply, can only assume she was looking at me. "Don't worry about him, he's blind as he is stupid!" Alas, birthdays were never a celebration, more a renewal of pain passed. Never considering myself worthy of anything up to this point, it was Pops who would reveal the beauty of hidden purpose."

"Woke me early bringing my favorite breakfast: Breakfast in bed. I could tell from the excitement in his voice he had the whole day planned. Pops worked for the California Coal Coalition, about the only job a black man could get in our town. Remember him putting-in long hours in the months leading to my birthday—I mean a lot. I'd rise and Pops was already gone, come home from school and half-hazardly make ramen noodles, wake next morning and sure-enough he was gone again. Nobody wants to deal with the aftermath of a blind child making meals few days in a row. After working eighty-hour weeks, saved enough money to do something very special for me. There was a fair that came into town every year, excitement swelled in my throat while practically begging Pops to take me, for as long as remembered, said we couldn't afford such pleasantries. Pops returned and picked my outfit, setting it on the bed. "Finish those eggs before they get cold, clothes are on foot of the bed, us men got business up-and-about town." I felt each article of clothing, ensuring I'd perceived outfit correctly. Turns out it was my favorite; plaid shorts, a pink, collared short-sleeve." Lighting in the great hall dimmed by twenty-five percent, transferring them to heart of the scene—one the man had never seen. "Fought writing-off birthday like every other. Smoothing the wrinkles on shorts and collar, I established a promise. "This will be the birthday I keep inside all the pain, letting it run down me like water from rain." picturing water droplets rolling off duck's back. Pops comes back, sees me with this wisecracking smile. I ask, "Where do us men take care of business?" "Downstairs into the wagon, I'll be along shortly." Descended to the entryway of our dilapidated home, stopping for walking-stick, climbed my happy-ass into vehicle. Pops loaded trunk, entering driver-side to explain, "Son, men travel up front, get on up here so we can cruise like we were intended."

Broski paused storytelling asking, "Remember how it felt first time riding shotgun?" funneled a courteous supply of alcohol, audience exuberantly cheered their response. "Ditching walking-stick, I clambered into front seat, getting all buckled-in." whistling, mimicking fastening seatbelt. "Before engine turned-over I rolled down window, you know, those old-school, hand-crank ones. We've had robots running the planet for how many years and they still put those, in that model? Hmm. Wagon in reverse, we backed onto our street, turning onto main thoroughfare leading into town. Had an idea as to our destination but like I learned from Pops, gotta be respectful when receiving what's given.

Air grew saltier along coastline where the county fair took-place. Unable containing myself any longer, "What all the other kids talk about during semester's start, thank you!" "Only place I haven't taken you that's still worth going to. Let's get inside and see what all they brought into town." First thing we did was walk around, getting the general vibe. Pops asked, "How's it feel?" Considering my complexities making life less-hospitable, had to find sufficient answer. Formed sentence in the way most children do—testing waters. "Well, it's my first time here." "You'll have to do better than that, us men have way more options describing a scene. What senses other than sight do we use perceiving?" Thinking with my stomach, "Everything here smells sweet!" One of the things I loved about him was his ability teaching, having fun along the way. "This word, though it describes taste, is also a good way describing what we're smelling. Remember it, so you can be real nice-and-easy with the ladies–*umami!*" Ten years old and umami was word of the day! Pondering this, I attempted another way describing how I was feeling. Tried overhearing some typical, fair conversations, but they were undiscernible over the general, uproarious nature of the place. "How many rides do they have?" Turns out, it was the right follow-up, spending remainder of the morning and afternoon sampling rides. Merry-go-rounds, side-street attractions where gentleman in a funny getup shouts catchy phrases. *"Whack-A-Mole, just one goal!"* There were bumper-cars…not going to lie, those were my least-favorite." not needing to go into finer-details of being rammed from any direction without notice. Getting-off one of the rides, "What's that *popping* noise?" already knowing what it was, having heard it at school–cotton candy machine. Reason I was so particularly focused on this moment, schoolhouse ritual became a point of contention between myself and facilitator. At school year's end they'd host Field Day, going no-holds barred on remaining budget acquiring ribbons, treats, year-ending goodbyes. Each year, I sat in a hard, plastic chair listening to children playing. Most consider it reasonable a disabled child sit-out during these events, however, situation was one of bigotry. I asked, "Ma'am, may I have some cotton candy?" Teacher, glaring, "Why don't you ask the *Make A Wish Foundation?*" cries of outrage filling room, "Other years I say in an empty classroom without air-conditioning."

"That's the sound of cotton candy being made. Since dad struck coal, let's enjoy some while catching the Ferris Wheel." walking to stand nearest, man there whipping-up a bag of the good stuff before getting in line. Apprehension mounted waiting our turn, Pops placed reassuring hand as people exited after ride's conclusion, guiding me to waiting bench seat. Ferris Wheel climbed upward, filling to capacity. Arriving at topmost portion, I blissfully reached toward setting sun smiling happily with my father. Then, I was ripped from ride's simple pleasantries to be reminded of life's remainder. Seat perched like umbrella in the sky, boy underneath jeered, "Look! A blind, black boy's trying to see the sun!" breaking into riotous laughter similar to a stuck pig, everyone getting a look at the monster I was made from birth. Clenched railing trying to ignore the dozens below, glasses slipping, breaking on hard concrete. I asked myself, "How do I, a child ravaged by hate, find the will creating life from my own plate? How can I defeat this malice when I'm unable telling you the face of my enemy?" Finally, Pops intervened.

"You know, it doesn't get much easier. People like us work hard our entire lives–*not* for ourselves. The loneliness you're feeling isn't solely your own; think of all the mothers and fathers bringing us into life, unto this world without a clue. Don't expect you to grasp what I'm telling you, but do ponder this; if you cry, families leading up to God cry too." "If God knows pain such as mine, why didn't he take something else? I'd go without walking if I could understand what it means to see–it isn't fair*!!*" "Son, fair is where we're at. My opinion: No one can say what is and isn't fair. People in charge are supposed to have it all figured out, our plan to survive. They spend entire careers campaigning, championing for change, reformation, yet never deliver on their promises. The boy underneath us is *beneath* us. I don't blame him for his ignorance and neither should you; like leaders, blinded though gifted to see." A calmness came over me as I considered it was ignorant humanity who was blind and not me. Regained composure, shaking dread of being alone and misunderstood, enjoying the kind of resolved silence father and son can share. If I were to describe feeling, similar to walking along an undetermined precipice, watching everything burn while venturing through it."

"Pops guided to bench overlooking the bay to avoid further confrontation. Between bites of cotton candy, "Hell of a year; secured position another six months, watching you grow in my free time*!*" "Free time about covers it. Maybe they'll give you another day off–that or a raise." "Coal's a fading industry, be lucky staying another two years before moving east where remaining profit is. Now, my ten-year-old, ready trying something new?" "I don't know…fourth of July I lit myself on fire playing with that sparkler." Letting-out one of his boisterous, rolling laughs, "Sorry son, know you were scared, but that's only time I've seen you strip, running to hose absent guidance*!*" From a large bag, he retrieved a long, wrapped tube. I picked at the tape holding the slick, delicate wrapping, unable determining what it was. "Describe it to me." gently taken from my hand, hearing popping noise, "This, is called an easel." "For painting and drawing?" "Absolutely*!*" rubbing my back encouragingly, "Spent many hours brainstorming what to get this year, something with meaning, thought-back-on the rest of your life!" Finding myself feeling not the least bit happy, said, "How am I supposed to do this? I'll be laughingstock of everyone!" "Doubt yourself too often and far-too soon." removing easel from it's holder, producing three, artist sketchpads, "Paper, may be blank now; what happens on each page, mentored purpose. Artists find a process removing themselves from pain and tragedy, receding deep within the confines of their imagination. Born blind, you've advantage they won't see coming!" Frowning, I asked, "You mean you've planned buying all this for awhile?!" Expression must've been borderline-tragic because he promptly reassured me with his final present. "An artist remains a blank tapestry until finding tools created in his/her likeness, allowing for controlled, curtailment of craft. Take your time opening these, so you can get a feel for what you'll be doing." I'm going to be one hundred percent honest: I HATED my birthday presents! Turning colored pencils over I wanted to scream! I began thinking I would never accomplish what he wanted, that I'd find no joy in this activity. Increasing volume of my voice to likes of which I never had before, ***"WHY WOULD YOU DO THIS?! ALL ANYONE DOES IS LAUGH AT ME! HOW YOU EXPECT ME TO DRAW A STRAIGHT LINE?! I CAN'T SEE COLOR!!"*** Though in the midst of a ten-year-old temper tantrum, I couldn't shake unyielding desire of pleasing my father. Tears weren't from one, unhappy birthday, but years of torture and abuse, all the while letting him down. Sunlight disappeared then reappeared, Pops retrieving gift dropped during outburst. "I apologize for springing such a complex concept, not my intention for you to experience defeat before you've begun. How does one see? By *feeling!* I'm no fool, how you perceive things is drastically different, there's no question you're meant to be an artist." Broski paused explaining, "Brain's malleability allows repurposing certain portions, heightening functionality of other senses. Think of it as God balancing deficit."

"Having embarked upon journey of artful rhetoric, child-version of me pouting like a sore-loser, maintained my status-quo: These gifts aren't acceptable. "We've walked road before, let's do it again surrounding the subject of art." I understand why he told it way he did, though how he started angered. He said, "Son, you're blind; learn differently in every sense. Redirect sensitivity away from what others think. If you react this poorly to life's inevitabilities, thankful it's now rather than later. Unable seeing, I'll give you that, but it doesn't leave you incapacitated from conceptualizing. No color, no problem; exercised great care sourcing useful guiding-tools. Since gift challenges in many aspects, thought it fair giving you what's called a waypoint." Pencil erasers were all the rage, with varying shapes and sizes, placed on the end of individually-chosen pencils. "Kids take these things for granted, can't tell you how many classmates were caught eating ones smelling like cinnamon rolls." audience laughing, eraser eating commonplace amongst school-age children. I turned eraser over noticing it was in the shape of a star. "What's color? What we see, something more? From what I can tell, what's observed is least-important part about it." reaching into pencil box, passing one off, "Purple pencil you have reflects purple, absorbing the rest. Suddenly, purple's been holding-out. What do us men gotta do to stop purple from being so greedy?" Catching-on to what Pops was saying in my own way, "Convince purple to share?" "Exactly! Don't forget, we're artists; plug into things, teasing heart's eye. Don't need eyesight knowing it's the right color, your blindness allows colors to describe openly. Given thoughtful identity, a color will then share it's secrets. Place eraser onto pencil." Enjoying what he was teaching I did as asked–the eraser was just what it needed! Pops, "Say hello to Purple! This is how you'll differentiate and connect with each color." Pops then created a palate for me to practice. "Use your feelings, it's important being yourself around your instruments so they're privileged doing same."

 Picking my first color, I attempted visualizing what eyes did not provide, channeling my energy believing purple would whisper to me, a secret. Fifteen minutes later, stepped away declaring, "Did my best, even came-up with a name." "What would that be?" marveling at my drawing of the sun resting atop bay, "A fair day." Broski reached into coat pocket revealing a small, orange colored-pencil sporting worn eraser shaped like a ball. "What's left from the original set. It truly was a fair day at the Fair, also the last birthday shared with my father." sudden mood-change, audience falling silent, "In the back of my mind I knew those long hours were going to catch-up with him, diagnosed with a lung-related illness laboring after coal. I was forced living remainder of my childhood holding onto memories, what matters with every stroke."

 Thunderous applause concluded Broski's story, making-way for next segment. "Before you go, tell a man how he did?" Siski, "Like always, stand awash from your resounding, emotional conveyance! Julio, please guide me where I'll be comfortable." Everyone fell silent as security rolled and lifted their prized masterpiece on-stage, *Destiny's Sanctuary*. Colors fused together, layer-upon-layer conveying the mysticism this spiritual vision radiated. An eternal land cast into dusk of evening, forested landscape leading to foothills gracing mighty mountains. Earth-tones swirled together, focusing painting's center; a majestic lake, lighter shades of blue suggesting primal energy beneath. In sky, a floating island, waterfall roaring from Heaven-itself, rainbows traveling-down length. A cozy cottage was nestled along southern embankment, double-doors painted slightly ajar. Animals of every kind greeted throughout the landscape, carrying a Zen-like effect to anyone gazing upon it. "Painting tells timeless story of a safe-haven, an intersection-point between reality and the eternal given after, where virtuous, love-driven spirits come to rest, waiting for family to join them in Heaven. My husband and I believe *Destiny's Sanctuary* ringing truth; an oasis belonging to personified life-essence, the seed of creation, Zion. Opening tonight's auction with the selling of our most-prized offering! If you don't intend sharing our art with others, we'd prefer if you'd rise from your seat and leave–we don't do business with fake individuals." Returning to seat. Broski smiled, "Appreciate the little shot you gave Veronica!" Siski, "Geist won't get away with her heist!"

Price soared to half a million, audience craning necks watching each, declared bid. Veronica was at the front of it all, infringing upon security. Julio remained seated, allowing the majority of bidders to be bought-out. Broski, "Looks like our favorite piece is moving faster than expected, if we don't make waves soon we'll have done-little deterring Veronica. Go ahead Julio, smallest increments." With the raise of a flag Julio joined auction, ringing-out, "Six-hundred thousand." Siski, listening Veronica's direction, "Working around me– you're finished! Six-seventy-five!" Broski, "Goaded after first nibble. Keep her pace." Exchange continued for several minutes, price soaring to one-and-a-quarter million *(bid by Julio)*. Veronica, raising an angry fist, "Two million!!" Leaning heads together, Broski, "Done all we can. When the lights come on, look for the bag."

Lights de-energized, sending everything into darkness, man's voice coming through sound system. "Sorry for being late...kind-of got lost on the way here, streets are so confusing! Might be hypocritical saying we come in peace, some of you aren't the types we'd bring home to our mommies and daddies*!*" Veronica cried, "What's happening*?!*" *Paging Aries crony:* Smelled the preservatives soon as you climbed from that tin can you call a car*!* A little bird told me you'd be here, for he too, smelled malodor*!*" pausing, looking-about the room, "Since no one's informed you, allow me to enlighten*!*" ***"DON'T YOU DARE, COLLECTIVE CONSCIOUS FILTH!!"*** "Oh *Dan,* if you'd be so kind as to relieve that ugly creature from her misery..." metallic thud, Veronica cracked in the head with a flashlight. "Relax*!*" the voice cheerily exclaimed. To everyone present, it sounded like he began munching on shelled peanuts. "We're actually pretty-sweet folk. Fancy, rich zombies have infiltrated our government, corporate industry, sports and entertainment, and our failing, black-market economy. Hell has arrived in the form of an international money-making venture brought forth by the men and women at Aries. I'm assuming most of you have what's called a brain, useful item really, it's located in the skull. Unless fuckshits already turned them into melted ice cream, it should be painfully-obvious. Each years, thousands of men, women, children are murdered by robotic creations." An agent near the entrance, "Cheer-up boss, still haven't got us*!*" "Without further ado, *smile!*" bright flash, musculature outlined while taking panoramic photo, "Thanks for your time. Above all, God bless." exiting, promptly picked-up by waiting minivan. Lights flickered on revealing biggest heist in recent history; forty-three paintings, artists vanishing into thin-air. Julio retrieving duffel, leaving for sedan. Grinning at himself in the rearview, "No matter how you explain process, there are still those who won't listen."

    "Jump out the seat dummy, how else do you expect me to control a vehicle going seventy*?* Shift laterally*!*" With some fast footwork, Laz was in-control behind the wheel. Plan-execution was flawless; height-dimensions allowing paintings to stack one on top of the other, agents moving forty-three paintings, snagging husband and wife on their way out the door. Artwork was hurriedly tied to roof racks, distributed amongst four, aging minivans struggling to reach the maximum miles-per-hour described in user-manuals. Wiggles, now riding shotgun, "Boss, why'd you take their microphone*?*" Looking at his right hand in surprise, tossing it into back, "Don't know to be honest, maybe it felt right, maybe I wanted a memento—the charade continues*!*" stepping hard onto accelerator, Broski yelling, "Careful Laz, paintings weren't tied very securely*!*" Staring into rearview, "In case you weren't aware, we're being tailed by blacked-out sport-sedans. Get on the radio and inform Dan we're changing our rendezvous to the *iBop Pancake House* after the Golden Gate Bridge*!*" Wiggles radioed the others, which was good given situation, as they were promptly rammed by pursuers. Siski, "Through acquisition or destruction…" Laz glanced rearview commanding, "Get down, I taste fire*!*" slaloming, sending couple reeling to floor, "We'll try outmaneuvering. If that doesn't work, I'll proceed ramming until we crush the ever-living life out of them*!*" Wiggles turned around and said, "What he's saying is, everything's going to be just fine*!*" automatic gunfire cutting their conversation short. "Situation's as originally feared people, how about things to throw*?*" Wiggles, "What about the paintings*?*" If Laz hadn't been dodging traffic and bullets at the same time he would've hit him on the shoulder. "Smooth Wigs, throw the one painting they want, right at `em. We need to intersect onto the 101 and get our asses lost in traffic*!* Couple miles maybe…" bullets shattering both windshields, streaking into traffic. Laz's radio beeped indicating a nearby radio-transmission, swiftly turning dial, discovering channel law-enforcement was using. Wiggles yelled at artists hunkered-down in backseat, *"HOORAY,* police officers are on their way to save us*!*" Laz rolled his eyes craving a cigarette. "How many Countries are you wanted in*?* If anything it makes things monumentally worse, having kidnapped two, famous artists*!*" Broski, "Oh man, this feels just like the movies*!* Hey baby, feel around for a tire-iron*!*" "Don't get any crazy ideas Broski. I know you're feeling rather artsy but please continue spooning your wife*!*" bullets shredding rear tires, enemies overtaking them nearing the 101. "Hey guys, your driver always comes through."

Hearing automatic gunfire, Julio floored the eight-cylinder engine, braking four-hundred feet from pursuers, ramming them into oncoming traffic. Wiggles laughed as Aries agents broadsided commuter, smashing into a windowed storefront. Emergency sirens blared as police and ambulance scrambled assisting gunshot victims, vehicle accidents. Van fishtailed limping onto their desired straightaway, Julio acting as moving roadblock. Wiggles cried, "Units converging from multiple directions*!*" Lazarus stood on accelerator, nearly jamming it in place. Attackers were persistent, identifying trailing van as their target, they aggressively dogged Julio, wildly aiming out windows to get a shot. Siski, "They're going to kill Julio*!*" Laz's mouth becoming a thin, straight line contemplating next move. "Time to get our hands dirty*!*" finding a piece of shot-off rearview, gaining Julio's attention.

Laz jerked right, then listing left waiting for an opening, asking, "How do you make a sinner kneel? The good, old-fashioned banana peel!" cutting sharply while slamming brakes, Julio overtaking them, braking to prevent flanking gunfire. Pursuers were not so quick to react; overcorrecting, toppling down oncoming lanes like a die-cast model abused by a toddler, another clipping Julio's rear. Engines roared to life once more, continuing their mad-dash towards freedom with only one pursuer remaining. "Another half-mile we'll be on rims!"

"We still have two tires left." argued Wiggles, "Floor this bitch to the Promised Land!"

"Wiggs, do-up your seatbelt and play the license-plate game." Racing through the intersection, everyone held-on with bated breath bottoming-out on a dip, leaving tire remnants behind as parting gift. "God-willing, this'll be the story we tell our kids before getting Driver's Licenses!" Emergency personnel sorting-out mess several blocks behind, only obstacle remaining was their final tail. Laz and Wiggles looked right crossing intersection, squad car missing them by three car-lengths, smashing into their pursuer. Vehicles interlocked in a twisted mass of moving metal, careening towards roadside, crashing into manmade embankment. Laz's deathlike grip loosening, "Those guys certainly were a nuisance! Everyone alright?" Broski, rising from cover, "Damn it's cold, can you roll the windows up?" uproarious laughter, escape party honking and cheering. "Wiggles, inform Dan we've earned our dine-in meal." Vehicles pulled into local pancake-joint celebrating their successful getaway. "One for the yearbooks everybody!" snapping a quick photo, saying to Julio, "Slick driving, glad to have you with us. Car's fucked but oh well, that's the price paid for using your head, saving all of us." turning to one of their most-seasoned members, "Dan, either you're taking this guy or he's coming with me to the field." Dan stepped forward getting a good look at Julio. Straightening his old, dirty snapback, "Dope. You're driving back to Colorado." Smiling nervously, "Sure Dan, dope!" As they stared across bay at the twinkling, red and blue lights, Broski, "Aren't social-outings marvelous?"

Veronica rushed to company vehicle, speeding to where agent was apprehended by authorities, a low, red glow reflecting off her headrest as A.I. device updated her on notifications and messages. "Should've known those blind monkeys were working with them*! What am I to do!?"* turning question to her microprocessor, finding result in the form of a strange, log-file. *"You should kill yourself."* Nearly swerving into a parked car, "What the fuck*?!* Close window*!"* action performed after a spike in latency. Reaching Golden Gate, she parked near tow-truck, busy ratcheting two, conjoined heaps onto it's flatbed. Climbing from her car, "Physical-evidence present, no painting, no life. " Disoriented, she wandered to waterline clutching head, ripping at her hair. ***"NO SACRIFICES! I FEEL THE POINT TURNING IN!"*** log-file exploding onto interface, copying, pasting, repeating, *"You should kill yourself."* Observing her peculiar behavior, tow driver ran from his truck yelling, "Ma'am, you alright*?"* Veronica turned slowly, gun in outstretched hand. ***"NO! I DIDN'T DO IT!"*** Veronica looked at him with blood in her eyes. Then, like she was already dead, said, "You should kill yourself. " A bang rang-out across bay, biometric diode on an Aries interface dimmed, darkening entirely.

CARMEN KARMA

Kyle sat in Bethany's office waiting for what he assumed was his termination paperwork. After becoming lead-anchor, the mountain of insults and underhanded behavior Hartigan displayed bordered on narcissistic. Bethany, privy to this mistreatment, exerted little-effort curbing, reprimanding. Biggest challenge he faced surviving this mishap without getting fired was the capitol in endorsements his co-host possessed through his lucrative partnership with Aries Industries. Monetary support received was astronomical, totaling hundreds of millions in exchange for countless hours of on-air endorsement.

"Can't change the past, remain steadfast, hope I can last." Bethany walked passed the long window overlooking newsroom, face flushed with anger, disposition somber—this was not going to be good. Door swung open slowly as she entered room, moving thin frame in front of door, letting her bodyweight close it. Kyle met her gaze, remaining silent, resisting blurting ill-formed apologies and excuses for his actions. Sighing heavily, she rebounded away from door and walked to office chair, sitting down to face him. Remaining silent, she opened drawer pulling-out several documents. He couldn't make out what each one was, but could clearly read 'Incident Report' at top of foremost sheet. Sighing, eyes traveled upward, "Any idea the predicament I'm in?" remaining quiet, knowing trying to rationalize events would anger, further solidifying his fate. "Network executives are calling for blood. Phone's not stopped ringing for last half-hour, and I can only imagine what this is going to do to our consumer ratings. I'm forced making a decision, however, choice has already been made for me by powers beyond my control—I need a cigarette!" smoothing hair impulsively, crossing legs tightly, "I've already berated Mr. Hartigan on his inexcusable behavior. He's useless, undeniably the worst reporter on live-television, but there's one thing making him asset; wealthy benefactors, contributions far-exceeding his worth as television personality. Steven informed me that if I fire him for this incident, all funding walks with him. I'm sorry Kyle, as much as I value and respect your work, bad-business letting him go, Aries totals to over seventy percent of monetary and technology donations received annually! Not to mention, my position as Director would no longer be an option, I'd have to resign due to the attention whole situation's brought!" Kyle, deciding it was his turn to speak, "You're telling me it's appropriate for our most-senior news anchor to say, "Stop mourning-over your wife, stop making love to her corpse!" over broadcast? Any idea the kind of status-quo you're promoting?" Tapping her heel, responded, "Nothing like this has happened before Kyle, in the entire, history of news broadcasting! Do you think me so-thick as to let him off scot-free? He's been placed on probation, working a month without pay for the part he played." Losing his temper, "I'm being fired for a physical altercation brought-on by years of mean-spirited, verbal assaults?" Bethany grabbed her pen and started filling-out the incident report. "Yes. As of today, your position with Channel 9, any involvement you've had with The Show is terminated. I'll give you the courtesy of paying you for remainder of the week, so you can get affairs in order. Finishing the necessary paperwork, then Rosie will give you time to collect your belongings." He'd stopped listening some time ago, though he appeared to be listening sullenly, already decided what his first destination would be; visiting his Mom in Kansas, asking questions he couldn't answer alone. After, searching for laptop-stealing punk. Reality came into focus while signing termination papers. "Like I said, you can file for wrongful termination and try collecting unemployment, but based-on charade you and Steven played, don't think anyone would buy it!" All he could do was look at her, somewhat shocked by the sudden harshness in her voice. "You know what, since I'm being fired, am I free speaking my mind?" Eying him cautiously, "Suppose you can confide in me this one, last time, your constitutional right after all. You're still fired no matter what you say, so, don't try convincing me!"

"I've always defined myself as individual who seeks truth. In the last five years, I've helped turn this second-rate, news network into one of the hottest in the Country. Steven mutilated his brain for some corporation, then gets-off telling viewers I fornicate dead bodies. Here's the real-kicker, next, I'm hauled into office and fired—situation reeks of conspiracy! Plenty of dirty business deals crossed my desk every week, that I choose not reporting out of respect for Channel 9!" Bethany listened with little-interest, practically just waiting for him to finish. "What I'm most-upset about is how you callously and almost instinctively sided with Steven when he's hurt our credibility since day one. Getting to the bottom of it; what Aries Industries is really doing behind closed doors!"

Placing hand on his, "May be you're right–always been a great reporter. I urge extreme caution; normal, healthy people like me and you end-up missing, wind-up dead." Removing his hand from under hers, rose saying, "Thanks for the advice. Since I'm no longer employed here and can't be trusted, might as well call Rosie." As if on cue, Rosie rolled by Bethany's window, optic-eyes entering before anything else. "Per Mr. Hartigan's instruction, I'm to escort Mr. Kyle Clark to his office so he can collect belongings." Glaring angrily at Bethany, "Now he's ordering me around through aftermarket accessory just to get the last, proverbial ball-kick! You remember this moment, since you've invested so much of your self-worth in it. Hope you bought Aries user-manual for all the soulless robots you have working here!"

"Alright Rosie the Riveter,

escort me to my office–we can

do it!"

Finished with exiting theatrics, Kyle and Rosie exited Bethany's office, Kyle giving a silent, parting goodbye to the studio. Rosie, "My condolences regarding your sudden termination, found myself wishing I'd learned apologetic one-liners to better-ease your emotional instability." He gave her a backwards glance and continued walking, not wanting to provoke the robot receiving orders from Hartigan. Nearing office, "You've ten minutes gathering belongings, after, I'll insist on completing your termination process." Staring blankly, opening office door, "Thank you Rosie, for being absolutely creepy. I'll be ready continuing when you enter."

He opened desk drawer, discovering that the miscreant made-off with the mug shard he'd planned keeping. Finding pink sticky-note, rereading message, "Maybe Mom holds answer to understanding my vivid nightmares, then, I'll be tracking-down this girl who absconded my laptop." Rosie muttering, "Mother's boy, obsessive, possibly a pedophile." Kyle packed belongings inside cardboard box found wedged behind file-cabinet. Closing flaps, sighing, he looked out at the twinkling metropolis around him. Late Fall; smog trapped in lower-atmosphere pushed against the foothills, forecast threatening snow as large, billowing clouds developed over the high-country, bringing with it, a drop in temperature, potential for traffic-delays. "Suppose it wouldn't hurt to pack and catch first plane out…staying is bound to make me do something I'll later regret." Her software detecting a change in the room, Rosie opened door with an optic-eye, peeking at Kyle through the opening. A human with sensitive hearing can detect the high-pitched hum Aries robots deploy focusing on an object, similar to the noise a cathode television makes on an empty station.

"Yes, I can sense your prying, snail eyes." What she said next was as simple as it was eerie, *"I know!"* blinking eyes one at a time entering doorway. Having enough of the creepy quiet, "Let's blow this popsicle stand." Allowing him to pass, *"Good one Mr. Clark! All newer models have improved, personality identifiers, processing mannerisms through advanced microprocessors."* Kyle felt uneasy walking in front of this living machine, capable decimating entire neighborhoods with ease. "The last thirty-seconds, I've come-up with three hundred different jokes. Would you like to hear one? It might help mental-health if you laughed more." "Not really, but if you insist." "How many anchors does it take running Channel 9?" "See where this is going—how many?" Closing distance between, extending eyes over Kyle's head, "Since having sex with the dead isn't part of the requirements, only one." "Let me guess, Steve's watching." voice coming through communication-array, "Four out of five stars for entertainment value, truly are a blubbering man-baby Kyle!" "Can't believe how low you were willing to go to bring out the Devil in me, there'll be a reckoning for it someday!" jamming finger into elevator call-button. "Empty threats, coming from a jobless lunatic!" "Calling me lunatic, but you're the one needing a robot and microchip to help you make decisions!" Rosie, *"You know I'll outlive you, right?"* Steven guffawing, "She's got a point; body's halfway to retarded already! Someday, your hand will look like a withered crypt-keeper's!" It was taking incredible willpower not yanking on Rosie's eye-stalks, beating her with them until she inevitably killed him. Exiting elevator, "Either way you look at it, rather be crippled than willing-part of a hostile, corporate takeover!" Steven, from behind him, "You're right about one thing spazz-hands, there's war on all fronts of this planet. Thing is, you're unfit making the draft-cut." Kyle whipped around, blood rushing painfully into arms. Ignored his first reaction, which was throwing oxygen tank at the incompetent man's head. Instead, found the most unpleasant expression he could produce retorting, "What're you rambling about!?" Noticing how hard Kyle tried being intimidating, "Know exactly what I'm talking about, useless prick!" saying words like spitting mouthful of chewing tobacco. Extending hand toward Rosie, "Your conversation with Bethany; intend doing your own, cute investigation. For the sake of the years we worked together, stay away from Aries Industries–far, too powerful being stopped." "Didn't think you had capacity thinking five minutes into the future, let-alone my situation, but then again, probably why you have Rosie Rivets." "I don't appreciate being referred to as human pocket planner!"

Stepping into Kyle's path, "This part I'm going to cherish; surrender your Channel 9 access-card, *The Show* is no longer needing your services." Choking back angry tears, he ripped ID from lanyard, throwing it into Steven's chest, exiting. Calling after him, "Suggest visiting Aries Museum of Technological History, learn what you're up against. When Skyson's done grinding you under heel you'll learn your place in this World; beneath the weight of those forced supporting wastes of space like you!" leaning against an outside window, lighting a large, expensive cigar watching Kyle disappear down street. "Look forward to reporting your tragic death in the near-future." brushing large ember, strolling into lobby, turning to make a remark to Rosie when something caught his attention. "There's movement atop parking garage. Rosie, perform bio-scan." Optic-eyes emitted high-frequency pulses utilizing disciplines of both sonar and surface-resonance, differentiating between objects in a predetermined space with impeccable accuracy and detail. "In-total there's forty-six vehicles; twenty-three sub-compact, twelve trucks, seven SUV's, three derelict, one motorcycle." Exasperated, "Are there any people?" swiveling eye his direction, "Two are engaged in sexual activity, and the other..." voice trailing, "fell from scan. Possible anomaly, heat-pockets where motor-vehicle traffic's commonplace." They stared into the night a few minutes longer before Steven decided to tie a few, loose-ends before ending workday. "I'll be in my office, don't disturb me unless it's for hookers, something worth my time." Rosie backed current memory-session, taking her place behind desk, starring one piece of information as important; email containing PDF image of a handprint–that of fourteen-year-old Carmen Sanders.

MÖÑŠTËRŠ @RË RËÄL

View of Las Vegas from Braeylon Skyson's office was best the city had to offer. Skyson had his back to window, a thin, skeletal robot sitting on large bookshelf, flipping through pages of a thousand page novel, committing it to memory in seconds. "Scampers, ready elevator, we're making phone calls—one of our chess pieces is out of place." Skelenoid looked up from reading, his voice soft, eloquent, a British accent per his Master's desire. "What we get hiring prawns to be our pawns." "Unfortunately, they've yet to outlive usefulness." Scampers returned book, doing a clean summersault, landing on an antique rug Skyson imported from China. "Let me guess, first call's in regards to email received from one of our bots in the field. Clearly beating a dead horse, but I find it pertinent reprimanding our human operatives." Reaching Scampers location, walked toward double-doors positioned before an immaculately lacquered table accommodating twenty-two persons. If table, chairs, adorning walls developed voice, it'd be compared to wailing cries of the damned turning and burning in purgatory. "Not all men carry stomach doing what's necessary securing own future. Left to own accord, waste time and money teetering upon own, moral precipice." turning left, walking into waiting elevator, "It always boils down to the same thing my Lord, there aren't enough humans alive willing to do what Aries requires." Doors opening reaching lobby, Scampers placed hand in front of strange console, powerful magnet disengaging pneumatic lock, attractive, female voice informing, *"Good evening Mr. Skyson, we're at 93% World Compliance!"* "President's on more thin-ice than oaf we're making example of. I know it was my intention drawing unsavory attention, but now he's purposely stalling the whole process." Rapping his fingers scathingly, "Do you know *why* he's making fool of himself?" Braeylon's eyes filling with malice,

"BETRAYAL!"

"Isn't it time we end Ronald Tramp's rant, grown weary of his *'I can't.'*" Arriving at the desired floor, door opened revealing a long, white hallway, sealed entryways lining both sides, ventilation fans pushing trapped, heated air upward. "Preparations remain; distribution of microchips.

Soon, we'll have control over biggest asset America has–the newest generation of adults*!* " Scampers laughed pressing fingertips together. *"Ah* youth, I find this tactic to be most-exhilarating; controlling the newest generation's critical to establishing New World Order." Skyson glanced watch, spinning outermost bevel, steel door opening to reveal another long hallway. "Favorite thing about this, particular strategy; collecting one thousand dollars from participants; insurance policy on every young adult drawing breath*!* " stopping before door situated in hallway's center, announcing, "Braeylon Skyson." Spikes protruded from ceiling and walls, deep, robotic voice asking, *"Mission protocol?" * "One hundred percent compliance." door sliding upward with a quiet hiss, spikes remaining long-after door sealed shut.

"Aries*!* " Skyson barked. "Engage primary system operations, get the shithead from Channel 9 on the line*!* " Skyson poured himself a drink from his crystal decanter, Scampers sitting cross-legged upon desk, video-call appearing upon walls, ringing five times before answered. Skyson, not bothering with niceties, "Was afraid you weren't answering." Wiping forehead perspiration, "Apologies, taking-care of urgent, company business." "As I'm aware, watched fiasco enfold on-air. Congratulations on regaining your lead-anchor position, found myself applauding your performance, even doubting myself, that I was too hard on you." Elated, he responded, "I can assure you, Kyle Clark will never work another day in broadcasting, I made Bethany ~~blacklist~~ him, isn't a news station in America willing to hire his crippled ass now! Rosie and I humiliating him was possibly the most fun I've had in years*!* " "Yes, job well-done. Isn't Rosie a superior work of craftsmanship*?* Even with her original hard-drive, performs better than newer models, given all the bells and *whistles*–like having a son or daughter." observing discernible rise and fall of his Adam's apple, "I said, isn't it like having a son or *daughter!?* " *"I–I–I—"* Skyson mimicking him until silent. "Look at him my Lord, you're a liar–useless and pathetic*!* " Standing, drink in hand, "How many years has it been*?* " Steven remained silent, fearful speaking or moving. Scampers and Skyson exchanged looks, then smiled nodding. "Aries, give demonstration of Steven's modular chip, one discussed earlier, I think he should find it enlightening." Hartigan immediately fell to his knees screaming in agony, curling into gyrating ball.

Disengaging the damaging, electromagnetic frequency, "Microchips we've created truly are a marvel of engineering, more uses than you so-generously advertised." His glare cold and calculating, Scampers ordered, *"Sit."* forced sitting like woman wearing a tight skirt. "We've arrived at a crucial phase, cannot afford liars who're unwilling to fulfill contractual obligations." satisfied with his presentation of power, "I'll ask again, how many years has it been?" Steven wheeled chair forward burying his face in his hands. "Seven years." "There we go, incredible how time flies!" Scampers, infringing on camera, "What was needing done seven revolutions ago you so-cowardly avoided!?" "I was ordered to…disband my family." Skyson eyed terrified underling sipping his expensive liquor. "Why was this part of the contract, non-negotiable?" "It was deemed necessary to ensure complete compliance." Skyson angrily shouted, "If those were my instructions, why didn't you do it!?" Hesitated before saying with resentful hatred, "I was forced to murder my family because you fear my daughter's potential!" glaring *defiantly* across computer screens, look quickly dissipating, Scampers moving into camera's view. "How DARE you doubt Lord Skyson, he fears no one! Give the command, I'll make-way to his office and kill him myself!" resting a hand atop his polished cranium, "That kind of grunt work's far-too-belittling to the hard work we loyally follow through with at Aries Industries–I'll have Rosie do it. Wouldn't you like that Steven old boy, killed by upgraded prototype I allowed you to build?" Scampers laughed softly at Hartigan's expression. "Vital-signs indicate blood pressure's rising to dangerous levels, could we make him have a heart attack? Finally, we'd wipe our hands clean of this errant fool!" Skyson waved a finger at minion like lecturing a naughty toddler. "Now now, though I appreciate thoughts and mirror your desire, where's the fun? Tell me Steven, what did Rosie say over TeleTalk?" Nodding, choking on spit and phlegm, "Rosie's targeting-system was activated by an outside source, waiting for the given-command to end my life."

"Do you remember trial-runs performed on weapons last year, people we reduced to ribbons of flesh? How long do you think it would take you to die?" "I'd surely die before having chance to run. However, saying this in my defense, if I go down, it'll be the end of you and your aspirations, believe you're forgetting your part of the contractual obligation, old bean." Scampers began screaming in rage, Skyson firmly ordering, "Scampers, you're dismissed. If you do not oblige willingly, Aries will see to it that you do so." *"Fine!"* Scampers cried, sulking away, walking the dome-shaped wall to his little cupboard, hatch opening, tucking him away until called-upon. "Robots get very emotional sometimes, don't you think*?"* Hartigan remained quiet, poised in his defensive strategy against this monster of a man. "How often do you think of stabbing me in the back*?"* Steven straightened his posture replying, "Far as you and I know, as many times as you. I've been your trusted understudy for twenty-six years." Eventually Skyson nodded saying, "This is your last slip-up. I don't care if you're carrying answer to the question of life-itself, I'll have you terminated–permanently." Nodding, confidently retorted, "Nothing like the checks and balances of power." moving to end call. Skyson, "Now that you have a microchip, there's nothing you can hide, soon as you think it, information's good as mine*!"* Looking at him carefully, Steven cracked a strange, wide smile responding, "Isn't an idea powerful*?"*

After fifth, failed attempt, "Why won't man answer when ring*?* Silly nitwit must think himself some celebrity*!"* Skyson considered returning minion to cupboard, deciding his banter would steel some of his own, impatient tendencies. He'd never admit it, but Scampers was created as a therapy robot for the aging man. "It takes all cogs and wheels keeping this clockwork engine running." On the sixth time, the proud image of President Ronald Tramp was front-and-center inside the White House's Oval Office. "Hello Braeylon, *so good* of you to call*!* Would've answered other times you rang but you see, was on the other line with family dentist, who was busy *teething me* the finer-points of flossing*!"* waiting for the audio-recorded laughter in his head to subside. "Amazed seeing you in at the White House, warms heart seeing our Country's tax-dollars *hard* at work." Shielding face from a nearby agent, whispered, "It's actually my first time in here*!"* gazing around in admiration, continuing, "I usually hold picnic meetings. Read in an article online, conducting meetings outside, especially when food's involved, does wonders reducing work-related stress–God I love *WonkyLeaks!"* Scampers, coming into view, "Aren't you slightest-bit curious why we've called*?"* President's eyes widened in surprise, then softened cooing, *"HELLO SKITTERS!* How *ARE* you*?* Is daddy feeding you *WELL?"* Infuriated, "Think the job finally cracked him, too bad we didn't install a kill switch in man's head when rigging the election." "Speaking of kill switches, thinking about passing into regulation, new law placing additional taxes on music deemed too scary for the general public*!"* Skyson poured himself another drink and said, *"Fascinating*–go on." "Charlie over here—*!"* swiftly grabbing pencil, chucking it at agent beyond camera's view, someone crying, *"OW!!"* while other men jeered. "Okay, let me start over. I was nice enough to let that bleeding, pencil holder pick the tunes on the way home, he puts on screaming metal music, making me have to do my breathing mantra*!"* Skyson nodded asking, "Isn't this why they place PARENTAL ADVISORIES on the front and back of cases, imprinted upon disk*?"* "Hmmm…" concentrating, fidget-spinner appearing, "That's *it!!"* sitting forward, spinner reeling toward man named Charlie, an agent exclaiming, "Now we have to patch the drywall." "We shall tax the music sold online, make a nice, little business out of it*!* Since you own the entire internet, I'll give five percent if you agree to make the tax-adjustment." Skyson, "Aren't there checks and balances to go through*?* Legislation, votes, things of the sort*?"* Tramp laughed while ripping into a bag of gummy bears retrieved from desk drawer. "Legislation*?* They tell me that fifty times a day*!* Just do it*;* it's not my fault those squares don't have good relationships*!"* Oval Office breaking into laughter, Tramp standing to bow at the men in his company. Scampers raised fists in anger, moments from slamming them onto table he had an idea. "I'll be right back." disappearing into his private dormitory. Hearing rummaging, Skyson grew interested, Tramp busy bowing to the unknown number of men *"kicking it"* inside Oval Office. Scampers returned carrying large shoebox, set down with a **thud** hoping it'd startle him back to reality. President Tramp picked up laptop, carrying it so it'd face in front of him, proceeding around the room giving high-fives to the ten or twelve present, saying things like, *"OOH YEAH!"* and *"MAKING MONEY!"* For reasons unbeknownst, Scampers ripped box from table in disgust, Braeylon stopping him, peeking inside. "My boy, how'd you manage these*?"* "Sort-of a hobby I picked-up." Skyson laughed jovially, spilling his drink, gaining Tramp's attention. *"Oh no!* Please tell me I didn't miss it*!"* *"Mr.* President*!"* Skyson laughed, "You have to see what Scampers brought–they're an absolute delight*!"* Tramp sprinted to desk,

roughly dropping laptop, nearly toppling his chair jumping
into it like a suede-styled layback. Fixing disheveled hair,
"Whoa, think I felt screw break*!"* "Quickly Scampers, before
we lose him*!"* "Mr. President, made presentation showing you
why we called.*"* Tramp, looking-about ecstatically, "Skeeters
made a skit just for me guys*!* Hold on a second, don't show
me yet*!"* Waiting for what appeared to be the entire Secret
Service to position themselves around the tiny laptop,
Scampers revealed several, meticulously-crafted puppets,
tossing one gently to Skyson, sliding own hands inside a pair.
One, replica of the President, second, identical to him.
Tramp's jaw dropped, grin materializing, "You made these all
by yourself*?!"* robot nodding, pleased with his handiwork.
"They help me going over day's events, planning, strategy.
May we get-on with the show*?"* motioning Braeylon to lead.

   "Ring, ring, ring.*"* Scampers brought his puppet
around, speaking in a military voice, **"The President must be
very busy on this night*!*"** Skyson replied, "We shall keep
being patient, I know he loves talking to us*!* Let's try one
more time before calling it a night.*"* Tramp resembled a child
in business suit, spurious presentation working to perfection.
Finally, Scampers brought the President's puppet into view,
Tramp exclaiming, "Look it's the President, *hush-up* and
listen to what he has to say*!"* Skyson gazed at his minion
expectantly, waiting for him to answer. "Ring, ring, ring,
ring–dammit Scampers, answer the call*!"* Scampers brought
puppet's hand to ear mimicking like he was holding a phone.
"HELLO!! THIS IS PRESIDENT RONALD TRAMP!"
choosing a high-pitched, squeaky voice. Skyson cast him look
of forewarning, then relented, allowing use of the hilarious
voice, men on other side bursting into laughter, jostling each
other like a college fraternity. "Good evening Mr. President,
my, you're looking dashing tonight*!"* Tramp puppet, ***"GOT
THIS FACE CREAM IMPORTED FROM CHINA MADE
FROM CHILDREN'S TEARS, IT TAKES YEARS OFF MY
APPEARANCE!"*** Scampers puppet barked, **"We've called to
discuss an urgent mission needing completion. The world
needs a hero at the UN Summit, making a proposition*!*"**
"A PROPOSITION*?!*" Tramp puppet retorted, ***"SOUNDS
LIKE A LOT OF WORK–WHAT'S IN IT FOR ME?!"*** "I
like his thinking*!"* Tramp said happily, "This guy's DEEP*!"*
Skyson shook puppet like a rattle saying, "Mr. President, if
you accept mission, what you're providing the world with is
invaluable…*"*

Aries activated a spotlight over the Skyson puppet. "For what we've made will blow your mind, let's take this one step at a time!" Scampers puppet, **"We've created microchips passing a series of rigorous tests!"** "Yes rigorous tests!" The way Skyson and Scampers threw together impromptu puppet show was impressive. Skyson puppet sang, "This technology provides quality life, giving people relief from strife! Small incision with a knife, you'll be a new man, better wife!" Tramp puppet cried, *"STAND AND DELIVER; WILL THE COST MAKE ME SHIVER?!"* Everything fell quiet, Skyson boldly saying, "Supply and demand? I'm helping people, I don't understand. Operation's only costs a cold, hard grand." Tramp's puppet falling over in shock, regaining composure. Tramp, "Good bargain, reacted the same way!" Smiling, Skyson, "Will you accept mission?" Secret Service agents stared *expectantly* at Commander in Chief, waiting reply. Man named Charlie complained, "Mr. Pres—" "Hush Charlie, I want to know if he's accepted the mission!" Bewildered, Scampers fixed puppets' posture, Tramp puppet declaring,

"I ACCEPT YOUR MISSION!"

Tramp exited chair celebrating, *"WE'RE GOING AROUND THE WORLD BABY!* Bravo Sneakers, Mr. Skyson, on an award-winning performance! My favorite part was when he said 'I accept your mission!', shows initiative and I like that in a man!" While Scampers returned hand puppets to shoebox, "Appreciate your *hutzpah* gaining support, these microchip's are rearing to change lives." "We'll leave first thing tomorrow–ten-thirty earliest! If any of you dickheads wake me up before my coffee-timer goes *"Ding!"*, you'll be incarcerated at Whowantonamo Prison while rest of us party at fourteen thousand feet!" Skyson, moving things along, "Expect a full-debrief shortly after Summit." Pausing celebratory gestures, "This is a Summit? You mean I'm legislating a legitimate event and none of you assholes told me?" Charlie, the President's main aide, "We've been discussing the Summit, various, foreign dignitaries all week Sir, even went over our iron-clad plan for a fair-trade agreement with China." Blinking vacantly, staring into lap, "Huh." smiling childishly, "Thought we were talking about sexual conquest! In hindsight, Summit makes more sense, especially since I was the only one doing any talking." Charlie complained, "All you did was *hum* while eating omelets!" Skyson, smiling politely, "If you need anything during your travels, please *don't* hesitate." Giving a half-assed hand salute, "If there's one thing I've gotten-down aboard my jet it's two: Television remote, connecting to Wi-Fi! Though it was a last-minute, promise trying my best." Charlie groaning, "United Nations agreed to block-schedule a year ago!" Offering the irritated man a gummy bear, "Don't you love it when Nations unite?" Scampers fought urge celebrating call termination, Skyson reminding, "One more needing follow-up, asset procurer, Veronica." "Quite right, Tramp made circuits go haywire." Aries performed required commands, the name *Vexing Sock* appearing on walls. "Who gave permission altering names in the Aries Legacy Directory? Wasn't something *I* authorized." Avoiding his gaze, "Sorry, was on a puppet marathon, found it appropriate." Scampers blinked, nickname disappearing, replaced with pawn's proper name. After three tries, decided the call could wait. "Unworried about this particular part of our plan, given her plenty of expendable cash. Either through acquisition or destruction, it's essential this piece doesn't see the light of day."

Scampers held shoebox, brooding over Tramp's ineptitude. "Sit back, watch him go." "Aren't you concerned he's going to make a fool of himself?" "*Will* he–this is certain." inspecting hand puppet, "However, this is no responsibility or concern of mine, already prepared dossier for his presentation. He's merely the catalyst solidifying our glorious moment." Scampers, staring at his favorite puppet, "It's a wonder the Country hasn't fallen into premature anarchy." Skyson smirked saying, "Know what you're trying. Conveying our demands through a presentation was genius, but I'm unsure how I feel. Weren't planning-on sticking me full of pins?" Scampers wailed, "Don't take my hand puppets my Lord, I wasn't doing anything bad, promise!" rummaging contents, "I even made Kyle Clark, the news reporter whose career we just ended!" held for viewing in the dim, auxiliary lighting, "Without them, my processor overheats!" Taken aback by his emotional display, "Have no desire keeping your belongings Scampers, what's yours is yours. However, discovering there's a puppet in my likeness is off-putting, please leave it here until tomorrow morning, need night's rest refocusing. Rather like the idea of my puppet remaining here in a constant, state of vigilance. Soon, our enemies will cower at mere glimpse of even this, sleepless sentry." puppet receiving a gentle pat. Bowing in obedience, "He'll remain here, all night–shall I double coffee made in the morning?" sharing laugh, "Rest well my Lord. Sun rises, you'll be one step closer to becoming rightful ruler!*" "Goodnight my little Scampers. If by some miracle I do find love again, you'll have to make a puppet I can gift." "Now that, would be the cherry on top." waiting until Skyson reached elevator, holding hand high as a sign of respect. After departing, he walked to table, tucked the mini Skyson under his arm and relocated to bed chamber, placing shoebox on floating shelf installed between bookshelves.

The room Scampers called home was larger than it appeared, a hardwired thirst for knowledge leading him to collect many books, leaving only room for the small, floor-bound mattress. Pulling a weighted blanket over his skeletal frame, poking favorite puppet out, "I'll make sure he lets me keep you." Auxiliaries darkened inside the control-room, line of traveling text reading, "94% World Compliance."

 SCAMPER

Innocence had a home in this beautiful girl's heart, bursting at the seams from the renewed excitement each school year brings. She thought about what to bring to Show and Tell Friday, quieting the early-semester sentencing of shudders and stutters, hopefully making new friends. That one girl in front has nice hair bows and smells pretty, tall boy holding door for everyone made her blush something fierce! Sat quietly at bus's front, fidgeting, driver taking distracted notice in rearview, oftentimes admonished being distracted introvert with poor social-skills. Despite what others thought, no situation, preexisting disposition ailed, simply a matter of sensitivity to surroundings, happenings of others.

Parents worked extremely hard becoming counselors with specializations in Child Psychology. Brilliant flagships; creating an idiot-proof guide becoming a better caregiver, aspirations set on answering long-discussed questions within child-rearing. Minutes turned to hours under the steady hum of their vaporizer, ambient flow of piano music, gentle aromas of bamboo orchid, human skin settled agreeably in their bedroom, blanketing space in a relaxed, lucid design. Weeks later, after repossession of family vehicle, discontinuation of power, hard work was rewarded with prestigious opportunity transforming ideas, hours of empirical data into creating a software program streamlining child-rearing into a step-by-step process.

Walked short distance from bus stop, earbuds blaring Billy Joel's, "We Didn't Start the Fire.", remembering not to let neighboring dog startle her again. Routine clockwork, pace slowed reaching cross-street, looking both ways before shouting, "I'M HOME!!" until firmly planted on family's "Wipe Your Paws!" doormat. Bursting through door, she listened for familiar footsteps of her very first dog, Mr. Bigglesworth, expectant smile changing to lines of worry, silence greeting her return home. Peering into adjoining family room, "Dad? Mom?" voice echoing around high-ceilings, "Maybe they're in the bedroom..." tossing bag into coat closet, running up steps and small landing in bounding leaps. Opened door slowly, creaking upon single hinge, revealing an empty bedroom.

*Migrating from room to room, she eventually found her father at his workstation inside garage. Wrapping arms around his midsection, "Daddy! Where's Mommy and Mr. Bigglesworth?" Returning hug, relocating her to chair between parked cars, "Mommy had to work late sweetheart...may have a last-minute, business trip if she doesn't finish." Staring into father's eyes, "If Mommy's at work, why's her car here?" resting hands on front tires of both vehicles. His face etched with lines of stress, exhaustion, began returning various tools to proper places. "What about Mr. Bigglesworth, did he go to work with Mommy?" father picking-up wooden saw, running hand along worn, rusted edge, taking-note of the oxidizing metal, bend in edge. "Listen carefully, okay hon." perking ears, nodding sweetly, "Remember when we first got Mr. Bigglesworth? Must've been...what, three years old?" "Yes Daddy, I got him on my birthday so we could be bestest friends!" Father returned smile, tilting head from side to side, "Funny thing about Mr. B—we almost didn't. Your mother and I were torn on getting a puppy, or investing in a teenage babysitter!" chuckling, daughter too young understanding. "Turns out, should've gotten the babysitter. Mr. B ran away and is never coming back." Shock soaked bewilderment, blending into a puree of emotional trauma and abandonment. "What do you mean? He always waits for me before going outside!" "I know he meant a lot sweetheart, but he's **gone now,** moved-on, finding new family to care for him." Passed the point of reconciliation, "I Want Mr. Bigglesworth—BRING HIM BACK!" Father's face contorted with rage throwing saw against garage paneling. "Maybe if you hadn't ignored him he would've stayed! Instead, found another family who'll take better care of him!" Pain of friend leaving abruptly faded, replaced with a strange, unidentified feeling. "He ran away because I ignored him? I didn't mean to! How do I get him back?!" "It's too late!" he yelled, wiping at sweat and grime, "Why I'm never buying a pet again! All you did was pull his tail and smack him half his life! Just an innocent puppy, and you made him wish he'd been given to __ANYONE__ else!" Looking into father's eyes, chest rose and fell with each, spastic breath.*

"THAT'S NOT TRUE!"

Exited garage heading to backyard, using entire bodyweight pulling the sliding, glass door open, tears bouncing off blades of grass near Mr. B's doghouse. Crawling into best friend's home all that greeted her were four, bare walls, pile of chewed toys in far corner. Falling to floor, "I'm sorry Mr. Bigglesworth, please come back!" listening intently, hopeful hearing the jingling of his nametag, rabies certificate. Sitting, sniffled gazing at toy pile, grabbing their favorite—tug-of-war rope played with since pull-ups. Exited structure carrying toy, not long before finding herself in garage staring at her father. He looked to be in the middle of something, inspecting object veiled by a large, grey sheet, refusing to acknowledge daughter's presence, even after grasping for his hand.

 "Did Mr. Bigglesworth come home?" Eyes sunken like a mummy at the Museum of Natural History, "You came back Carmen! Underneath's a little surprise Daddy brought home from work!" Carmen's eyes brightened, smiling through tears, "What is it?" quick flourish revealing large, terrifying machine. "Since your mother and I've been forced working later, created a nanny to care of you. Come; stand in front of Rosie for initial setup." positioning her before the metal monstrosity, pushing buttons along the nape of it's neck. A humming sound increased in volume and intensity, machine growing taller as system, primary, software functions engaged, two, optic-eyes revealing their deep, ember glow.

 "Rosie, meet your new task. Initiate the Parent Perfection software, starting a new, child profile." Optics abruptly focused, locking onto Carmen. "Opening requested software, creating profile. Load preset parenting styles, customize parameters?" For Carmen, every childhood nightmare, bump in the night amassed into the fray, there to stay, her thoughts simple as they were tragic. "Am I having a bad dream? Daddy isn't the same. Mr. Bigglesworth!" Eyes desperately searched her father for reassurance, to him, she wasn't in the room, had to keep fooling himself she wasn't his daughter. Looking away, steadied gaze upon Rosie saying, "Was going to go with preset parenting options, but I've changed my mind, child's as bad as they come; filthy, animal abuser, he deserved dying because of you!" She recoiled in fear, nearly falling backwards into chair between parked cars. "Have a customized profile on thumb drive here in my pocket!" retrieving USB, inserting into available port. "Downloading driver software, transferring files." Encountering a system-error, muttered to himself, "Boys in the lab said this might happen." sighing heavily, forcing shutdown. "You're to go upstairs and go to bed—no dinner for naughty girls!" Not pausing to breathe, Carmen tore from

*He threw outside latch leading to garage, returning
to work bench, opening tool chest, retrieving bloodied
pillowcase with a unicorn on it. Lifting pant leg, exposing a
rather nasty wound, "If only you hadn't bitten me." tossing
sack carelessly on top of wife's body, entering vehicle.
"Plenty of places hiding bodies in the Rocky Mountains."
Lighting expensive cigar, pushed garage button on sun visor,
leaving Carmen to suffer in a dark, silent house.*

Wind blew forcefully along parking garage's upper-portion, concrete, masonry providing options climbing where pleased. She regretted accepting this, beginner's mission, Kyle's life revolving around two places–work and home. Plus, it was getting late, last thing wanted was being detained by police for curfew violation. Concentrating, climbed onto tippy-toes, gloved hand providing leverage pulling her one-hundred ten-pound frame to next level. Swinging legs around, hopped down from barrier, dusting concrete residue from hands, faded black jeans, looking moodily at parked automobiles, picturing herself driving alone–*friendless.* Kicked small pebble near her foot, bouncing, rolling to stop underneath blue SUV, a startled rat scampering out of sight.

Carmen stood five feet, six inches, brown hair graced a reddish tint, wearing black beanie, hoodie over raggedy T-shirt. She bears pain many carry; whether or not a child's received any, familial structure, state of decay's produced from society driven by screens, less by genuine-means. normality a family purchase robot meeting requirements sustaining. Designed with essential software programs hashing a most-complex algorithm, generating code not in binary, something scientists named binary supplicant. Language grants a system unique functionality, absorbing events, executing automatically. On all requested actions, system numerates by one of three, nominal values: ***1, 0, OR ±1.*** Astronomical design of coding language grants ability retroactively adding to database, choosing preferences from a straightforward regiment maintaining survival. Experiencing binary supplicant firsthand, Carmen made decision providing for herself on the streets at age seven, developing into a stubborn, hard-nosed kid who was more comfortable observing others at a distance. Outside, discovered pile of rubble, lazily tossing pebbles to street below, doing-so for all of ten minutes until passerby howled in pain. Stricken man some distance away, sighed, "Wondering about news anchor." Though dossier pegged him a widowed workaholic, didn't expect him staying late. Reached into hoodie pocket grazing porcelain mug shard. Activity stirred, balding man strolling toward elevators, "Nut-job one for evening news. Soon, I'll be enjoying nice, cup of cocoa!"

Kyle was engaged in conversation, thinking it usual behavior until surrendering ID. "What's he gotten into? Off-chance he's gotten canned, mission may've taken pleasant turn." Picturing herself sitting in nearby park after stealing a sandwich, watching Mr. Clark waste-away. Blame it on her inner gossip-girl, self-driven desire learning everything about person tracking, had to catch piece. "Suggest Aries Museum of…" entirety explained by tone used delivering message, Kyle even carrying sad, little box solidifying shameful walk home. Should've descended stairs yet for some reason, drawn to larger man, lag time making her unable escaping eyesight entirely. Quickly and quietly, Carmen crawled backward, spanning sixty feet in seconds. Nearing roof's edge, pushed upward with lean arms, ensuring feet cleared ledge. Recruited recently, debriefed ad-nausea about technological advances at Aries, Lashbrook drilling importance of placing objects between scanning robot to prevent detection. Letting go, rappelled structure without rope. Trick, as she'd worked it, keeping momentum toward direction of travel–strong legs, tough arms doing the work. Acquired mindset deepened learning experience, defeating obstacles sending most to their death. Feet landed on second floor of garage, pushing away, pivoted, rotating hips until facing head-first, transitioning into clean, barrel-roll. Finding feet, quickly followed Kyle's route via parallel pursuit, matching speed of target. Everything pretty much wrapped itself up and to knowledge, Collective Conscious only found "valuable" for wealth of resources. "Pranking Lashy for pointless errand!" picturing waking Commander, "Weapons training *and* first pick of goodies next time Laz makes supply-run." Block from residence, sought location giving direct-view into living-quarters, never closing blinds, rarely locking apartment. Bench half-block away, Carmen made *beeline*, overtaking Kyle. Thinking fast, jumped atop bench singing, **_"THERE'S HOLE IN THE BUCKET, DEAR LIZA, DEAR LIZA!"_** Assuming she was drunk, muttered derogatorily before entering apartment.

Tossed box against stool lining breakfast bar, overturning on big-toe. **_"DAMMIT!"_** stumbling, tearing at laces revealing bloodied toenail. Call it reporter's intuition, happenings more than coincidence. Looked forward to visiting mom, asking clarifying questions, discussing recurring dreams. If to go with own diagnosis, workplace abuse combined with unaddressed trauma from wife's premature passing. Over to closet, pulled out a carry-on bag buried under laundry, kicking at dirty socks formed into balls amongst unkempt wardrobe. walked to dresser pulling last pairs of clean pants, socks and underwear–stuffing them on top. About to turn and leave bedroom to call a taxi, something grabbing; picture of him and Aspen during wedding. Picking it up with good hand, gently placing it on top of clothing, zipping bag shut. "Taking you wherever I go." Replacing socks, gingerly slipped into dress shoes, flicking lights, locking door.

Many social interactions didn't make sense to Carmen, having practically raised herself. One of these: Proper amount of time spent awake before retiring. Own place, life would revolve around cartoons, eating junk food. Not that thought had anything to do with task at hand, but did help repelling omnipresent boredom accustomed experiencing during surveillance. At twenty-minute mark, lights turned off, joyful cheer escaping; instantly fixating on cup of hot chocolate pondering earlier; noticing streets empty with exception of lone taxicab. Stuffed hands into pockets, scrounging for change to avoid walking. "What the—" concealing face, Kyle flagging approaching taxi, hoping he'd give destination, gleamed word out of the bunch–*airport*. Though desired endpoint, no position calling a lift. Quickly and quietly as surroundings allowed, scampered across road squatting behind rear quarter-panel. Hearing driver hit automatic latch on trunk of cab; letting muscle memory take over she pushed on trunk, forcing it swing fully open. Having done this number more times than cared to admit, knew driver's rearview would be obscured, giving coverage to lightly ease into trunk. No sooner she'd gotten inside, Kyle threw bag on top, shutting trunk. Inside, wafted menagerie of smells; whoever owned vehicle was a drinker, smelling wet spot, fought urge to retch. Surveillance mission in full nose-dive, orders remained same: Track until reporting.

"I taste coffee and whatever's in my front, jacket pocket, what about you Charlie? Let's take pictures of us pretending to poop in the Embassy's mailbox, ought to rile-up Postal Service!" In a wave of mysterious fog, President Tramp went into deep recess, all other thoughts vacating while assembling a strategy presenting Skyson's microchips, returning to conversation had aboard *Air Force Fun.*
(Many harps being played)
Air smelled of cigar, acrid cigarette, a loud clatter from the President's executive bathroom, Charlie exiting with a lit match. "Can I ask why you dismantled bathroom fan? Doing-so is technically a federal crime." Tramp looked away from television scolding, "Close the damn door! I'm huge fan of curry, just not on the way out. I needed a new fan and everything on this damned plane uses two-plug!" pausing explanation, appearing as though a profound thought entered mind, whispered, "They're trying to kill us all!" "Sir, you need to reel-in your focus, going to a Summit, not getting high. What was in your cigarette anyways?" "Think the *cool kids* these days call them spliffs–I rather enjoy them." "Is something bothering you?" searching boss's reddened eyes. "You know Braeylon—good pal of mine by the way—and his weirdo skyscraper that's actually a sprawling labyrinth of bunkered, isolated, testing facilities..." happily pointing to his head, "I've got a good one of these Charlie. While I forced you to make sushi, watched documentary about when planes hit the Global Stock Depot–it was an inside job!" hyperventilating, settling back down, "What I'm trying to ask is, do you think Mr. Skyson—like a *father* to me by the way— has ulterior motives for making me do this?" standing, walking strangely, "What if he's trying to enslave my mind?" Always a man known for dramatics, he crumpled to floor in defeat. Inspecting the bottom of his shoe for dirt, "I just don't want my business partner and buddy betraying us, he's the only one who calls with good news and smiles, the other fellas in the big people world run away from me–you've seen how they treat me!" Charlie helped return besought man to his recliner. "Pretty-sure we've all known what kind of man Braeylon Skyson is; produces incredible leaps in technology, effectively strong-arms Nations beckoning at his every call." Tramp uncovered face considering Charlie's words. "Now you

mention it, he's pretty-persistent calling me. One time, he called me a "lollygagger", made me feel fat and depressed*!"* Charlie looked around hoping more were paying attention to his antics, turns out, they were doing their best avoiding eye-contact. *"Well..."* he sighed, "have you considered looking-over information and video emailed this morning*?* Only way we're pulling this off is by making-good on our campaign promise, establishing a fair-trade agreement with China. *"* Straightening posture, replied, "Shouldn't be too hard, I mean, think about it*; we,* The United States of America, pay quite a lot of dollars in stock market revenue, and in tariffs they enforce in an unfair manner*!* Why's it my fault they're forcing their youth into sweatshops creating our toys*?"* airplane erupting into laughter, Secret Service agreeing with Tramp's opinion. Ever the strong debater, Charlie offered rebuttal, *"Mr.* President, you do realize we've voluntold China to manufacture not just for us, but everyone*?* We pay average, Chinese worker cents on the dollar for what's made after Global Market Return On Investment. We have literally, as a whole world, forced the Chinese people into indentured servitude.*"* Tramp brought finger to man's lips silencing him. Face coming within inches, "Don't you **DARE** start the conversation about rerouting toy manufacturing to Taiwan*!* Have you ever felt a toy with no soul*?"* receiving no response, smoothed Charlie's suit quietly saying, "Good, you don't want to.*"* Returning to topic at-hand, "Aries Industries has been an underground, criminal empire for number of years. Although we can't place full blame on Skyson for crimes committed on his networks...*"* Tramp pulled a newspaper hat from inside jacket, placing it on his head with impeccable precision, everyone continuing their usual activities, used to President's laidback personality. "Bottom line*;* someone has to stick to their guns on the mountaintop*;* chosen trusting the friendship, business partnership I've with Braeylon. Besides, we both know if any other man was in charge, if the World was set up differently, whackos would still claw and catapult their way in to commit crime. I'll first be giving introduction explaining the relationship, investment of trust I have in this man—he did help me win the election after all*!"* happily looking at Charlie, busy inspecting large Band-Aid covering the pencil wound received night prior. Tramp slapped it advising, "Should've gotten the *My Little Phoney* ones*!"* After intake of breath, "If you're sure I'll stand behind you, just try not to blow it. Though you're pretty-comfortable with several foreign dignitaries, best keeping creative elaboration to a minimum.*"*

Tramp returned to reality as Charlie concluded response to questions asked of him. "Anything you guys wanna do? Antique shop for something special?" Secret Service *(large posse; two lines, six abreast)* cheered agreement. Charlie, only one caring, "Delightful, well-and-good. Strict schedule, so…" Tramp sighing contentedly, "Who's ready for some sightseeing? It's fantastic being here in…" "Italy Sir. Remember your *clever* catchphrase being nice? *"Even Its are Allies!?"* Summit starts in fifteen." pointing at large building, "That's where we're going, nice and easy…" "Next time, we're having this at one of my hotels; pamper diplomats with steamed, towel-treatments while emptying their travel accounts!" idea producing bout of laughter. "I've thought it over Char, since I've been running this Country last thirty years or so, opening playing hardball with China!" Charlie wearily asked, "Do you think it wise opening a peaceful assembly aggressively attacking others with trade regulation? Trust me on this; require a clear-air if you're getting Braeylon's needs fulfilled." Upset having to deliver message differently, "Alright, I can improvise with the best of them! It may take minute or two to, you know, *get in the zone.* After waggling my tongue at these guys for a bit, I'll have them right in the palm of my hand, my **PALM!** See Char, I know what I'm doing!"

There's little to be said about the aesthetics of politics. What used to be inspired discussions geared toward heightening mankind had in later years, turned into rude moments displaying open favoritism. It had been decades since prominent Nations had taken responsibility for things such as reparation, pollution-control, implementing strategies searching and eliminating terrorists. It was in Aries Industries infancy those desiring to impact such areas disappeared, tumbling in sullied investments, capitalism leaving communities refined, unveiling a degrading, moral precipice.

"I'd like to thank my mother for giving-birth, providing the opportunity speaking amongst all you doers and triers."

Charlie held stack of notecards directing the opening of the U.N. Summit, respected officials listening patiently as

Tramp produced polarizing jargon. "Thank you America, for elected me into office, offering insight to a despairing Country desperately seeking qualities I carry, each day. If it wasn't for the deliberate, self-forged energy I was able to instill in others, I don't think we'd be here." leaving podium, wandering perimeter of political coliseum, Charlie fearing he'd suffered his final, bout of cluelessness. Inches from fire door there was a discernible change in atmosphere, everyone present hoping he'd exit, not to return. Resting hand on doorknob, gently caressing it, "Don't you love the way a door handle shines? Got to wash them every day mind-you, a lot of germs going-around these days. It's a bit stuffy, will an alarm sound if I prop the door?" politicians voicing protest. Disappointed, Tramp took-hold of nearby folding metal chair, expecting onlookers to notice it was left inside the yellow lines drawn preventing obstruction. Noisily dragging it, "Having this chair where it was in an OSHA violation. I know I know, don't have to thank me, just make sure you pay it forward during next visit to your local grocery store." opening chair, flipping it backwards, sitting, smacking lips, sighing in satisfaction.

"Let's get down to business–any questions so far?" everyone silent, waiting for theatrical performance to draw to a close. "Good, didn't come all this way to babysit. What I've to discuss is of utmost importance, as it's something we've all grown dependent on: Technology." As you know, Braeylon and I are friends...he even sends virtual Christmas cards. Our cybernetic Santa manufactured new technology, outdoing all the rest, establishing *more* for us than universal connection. In our modern age, internet, service robots, things of the sort, we've learned there are no shortcuts when it comes to disseminating information from alternative facts. What Braeylon's created; it isn't a robot helping with daily chores, such as raising children, playing house." looking joyfully at unamused cohorts, giving reassuring, *thumbs-up* to translators abjectly recording everything said.

Placing hands in front of him, tucked fingers into palms creating shadow-puppet rabbits, one following other hopping along chair's backrest. "Braeylon and his little robot Squeegee did a wonderful puppet show explaining the benefit of establishing an agreement between Nations authorizing immediate use of this technology." Denmark used the time between Tramp's breaths presenting a clarifying question. "Do not see discussion continuing unless given tangible metrics outlining this new, innovative idea."

Tossed medium-sized bag, everyone questioning his peculiar, political strategy, Tramp revealing a child's See-and-Say. Smiling fondly, pulled handle activating spinner.

Groans, low muttering. Representative from China, "We've travelled many kilometers discussing important matters! What does a toddler's toy have to do with any of this?" Tramp frowned like he was the one being ignorantly pandered to. "Excuse me Sensei, you holding the microphone? Didn't think so. Toy happens being the first I remember playing with as child. With this, little memento, began the hard, mental training preparing reins of today, for the reign of tomorrow. How many of you agree with statement, "Animals, the only living things you can trust." none responding, everyone hoping to shorten his time with the mic. "It's irrefutably the mindset of us all, but worry-not my friends, I have great news, humans are animals too!" heaving sigh of relief, "One of those profound moments leading-up to me becoming President. What I'm trying to say is, we can trust Braeylon Skyson; a dog can only bark, a cat only meows. Not to mention, a Billy Goat gruffs, and a cow and pig can dinner plate."

Tramp reached for pocket, producing small box. Arriving at platform's edge, getting on bended knee, opened box with a question poised for poisoning. "Will you buy and sell microchips?" Diplomats finally understanding the deal Ronald Tramp was pitching, China chose weighing-in. "If these were to be purchased by any of us, like a display better than this!" "Oh yeah? Charlie, activate the video!" relocating behind podium, pressing button, projection screen displaying video-clip of Steven's news broadcast. Tramp, holding arms in a welcoming gesture, "This is why I trust my pal Braeylon! He keeps driving and striving, pushing the limits to provide life-changing benefits! Thanks to this artificial intelligence, we can effectively streamline students, choosing which ideas are cultivated! These dynamos are under constant supervision while we breathe intelligence into them like a lifesaving ventilator! Combining technology and humanity helps us perform and complete our daily functions, allowing more time focusing on fun! What if you could do Sudoku and crossword at same time? Sudossword is what you'd have!"

Russia, "If we're to sign for such a device, need an insurance policy, *посул*, they're free from defect." Trump laughed heartily at his concern, underhand tossing box, "See for yourself, thing's squeaky clean. I won't be getting one, medical procedures terrify me." After inspecting, asked, "How can we be certain Skyson isn't infiltrating what little privacy remains?" President shrugged understandably in relation. "Had same debate, laboring in my personal office aboard plane. Fortunately for you, he's like my best friend. If it wasn't for his campaign contributions, would've never acquired money traveling, winning the hearts of millions." Everyone was still concerned about subjecting their youth to unknown device. Waving an arm airily about, France forewarned, "Relationship with the United States wavers, France, no desire being plagued by malfunctions. Histoire apprise, trust Mainland first." "You keep enjoying crappy crescents, we have *Pillsberry, Mhmm!* We should invest; no way we're being lured by man we've already given world to. If we object, will eventually hit bottleneck where machines no longer let us in because we refused their wishes..." staring dreamily into distance, imagining world spoken-of. "Far as I'm concerned, these are the next, big thing! No side-effects; give those kids in Vegas calculators and before you know it, driving sales, repurposing taxes!" After five more minutes of Tramp rambling, manipulating entire gathering like party he'd organized, pointed a finger toward fire-door curtailing his approach.

"The document I'm passing around, when you get it, sign your name on the dotted line, don't be a lame guy on that fancy fence! After all, I've only recently obtained Presidency, but due to knowledge in macroeconomics, have a longer run than Kennedy. I know we'll be fine because Braeylon and Squilly are really, quite nice; we talk and one years ago, he sent a turkey for Thanksgiving–t'is the Season!" Charlie yelling nervously, "Okay Mr. President, place issue to the back of the line, only two hours for open-floor debate." Wrapping things up, explained, "Whether you sign for device or not, they'll probably land on your doorstep, those who've had the surgery moving-in to replace you." Tramp dropped microphone, exiting fire door, sprinklers activating, raining down upon those inside.

SPEAR & THE ARCHER

Water trickled down the steep landscape, thousands of seafaring birds journeying from habitats foraging insects. Gentle breeze swirled, gathering all clouds from night prior, stretching across horizon in a thin veil. Lizard skittered along length of fallen log, disappearing from sight. Westley regained consciousness, wiping at dirt and grime, filled with a deep, gnawing pain. Regained vision, mind spinning from events leaving him clinging to life, comrade, meal for vicious jungle. Word formed describing: Carrion-feed. Coming to sitting, observed surroundings–no idea where he was.

"WESTLEY SURE CAN TAKE A BEATING!" Joe, "Have to cut our losses, map drawer…brave weakling." Martha, "Came in partway, but I rather liked Timothy!" Daisy, glaring at Joe, "*You* fucked him over!" "Last I checked, not a panther–Jesus Christ!" Byte, "Precisely." "Wait, Jesus was the panther?" "Unbelievable. Remember last night, when you were disappointed with part, rising action? Something you missed about the importance of Him dying." "How can something said jokingly kill Timothy?" Byte to Daisy, "You understand his stupidity; please enlighten, saving patience for something less-rudimentary."

"Jesus lived so sins would be forgiven. No one understood why he was the Son of God, or why it was his job informing others they're also Sons and Daughters of God. Essentially, your callous remark of one of us playing Jesus desecrated his reason for living." "Nicely-put. Remember this and never forget it, otherwise fate will surely crucify every chance left. Instead of accepting possibility of selfless sacrifice, you were busy fashioning a crown of thorns, spear needed in that ruminating head of yours. You carelessly spoke the Lord's name, making it appear like his intention was to become a glorified Martyr." pointing strong finger at Joe's cranium, "Soon as idea was obtainable, you decided for all of us, *one* of us, as result, Timothy has died–happy?" Martha nodded saying, "Yep, Jesus was the panther!"

Joe slid from booth, walking to bathroom, resting forehead upon door. "Mrs. Bit," loudly so he could hear, "since you've whole *kit-caboodle* inside noggin, help discover a feasible strategy, slim-chance reestablishing redemption absent retribution." resting eyes on Joe, not used to intelligent, spiritual banter." Mrs. Bit smiled brightly doing the Macarena. *"WE'VE MULTIPLE CHOICES, PREVENTING DEATH FROM EXPOSURE– THIS IS NOW A BRAINSTORMING SESSION!"* Joe returned to table, instantly providing input. "Westley's broken as a used condom, need to utilize some sort of…" Martha, saving the group from useless banter, "He's resorted to crawling anywhere he goes, unless dying animal walks into him, he's going to starve." Daisy, "Canteen's inside Timothy's tomb…don't have the heart sending him back there!" Joe, "There was a rainstorm, get him hydrated, figure something out. Just brainstorming…when did they invent the wheelchair?" Byte laughed picturing Westley traversing jungle in wooden wheelchair. "Hilarious–less storm more brain. How about berries? Knows what they look like, already crawling-around like a bug, might as well shed uniform, returning to nature." Mrs. Bit, *"WHEELCHAIR WAS INVENTED IN 1665 BY PARAPLEGIC WATCHMAKER STEPHEN FARFLER!"* Joe, "Agree to disagree pal. Westley needs to make sure he's ready to dance, going to wither away like my mom's box without a real meal!" Martha, "Gather components, making trap." *"OOH, BRAINSTORM HIT HURRICANE-STRENGTH!"* Byte, "Mrs. Bit's taking over, about talked-out until Westley's condition improves."

Precipitation trapped in various, earthbound plants blanketing–*advantageous*. Travelled some distance, gasped between mouthfuls, relishing in the cascading liquid. Resting against tree, inspected body; through soiled trousers, discernible difference in size between legs, resisting urge removing, fearing pain too intense. Condensation dripped from foliage above, soaking Westley into a dank, miserable mess. Rolling onto stomach, crawled ravine's bottom, hopeful coming-upon area providing his next meal. "Berries it is. Day I'm eaten by filthy underfoot will be the day I'm sent to Hell, reborn as a Rabbi!" Wildlife here was unlike anything he'd encountered; many a fowl, foal and foul fool had met an end from his arrows, yet there was something savage, unyielding in the beasts proudly living here. "It's in their eyes; chiseled experience seen upon charge. Cannot say fear, something else; that headlong stare, it smothers, snuffing-out like candle."

shivering, pushing the feeling of being hunted from mind, knowing his morale played a key-role in winning battles. Thirty minutes, gained promising location, foliage bearing a darker hue, coming-upon bush similar to what Timothy and him discovered earlier. Though he'd experienced death frequently throughout his life, Timothy's death resonated differently, calling sacrifice casualty of war didn't befit the man. Hunger took-hold, allowing respite from guilt and sorrow, acidity in berries turning stomach. Having his fill, set to work on what he considered a more-fruitful approach, digging large hole, achieving depth of one meter. Grabbing bush, removed branches and thorns, breaking it into usable cover. Placing over hole, allowed hand fall lightly on top, as imagined, covering collapsed easily into hole's bottom. Fixing trap, placing handful of ripe berries, "Things go my way, something worth eating by day's end." Reeking of body odor, Westley labored in a northerly direction, keeping in mind the possibility of panther giving-chase. From what he knew, they're predacious creatures of superior intelligent, alpha-instinct hardwired into DNA, one of few animals known engaging in tortuous, killing-tactics. Single attack's placed to inflict grievous wounding, then observed, panther grading the efficiency of it's marring strike, all-the-while remaining from sight in the shadow of trees.

Five had no interruption, Daisy returning to her sluggish, subdued self. "Smile bright eyes, chance refreshing, skipping ahead." Mrs. Bit's head plopping onto arm, Joe asked, "We're allowed to sleep!? What *else* haven't you mentioned?" "Great question..." Daisy pried curiously. Smirked responding, "That's for no one to know, not even me." Joe, "Telling me you and catnap have been winging this?" Byte to Martha, "You're the most-viable candidate posing this question to. Kids, do they come with manuals attached to their scrawny legs?" "Suppose not. However, parents didn't raise an idiot." Byte gestured toward Joe saying, "There you go. *"Winging-it* isn't my preferred way describing it. The first kid's always most-impactful, each after theoretically becoming a better-curtailed syllabus. Of course, there's schedule rearranging, tragedies, things of the sort..." voice trailing, Joe inquiring, "How'd your kids turn out?" "They grew-up. Was never around long-enough giving them the one byte kept for me. Knowing this, I was the fool who promised being in every part. They don't know it, but I love them." only sound was Mrs. Bit's snoring, dreaming of Broski walking the stage in San Francisco. "Wow." Daisy said, "You truly are a profound man." "Yes, you're lucky having me. Listen my children; we're jumping forward and backward in story—three days, to him, hundreds of years. Lost his longbow, but it will be returned, up to us if he lives for message to be spread." Daisy, "Should we be writing down what you said?" "Don't care, all I ask is don't fail." gesturing toward wife, "Look at her." Martha, "You love us because you need us, whereas you need her because you love her!" Curious expression crossing face, retorted, "You've no clue about the game I play, you do however, get me."

Subsisting on berries, stomach burned painfully, physique altering drastically since comrade perished. Clouds remaining absent rain, thirst-alone drove him from grotto. Late-morning until next day he crawled, trousers fraying, revealing lower-torso ravaged by abrasion. It became obvious why he'd refused handling death rightly, he was afraid of it, position in military finally besting him. As he'd grown harder in physical nature, so did the balance within; forced coming to terms with all the tiny fractures an act such as war creates with it's iron chisel, nigh impossible. As he unraveled, considering the errs in his past, sins he'd committed were not limited to battlefield. "Commendations received for the marvel I was, how are they helping me now?" hushed quiet fell around him, Mother Nature relenting in torture, leaving him to thoughts. "Killed, dodged consequence, save for hangovers used receding guilty conscience. Cannot hold onto survival, those coming before taught incorrectly. Timothy was better-fit for this jungle than I! Sensed beast's approach, weapon in hand, yet it was *he* giving it a damn hug! And for what? So I could crawl as worm does, searching for morsels between choking roots! Why did I even save the damn man?! Whether ship and crew were laid-waste by sea or not, he'd still be here, creating peace treaties for primates!" tears rolling, accepting his part in misfortunes, "Wanted to stand alone, now know being alone."

Soft thudding, two humans running dirt path. They were considered original Natives. As civilizations advanced in industry, theology, religion, indigenous tribes resisted, remaining inheritors of surrounding region. "Come, instrument must be studied!" longbow in outstretched hand. Girl panted, "Something bad happened in there…" Woman nodded, observing a pool of dried blood near weapon. "Move *faster*, we go over this every time!" Ran path northwest, Mother glancing behind, finding herself alone. Returning around bend, "What is it?" she snapped, "Remember what happened to cousin when he stopped moving?" Child's eyes fixed downhill, "Strange sounds momma." Hearing moaning beyond the obscuring thicket, "Possibly an animal nearing grave–stay close." Holding bow like bludgeoning weapon, peered through leaves, keeping daughter away. "Father lets me see." "Shall have talk with father! Wait upon path, only staying long-enough seeing what it is." obeying her mother, running from potential danger. There, lay Westley, covered in bruises, cuts and abrasion. He was a white man from lands to the north–her people wanted nothing to do with his kind. Displeased, "Shall fetch the men. They'll carry intruder to my husband's hut, retrieving remaining value before he's put down." Westley, "To haunt jungle starved, foot soldier. Suppose if cannot get into Heaven, and Devil refuses for regretting, ghost could be something of a delight. Guess this is it–dying in discomfort. Leastways, proper amends for rotten things done. Enjoyed living; go today or tomorrow, die proud, British man!" Occasionally, one of theirs would venture into the wild, only to be found days later in similar condition. "Look at it this way, if both the Cardinal and Monarchy got it wrong, and I somehow make it to Heaven, Timothy will have proper map drawn to our desired destination!" hearing noise, over his fear of death, "Must be that panther…should've punched it harder. Wonder what would happen if I laughed at it really loudly." quickly rolling, yell-laughing sound's direction, spurious call making woman lose balance and fall into the open. Not having any human interaction for some time, "You help!?" She watched him closely, seeing if he'd lunge at her, making it easier watching him die later. Westley finally got a good look at the indigenous people inhabiting region; complexion dark, free from scarring, hair extending past buttocks, slender, shorter than what you'd find in England. She was strangely alluring to him, resisting lingering upon her breasts. "You're beautiful, help?" smallest of smiles forming–maybe she understood what he said. She maneuvered to his place on the ground and began looking him over, allowing her do as wished. "Leg's broken, cannot walk." discovering she wasn't alone, "Your daughter?" Understanding body-language more than his words, turned around scolding, "Said wait on path!" "What are we doing with him? White men are mean in stories told at mealtime!" "Too young knowing this, the men make-sport killing them, as they have our ancestors." Could tell from tone, deliberating over what to do. "Excited watching chase with spear!" "They will do such thing! A blind bird can tell he's been hurt, soon to perish absent help." "The village will serve him no better! Why are you changing your mind about the white man?" "Mind remains the same, there's something making me resist bringing him to our people." Shjoza peered curiously at Westley, eying him like a large, slimy snail. She pondered options saying, "We can keep him secret, nurse to health, learn while doing."

Moods improved since Westley's discovery. Mrs. Bit, bouncing joyfully, ***"NOT ONCE HAVE I FALLEN ASLEEP, ARRIVING IN BETTER-SHAPE!"*** "Last time, we lost two-hundred years off the Roman Empire." sharing laugh, ***"I THINK WE DID THE WORLD A FAVOR THAT TIME!"*** Joe, remembering middle-school, Joe, "Holy shit, you guys caused Pompeii?!" Eyeing Joe as if *in* middle-school, Byte, "Slumber allowed for creation of too many bathhouses. For years, debauchery distracted from warning signs. Fifteen minutes is all it took to be burned by holy fire." Martha supplemented, "What's mind-blowing, back then, no different from present; can't get on social media without losing faith in humanity. *FacialBooking* used to be platform where people connected, now graveyard of scammers, date-rapists." Daisy, "Year ago, posted about vaccinations developing generational illness, removed violating terms declaring it caused those viewing distress." Byte, "Like Martha said, today's no different. Idiots refuse completing challenge originally charged achieving, rest of us overworking while they dick around. Withholding, altering, outright disregard of information's indicative of sinners turning to sand against grain of adversity. Most-frustrating aspect; Mrs. Bit and I meet somewhere hoping people finally gotten shit together—visits only delaying us further. Fortunately, Martha has enough brains counteracting Joe. Here's what's coming next: Love." Joe burst into laughter. "Westley and Native going to hook-up?! *SWEET!!* She's doing all the work on account of his messed-up leg!" laughing, enjoying outlook during precarious situation. Byte, "Yes, *love*, crazy I know. Amidst adversity comes someone destined to meet. Week passed, mystery woman returning daily, bringing food, water, natural salves healing minor blood infection. Movement along jungle floor made broken bone move freely, causing seepage into surrounding tissue." Daisy interrupted, "Isn't that the definition of internal bleeding? Shouldn't he be dead?" "Stand corrected, *suffered* internal bleeding–better?" suppressing yawn, "Take over Mrs. Bit, know I'll dance over lovey-dovey details, leaving us short." Climbed from place via low-hanging wall, running around to stand in front. ***"SENSE CHEMISTRY BETWEEN WESTLEY AND MYSTERIOUS MUM!"***

    Listened hopefully for familiar footsteps. Shiva; unlike any encountered. Expectant smile remained fixed scanning hill above, waiting appearance upon path. Week since Shiva and Shjoza discovered, remained where found, patiently waiting return. Rumors heard about humans inhabiting turned resoundingly false; recalling drunken nights surrounded by shipmates, trading rumors about vicious, wild cannibals. Recently formed opinion, language didn't prove impasse; reading body language, attempting repeated vernacular easier to stomach than longwinded conversations with Countrymen. Looked at filthy hands thinking fondly of friends, then at Shiva's mock-splint. Crafted from three, fibrous plants grown naturally in those parts, great care was taken weaving. Upon administering, produced sturdy sticks fitting perfectly inside inner sleeve created sewing ends together. Westley's condition improved to such a state, had enough support coming to standing position, nearly all bodyweight on good leg. Absentmindedly fidgeted with pebbles waiting, later than usual. Was an undefined feeling whenever sharing space or jogging through mind lightening spirit. Able to tell from way caught her looking at him, feeling very much same way. Ears perked hearing familiar sounds of footsteps approaching direction from path, eyes meeting Shiva's soon as pair trotted downhill. Both smiled happily coming to halt, daughter carrying basket covered by rabbit pelt. Rising to sitting position, Shjoza lifted pelt away to reveal lunch gathered night before under cover of darkness.

    "Morning, how are you?" Adept at learning, Shjoza, "Morning good, yes." mother eyeing in surprise. "Friend's taught too much. All it takes is father hearing, gather every warrior in village finding!" "Like father wants to spend time, all *he* cares about are warriors! Maybe this man has friends; board ship, leaving for paradise!" "Not to speak of things! Remember last, village idiot thinking he belonged amongst

white man? Tied to log, pushed to sea on northernmost tip."
"I was told village permitted joining–how terrible!" Shjoza
tossed several, thin squares comparable to rice cake. "Too
young dealing in affairs of elders. Why find it necessary
wedging?" Smiling triumphantly, "Think those old birds
know what they are doing? *Ha!* Sent most-recent casualty out
to sea tied to a log!" Shiva wanted to disagree; no denying
impact members of community have settling on salty
disposition. Outlanders always pose danger to culture, way of
life. Historically speaking, reason people came here was
escaping tyranny from early, Spanish Inquisition. Decades
ago, viewpoints held against white man were instinctual. "No
matter your opinion of elders Shjoza you must respect them;
from greater adversity than either you or I. Ignored white
friend too long, see way he looks at me?!" attention on
Westley, watching, munching food. "Westley." moving hands
demonstrating work. "More next day. Find way, how say…"
Looking deeply into eyes, held-up hand telling was not
problem. "Saved from death; wait, even coming late." Shjoza
explained, "Hide from all in grasses tall. There, I stare,
looking everywhere for mother while she weaves." Language
skills developing, impressed with intelligence of young child.
"Know it skin." gesturing toward arm, "Cannot win." Into
basket, Shjoza retrieved drinking water contained inside stone
with bored-out center, gulping contents in seconds. "Shiva,
how long? Beasts looking to erase." Helping translate,
"Wants to know when can come with, afraid being eaten."
Nodding, searched sign of anger, ill-will. "No outlanders.
Fight there, now, we are here. I like you, them, kill." Having
lived entirely different way, sincerity was found written on
face, accustomed to typical, showboating style of era. "Can
wait, not bait." reaching, hoping would do same, hesitated,
then reciprocated. "You, guest, leave you to rest." Shjoza
bouncing around in joy. "Quiet down, last thing needed is
Crygal finding." A deep, guttural voice, "Nothing remains
from knowledge!"

Warriors wielding spear ambushed from all sides
dragging Westley from reach. Shiva tried getting to him,
easily subdued as Crygal entered scene. "Heard from sighing
wind carried forth by nosey neighbors, *"Shiva's out all night
in tall grasses!""* striding through warriors gazing upon
newest prisoner, "What more have you been hiding?!"
placing foot on Westley's chest, forcing air from lungs. Held
by family members, angrily shouted, "What was I to do
Crygal?" Stormed wife's direction striking with hard

backhand. "As we always do with. They rape land, leaving it smoking and empty! Know nothing of nature, what it truly means living under endless sky! Know nothing of us, return them to dust!" warriors cheering, beating Westley. "*STOP!*" trying to free herself, "Kill him, kill me; know of nothing but war, attacks never coming! White or not, love more than you!" party grew quiet, all staring at Westley. Filling with rage, "You *LOVE* him!? If this is how moon separated from sun, ripping far away!" pointing weapon threateningly, "You will bleed throughout jungle—not in death! Spreading remains across island so place learns your wickedness! Take this *thing* to village, let's see how worthy your love is!"

"Nice knowing everyone, should I just, let myself out?" *"DON'T QUIT UNTIL REFUSED ANOTHER PAGE!"* Daisy and Martha were busy going over Byte's riddles to help Westley's chance of survival. "Don't need that, explaining what's happening." Martha, "We're thinking *now;* what good are details used in hindsight after we're dead?" Impressed, "Alright; you first—make it snappy." Daisy, "Shiva and Shjoza found longbow, what they did with it, mystery. Up to us if message is spread…" Mrs. Bit, *"SOLEMN DUTY POSITIONING, FOSTERING ENERGY INTO STORY WORTH REDEMPTION!"* Concerned, Joe, "You guys haven't been listening, prisoner to crazy spearheads, about to be delivered like passing sprinkle! Newfound love's preventing that?" Byte, "Held prisoner until Crygal faces in fight to the death. Mindfulness is our biggest ally; injured, but Westley is a warrior, born fighter for this moment." Mrs. Bit continued dancing-about adding, *"REMEMBERING WESTLEY'S STRENGTHS, INCORPORATING NEWFOUND FEELINGS—POINT NO ARMOR CAN RESIST!"* Joe, amped about upcoming battle, "Beating Crygal at his own game while winning the heart of his woman!"

Westley crumpled onto ground, restraints severed. Encircled mass opened, Crygal yelling at fellow tribesman. "How he came amongst; water moccasin winding through water! No interrogating; slight will be addressed sundown." Westley scanned crowd for Shiva and Shjoza, too many villagers gathered witnessing commotion. Grabbed roughly, carried to where wooden cage sat, barely fitting canine. Forced inside, peered scene around, remaining calm while villagers stared as if animal for sale. "Dealt with men like

Crygal, intends fighting." courtship taken seriously back home, only imagine punishment in third-world cultures.

Village rested atop northern peninsula jutting into Atlantic like bent needle. Released from cage, approached Crygal stood. By looks of it, whole village present; majority cross-legged in large semi-circle. Looked left and smiled catching Shjoza and Shiva. Fear and concern filled eyes, both aware of ritual taking place. "Opportunity redeeming ancestors from deeds of the white devil! Fled burning villages, leaving elders to die while pale-skins advanced! With forked tongues persuaded, killing us while we slept!" cries of outrage, "Again, white man pushes into home trying to live amongst! What do we say to the white man?" Whatever Crygal said struck personal, warrior jogging to Westley, looking him up-and-down before handing battered spear. Words Timothy shared regarding natives did nothing stirring confidence, knowing men and women in Amazon wield spear for most their natural-born life. Taking spear in both hands, hobbled to area's center where Crygal stood orating. Aiming spear at chest, "Creeping around our lands searching weakness! Poisoned minds of Shiva and Shjoza, tricking with strange charm! Breaking smolder; filling with holes so we can see evil pour from his flesh!" Jeering quieting, Shjoza yelled, "No bait!" Pivoting, readying spear, "Need more stopping, telling now." Not understanding, Crygal jabbed to skewer shoulder, Westley swiftly countering, knocking lethal end away. Never wielding spear, chose approach similar to fencing, keeping from harms reach while remaining standing with broken leg. Knew if not cautious on weight transfer, leg would buckle under weight, left defenseless to any sort of assault. Observed enemy, switching between Crygal's stance and own. Westley smiled, frustrated from single parry. Correcting stance, Crygal lunged for abdomen attempting to send onto back. Westley parried early, countering with move practiced during swordplay. Spear deflected toward face avoiding glancing blow, parry completed, transferred spear into right, reaching with left, grabbing ahold of Crygal's, delivering solid punch with spear-hand. Stared at confiscated spear in disbelief, driven into tantrum from combat poise. Audience roared; lone man humiliating leader. Inspecting spear, tossing Crygal's near feet, "Shiva; unworthy being husband!"

Crygal assumed untrained fighting—piss-poor appearance working to advantage. Enraged, disregarded proper form charging, shrieking like banshee, substantiating enough force testing. Charging dead-center, Westley twisted on broken leg, falling, watching deadly spear thrust into empty air above. Pushed mightily on broken leg, rolling, rising to one knee, countering with quick swipe, making contact with hipbone. Resolve increased with each successful parry and counter delivered until Crygal screamed string of guttural words–battle becoming unfair. Three warriors strode forward at command brandishing weapons. Ball formed in throat, searching area for anything leveling playing field, sizeable rock short distance away. Lunging leap, grabbed with both hands rolling onto back, rising hard as he could bringing arms over head. Aim was true, bludgeoning two, bouncing off faces–rendering unconscious. Panting, recovered holding spear like bayonet, "Join forces with him, otherwise…" comprehending, retreated to Crygal's side combining forces. Aware of weaknesses Westley couldn't hide, Crygal swept furiously at legs. *"FUCKING ARSE!!"* staggering backwards. Battle had to end now, *decisively.*

Tested spear flexibility, seconds before Crygal resumed slashing, sending into waiting points behind. Years of downrange battle took hold; transferred weight from bad leg taking aim, arm coming forward in a blur, crowd gasping. Arriving upright, lips became thin line; spear piercing neck clean-through, penetrating halfway down shaft. Weapon fell from hands, clattering in a cloud of dust, falling to knees gurgling blood. Crygal eyes met Crygal's across square; devoid of emotion, watching archaic modality held onto die with. Fell limply to ground, thrown spear piercing into dirt. People gawked at fallen leader, uncertain how to respond. Was Shjoza breaking rank, running to center of battlefield, none stopping as she threaded through family arriving beside Crygal's crumpled body, "Mother and I disagree with father about the white man! Not color of skin need being afraid of, but what war brings! If any is against Westley, speak now, joining father in error." approaching Westley, raising hand, "Life is spared!" Approval, villagers clapping and shouting welcoming to family. Shiva made it to where Westley and Shjoza were, hand finding his. "My King."

"CAN'T BELIEVE WESTLEY DID THAT!!" Joe screamed, "When he went to throw, thought for sure he was going to miss and die in shame!" Daisy wiped tears saying, "Liked part when she called him her King!" Joe looked across table like she had cooties and said, "Admit it babe, Westley reminds you of me." Smiling coyly, "Depends, would you throw a spear through crazy guy's neck to be with me?" barely letting her finish, "Of course–unless it was him!" nodding at Dr. Byte. "Fortunately, spears are thing of the past. Speaking of..." heading to kitchen for speared pickles. Martha, pushing thoughts forward, "Rescue's about only thing left." *"WESTLEY'S DISCOVERED LOVE AND ACCEPTANCE–RESCUE HAS CONSEQUENCE!"* Inside kitchen, "Absolutely. Focus energy into family Westley has." returning with jarred pickles, "Should've grabbed these hours ago."

With diligent work, Westley learned new language, inheriting something no white man ever had. Not permitted Crygal's position, Shiva continued leading, leaving Westley practicing spear and archery. Finely-crafted arrow drove deeply into tallgrass target. Shiva, looking away from shot, "Fit hunting before Winter's roll!" Laughing encouragingly, "Warriors will be thankful. Tip; hold too tightly on string. Pull not on string but arrow." Shjoza sprinted downhill yipping, ramming into abdomen. *"Oof!"* collecting for hug, "Wish catching unaware, yell after closing gap. What good's war cry if intimidate nothing, giving location?" Pouting, "Training, develop style formidable as yours!" Shiva, "Not to learn until weighing more than strength required shooting." "How will I know?" Westley, "Shall weigh!" cuddling in fatherly affection, Shjoza cackling. "Not quite heavy en—" not believing eyes, sailing their direction none other than *Cortana.* Part of him clicked heels cheering, newer part experiencing something else. Shiva, "Your people?" nodding response. "What will happen?" Stared into distance trying to sense intentions carried by easterly breeze. "To retrieve myself, late comrade. Must return to beach, what they would have of me." "Going also." Jogged path, on same beach in two hours. Ship made progress toward location, man peering at him from crow's-nest. Dropping anchor, rowboat splashed into ocean, four men dipping oars rhythmically into water. As boat's underside graced sandy shore, Westley walked to tide's edge meeting. "Stay where you are, identify yourself!" staring at destroyed uniform in disbelief. Pointing at ship anchored some meters away, "Colonel Westley Overturf of *Cortana,* ship battered by storm last summer." "Aye." sailor replied, *"Dreariest* in expedition history. Night alone, lost ten." continued, "Anyone else ashore? Private Timothy Whittle?" "Timothy and I washed overboard, managed making-it some time until cornered, eaten by panther." dismay crossing faces of sailors before him. *"No good; reason sent retrieving–most-valuable cartographer in British Navy!"* Westley frowned, search-and-rescue encompassing recovery of one, Timothy Whittle. *"No bearing to his level of importance." "Savant in area of expertise–sorely missed. What of you, ready leaving?"*

"See no one representing themselves as family." gaining support, *"Returning to ship with us!" "NO!"* Westley yelled turning to escape. Boots in better condition, overtaken and dispatched without difficulty. Face shoved into sand, grabbed roughly at arms and legs, carried to waiting rowboat, clubbed with bayonet to obtain compliance. Eyes refocusing ten meters into ocean, resisted with all his might, kicking and elbowing until restrained with rope.

Brig clanged open, Westley stuffed inside. Shaking barred door, ***"LEFT FOR DEAD! SHOULD'VE STAYED!"*** sailors ascending narrow steps. Rage filled chest cavity, yelling until throat tattered. Voice called, "Year in isolation, first thing heard is wished deserting responsibility to remain wild animal." Commodore's outline stepping into sunlight filtering through porthole. "Left a proud member of the Royal British Navy, returned savage as people claim befriending! Have you gone *mad?"* "Found clarity. Only disillusionment done by hands of Countrymen, training ourselves to kill." Commodore laughed uncaringly, keyring flipping around index finger. "In case you've forgotten Colonel, do not have authority making such judgment calls. Returning to homeport, there, brought-up on desertion charges. Errant fool refusing rescue, now, you'll suffer for it." moving returning to quarters, banging hard against iron bars. ***"UNHAND ME MUTINOUS FOOL!"*** Westley found Commodore's throat, twisting, man crumpling to deck absent whisper. Keys from lifeless hand, unlocked cell, walking boldly onto upper-deck, climbing into rowboat, escaping without notice.

Shiva and Shjoza watched events, retreating fearing men would cause great harm. Gathered villagers telling what happened as ship disappeared beyond Earth's curve. Shiva and Shjoza remained atop peninsula all night.

Using moonlight, Westley struggled maintaining course, gliding lonely water two days, managing large, arcing circle. Strength exhausted, lay moaning, rubbing bleeding blisters. *"Shiva!"* through cracked, bleeding lips, *"Please, like first time."*

"Feel him out there fighting course of tides, growing weak! We must *do something!"* Shjoza blinked away tears while looking up at her mother. "Can you *feel* where he is? Never heard love spoken of in such a way." To Shjoza, Shiva felt as if she was vibrating. On cliff's edge, posture poised, hair blowing gently in seafaring breeze. Sun setting, could wait no longer. "Stay Shjoza; sense something. Ground rumbles beneath, Great Spirit urging action! Cannot sit any longer, allowing *only* man ever loved to die alone absent stormy seas!" Shiva rose and tearing-off in direction of path leading where her people stowed canoes. Confused by actions of love-struck adults called after, "Left on ship! Can you be certain he's ever coming back?"

Days of constant exposure had taken toll; scorched skin blistered and raw, taking likeness of reddened, worn leather. Was still too dark to scan area around for land and given hope on finding way back home hours before. Gentle, lapping of waves was all senses allowed record; almost gone, slowly dying of thirst inside wooden tomb. "Even bird pauses for laugh." calling noise in distance. Waking world slipped away, falling unconscious waiting to meet Maker.

"Westley! Westley!" Shiva yelled out over darkness of early morning in canoe, guided by nothing other than heart. With each pass of small oar longing reached out into cold sea searching for purpose. She continued shouting into silence, carrying with her all hope left in Creation. Pace matched racing heartbeat; unable to give up whom believed so strongly in. "Row into sea until perish if means staying with you. Please love, my heart song, gone so long. Cannot imagine jungle without jingling laugh or canopies without sheltering arms–return to me! Do not let ocean tear us apart!" crying, unwilling to relent in search. Response to emotional outcry– *empty waters*. Called again to quiet sea around, seeking deliverance.

There you were unable to stir, where are you now handsome sir? Where is us; can it exist without being rushed? Please

Seagull pierced morning sky with lonely cry. Nothing, then, rowboat materialized. Shiva dug oar into water, crying at sight of Westley's prone form. Abandoning canoe, made the seven-kilometer journey home.

Daisy, "Wow, Shiva's *dreamy!*" Mrs. Bit returned to seat sighing, ***"FANTASY AND REALITY WOUND INTO PACKAGE!"*** Byte glanced watch, snapping fingers getting attention. "Time's running short, seconds to prepare for story finish as destiny intends. Joe, if you speak out of turn I'm throwing brine all over you." settling into seat, remaining silent, "British are coming; angry–looking for blood. Westley had no option; killing Commodore chance returning to Shiva. Heading direction are three dozen, armed British soldiers, arriving in ten hours' time brandishing muskets, killing anyone in the way. Only choice is how we choose handling. Ideas?" Joe said, "Probably bringing every able-bodied person!" Daisy, "Remember Westley's trap? What if we created another?" Impressed, Martha said, "Might be clever enough to work! Infantry's following path single-file. If managed drawing-out Westley, muskets inferior to ambush tactics." Byte smiled happily at Storyweavers. "Won't count chickens before hatched, good feeling about second strategy." Joe pumped fist into air and cried, "Let's take the jungle to these assholes–*where's* that panther?" "Stick to strategy; creating masterful plan disillusioning enemy."

"White sails!" Shjoza pointing toward far horizon. "As expected." Westley turned addressing those gathered, "Not enemy because of skin, threaten everything worth keeping! Must band together, taking battle to jungle!" Many weren't used to hearing Westley talk of battle. Shiva, "Cannot fight a war not prepared for. Remember hunting cliffs taken to?" "Swine Line. Misdirect, entrapment within crevice?" "Only way boar are hunted without serious injury." Thinking strategy, "Shjoza as bait..." "What?" removing from earshot, "Particular way these men operate." Shiva interrupting, "No bloodshed, forcing people engage in battle!" "Plan requires none perish, using Shjoza as lure–off-guard at sight of young child, then, have her run. How goading–Countrymen aren't stupid." Tone softened realizing plan involved pacifism.

"Skilled weavers capable doing great lengths; disguise Swine Line." Nodded asking, "Throw Shjoza to other side?" "What if cannot run?" Never once allowed venturing alone, danger found even along path. "No stopping, no getting cornered." Plans set, women wove cover fooling keenest-eye.

Men hastily exited, forming rank. Last boat touched sand and Captain Jill jumped swiftly ashore. "As you know, here in search of one man and one man alone. Colonel Westley Overturf is wanted for crimes announced: Desertion, murder, treason–killed on sight. Delusional, most-likely lying in wait. Not leaving until recovered corpse!" Focused militia maintained seasoned alertness, none taken to environment such as this. Humidity robbed breath, sweat stinging eyes, majority drinking canteens. "Mustn't disturb wildebeest; single file, limit noise." Slow-going first two hours, holding shoulders in some cases, eventually reaching a clearing. "Fan-out, could be him!"

"A CHILD? HALT!"

Shjoza locked-eyes with Jill leaning against boulder. "Catch in game of hide-and-seek, maybe Westley's yours to keep!" climbing boulder yipping, vanishing. "Person nabbing gets commendation upon return!" Shjoza dashed, constantly drawing militia to location, jumping obstacle, maintaining distance from approaching war party. Not once for two hours, did she stop, nearly running headlong into trap. Reaching Swine Line, fell exhausted. "Shjoza!" yelled Westley, "Are the British coming?" Gasped, "Bait good!" Villager beside, "Cannot suffer open war!" Soared over masked covering, crab-walking embankment so enemy would cross, hoping British followed standard engagement, forming ranks entering, discovering Shjoza. Tribe's finest Amazonian Spearman, Westley, Shiva with longbow lay in wait, ready defending village. *"YOU!!"* Jill screamed pointing bayonet her direction, "If don't reveal whereabouts of Colonel Overturf, shall open-fire!" *"OW,* hurt and no move!" Scoffed, "Went through jungle silly girl!" advancing toward camouflaged trap–not fast enough. Shjoza recognized this yelling, *"COME GET ME SIRS!"* scampering uphill, Jill screaming, *"GET HER BEFORE I SHOOT HER!"* men sprinting, stepping onto woven covering, tumbling into inescapable depths. Warriors charged in well-executed ambush, Westley engaging Jill in close-quarters combat. "Should've known!" swiping bayonet in long sweep, stopping advance. "Forced into brig aboard own vessel, what did you think would happen?" quick thrust agile man dodged. Sidestepping, assaulted upper-torso in a slashing motion. Injuries long-since healed, Westley fell backwards pushing away with feet, pressing shaft hard into dirt, rebounding with a strong attack, piercing abdomen. To those trapped, "Remaining until surrendered. Once offered, board ship never to return, or join."

Everything grew comfortably quiet. Byte gazing at traffic, "Three days; how long it took for British troops surrendering, unwilling laying down lives accustomed. Returned delivering message to the King in Westley's handwriting."

"Those lost to storm perished, crushed to bits by relentless waves."

"GUIDED WESTLEY TO PARADISE; REMAINDER OF DAYS WITH THOSE MEANT TO BE WITH, CONTINUING ADVANCEMENT OF PEOPLE UNDER HIS GUIDANCE!" Daisy fighting yawn, "Can't believe we did something right!" Joe stretching, "Knew Westley had the balls fighting own Countryman!" Byte regained everyone's attention over eggs, decaffeinated coffee. "Earned liberty; three days, however, event could trigger any time." Joe complained, "What are you talking about three days?! Are you out of your damn mind?" Byte, unwilling to hear anymore complaining, "Tough shit, nobody else's complaining." Mrs. Bit, ***"NOW SLEEP!"*** Storyweavers falling asleep.

Car doors slamming in constant, typical drone, travelers aiming for work appointments, brief, moments of leisure. Kyle thanked groggy driver, tipping, reminding about luggage. Part making Carmen nervous; snuck into vehicles unnoticed dozens of times, caught at this, crucial point. Pushed Kyle's bag against trunk lid, praying when opened, promptly fall to ground, decreasing likelihood being spotted. Foot quickly pushing bag downward, did body roll tucking legs–passing as pile of worn clothing. Ploy in positioning paid off; duffel falling to asphalt, unnecessary looking inside. Carmen waited to count of five, giving Kyle time walking through doors separating drop-off from ticketing/baggage claim. Depressed latch allowing passenger seat swing forward, climbing casually out, sliding over, lifting seat to rightful place. Stowaway procedures completed, glanced at dumbstruck driver in rearview. Smiled innocently saying,

Inside, paused near elevator ensuring she hadn't been followed. Peeking through entryway, found Kyle standing in one of several ticket lines. "Wonder where he's going…" unable imagining him going anywhere noteworthy. Observed woman wearing oversized moo-moo get in line behind Kyle and start talking into her purse. "Sorry *SNOOKUM'S*; left a sticky-note, they'll stow you safely!" Turned away from baffling scene admiring unique atmosphere only experienced at Denver International Airport. Lofty ceilings rose more than forty feet, smell of sweets from tourist-traps throughout concourses titillating. Most-impressive feature was miles of track underneath; ideal for international transport hub, allowing optimum tarmac usage, safe transport to and from concourses. Leaned against wall before women's restroom, viewing primary walkway prior to security. Unusually busy for Tuesday, so distracted by cute boy, almost missed Kyle entering bathroom. "Stay focused, wouldn't know what to do with him anyway." Target exiting, proceeded-on to escalators. Overhead, *"Please have documents ready prior to security."*

Discovered area right of security where offices and detainment rooms existed, moveable wall with security glass.

Rummaging pockets, fingers enclosing around circular object–
1620 battery. "Can't believe how lucky I get*!*" enough metal
setting-off detector, person ushered into additional security.
Didn't take long spotting man behind Kyle engaged in phone
conversation. "Bingo was his name-o." Searched shabby
clothing for inconspicuous, time-consuming place. Reaching
escalator, used higher-vantage lodging it in bulging waistline.
Suddenly, he yelled at person having conversation with,
backhanding Carmen. Fell in stunned shock, landing hard at
escalator's start, travelers making adjustments preventing line
from toppling. Strategy botched prior to execution, "Piece of
shit*!* Hard to believe, but there's more people here than you*!*"
grabbing phone, chucking it to floor twenty feet below.
"WHY'D YOU DO THAT ROTTEN BRAT!?" onlookers
outraged by his audacity, bulldozing everyone rescuing phone.

Reaching security*,* walked along shop entryways
dotting perimeter. In minutes, Kyle would be on to departure-
gate, Carmen, flaw on mission success-ratio. What happened
next was described by the news as "puzzling airport incident".
Screeching followed by a thunderous crash, escalator
malfunctioning, one most-unfortunate, plummeting over
railing, breaking his leg, procedures coming to standstill.
Carmen neared moveable wall carrying security glass, putting
years obstacle training into action. With a running start, leapt
placing foot on round, silver doorknob, pushed extending
arms, fingers curling onto other side. Up and over, pushed-off
pivoting, transferring impact into roll. Disappointed skills
went unnoticed, "Can't wait telling Lashy*!* Pull that off again,
uploading to *MeTube!*" Considerable panic and confusion
other side of barricade, personnel moving diligently reaching
injured, Kyle onlooker to peculiar accident. *"Extra time…"*
plopping onto floor, practicing finger exercises. Hand
following other in smooth, liquid-like motion, "Miss my glove
lights*!* Maybe after this, Lashy will let me keep them*!*"
Enjoyed testing physical limitations, but favorite pastime
would always be gloving, relatively-new form of expression
following dance music. Unfortunately, considered precursor,
accessory to underlying drug culture. Alas, place world had
come to–self-expression came a with price. Last decade,
discrimination against various flow arts*(hooping, poi,
dancing)*, way for those with pride and prejudice controlling.
Even at adult music venues, freedom of expression banned*;*
stories of confiscating possessions, employees not willing
return unless offered money. Paramedics transferring man
onto wheeled stretcher, "How do I sneak onto a plane*?*"

Kyle witnessed snob violently push a little girl, then, tremendous screeching, citizens falling due to malfunctioning elevator. Reporter in every sense, would've loved sinking his investigative teeth into story like this, recalling an incident at Kings Cross Station in 1987. Subway transit system used old, outdated, wooden escalators lacking proper maintenance, catching fire from a buildup of oil and grease upon rotating mechanisms. This residue ignited, killing thirty-one passengers, injuring hundred thirty-one.

Lines zippered into one, intercom directing traffic to stairs between escalators, elevators behind. Belongings searched, located gate amongst numbers and letters printed on ticket. "C38. They would put Kansas at last, available gate." Navigated toward underground tram thinking about recent contracts D.I.A. signed for–controversial to public. Tons of additional dirt was removed during excavation, supposedly done increasing tram safety. Officials were unable accounting for volume of material removed, ridiculed unkempt, tonnage remaining piled outside airport for months. There was also conspiracy involving horse statue with glowing, red eyes named *Blucifer* positioned outside entrance. Stirred adoration much as it instilled fear, rumors of government organizations forcing personnel to remain silent about the nature behind it's creation and placing. Conspiracy theorists were certain they'd linked construction project and *Blucifer* to fallout shelter built protecting the World's "most-valuable" from nuclear winter. Regardless of reason for construction, wasn't end of negative attention received, blaming renovation delays on numerous, safety violations. According to those involved, errors made in purchasing materials, combined with inability putting-forth progress, airport hemorrhaged profit. Whatever reasons for strange happenings at one of the busiest airports, pushed thoughts aside, tram stopping other side of stainless-steel doors. Chose standing, avoiding frustration upon exit. Family and woman in hoodie sat in front enjoying the architectural designs lining tunnels. Little did Kyle know, this was the beginning of his new life, freed from the influence of others.

Climbing to feet, excitement swelled anticipating underground transit system, sitting on carpeted bench watching hundreds of pinwheels oscillate. Snuck-in ahead of deliberating Kyle, turning to curved, front-windshield, prerecorded voice saying, *"Doors are closing, please keep clear and hold on for departure to, Concourse A."* Marveled at train's speediness, fighting giggling with toddler alongside. Concourse A and B came and went. At C, tied shoelace allowing Kyle exit, struck by brilliant idea. Galloped stairs, smell of food overpowering, salivating from idea of eating McBurger's. Quiet as a mouse, snuck-up behind Kyle deftly retrieving his wallet, landing comfortably on moving-platform opposite direction. "No pictures, no cash." Carrying bankcard, walked into open lobby of McBurger's. "No line, just the way I like it!" slamming card on counter, "Number one please, freedom fries!" "Airport rules require ID matches name on the card to make a purchase, we've had complaints about unauthorized charges." Mimicked searching, finding pair chatting near entrance. Straightening posture, "Father's very important and doesn't like interruptions, okay if he just waves?" Cashier hesitated, relenting.

Carmen shouted, "*DADDY!*" praying businesspeople would notice, shorter, Oriental man raising hand.

"Didn't take after your dad." "Everyone says that. Should see mom; six foot three, two hundred fifty pounds." grabbing to-go bag, leaving cashier ogling. Walking past men, "Thanks pops, have some fries!" tucking greasy handful in suit's front pocket before waltzing away. Leaning against platform railing, hungrily unwrapped burger, shredded lettuce flying all directions. Scanned concourse looking for Kyle, easily seen from a distance. Eating, "Think I'll keep wallet for a bit!" stifling laughter seeing destination. Sitting at gate across, "How am I sneaking onto plane heading to Kansas at night?" Minutes performing act of terrorism before aircraft departed, reporting failure. Hardened gaze toward C38, monitored by sleepy flight clerk. "Time to get ninji!" Walked along rows of seating, waiting caddy-corner of smaller gate. Scanning with peripheral vision, Kyle was seated twenty feet away, back facing to her. In a lucid blur, mapped projected path avoiding possibility of recognition. Needing distraction, foot traffic minimal, bit lower lip anxiously, beginnings of mission failure creeping-in. Seeing family of five approaching flight desk, moved for open concourse door while distracted. Performing slalom into passageway, waited hearing someone shout, forcing her into mad dash. Slowing, awkwardly tiptoed through loud, reverberating tunnel hoping footsteps wouldn't alert. Nearing hallway's end, "Carmen, may've pulled this off." nearing door to steps descending to tarmac. "Pray for open hatch*!*" Pulled roughly, hastily opening, climbing down metal steps to ground, walked to plane's nose searching for baggage crew, spying them working together at aircraft's rear. This hour, passengers were occasionally offered front seats due to odd traveling times to closer destinations. Due to nicety, luggage was stored in spacious, rear-cargo hold. Carmen whispered, "Impressed use normal-sized planes to Kansas, figured only options were biplane or medium-sized tornado. " At plane's nose, ran to rear wheel, gauging location of luggage loaders. Guy nearest, "Yeah, thought about calling her, but read online there's mandatory forty-eight-hour rule I should follow to not look desperate. " Other, tossing bags from trailer, "Ain't no forty-eight-hour rule where I come from*!* In my hometown, either you got it, or you don't. " In her opinion, both lacked minimum requirements necessary catching a woman's interest. "How many times do I have to tell you, Mom's sick and needs help. " Heaving large one over, "Change excuses why ladies won't date you, sickly mother angle only gets pity lays*!* Probably land someone who owns dozen cats and dresses them*!*" "That's Mom's friend Wilma, comes over Friday nights and watches *My Feline Failure. **DON'T THROW THAT!*" Looking at what he was about to throw. "Probably would've done it a favor, come look*!*" walking to coworker, getting look at whatever it was. Distracted, Carmen successfully stowed into cargo-hold while men gawked inside luggage. Pulled large bag over small frame, hiding from view, nearly choking on horrendous smell, "Why'd it have to be a hockey bag*?*" outside, "Loading last so we don't squish it. " Made quick work of what was left, bringing purse into hold near Carmen. "Here; best chance surviving takeoff. " gently onto floor, strolling away. Sat in eerie silence, waiting hearing alarm, announcement indicating stowaway terrorist. Sudden hissing noise, hatch slowly closing. Thrust bag off, clicking heels of worn high-tops, "There's no place like home*!*"

Kyle worried about upcoming rent. "Guess Mrs. Cantwell would take me. Mumsy and I could fend for ourselves on mattress in living room. " Was vendetta against Aries Industries worth the effort? Many done same, ending one of countless, raving lunatics. Wasn't something spoken-of, World taken notice of glaring coincidence and turned blind eye, deciding connection to Aries worth more than life. Certainly no going back, nothing about old life valued, Dr. Jekyll/Mr. Hyde version. Personality change thought temporary ingrained, resulting in fluctuating self-worth. If didn't make good on past mistakes, vindicating from career disaster, next setback would be far more costly. No turning back; visited aging mother, sourcing reason behind recurring night visions. If it hadn't been for Gloria helping deliver, likely shipped to Denver orphanage. Unemployed, best spending frugally affording living in Denver, settled for peanuts and canned soda. Elderly flight clerk breathing into microphone, "Attention: Twelve-thirty departing to Wichita is now boarding. Small flight of only thirty-six passengers, all sections may approach and begin boarding." Kyle walked to podium, first in line, "What's point of establishing procedures if *choose* disregarding? Are handicapped to be muddled in and injured?" looking at ten or twelve people boarding.

Flight clerk tapped hearing aid yelling, "WHAT?!" in his face.

"Heard him all along, didn't want to deal with him." considering continuing conversation, instead, boarded without further issue. Stowing carry-on, settled into seat realizing he made plans without consulting Gloria. "Mom's game for spur-of-the-moment company, what I was in first the place. Better give her a call." retrieving beat-up, flip phone used since high school, pressing appropriate speed-dial, receiving greeting from kind woman raising since birth, "Hello?" "Hey Mom, surprise!" "What would that be at thirty after midnight? Don't tell me sending gift cards, have three you gave!" Made habit sending cards to favorite stores not in Kansas. Remembered response fondly, "Kyle, what you expect me doing with card to store I can't shop at?" "Age where robots can replace our military, it's called the internet. Let me walk through steps purchasing something online…" back to present conversation, "Sorry for calling late. On a flight heading for your town, interesting career developments, wanted to stop-in." "Happy haven't been forgotten! Cab for when you arrive?" Remembering no income, "Pinching pennies waiting for first client, would you?" "Taxi and piping pot waiting!" "Thanks Mom, better mood already."

No sooner closed cellphone, "I know you!" "Look buddy…" stopping, recognizing. "Yes you recognize me! For *I too*, am a news anchor! Kansas's on-scene news anchor, Channel 4's own, Marshall Zellinger—can I sit next?" Not feeling sociable, wanting nothing more than sending on his way, nodded. Sitting for roughly a second, asked, "Mind if switched seats? Deathly afraid of flying; seeing crash-site plummeting to our doom somehow soothes." "Makes sense." switching seats, Kyle retrieving magazine to deter additional conversation. "Probably aren't in the mood, asking anyways seeing you're Nation's current, conversation piece." Leaned seat prematurely replying, "Don't bother, fired for entire mishap." Raising eyebrow behind rimmed, designer glasses, "What about other guy, pizza guy? Please say they fired that Aries pet!" Returning upright, "Thanks for saying that. No, did not fire him, in fact, weird, lateral way *promoted* the bastard because now he's only anchor, running both segments." Laughed, "Channel 9 biting the big one! It's all the money invested." Impressed with investigative skills, "9's become so dependent on Aries, severely under-sourced contributors, nothing they can do but be advertising-plug." Woman startling earlier was also traveling to Kansas. In effort lightening mood, "Was upset she's on our plane, now I'm relieved; event of turbulence, balance-point or arguably, jettisoned cargo." Marshall blinked. "May not help your viewers Kyle, Kansas is top-fifteen in most-obese States." Embarrassed, "Second, worst day of my life; career ruined, investigating Aries Industries." Marshall stood ensuring none prying. "You know what happens to people investigating." "Working with Steven Hartigan, gleamed information making Hitler clap heartily from the afterlife." Gazing intently, "Level with me, investigation worth your life?" Pondering, "Guess you'd have to be me." Noise of disapproval, "Homebound flight next to newest scandal Country's seen in years–I'm your asset." "When I look at Aries robots something disturbs. Machines living amongst, if given command, perform mass-genocide." unloading, "Ex-coworker implanted microchip granting impunity, someone needs to put Aries under radar ASAP–not so far removed from history I can't smell hostile takeover." Jawline tightening, "Interview with Kansas Agricultural Board this month, facts proving helpful." "You dug it, out with it." "Seven separate counties report equipment responsible dispensing pesticides and hormones are malfunctioning." Hoping he'd misheard, "How bad is it?" results potentially catastrophic, creating foodborne illness, disease, genetic mutation. "Information from afflicted counties, *Computer virus laying dormant within Codex*". Messages to White House constituents have fallen on deaf ears; everyone's brushing whole thing under Auntie Em's rug. What I think; plan blowing us away, abandoning Earth altogether, leaving humanity in what remains." "If what you're telling's true, Food and Drug would be all over it."

"Behind in World Commerce–Ronald Tramp material!" Surprised, "Comes to information on current President, no one knows more." "Well-aware. Made habit watching broadcast every week. Used to think you obsessive, borderline disrespectful, however, information from correspondents every news outlet has redeemed you in that regard." Enjoying a deserved, moment of triumph, "I'll admit, thought I was making bad career-move digging-up the President's skeletons. What is it Tramp's done that I don't know about?" "Remember the recent, E-cigarette scare?" "Vitamin-E Acetate culprit behind lung-related illnesses." Reaching runway, "Go figure, substance described *'external-use'* making someone croak. With help from big tobacco and FDA, Tramp focused political sway into lobbying for banning E-cigarettes. FDA's preoccupied with controlled ban, little-resources responding to catastrophe." Deductive reasoning putting pieces together, "Lobbying this could be coincidence, does allow computer virus to operate unchecked–blaming persons unknown." Another grim fact, "Tramp's cut what he considers unnecessary funding, if it wasn't for electronic umbilical-cord…" "Think diplomats appreciate headline, "Technology giant **DOOMED** us all!"? Won't be hearing it from me, different approach no longer having 9 as resource." "You're great reporter Kyle, don't go mad chasing ghosts." Midnight moon shimmered atop crests of cloud, congregations of heating and cooling water-molecules hanging from invisible thread, light-pollution reflecting underside of storm front. Drifting to sleep, "Ghosts are least of my worries, greater shadows forming on-scene; rebuked renewal signifying chaos." Marshall powered cellphone, sending text to contact marked 'Copyrighted Criminal'. "Initiation approved."

Carmen brought head between knees stifling noise from whining engines. Had trip been less spur-of-the-moment, would've flown as underage minor through airport's VIP travel system; allowing first-class amenities, personal flying buddy. "No vomiting. If do, making sure it's in dude's hockey bag, might force him to do laundry." fighting phobia of death by falling. "Getting wherever headed, must consider revealing myself, carrying his wallet, don't see rightly returning." picturing Kyle ripping wallet from hands, pushing her to the ground, kicking repeatedly. "Whatever." Mindset Carmen used getting-over longing for companionship. Easier having foot out, planning payback. Despite beliefs on what love should be, best way avoiding hurt and disappointment, pushing all nearest away. "Just like you, caring about shmuck tracking, *why* is it so?" Dilemma, drain on happiness, though doing little perpetuating. Thought back to when placed before Commander Lashbrook, exposed to cruelest critic–herself.

Trembled in plank position, man reaching for heart buried amongst homelessness. "To everyone's surprise but you, deliberate act rendering us operationally limited. *Why* are you here? Streets will treat you better if do not participate!" Shifted weight noting how concrete pained elbows. "*Guess* I failed in self-control, caught for reprimands." Remained planking, defensive yet subdued, waiting for him bringing steel-toe onto small of back. "If toe-line was drawn on floor, keep from thinking way anymore. On your feet." Attempted rising, captor forcing posture downward–planking she remained. Stared defiantly at whom she considered new master. "Submit to no one, you're not my father!" Kidnapper relented dogged-focus, laughing, "Blessed being me rather than heart-stealing hooligan." With look cold as ice, "Far as I'm concerned you have *nothing*, it's already been taken. Streets remain; child in exile can still make her name." Kneeled, chiseled expression inches away, smelled of hickory and…. Lashbrook snarled, *"STAND UP!"* Rolled away, leaning onto backside, "When I stand, getting whatever I want, when I want." Crossed tan forearms shrugging, "Found you scrounging in a dumpster, accept humility. How you perceive yourself, worthless." Carmen looked away, remark hurting feelings. "People are watching my activities…was looking for a good shank. Soon as we're done I'm dipping, memorizing steps, haunting molesting ass from afterlife!" "No desire using in base-gesture." Whirlwind of nervous energy and anticipation sprouted, importance introduced to propagate potential. Watching suspiciously, "Kidnapped for *good*? Think you need to be replaced…unless have some, profound use for size one jeans!" "Dangerous men; cronies, sent to dumpster bothering–testing wit." squatting, gravel within tread scraping concrete, returning stare in moody, defiant glare. "Not sure how I feel; freak who sent goons enslaving, or you care." "Gain nothing aiding illegal trafficking; eternal thorn in lion's paw in war against evil." "Evil*?!* *GEE-WILLIKERS!*" Sat heavily at desk in room's center, grinding greying stubble. Irritated, "Don't deal with kids. If manage being an adult, sit in chair here and we can start over." Resting hands behind head, "Depends…trying any funny stuff? Let me tell you about three—wait *five*—losers sent tagging, thought they were clever, now they're where I wanted–***BOXED-IN LIKE SARDINES!***" Lashbrook stood from leather chair so abruptly, careened from imposing form, bouncing-off parked motorcycle. "Exactly what I need to know*!* Sent entire squad bagging your ass, yet to receive correspondence*!* What did you do to my subterfuge team*?*" Carmen laughing, "Can't figure out what happened to your X's and O's, crying to girl who bested asking forgiveness and favors*!*" Lashbrook marched toward, sitting down beside. Removing gravel wedged in boot tread, tossed it gently her direction, eyes meeting; man grasping elusive coattails of purpose, given memento of possibilities-lost. Life isn't ill from God's will; of deeper muscle, beating for those remaining still.

"Name's Brandon Lashbrook. Problem had is beyond where hailed and what we've done.*"* "I've been through a lot and don't process like you can, best if you're to the point. Can't deal with people when they're in front of me because I'm forced watching everyone live while fleeing from life*!*" "Why I spent effort getting you here. Organization's failing, remembered from narrowest window. Compromised; tested by World's One Channel and failed.*"* Unsung precedence; inner-workings of operation no longer confined to power-hungry strategists. Truth conceived, considered, confronted by aging, military traitor; if cannot place entirety in those coming after, won't have empty room filling with laughter. "Algorithm combed recesses, warning weakness. Obtain information, growing bestial during transmittance. Truly understanding, no longer fit being leader.*"* stood, removing USB from around neck, "Exchanging hands impassions commands. To those able, tomorrow's earned despite cat's cradle.*"* Titanium-alloy gleamed under incandescent lighting, *"Twitch"* etched into sides, low-resonance frequency producing noticeable humming. Carmen, "If God needs help, why kidnap*?*" Ignoring, "Listening to dead man's robot, giving everything to adolescent. Book inferred moment, cannot find wherewithal conveying. Confident intent will take root, emboldening purpose.*"* Despite inability answering questions, managed earning trust. "Let me put it this way, homeless, have nobody. Live on the streets and met spoiled sandwiches easier to swallow.*"* "Stop changing subjects, join and spare suicide by sidearm.*"* Wearily, "Does everything need to sound so dramatic*?*" Staring expectantly, "While we have you, see what Twitch thinks.*"* "*While we have you—* where do you get off? If part of this operation, gotta treat me right. Lashbrook beckoned follow down adjoining hallway, stopping in front of large, two-piece door identified as *CUSTODIAL CLOSET*. "Better not be an imprisoned cleaning slave*!*" "*Silly child!* Where creator's invention lives, The World's One Channel*;* us, God-loving folks prefer his pet name, Twitch.*"* knocking, standing attention, "Commander Lashbrook reporting to Twitch for inspection*!*" Banging and crashing, optic eyes darting from bronze-plated mail slot. "*NO!!* Thanks for showing your hideout—*!*" "Get over here*!*" dropped in front of Twitch.

Turbulence between stratospheres shook Carmen, reaching for USB, tucking beneath hoodie and T-shirt. "First thing, buying apology present with his money for stealing, ruining life past week.*"* Wasn't always privy to inner-workings of Lashbrook*;* considered methods doing business downside compromising split-leadership*;* man of direct, military strategy, whereas preferred hands-on approach.

Whimpering, purse-like bag moving. "Didn't think she had living thing inside*!* Surprised this an approved, TSA travel-method transporting domesticated animals.*"* On hands and knees, scampered to where bag sat, whatever was inside squeaking fearfully. Hands found golden zipper at far side and pulled gently, intertwining rivets giving, tiny, *adorably ugly* Chihuahua nestled tightly within confines. "Worst method of animal transport witnessed*!* If I wasn't in middle of something, lady would have new home for purse, up her rear– *HEY!* What's the matter with you anyways*?*" terrified someone other than owner accessing satchel. Carmen removed dog from bag, placing him gently in front of her. He flopped on his side before coming to rest, looking frightened. "You can't walk*?* Here, let me try standing you up*!*" lifting once more, setting upright on legs. Chihuahua teetered in place, falling with a thud. "Climactic. What's your name*?*" reading nametag. "Skittlez." handling newfound friend, "Your mine, hungry?" Shivered considering offer, hoping she's nice as seemed. Carmen ripped apart fries, placing them in front of his nose. Licked at salty morsels vigorously, whimpering to get her attention. Pushing bits into canine's mouth, "Befriending dog when can't take care of yourself!" Munching fries, lay onto side listening to engines, whipping of wind. Cradling Skittlez, "Best flight could've asked for."

Pilot announced descent into Wichita. Marshall, "Would've woken before descent, but you looked *just so cozy.*" Kyle yawned, stretching, "Don't see how you can be so cheery at…what time is it? Watch stopped working sometime after takeoff." "Some kind of day, encroaching upon two A.M." Debated telling best sleep in nights, passing for memorable approach. "Aren't doing some, crazy story on me? Trying to avoid embarrassment. Window watching, "If thought you bad company, wouldn't have asked sitting–friend in Channel 4." Gazed at one of Kansas's largest, sprawling cities. Based around agriculture and livestock, Kyle's mother chose Wichita for retirement, offering amenities no other community offered; rolling prairies, fast-paced city action short driving distance. "After handling business, look you up for a reference." Marshall jumped as landing gear engaged. "Sure, if there's anything I can do. Took liberty putting number into phone." Gesture strange, thanked feeling for device. Descent completed, passengers accessed overhead storage. Roughly slinging carry-on, "Why choose midnight flight? 4 trying to save a few bucks?" "Think you know more than most, on-scene reporters don't have routine schedule. Tomorrow, off to next killer story!" After passageway, extended hand. "Can't say when you'll be hearing from me, sure to watch–glimpse reporting poise." Returning handshake, "Watch evening; recap of recent, on-scene report. Won't give anything away, this way you'll watch!" "Long as I don't see grainy footage of me being fired, I'm in." Marshall traveled in direction of news station.

Landing-gear startled from sleep. "Sorry! Want more freedom fries?" Between elbow and forearm, answered staring with wide, wet eyes. "Better plan busting-out of this joint." walking to exit sealing from outside, "Would go au' naturale, carrying, since there's to be upset person looking for you, best keeping hidden. *Ah,* here's handle! Won't pull it yet, probably signals cockpit." Skittlez barking agreement. After grabbing purse serving as kennel, got him inside and sat against stack of luggage positioned right of exit. "Tucking you under hoodie keeping out of harm's way." dog kicking inside little bag, swaying gently back and forth. Daunting question presented; open cargo after taxiing, possibly alerting personnel, or wait for luggage crew, risking quarantine?

Go-cart and trailer rounded corner, employees handling baggage navigating toward aft cargo. "Don't care how many times try explaining Spirit Science, refuse believing there's some "Collective Conscious" life taps into. If this were true, why can't I hit on celebrities through the TV?" "Shows you were half-listening. Someone with only sex on their mind's incapable harnessing concept. Until you stop flaking, watch these videos, never will." grabbing for talkie, "Baggage crew to cockpit: Open aft-cargo for unload, thank you!" "Not Friday, pick day working for–*WHAT THE HELL!*" luggage falling to pavement–prior loaders playing twisted prank. "Got to be a first! Think we'll file report?" "Depends if anything's damaged, let's hurry before anyone sees this mess." Skittlez over shoulder, grabbed handrail, swinging with both arms, shimmying direction of side-entrance. Distance of twenty feet covered, suction-like grip weakened, unable eliminating noise sliding down winged vessel. Dropping, absorbed impact transitioning into a roll. Grunted standing, pair still removing incident. Course-of-action; sprinting toward staircase. Grabbing doorknob, "Got to be a glitch in the Matrix! That or flagrant disregard." Stalling, came upon maintenance staff getting floor cleaner operating, stating with much authority, "Gas goes here, oil there, cleaning-fluid everywhere!" Righting posture, "Don't get paid for this–where's your people?" "Soon following!" handing wallet, His daughter's waiting outside restroom, thanks Pumpkin!" handing wallet, walking away.

Worst part over, possibly-fruitful opportunity revealing herself, briefly imagining, "I'm from the "adopt a kid at the airport" program!" Darting around brick pillar, "Waiting here won't be too bad of a gig. Catch by surprise, maybe he won't be upset." slapping mouth harder than intended, forgetting buying present. Area deserted with exception of Skittlez's owner near baggage claim–looked forward to exiting theatrics. Despite how charming fourteen-year-old could be, some things not bothering and petty theft considered necessary. Target approaching, stuffed hands into hoodie finding fragment swiped from desk. "Perfect transition softening blow." Kyle's eyes filled with recognition and anger. "Why in hell did you think leaving damn sticky-note fair consolation invading privacy for your sleazy, criminal empire*!?*" Revealing peace offering, "Doing what I'm told. "Don't see why you bothered, how you stole my wallet*!*" reclaiming, "Did you buy anything*?!*" "Snagged McBurger's before cram-packing into plane's underbelly." Kyle's eyes bulged, interrupted by shriek from luggage reclamation, ***"WHERE'S SKITTLEZ?! WHAT DO YOU MEAN TINY PURSE CONTAINING TEACUP NEVER ARRIVED!?"*** Carmen stifling laughter. "Something to do with little development as well*?*" High-tops rubbing together, "Also threw phone, made an escalator break…poor, innocent traveler falling to injury–what a day*!* Can I crash with you*?*" Kyle's eye twitched, imagining handcuffing, never letting out of sight. "Might as well get thumb on you now before finding Earthly belongings plundered*!*" "Why'd come all this way*?* Can't imagine you having too many options." "Not like it happens to be any of *your* business, family here. It's my turn*:* What compelled you *stealing* woman's dog*?*" Brought finger to mouth as if pondering question, retorting, "Well, what would *you* want if were traveling in cargo hold, left to luggage of the Universe*?* Let me show what she put him in*!*" pulling hard at hoodie zipper, revealing breathing purse resting on hip. Remembering woman screaming into purse earlier, "Oh. Still remember larceny being punishable offense in our society. Try this one on for size*;* did you know your a terrorist*?*" Carmen snorted. "Can't say you're terrorist-worthy material." Exiting airport, observed purple colored taxi-van, tall, black man nearby holding cardboard sign, name written on it. Looking back in annoyance, responded, "Do I look like I have time for your problems*?* Going to have to solve them yourself. Keep-up if you want to pull orphan card getting fed." Somewhat impressed teen listened, clambering into open van. Cab driver smiled warmly, extending welcoming hand. "*Mr.* Clark– pleasure finally meeting*!* Name is Michael. Your mother's been using me as driver for last four years, getting about town when hip starts acting-up." smiled tiredly saying, "Thanks for helping mom about town. Let's get home before I fall asleep and forget I'm babysitting." Merging into left lane of Eisenhower Airport Parkway, Carmen smiled, yells of dog's prior owner fading in distance.

Shortly after three-thirty A.M., arrived at outskirts of Wichita, parking in front of Gloria's. Kyle approached driver-side door and shook hands with Michael before pulling away from col-de-sack, leaving in early-morning darkness. Creaking of porch door swinging broke quiet serenity, both turning around. Out from enclosed patio came elderly, silver-haired woman. Gloria Abadacoa was no ordinary woman. Lifelong career performing as CNA and midwife; hero in a flash during Misty Clark's death; example of woman destined mother, learning burdens involved through alternate means. Many attributes making Gloria worthy mother; blessed opportunity loving another, married and divorced, suffered watching those grown-up with, develop large, flourishing families–struggling with own mortality. "Hey Kyle! Told you I'd have someone waiting; Michael's been such a sweetheart! Plus, got a nice backside! *Who* do we have here?" woman's eyes falling on Carmen. Hands were shoved into pockets, kicking at fallen leaves grounded at autumn's start. Gazing disappointedly at forced, travel companion, "Name's Carmen, owes favor for stealing." "*HA!* Karma borrowing from my wallet! Good job young lady!" approaching for high-five. "He was *too easy* Mrs. C!" Finishing high-five, sweetly replied, "Call me mom, Gloria if you must. Quickly find mom's about only thing respond to nowadays. Sometimes, someone gets lucky and gets a ma'am out of me. Let's get you inside and caffeinated!" Kyle couldn't believe it; put in his place by teenage delinquent before breakfast.

House was situated on one and a half acres; maintaining large, vegetable garden, chicken coop. Paintings and memories covered walls inside her one-story home, Carmen finding embarrassing photos with ease. "How old were you, *twelve!?* Surprised it's not your mom!" Kyle lodged himself between, blocking picture in question. "Day I tell thieving dropout my story will be day I kick the can!" Gloria, "If can't learn to behave, giving both decaf. Sit, fill me in." Carmen didn't have to get invitation twice; no sooner did he take eyes from prom picture, newest annoyance made it into seat next to Gloria. Sitting, "Appreciate opening your home to us, may be biggest asset moving forward." "What's debacle making you drop everything?" "Quoting man, Steven Hartigan's "a fat furry fuck" who (A), got microchip implanted during lunch, (B), announced on live-television I violate Aspen's corpse!" Carmen recoiled exclaiming, *"EW!"* Angrily kicking chair foot rested on. "Feet off the furniture Smudge–*my* mom's house!" Gloria commenting, "Manners aren't your strong suit. Change of subjects, you employed?" Fighting lying, "Make more than him!" laughing at his expense. Sighing, "Like you said, change of subjects, talk later after toddler takes nap. Forgot what you feed teenagers putting them to sleep…do you have turkey?" Walked to cupboard sorting coffee mugs, delicately moving them about.

"*HEY!* Going to pour me cup, or leave newly-claimed dependent hanging by her heart strings?"

"How about grab a stool and find your own, or you going to swipe those too?" walking from kitchen into guest quarters, closing door. Listened wondering if he'd called it quits. "Guess it's coffee and sleep time for me as well! Where do I go?" tilting head sweetly. Waving toward family area, "Furniture by the front. Game chatting…but you've had quite the trip." Carmen gasped. "Hungry, dehydrated dog in hoodie, can you help me feed him?" Eyes widened then relaxed. "Isn't most-bizarre thing. Pretty sure your old enough, help yourself to whatever. Don't think me fool; to this day count number of beers left." Removed Skittlez from cramped traveling space, Gloria gasping, "Can't believe my eyes! Don't go leaving on table, set him down in living room, returning with what's needed." Clattering of dishes, water spilling in scattered droplets hurrying to companion. "Dog has weird, walking problem. Do you have way helping him balance? Feel like he's small enough, all we need is to cut some holes into toilet paper tube." Not willing involvement, "Only *people* nurse dear, have to devise something another time. This is a home, not inventor's workshop." Carmen looked around for pillow, small blanket supporting Skittlez. "*AHA!* Knew you'd own fluffy things!" Grabbing throw, situated dog nicely, giving filtered water and consuming remaining freedom fries. "There you go little guy! Tomorrow will be much better, *promise!* We've new, adopted Daddy who'll buy us food! Mom, wake us for *Happier Hour* at TacoDong!" Gloria chuckled softly. "Thought *I* was to be wimp, falling asleep first." flipping light in family room, leaving Carmen and Skittlez to sleep.

Yelping woke Carmen. "Who's hurt?! Did I lay on you?" Skittlez whining happily, hopeful receiving praise. "You did good pup, however, do you get your thrills kicking humans while they sleep?" observing scratch-marks on lower abdomen, Skittlez licking his nose in response. Looked across family room, voicing opinion as eyes came across teenage Kyle wearing braces. "At least now I know you never would've been my type." gently petting Skittlez, sneezing, hands covered in Chihuahua fur. Down at ailing friend, asked, "Not long for this world are you, unable working hind legs and all…can you do a handstand?" setting on front legs. *Amazingly*, little guy still had strong front legs, managing three-second handstand before plopping over gently into waiting palm. "I feel better! Let's find out what we're doing." Without hesitation Carmen walked boldly Kyle's bedroom, placing annoying knocks along door, loudly singing,

Brief clatter, phone hitting floor, Kyle unwillingly stirring. Turned knob, curiously poking head inside. Peering from under covers, "What are you doing?" Startled, closed door to thin line replying, "*YO!* You were one wanting to make big, important trip to Tornadoville! Also…beginnings of *rumblings* in tummy." leaning door wider, blue eye peeking from underneath comforter. "Let me get this straight." pulling covers back, "Wormed way here following, suddenly up to *me* caring of you?" "Didn't make the rules pal. Wanted to drink hot cocoa but no, you, had to jump on random plane!" Rolling over, "In case forgot, came to mother's house, what most people with families *do* during hard situations. Waking for anything other than what's assumed as neediness?" Carmen bit her lip thinking of excuse rousing. "Guess what I'm interested in, why choose visiting your *mother*. Might as well dish what you're up to. Like it or not, stuck with me and I, you." Exhaling, ordered, "If making conversation, want to be in clothing deemed acceptable." Returning to living room, found Skittlez using bottom-half of sofa standing upright. Carmen couldn't help admiring fighting spirit. "*YOU* Mister, aren't to be wandering!" searching back door, "Adults will be in backyard when deemed acceptable!" Exiting front, walked around patio, through white-picket gate, accessing backyard. Leaves were nearly done changing, early afternoon sun shining, burning strongly in cloudless sky, clucking heard from nearby chicken coop. Backyard itself was enormous and opened from small, aging porch area. Here, knickknacks designed blowing in breeze hung on nails and iron angles, wind nonexistent, various ornaments dotting not stirring. Set Skittlez on grass to be reachable, but not far enough falling into garden patches. "Be a pleasant pupper, do

business with quickness–promise not to watch*!*" startled
finding Gloria sitting behind.

**"WAIT ANY CLOSER
WOULD'VE BEEN IN
TROUBLE!"**

"I'm a quiet woman about my own house. Midwife,
nurse in delivery, can't say carry I desire anxious energy.
Come, sit." Laughing nervously, settled into chair, fidgeting.
Fortunately, Skittlez was perfect conversation piece. "See
what you mean…poor thing. What's wrong with him*?*"
coming to teetering, standing position, chin pressed firmly to
grass. "Don't know. Assigned to your son and long story
short, stole Skittlez from inhumane owner at Denver airport."
Interest alighted hearing son was assigned teenage girl.
"Confused as to how you know Kyle. Assigned*?* Sign-up for
youth-mentorship program*?*" Thinking how to explain,
"Probably should ask him, have no formal education." "Are
you a biter*?*" "Usually play by myself is all." Ladies defaulted
to Skittlez, smelling dandelion while using restroom. Gloria,
"Funny, first time meeting dog-thief I actually like." Kyle
rounded backyard, spotting females together, *bonding*. Rolling
eyes, "Looks like I'm outnumbered…bratty teenager sure
knows how to win them over. Morning folks*!*" entering
concreted patio area, "Plans for today*?*" Gloria, thinking
about dogs, "Do you remember Oopsie*?* Very young when
she ran away. After listening to this sweet girl, like to admit
she was stolen by dog-sitter while on vacation." Jaw dropped.
"We had to do this now*?*" distressed, striding Carmen's
direction, "What's your name*?*" Teenager looked from lap
asking, "Who, *me?*" "*No*…asking mom. Course you,
pipsqueak! Forfeit chair, I'm handicapped."

**Rising, extending hands in
flowing, exuberant manner,
"HAVE YOURSELF A SEAT–
name's Carmen by the way."**

Sitting, "Oopsie got nabbed*?* Made posters and
everything*!*" "Nice as they were, threw them away." Carmen
giggled, receiving disapproval. Kyle coolly, "Dog appears to
be practicing fish moves, suggest you handle that." Gloria,
"Aren't doing anything until chatting about flying out here

with runaway teenager." Carmen looked back and forth
between, eager hearing explanation. Many options entered
mind how starting, chose most-direct, saving mother sleepless
nights, retirement drawn to close with concern for son's sanity.
"Aside from termination, office was broken into by none other
than teenage sweetheart, taking laptop, leaving *cutest* sticky-
note. Go ahead Carmen, tell mom who you work for." "Do
grunt work for Collective Conscious, *which*, by the way, don't
understand why everyone hates us–we're the *good guys!*"
Taken aback, eyed young woman while Kyle laughed, "Don't
remember too many stories where heroes were thieves and
bandicoots*!*" "Doing this at such a young age–where are your
parents dear*?*" Carmen sat cross-legged on concrete saying,
"Ready for me to blow your minds*?*" in melodramatic voice,
moving Skittlez's paws, ***"WORLD'S COMING TO AN END,
DRIVEN BY BLOODTHIRSTY IMBECILES!"*** Assigned
following Kyle because of his precision at finding information
on our Country's President. Failed to mention Kyle, man
fitting character profile is mentioned in some book Lashy
has." *"Find the book!"* Dark and powerful monstrosity was
form unlike any could imagine–even in own worst nightmares.
"What do you mean? Does your boss have an M.O. on people
he assigns *stalkers to?*" blank look replying, "No. Pretty much
get anything we want at drop of a hat anyway. Book Lashy
has is like old, *really old.*" "Alright you, you…*developing
degenerate*, you've got me on this one." toward Gloria,
"These things are happening to me on the regular, almost like
God forgot dialing down temperature in purgatory." throwing
hands teen's direction, "Having horrific nightmares about
World ending, about book pipsqueak here mentioned! I have
got to be going *crazy!*" Carmen boisterously, ***"OOH, OOH!***
Might explain why assigned following*!"* Gloria, "Guess can't
be surprised–always been a very special*!"* teen laughing
before quieting-down. "Doctor convinced to fulfill important
purpose. *No slouch* of a man! Few times years worked
alongside when could not deliver or provide care to patient.
Bit of an ass if asked others. Ask me, most-mysterious man
encountered." stood with surprising quickness, barking,
"Rummaging boxes for heirlooms*!"* Carmen celebrated
realizing she wrangled her first, new recruit. "Let's go noob*!"*
Cutting-in ahead, "You'll touch nothing. Carry oxygen; slows
me down when it's full." roughly passing, nearly bouncing
concrete patio. Observing him go around corner, shrugged,
cutting-through Gloria's patio, in living room before either
reached front. Gloria looked at her approvingly, Kyle not so

much. "Why the heck would you cut through lady's bedroom*?*" "How about you remember I *am* a lady*!* Plus, now *I'm* handicapped, call these things portable*?*" "Give it back then*!*" he snapped, "Left a job where nut-bag threw handicap lines left and right. " Gloria, looking over shoulder, "Can't get in the door without yelling at her can you? She's doing all the rummaging, no way we're climbing into crawlspace. " Delighted, *"YES!* Take Mr. Puppers–little guy shakes all the time. " Unsure if subversively picking-on him, eyed suspiciously approaching. "No stealing, checking pockets if necessary. " After exchange, Gloria led to partially finished basement, coming to area elevated from foundation. "Have at it any way you please, watch out for spiders. " Carmen peered into crawlspace, hoisting herself inside, "Got a light*?*" "Pull-string, might break bulb with your head. " Swipe of outstretched hand, smiled satisfaction, six boxes of varying sizes. "Hand Skittlez to mom. " Gloria saved Kyle trip, kidnapping dog, "Have at it, grabbing foldout chair so I can watch. " Didn't take long getting boxes on concrete like performing police lineup, reused numbers of years, different persons' handwriting upon fading lines. "Going to just *stare* at them*?* Prefer others went through these; let go most things– whittled to six boxes. " Concerned for her health, "Trying to tell me something*?*" Waving reassuringly, "Blessed with long life. Are things left on a person's plate enjoyed sharing with others. Besides, mostly filled with clothing. " In Carmen's mind, like entering shopping mall. "I'm going in–Carmen needs a new outfit*!*" Kyle glaring, remaining calm while invaded Gloria's privacy.

"Guess you never really had a Christmas. "

"If teasing, insulting nickname; same we call our disgusting robot, Twitch, maybe it'll fry his circuit's*!*" Kyle approached box and ripping tape off replying, "How about talking less about creepy robots–no fondness for them. " *"No shit?* You and me both Bucko*!*" First boxes, clothes worn by a younger Gloria. "Okay Mom. " said Kyle respectfully, "Outfits must've looked *great* on you, remember this. " holding nicely-crafted overcoat, fur-pelted, pleasing to touch. From foldout chair, "Yes, I too, remember that one*!* Used to wear it in *fiercest* weather conditions, surviving Colorado blizzards. Many winters Kyle fogged kitchen window watching me shovel it away*!*" pausing, seeing Carmen's

194

longing. "Um, is there such a thing as dibs? Gets cold during winter, also, per nature, need something heavier, with more pockets." waggling arms showing worn, ragged hoodie. "Consider it yours, all I ask is it gets put to use, see you growing into it nicely." Kyle said, "Mistreat it in any way, shipping where it belongs–not talking about the coat." Wasn't until last, two boxes Kyle came upon yellowed envelope. "Isn't this a gem-piece, mail left to me!" "Know letter you speak of–read it aloud." In swaying, crawlspace light, "Doesn't give indication who sent." Carmen inched closer, rallying, "Open it, want happier hour at TacoDong!" Kyle snapped, "Can't open without shredding contents!" Hand extending, "Ask for help." "Does know how to listen for something other than chasing footsteps." gauging sincerity, "Promise won't read." letter passed to Carmen. Brought within inches of face, fingers coming around edges, dirty index finding envelope's lip. Soft, peeling, opening with great precision. "Here you go!" "Must get into mail frequently." Gloria, "Read the letter, girl did you a favor." Opening, removed three, yellowed sheets of aging paper, one, brief message, other two blank. Small, silver necklace rattled inside, handed to Carmen, "Deal with this."

Mr. Kyle Clark,

Good job today kiddo. As you're aware, mother died in childbirth…God has different plans. Lacking better explanation, you're important establishing story of tomorrow. There's a book–don't get panty's bunched wondering how I know. For all I know, I'm in a diner watching idiots dodge traffic. Remaining space is how we'll communicate, use it wisely. Good luck.
Signed, Dr. Byte.

"**WOW!**" Carmen exclaimed. "That's really cool! Can I try it?! Want to ask magical genie a few questions!"

Gloria, "Always something curious about Dr. Byte, never put-a-finger." "Use communicating…?" Smiling politely, Carmen, "Do you have a pen? I'd like to say hello." Gloria held hands in the air. Whined, "*Kyle,* I know you have a pen!" Recovering, "***LIKE HELL!*** Do but it is *I* who will get first whack, letter's addressed to me." sitting beside, taking papers and pulling writing implement from pocket.

"Hi, I'm Kyle Clark."

Everyone leaned closer, trying to see what magic would occur. Thirty seconds later, Carmen was *done* with waiting. "This is why I wanted to go first! The genie doesn't like you Kyle." Swiftly grabbing, wrote.

"SQUIGGLEBUTT."

Wrestling over pen and papers, tiny, bold letters appeared.

DR.'S UNAVAILABLE. PLEASE, CONTINUE WASTING SPACE.

Kyle laughed complaining, "Response expected from man going by Dr. Byte. Told me about his brilliance, never once granted meeting." "Giving same response always have; Dr. Byte is a busy, private man. Didn't make himself available to others outside work, nor attend parties or charities, yet it was he who acquired funds. Commendations, funding received, all due to his excellent work." Walking to her new coat, "Probably knows what he's doing. You trust me and I'm a kid!" "Don't stretch the truth. Owe me laptop, some sort of reimbursement on my debit. Obvious course of action is accompanying to your gang, seeing book." Gloria nodded supplementing, "Who would've thought in world discovered as ours, adventure!" Carmen, "Simple mission, all we have to do is fly home—enough money for two tickets?" Frowning, "If want to lose apartment, becoming street hoodlum." Satisfied with response, "Isn't *too bad* there…" "Where's home exactly?" "A covert, dwelling facility underneath Denver International Airport."

Ladies relocated, engaging in small chit-chat. Years of minimal interaction, Carmen dove to heart of Kyle's insecurities. "Think he fell asleep—handicapped thing?" "Sorry for look, accustomed defending; delivered stillborn during emergency C-section. Endured incredible fetal-distress, considered miracle he survived. Something Misty said, Kyle laying dead on implements table…" noise heard, given-up sleeping, rejoining. Carmen from laidback position, "Can I have hot cocoa? Don't think he's happy enough for happier hour." "Cocoa always works sweet-talking into TacoDong— least in these neck of the woods." Kyle entered observing Skittlez carried by Gloria. "Mom's carrying *your* dog?" "Enjoy a spot of hot chocolate before taking us to eat!" Gloria backed her saying, "I'm a retired lady at the end of the block,

196

think there's food here feeding?" Expected a fight, surprised when said, "Works for me." sitting next to teenager, cracking knuckles on good hand, "Since I'm paying your upkeep, questions shall be asked and you're to answer. How much money's this boss paying?" Hands hovered weighing salary.

Technically, worked last four months at initiate-level. I do however, run the whole organization!"

Kyle, "Starting to question the skills of this criminal empire if they're reduced to hiring orphans off the street." "Like I said, technically run the joint, but I only get food and shelter if I choose remaining inside. No offense to those guys, but all I see *them* do is stare at charts, talk about science mumbo-jumbo. That, and stupid, freaky robot I told you about is *obsessed* with me!" Gloria joining, Kyle, "They must pay adults a living wage, credit maybe?" Carmen chortled explaining, "Let me tell you order of operations in Collective Conscious. There's me, *CARMEN AT THE TOP.* Next, Lashbrook and Twitch; buddies, but don't do business unless necessary. *LAZARUS!*" eyes glimmering, "Dude *I* want training from–*pew-pew!*" Gloria interrupting, "How does one acquire wage?" "According to Twitch, prophetic robot, money's meaningless; technology moves enslaving at command of entitled few." "Money's useless; good, hate it– keep them coming!" "*Cocoa!*" taking long, frothy draw, "Thank you mommy. Anyways, below Laz are technical guys. Dan built *COOLEST* shield–protecting from Armageddon!" Imagined impregnable fortress beneath airport equipped with a complex shield-system. "I'm in. Mom, coming with us!" Quiet fell. "Not going. From toddler in Sunday dress to womanhood I've chased dreams, delivering life unto world in form of precious babies. Lived long, happy life, saved good souls along the way–it's your turn." Carmen, "Guess it's something you and I will learn with age." Skittlez groaned signifying mealtime. "Does this mean we aren't going to happier hour?"

Carful of smiles returned from local, fast-food joint, that is, except for Kyle, mulling idea of abandoning his mom to join a crime syndicate. Group was either on verge of collapse, or going beneath the radar surviving whatever fresh evil was coming. Only option: Obey mysterious, self-replying paper. Carmen, "Told you it would hit the spot, only ten bucks! Few years back, used to fly a sign for money and four dollars would feed a whole day!" "Once inside, are to use my phone and call your boss." Loud yipping came from backseat, Carmen choking on a soft taco. "Let's get inside."

Around kitchen table, "Sorry denying you there but you know we're terrorists. Lashy doesn't have contact number, least I'm aware of. Whenever I need him I start rummaging, finds me about ten minutes later." "Gotcha. As you feed your dog, making mess on the floor, what info?" Rice and beans falling, responded, "Our group's existed for over one hundred years fighting against Aries due to massive, hostile-takeover during rise to power. Story, told little from Lashy or Twitch. Frustrated regarding original purpose." "You're a kid; don't imagine them being straightforward with punk like you. Does raise concern for own purpose, lacking physical strength, more to get on personal-record finding where I fit." watching Skittlez, held in position comfortable lapping rice and taco meat. To Gloria, "Against you staying, can't force you coming either. What I request is longer stay, possibly financial support. Let's spend days relishing, caring for teen and dog." forcing smile, "Why'd you decide it appropriate eating at the table?" Toward Skittlez, "We ate fries inside belly of commercial airliner!" whining approval, informing finished. "I'll clean-up if Mom does what Kyle requested." "Wouldn't say no to anything asked, nor doubt what you've told."

(Three days later)

"That was close." spotting mug fragment, tucking it away. Opened door, finding Carmen and Skittlez. "No way I'm checking-in Skittlez! Will be riding quietly, squirmy, but with me." Kyle looked her ^{up} and _{down} noticing mom's overcoat. "*If* by some miracle make it through, will have truly surprised." Carmen allowing exit, "What I want to know, can you **DIG IT!?**" "Dig what? Sneaking dog onto our only method of travel, something else your burdening journey with?" waving envelope it in front him, "You forgot–wasn't keeping it!" "Obviously don't believe you but thanks." tucking away, "All set on your end?" Shrugged responding, "Usually don't worry about these things; come as I am, leave as I am–with a *new coat!*" Found Gloria where expected, sitting front porch in remaining warmth Kansas would see for months. "Michael's here soon…anything else I can do?" "Restful three days, more time smiling than have in ages!"

Carmen interjected, "We'll find way communicating, Twitch can pretty much hack anything." Kyle, "Suggest placing dog inside pouch so aren't confounded from start." gesturing Gloria rise, "If it has to be goodbye, up you wonderful woman!" Hugging her tightly.

"Don't worry about me – GLORIOUS thing about life! Like all the pinwheels and windmills scattering peaceful countryside driven by wind. I am *precious remnants*: dust, vegetation, tumbleweeds in wind's breadth. For whether they know where they go, tamed by no one."

Fighting tears, "Consider finding roommate, lonely in winter I'd expect." "Can tumbleweed be tumbleweed unless free from undertow?" "*OOH!*" Carmen exclaimed. "One thing you should buy, bunches of portable chargers! They work like *pronto* and some have nifty flashlights when power goes out!" Hugging, "Probably won't. Thinking food, rechargeable DVD player!" Van pulled into cul-de-sac, Carmen, "Nice meeting bye!" running toward automobile. "Look out for her. May not be great company man your age, but she's bright and very agile!" "Goodbye Mom, love you tons, all the reruns. Watch Marshall on the news, catch his email and ask if there's shelter you can go to if something happens." Encountered same, pleasant demeanor from Michael, assuring he'd continue helping Gloria.

"Officially started *Mission: Indescribable Airplane!*" "It's still early; running your mouth, wait until after security ." "*There's* that positivity I was looking for! Short-term goal: Food." "Didn't you eat at mom's?" shyly, "Stood outside while you got ready." "Wait while purchasing tickets. Instincts classify you as a nosey person, so, away with you." Encountered no hassle buying tickets to Denver, reconsidering separating, knowing Carmen type to wander. "Come!" "Saw you coming, didn't have to yell. Might I get a gander at my ticket?" "Might I add, tampered ID of yours, absolutely ridiculous." Carmen admired ticket, burying it in coat pocket.

Conquering impasses, Carmen, "Skittlez had it in him keeping quiet! What else do I have to do to be treated nice?" "For starters, how about don't stand outside listening to sounds of me waking-up." "I'm not like other lame, spoon-fed pets called children." Righting expression, "Precisely why it's inappropriate; barely old enough passing as your dad, so, no lovey-dovey stuff." Slapping him on the back, "Definitely my type. Sorry, hate to deflate dwindling ego, have enough challenge loving myself." looking across torso, "Name your oxygen tank–conversation starter if you nail it!" Hiding embarrassment, doing little-more than sweating about collar. Out of arms reach, "No more childish antics! Interacting for as long as it takes getting to whatever hideout you call home, then, men will take over, leaving you to your creepy robot." Falling in-stride, "Pretty-much what they do. Thing is, guy lives in a broom closet! Tried hanging with him, smells of mildew! Point is, no one can get rid of me! Tried, here I am–calling all the shots!" arriving at departure gate, "Aren't going to Chicago!" "Flight leaves in eight hours. Distracted by thought of sitting far away, didn't realize takeoff wasn't until four." Finding seat nearest, "What I mentioned earlier, food. I'll sit here like a lonely girl waiting for her plane ride home." Looked at her wondering how much it'd cost feeding based on size. "Getting my bank statement at the end of the month." Fifteen minutes later, Kyle returned carrying paper sack. Camouflaged by coat, exploded from seat crying, ***"THAT WHAT I THINK IT IS?!"*** "Lucky getting anything!" Carmen returning to seat, waiting to be served her food option. "Where's your breathing purse?" "Don't concern yourself! Needless to say, saving him freedom fries." Kyle and Carmen people-watched, boarding absent interruption. Teenager groaned, "Sure know how to shop." window seat taken by sleeping man, "Switch, don't do well with those I'm not responsible for." Throwing bag into storage, settling into seat, "Keep your voice down don't see him waking. Saying you have a thing against our sleeping friend?" "More of a people problem. Don't expect anyone to understand, but I do think the average person's a bit assuming to think I'd risk my skin saving theirs." Remembering comment made on their inbound flight, "Suppose it isn't the most-intolerant thing I've heard. At least I know you won't be providing resuscitation." "Never found first-aid my style. Rarely seen, rarely get caught; profile keeps me pegged between assassin and drunken hobo." Not interested in hearing her talk, "Have something called daily energy expenditure; what I allow for sniveling children such as yourself. If must talk, finding flight attendant, informing your dog-smuggling." "You wouldn't do that, Skittlez is practically you!" Struggled finding comfort placing fate in teenager, her underground ring of terrorists. Carmen whispered into pages of an *AirMall*, descent becoming experience burning into memory.

Reached altitude of twenty thousand feet, making course adjustment. Carmen climbed over Kyle reaching into overhead compartment, pulling at zippered, main pocket, rummaging–exiting with Kyle's letter. Repeating motion, relaxed into seat and placed worn, yellowed pages inside magazine, keeping from sight.

Combed contents, stopping after automatic reply. "No answer? Oh well, putting you back." Folded letter into sections returning to proper place when correspondence began bleeding onto page.

"That was interesting!" Kyle snapped, "If described way sending into rage regardless situation, waking abruptly!" Carmen stepped over him into aisle as seatbelt-icon illuminated, "Excuse me, wanted to tell me—I mean you—about Mister Genie." dropping magazine into lap, "Skip reading, look at the mountains." Carmen reached into overhead compartment and found zipper on Kyle's bag, finding shard. Had situation been different, would've celebrated how quickly she completed assignments. Sickly, red glow pooled from mountains and foothills immersed in an unnatural, funneling fire. Overhead, "Attention passengers onboard regional flight: Situation of unprecedented nature is developing, advised rerouting to area away from population. Prioritizing traveler safety, this is not an option. Locate nearest seat, fasten seatbelts for descent." passengers obeying request. Aircraft *lurched* hitting unexpected turbulence, wings bending several inches. Carmen climbed over Kyle into seat, buckling seatbelt, pilots aiming for D.I.A. in-lieu of jeopardizing passenger safety, no longer carrying fuel landing elsewhere. "Things just got real, what haven't you told me?" "Skyson uploaded a virus to Aries mainframe locating Twitch and allies for annihilation." "All this for homicidal man's vendetta against a robot?" "For stupid thing's ability backdooring anything with or without network-access. Considered sending him away, unfortunately, only way spying on enemy." losing altitude, passengers seeking consolation. "What're they doing!?" Kyle eying cockpit door. "Trying to land, what else do y—" finding where eyes focused, "That's why he said mountains were glowing! Can they get inside?" Glass imploded, oxygen masks fell uselessly blinding passengers, losing cabin pressure, strain jeopardizing ability remaining conscious. Carmen let out a deafening scream watching couple across; passed the point of screaming, arms flailing attempting to pry attackers from skulls. *Whirring* and threshing; spAIders entering through cranium's base, severing connection between brainstem and spinal cord in a gnashing of puncturing and tearing. They fell lifeless, blood running down necks. Plane nosedived, cockpit doors bursting open, co-pilot ripping at three climbing legs, yelling as they worked together puncturing thighs—defenseless to seven leaping for neck. Unfastened had no chance; pummeled by unrelenting whirlwind; gravitational force ripping plane into pieces, shrapnel, limp bodies soaring into open atmosphere. Shoving letter into jacket, worries were swept away, destined capture in cloud reflecting off a city in chaos.

Jet fuel smeared runway in **black gobs,** debris raining upon tarmac and landscape. Brush fires scattered area, emergency sirens piercing night sky, emergency personnel struggling against Armageddon. Crumpled debris impacted median, cratering between incoming and outgoing flight runways, sparks from severed electrical wire threatening conflagration. Area around hissing hulk fell silent, whimpering coming from inside return-flight, Skittlez returning Carmen to waking world. Streaked with dirt and another's **blood,** gagged foul soot, depressing latch releasing from aerial-tomb. Dried shrubs, grass underneath reached flashpoint, carcass becoming oven of flames and choking gases. Inspecting Kyle, blood trickled from ears, shrapnel penetrated upper-torso, tattering clothing. Fighting Kyle's restraints glanced window—flames melting it away. ***"COME ON SEATBELT!!"*** struggling with blown latch. ***"KYLE, WAKE-UP!"*** slipping, almost falling into growing fire. Remembering mug shard, desperately cut seatbelt, funneling smoke blinding while trying with every part of her to save Kyle. Through smoke and sparks read *"Before Me"*, yelling into lonely night, ***"BEFORE ME'S GONE, THROWN***

AWAY!! YOU'RE LIKE ME, DON'T DIE! Gashing material, pocketed bloodied piece tearing at what remained. *"BREAK!!"* individual strands of reinforced harness fraying and unwinding. In last-ditch effort fueled by desperation, lunged toward Kyle using teeth, bloody fingers ripping at remaining half-inch. Skittlez yelped inconsolably, overwhelmed by searing heat. Kyle's arm over shoulder for hurried transport, legs threatened buckling, third-degree burns forming on cheeks and forehead. With prolonged effort, pulled Kyle into chest, limping away from crash site, getting no more than thirty feet before legs would carry no further. Fell awkwardly onto runway, rolling so as not to crush Skittlez, Kyle falling like crash-test dummy. Wheezing, observed canopies, survival evaporating, night's sky filled with untold number of shooting stars, colored sickly red, swarms sliding airport canopies, not long before congregating, swelling numbers. Rumbling in distance, another plane crashing into air-control tower, shearing structure from base. Bringing knees into stomach, lip quivered watching wave leap from rooftop, swiftly falling, motionless after impact, serving as landing pad. Eye-stalks of several hordes swung Carmen's direction, identifying humans waiting to be upgraded.

"Guess we weren't meant to make it, goodbye!"

Constant, jingle of ammunition racing toward fallen wreckage, footsteps pounding tarmac. In minds, wasn't much hope for rescue. Lashbrook shouted, *"DOUBLE-TIME, FIND HER!"* Dan over roar of wildfires, *"TRAFFIC CONTROL TRANSMITTED; PILOTS DISREGARDED NATIONAL MAYDAY, CHOSE LANDING!"* Lazarus, *"STRAFE FOR CROSSFIRE!"* Unable maneuvering faster than their enemy, dash became matter of time-management. Go-cart nearby, Lashbrook, *"CLIMB IN!"* In driver's seat, stomped accelerator towards struggling teenager, firing weapons thirty yards out, splitting numbers sending swarms their direction. Caliber weaponry used combined with rate-of-fire proved effective slowing; surgical limbs tinkling asphalt—rendering robots useless. Cheers and laughter from experienced militants, men showboating, and competing. Finding gap in mayhem, Laz, "Swing around, if they get her, abysmal obituary for God." Drifted around smoldering wreckage firing weapons, strafing units away. In what little lighting remained, Carmen sat legs drawn tightly, waiting for spAIders to overwhelm—new master at helm. After Lashbrook completed turn, she spotted them. ***"LASHY!"*** watching in rescued admiration, enemy falling before launching counterattack. Splitting numbers, spreading-out to avoid cornering optimum, incapacitation tactic. Pointing at Kyle, ***"BLEEDING!"*** Loading amongst abandoned luggage, rendezvoused with those on foot, veering into sprawling labyrinth underneath airport. Rumble of engine faded, headlights disappearing into subterranean pantheon, leaving only echoes, metallic skittering.

HIDE WHAT YOU SEEK

In the outermost reaches of space, where everything is out of place came the Heralded Evils, searching for their source; reason why hearts' became barren and stale, self-worth and happiness lost at the fail. Hungering, toiling restlessly, searched any method reprieving them of despair and anguish. Where did they come from? Do they have inner-light, fire inside? Some say it's a dying ember; dark matters of dreams deferred. They surged effortlessly through time and space destroying, rending, killing and infecting.

Pride & Prejudice, the Dynamic Duo, consisted of two halves; one half, pieces ripped from Bæöbõb, other a sutured, mutated inscription containing many sparks. Passed-along by past evil from first Sheol, sparks describe captured essence *(a list if you will)* of living things awaiting rapture. Pride lunged forward with ten, long tentacles, traversing great distances with incredible speed, a shadowy **blur** to the naked-eye, Prejudice lounging lazily-about, letting him do all the work.

"You *do* remember where we're going, don't you Pride? I know you'll never stop and ask for directions!" giggling maniacally, bouncing up and down roughly on his behind. Pride sighed, rolling numerous eyes disapprovingly. "To farthest reaches of space, gathering our armies of old. Require no specific direction, for darkness is everywhere." Prejudice climbed along Pride's body to where his tentacles connected. Leaning against one of his faces, enthusiastically sighed, "Isn't it infectiously glorious!? We'll mincemeat anything with a soul to steal!" Coming upon a series of asteroid and meteorite clusters, Pride changed heading, ensuring they were in direct path of the free-roaming rock, compounds encased in ice.

"Where's planet Earth from here?" Prejudice elbowed Pride's eye replying, "It's unlike you, speaking-out to me, especially with questions asked many times before! Soul yearns for pitiful humans, isn't that the curse bestowed upon you? An unquenchable quench, un-scratchable itch; desiring a soul that's never received!" Ignoring his cutting remarks, Pride gazed closest meteorite, grabbing it with long tentacles, stretching his entire body until motionless in space.

"You insignificant wretch, I know what I am; unconquerable, overburdening aggressor! Think of all the glorious power received after we've bathed Zion's land in the blood of her pretty, little, animals!" taking-aim, allowing his undying need for living souls to triangulate a location, darkened heart focusing on one city–New York City. With legendary might, Pride thrust tentacles forward, meteorite vanishing from sight, speeding toward target with devastating accuracy, Prejudice slamming into nearby comet, "Two months." "Fine, I take it back–must've found touchy subject of conversation. Would you throw comet too, sweetening the deal? Idea of an asteroid I touched killing humans pleases me." Taking-up comet, repeating same motion, "Three months."

"Why's mine three months!?
Deserve better; I'm
Prejudice, I am most-

supreme!"

"If you want me being honest, comet's small in stature, contains less mass, susceptible to gravitational pull of other objects." Though upset, he swallowed his pride remembering they've armies to gather. "Bæöbõb commands destruction of Sanctuary! You know what lies within; Giving Tree, and the arch to Kingdom of Heaven!" Placing Prejudice next to one of three mouths, "Well-aware of what that doomed bitch has kept hidden! I've unfinished business to attend to in her lands; Azorius, fabled guardian of Heaven's pearly gates. I'll show all in Creation just how fabled his power is compared to that of mine!" Prejudice, bouncing excitedly, "Do you think after we've killed everything inside Zion's land, we open gateway and wage war with God?" "Is it not every day we exist we wage war against him? Trust me, battling Him now as we speak. He, who's always within us, trapped in futile effort of winning us. Never agreed to being weak, nor meek, for the glories we seek have nothing to do with that freak, or destiny to reek of emotions that leak." Prejudice brought hand up contemplating words*(although he truly wasn't)*. "Let's strike a bet. After slaughtering everything inside her disgusting home, let's stretch serpent's soiled corpse across the heavens and peek inside! If I find God, I get my demands met first–I've some great ideas for the New World Order!" Pride laughed at his little friend. "What would you know about establishing New World Order? You, who puts all others beneath, what kind of setup would that be? Hmm, one positioning you to steal name of God for yourself! What does this leave Pride?" Prejudice, gyrating excitedly at the base of a tentacle, "I'd LOVE being God, yes please! As for your position, I've always found you most-suited as my royal mount!" Pride snorted, resisting urge throwing him into another comet. "Think I'd waste time carrying around a flimsy puppet? There's reason why I've been given name Pride; how does one shackle beast that cannot be overcome? In response to your New World Order, in claiming the name of God, matter-itself would grant you your deserved place beneath. This is how you're to remain—forever prejudiced." Not having fun any longer, Prejudice sulked in defeat, then, a twisted smile formed. "That's okay my brother, for even at the end of things, Pride & Prejudice, you can't have one without the other!"

Invisible, you could look right at her and never see it coming, a reflective mirror pointing at you until death. She's been called many names, held responsible for all things bad under the sun. Remaining spark preventing prescribed fate no longer providing stability, silted essence left to stagnate in what remained of humanity's melting pot. Gaze spanning depths of time and space, "Always a glimmer of Sin inside Sanctuary, I was amongst the animals that day, wreaking havoc! How glorious fate did *fly*; wolf spirit submitted, dragged across ice and snow, taking life from the Alpha, making mate crow!" When last sun sets, Sin commits one, final act: Deliverance. Life-force will not just innervate, it will center fate; sealing all in specific place, single point, before dispersing outward all directions in the form of a single, unwavering emotion. Focusing on energy-source nestled halfway across Galaxy, "*There* you are! Zion, in three days I'll be visiting, bearing Good News! With all weakness removed from my body, I'll appropriate use of this newfound clarity!" Sin headed-off in the direction of Creation's last, hidden secret.

His story was truly most-tragic. Original once stood at pinnacle of enlightenment, watching his purpose chopped to splinters, reduced to ash, never to return. Unable being guardian, Original was taken-down path of endless pain, countless sorrows, forced siding against own people, losing his promised duty. Harnessed in chain inside Baeobob's fortress, hanging over Giving Tree's stump, blood splattering upon it, heart knew he was already dead. He no longer served anything, no purpose.

Jumping from asteroid to meteorite, he had quite the squandering order: Etch Baeobob's face into tapestry of Creation. Hadn't a shred of hope for someone evil as he; unworthy of redemption, on self-destruct. "Will there ever be a day not so grey, where I place my soul to rest, laying in cosmos as a star, instead of this pit of blackened tar. I now turn course to planet Earth, finding utopia fit for Creation's rebirth, waging war with all in my way, for I am unfit being born a new day."

"Must see this through to bitter end, I am nothing without my Great Tree, my soul, to tend."